THE NIGHT BEFORE CHRISTMAS

BY
ALISON ROBERTS

ONCE A GOOD GIRL…

BY
WENDY S. MARCUS

MILLS & BOON

Alison Roberts lives in Christchurch, New Zealand. She began her working career as a primary school teacher, but now juggles available working hours between writing and active duty as an ambulance officer. Throwing in a large dose of parenting, housework, gardening and pet-minding keeps life busy, and teenage daughter Becky is responsible for an increasing number of days spent on equestrian pursuits. Finding time for everything can be a challenge, but the rewards make the effort more than worthwhile.

Wendy S. Marcus is not a lifelong reader. As a child, she never burrowed under her covers with a flashlight and a good book. In senior English, she skimmed the classics, reading the bare minimum required to pass the class. Wendy found her love of reading later in life, in a box of old paperbacks at a school fundraiser where she was introduced to the romance genre in the form of a Harlequin Superromance. Since that first book, she's been a voracious reader of romance often times staying up way too late to reach the happy ending before letting herself go to sleep.

Wendy lives in the beautiful Hudson Valley region of New York with her husband, two of their three children, and their beloved dog, Buddy. A nurse by trade, Wendy has a master's degree in health care administration. After years of working in the medical profession, she's taken a radical turn to writing hot contemporary romances with strong heroes, feisty heroines, and lots of laughs. Wendy loves hearing from readers. Please visit her blog at www.WendySMarcus.com

Alison and Wendy's books are also available in ebook format from www.millsandboon.co.uk

THE NIGHT BEFORE CHRISTMAS

BY
ALISON ROBERTS

MILLS &
BOON

First published in Great Britain 2011
by Mills & Boon, an imprint of Harlequin (UK) Limited.
Harlequin (UK) Limited, Eton House, 18-24 Paradise Road,
Richmond, Surrey TW9 1SR

ISBN: 978 0 263 88617 7

Harlequin (UK) policy is to use papers that are natural, renewable and recyclable products and made from wood grown in sustainable forests. The logging and manufacturing process conform to the legal environmental regulations of the country of origin.

Printed and bound in Spain
by Blackprint CPI, Barcelona

CHAPTER ONE

'PLEASE, Mummy…*please*…'

The huge blue eyes were filled with such desperate longing, it was unbearable.

'But it'll be horribly crowded, darling. We'll have to stand in a big queue for heaven knows how long.'

'I don't mind.'

'We might be gone for hours.'

'Misty doesn't mind, either. Do you, Misty?'

Another set of blue eyes but without the sparkle. Framed by the same gorgeous, golden curls, but this face was much thinner and there were shadows caused by the kind of pain no child should have to endure. The brave smile as this little girl shook her head in agreement was even more unbearable. It was enough to create the unpleasant prickle of tears at the back of Lizzie's eyes.

She swallowed them away with a skill born of long practice.

'It's 'portant, Mummy. I have to tell Santa what me and Misty want for Christmas.'

'Christmas is weeks away, Holly. Santa will be there every day from now on. It's the first day of the big sale today and that's why it'll be so crowded. We could go next week.'

'*No-o-o.*'

'Why not?'

'Cos it's Santa's first day and he might 'member what I tell him and he might forget when he's listened to lots and lots of other girls and boys. Me and Misty's secret might fall out of his head, like things do for Nanna.'

There was a snort from the corner of the room, but no comment. Lizzie hid a smile. She also stifled a sigh, trying to think.

It would be overheated and stuffy in the famous department store, Bennett's. There would be a huge queue with dozens of children waiting with their parents for their turn to sit on Santa's knee and whisper secrets. Happy, excited, *healthy* children and she'd have to stand there for far too long. Feeling the pull back to this small hospital room. But if she stayed, she'd feel guilty. Holly needed her too and she was going to get even less of her mother's time in the next few weeks.

'For heaven's sake,' came a firm voice from the same direction the snort had come from. 'Go, Lizzie. You'll be seeing more than you want of four walls like this in a couple of days. I'll stay here with Misty.'

'Are you sure, Mum? You've done so much already today. You must be exhausted. How's your hip?'

The older woman smiled, looking up from a pile of felt fabric she was sorting in her lap. 'I'm fine. Think about yourself for once, love. Go and have some fun with Holly. Bring me back some of that lovely Bennett's shortbread and I'll be happy.'

Holly was whispering in her sister's ear and Misty was nodding. Smiling as she whispered back. They both looked at their mother and the solemn expression on two small faces told Lizzie that the secret was of the utmost importance.

She had to swallow hard again. Her two precious

daughters who should look identical but were becoming more different every day.

How ironic that she'd chosen Misty as the name for the twin who was fading away before their eyes.

What was the secret wish that Santa had to know about as soon as possible?

That this was going to work? That Misty would be well again?

Hope might be a vital ingredient in what made something successful. Lizzie took a deep breath. She smiled.

'Come on, then, Tuppence. Let's go and see Santa.'

Jack Rousseau had no idea whether he was heading in the right direction.

Why on earth had he thought he might as well pop into Bennett's because it was right beside the bank and get finding the only Christmas gifts he needed to purchase out of the way? He should have spent a pleasant Sunday morning in the markets last week, when he had still been in Paris, and found something original enough to make both his housekeepers smile.

Instead, he was here in London and it was freezing and grey outside and way too crowded and warm inside. And he only had an hour or so until he was due at the 'meet and greet' at Westbridge Park, the prestigious hospital where he was due to start his temporary specialist position tomorrow.

The sensible thing to do would be to give up and come back another time. Preferably when the sale had finished. Late at night, too, so there wouldn't be so many noisy children and pushchairs to avoid. He should have stayed downstairs and chosen something in the perfume department and ignored the flash of inspiration that had sent him in search of kitchenware. Now he was trapped on an escalator, looking down on a sea of humanity and Christmas decorations.

Christmas.

Was anybody quite as unlucky as he was in having the whole world building up expectations to a day that held a memory as unpleasant as the spectacular ending of a marriage? He had avoided the whole business now as far as humanly possible for many years. A bonus in the form of cash had always been suitable for the people he'd needed to find gifts for so why had he chosen this year to break his routine?

There had to be a thousand trees in this store. *Incroyable.* There was a whole forest of them when he stepped off at the top. Green trees. Silver and white ones. Even a fluorescent blue thing that looked very wrong. They were all covered with bows and balls and twinkling lights and it was all too much. Jack ducked between two of them and found himself in, of all places, the lingerie department.

Pausing to catch his breath and find an easy escape route, he found the shapely mannequins, wearing Christmas hats and very little else, quite a pleasant distraction. Jack was rather taken with a red and black striped bustier with built-in suspenders that were holding up some fishnet stockings.

A perfect Christmas gift for the woman with the right credentials. What a shame Danielle had given him that ultimatum only last week. She knew the rules, he explained silently to the mannequin, so why had she gone and ruined everything by demanding a commitment he would never make again? With a grimace that embraced both the current emptiness of his bed and the fact that he was trying to communicate telepathically with a plastic woman, Jack sighed and turned to scan the crowds once more, looking for a 'down' escalator.

There was a long queue of people making a human barrier halfway across this floor and Jack turned his head to find out what the attraction might be. A fashion parade perhaps? In the lingerie department?

No such luck. He should have guessed by the fact that everyone in this queue had small people attached to them. There was a Christmas grotto over there by the lifts and a Father Christmas was enthroned on a crimson velvet chair. A photographer was adjusting lights as a mother tried to persuade a toddler to sit still on Santa's knee to have his picture taken.

A nearby child was whining. 'When's *my* turn, Mum?'

Another was crying. The rising level of high-pitched, excited voices was starting to make him feel distinctly uncomfortable, like fingernails on a blackboard.

The stairs would be faster. Turning on all the charm he could muster, Jack edged rapidly through the press of humanity, excusing himself repeatedly. The vast majority of the people were women and they responded admirably to a bit of authority tempered with a smile. That they continued to stare at him after he'd passed by went unnoticed.

He almost made it. If it hadn't been for the little grandma practically fainting in his arms, he would have been half way down the stairs by now.

Instead, he found himself searching for a chair. 'Is there somewhere she could sit down?' he asked the saleswoman who had come rushing to help.

'Here. This way.' The face over the trim black skirt and frilly white blouse was anxious. The woman, whose name tag said 'Denise', was holding aside the curtain that was being used to screen the back of the Christmas grotto.

The chair was solid and wooden and the elderly woman sank onto it with a relieved groan.

'Keep your head down for a moment,' Jack said. He supported her with one arm, using his free hand to find her wrist.

'Shall I call for an ambulance?' Denise asked.

'No!' The elderly woman shook her purple rinsed hair. 'Please don't do that.'

'Give us a minute,' Jack said. 'I'm a doctor.'

'Oh-h-h.' Denise smiled for the first time. 'That's lucky.'

Jack thought of the minutes ticking past and how hard it might be to find a taxi once he made it outside but he wasn't going to contradict Denise. He could feel a rapid and rather weak pulse in the wrist he was holding and he noted the faint sheen of perspiration on the woman's pale face.

'What's your name?' he enquired.

'Mabel.'

'I'm Jack,' he told her. 'Dr Rousseau. Tell me, has anything like this ever happened to you before?'

'No. I'm as healthy as a horse. I don't want any fuss. I just…came over a bit funny, that's all.'

'Dizzy?'

'Oh…yes.'

'Sick?'

'Yes. I'm starting to feel a bit better now, though.'

'No pain in your chest?'

'No.'

'You're puffing a bit.'

'I walked up all those stairs. My great-grandson's here somewhere, with my daughter. He's waiting to see Father Christmas.'

This was where the man in the red suit must come when he was allowed a breather, Jack decided. There was a small table beside the chair with a carafe of water and some glasses.

'Do you think I could have a glass of that water, dear?' Mabel asked.

Denise did the honours. Jack stayed where he was, thinking through his options. If he could rule out anything serious, like a cardiac event, he could probably leave Mabel and escape downstairs. Or maybe they could take her downstairs. It was rather stuffy in this small, curtained space. He was in a corner and his back was right against one edge. Right beside the red velvet throne, judging by how clearly he could hear voices.

'Hello there, dear. What's *your* name?'

'Holly.'

'And how old are you, Holly?'

'I'm six.'

'And what it is you want for Christmas?'

'It's not just for me.' The six year old girl sounded so earnest she was breathless. 'It's for Misty, too.'

'Who's Misty?'

'My sister.'

'And how old is Misty?'

'She's six, too.'

'Oh...you must be twins.'

Santa didn't sound half as bright as Holly, Jack thought. He still had his fingers on Mabel's wrist and her pulse was jumping a bit. Maybe he should send for an ambulance. Just because she wasn't experiencing any chest pain, it didn't mean she wasn't having a heart attack. The pulse was faint enough to make him concerned about her blood pressure as well. Of course, if she'd nearly fainted, it would have dropped considerably but it didn't pick up in the next minute or so, he'd need to do something.

'How old are you, Mabel?'

'Eighty-three.'

'Are you on medication for anything?'

'Just my blood pressure. The doctor's given me some new pills for it. I just started them yesterday.'

'Hmm. That might well have something to do with how you're feeling. Can you remember the name of the pills?' he asked.

'They're in my purse. Oh, no...where *is* my purse?'

'You must have dropped it!' Denise exclaimed. 'Don't worry, I'll go and have a look right now.'

Jack watched with dismay as the saleswoman ducked through the curtain and disappeared. She might be gone for a long time and he could hardly abandon an elderly woman having a vagal episode, could he? He was trapped. Closing his eyes for a moment, he could hear that Holly was still chattering to Santa.

'It's cos we were born at Christmas. I'm Holly and she's Misty. Like, you know, misty-toe.'

Misty-toe? Jack felt his lips twitch and some of his frustration evaporated. He was stuck for the moment so he might as well try and enjoy it.

'And you and Misty want a daddy for Christmas, you said?'

A *daddy*? Jack blinked and started listening a lot more carefully.

'Yes, please. Is that OK? Mummy says we don't need one really but I'm sure she'd like it. You can manage that, can't you? I told Misty you could. She wanted to come too but she's too sick.'

'Ah... I'm sorry to hear that.'

So was Mabel. Her head was up and she was clearly

eavesdropping on the secret conversation behind them as well. At the mention of the sick sister, she looked straight at Jack. Horrified? More like…expectant.

As if *he* could do anything about it. He was a specialist surgeon, not a paediatrician. Unless they needed new body parts transplanted, he didn't have anything to do with small people.

He had to admit he was getting curious about this child, though. It wasn't hard to straighten a little and move his head to where there was a gap in the curtain that would allow him to have a peek.

He could see the back of Santa's head and the arm that was around the child on his knee. He could see a mop of blonde curls around a very pretty face that was staring very intently at the man hearing her wish. She had the biggest, bluest eyes Jack had ever seen. Give her a set of wings and a little halo on a headband and this Holly would make a perfect Christmas angel.

How sad that she had a twin sister who was so sick.

Santa must be feeling the same way. He was certainly giving this child a little more time than others might have had.

'She's going to be all right. Mummy's hoping she'll get a really special Christmas present that will make her better, but you know what?'

'What?' The tone was wary.

Jack's interest was firmly piqued. A special Christmas present that would make her better? It was the sort of thing a parent for a child waiting on an organ to become available might say. Bit much to expect a miracle before Christmas if they were on the kind of waiting list the majority of his patients had to rely on, though.

'I think having a daddy would make her feel better. It would make us *all* feel better.'

'I'll…see what I can do.'

'He has to be nice,' Holly said firmly. 'And kind. And he has to be really, really nice to Mummy so she'll like him too. That's my mummy over there, see?'

Jack's head mirrored the turn that Santa's head made. The woman standing beside the photographer was unmistakeably Holly's mother. An older version, really, with shoulder-length, blonde curly hair and a cute nose and, while it was far too far away to see the colour of her eyes, Jack just knew they would be as blue as a midsummer sky. Mummy was curvy in all the right places, too. In fact, it was a bit of a puzzle why she was alone. Looking like that, surely she'd be fighting off potential daddies? What man wouldn't want to be really, really nice to her?

Apart from him, of course. He'd been there and done that and the failure was a huge black mark on a personal history that otherwise shone with achievement. A wise man did not repeat his mistakes.

Santa stared for a moment or two and Jack could hear him sigh as he turned back. Holly's head turned as well. Far enough to catch sight of Jack peering through the curtain.

'Ooh,' she squeaked. 'Who are *you*?'

Jack had to think fast. 'Just one of Santa's helpers,' he whispered.

'Are you a…nelf?'

'Yes.' Jack nodded. His smile seemed to come from a different place than usual. It felt…softer. 'That's it. I'm a nelf.'

'Why haven't you got a green hat?'

He was spared having to answer. The photographer

was tapping his watch and the next woman in the queue was edging forward with a small boy who had a very expectant smile. It was clearly the next child's turn to tell Santa what he wanted for Christmas and Holly was distracted by the gentle nudge that was intended to dislodge her from her perch. Not that she was having any of it.

'He has to be nice to me and Misty as well as Mummy,' she told Santa hurriedly. 'That's 'portant. Uncle Nathan liked Mummy but he didn't like us, 'specially when Misty got sick, so Mummy told him to go away and never come back.'

'O-kay,' said Santa. 'I'll keep that in mind. But now it's time for—'

'Mummy said she wasn't sad because she loves *us* so much she doesn't need anybody else. She said we're the two best little girls in the *whole* world and I'm trying to be extra-good even when it's hard and everybody's crying because if you're good, you get want you want for Christmas, don't you?'

Why was everybody crying? Jack wondered. Was Misty's case hopeless?

He glanced at Mabel. *She* was crying.

'The poor wee pet,' she whispered.

'Mummy looks after everybody.' The voice was wobbling now. 'Me and Misty *and* Nanna. But there's nobody to take care of Mummy, is there? I'm still too little.'

The photographer was talking to Holly's mother, who nodded and marched forward.

'Come on, Holly. You've had your turn now.'

'But—'

'No "buts". Come on, we'll go and find that shortbread for Nanna.'

It was a grown-up version of the determination he'd been hearing in Holly's voice.

'Merry Christmas,' Santa intoned, but he didn't sound nearly as jolly as he probably should. 'Ho, ho, ho.'

Denise came back. She had a middle-aged woman with her who turned out to be Mabel's daughter.

The elderly woman was feeling much better. Her daughter said they were going to go straight to the doctor's on the way home. She thanked Jack profusely for his medical assistance. So did Denise as she dashed back to her duties.

Jack was free at last. He escaped from the back of the grotto. Heading for the stairs, he passed Denise, who'd been stopped by a customer's query.

The customer was none other than Holly's mother. Holly gave him a suspicious stare and must have communicated something through the hand she was holding because her mother turned her head to stare at him as well.

The eye contact was like nothing he'd ever experienced in his life. As though they *knew* each other. Intimately. A prickle of something he couldn't identify traced the length of his spine. His step faltered inexplicably. He covered the odd blip by glancing at his watch and seeing the time was more than enough incentive to keep moving. He had no choice, if he was going to have any chance of making his meeting on time.

Weirdly, what he was feeling now was a strong sense of disappointment. Because he would never know the end of the story about Holly and Misty and whether they would get what they wanted for Christmas.

No. It felt like more than that.

Almost as though he'd just lost something.

Something 'portant.

* * *

'He's not really a nelf,' Holly muttered. 'He hasn't got a hat and he's too *big*.'

Lizzie was only half listening because Denise was trying to direct her to where she would find the shortbread she needed to take back to the hospital.

Who was too big?

That astonishingly good-looking man who'd just given her the oddest look? He had the most beautiful eyes she'd ever seen. Chocolate brown and...interested? No. It had been more than the kind of appreciative glance she was used to getting from men. It had been more like he was surprised to see her here. As if he knew her from somewhere else. That thought was just about as strange as whatever bee Holly had in her bonnet about elves.

If she'd met him before she would have most certainly not forgotten the encounter.

Keeping a firm hold on her daughter's hand, Lizzie went in search of shortbread. Holly was happy and so was she. In a little while their mission would be accomplished and she could get back to where she really needed to be.

Maybe later...much later, when she had a minute or two to herself, she would indulge in remembering those dark eyes. Relive that frisson of something amazing that she'd felt in that heartbeat when his eyes had touched hers.

A secret smile tweaked the corner of Lizzie's mouth. She'd have to save it for later but there was no reason not to indulge in a harmless little daydream. After all, who didn't need a touch of fantasy in their lives now and then?

CHAPTER TWO

THIS was payback.

On a cosmic scale. Punishment for the very real pleasure Lizzie had found last night, dreaming about a pair of chocolate-brown eyes.

She had never expected to see them again. Certainly not at close range. But here they were, on the other side of Dr Kingsley's desk.

'Who are you?'

Oh…Lord… It was supposed to come out as 'Who are *you*?' and not 'Who *are* you?', as if she remembered him and was desperate to know his name.

He wasn't smiling. In fact, he was giving her the same kind of odd look he had when he'd passed her in Bennett's department store yesterday.

'I'm Jack,' he told her. 'Jack Rousseau.'

His voice was as smooth as the rich chocolate his eyes made her think of. Just as dark, too. And there was a subtle hint of a very attractive accent. Rousseau? Was he French?

Lizzie's mouth went curiously dry and she dropped her gaze instantly. Not that it helped. He had both his hands on the desk, fiddling with the disc of a stethoscope lying on the blotter. Long, shapely fingers and hands, the backs of which were dusted with dark hair. Absolutely masculine hands but they looked very clever.

Sexy hands. Like the rest of this man whose name meant nothing to her. He was a complete stranger despite this odd feeling that she knew him. A two-second encounter in a crowded shop couldn't account for this feeling of familiarity but illicit fantasies in the privacy of her own bed certainly could.

This was appalling. She had to say something before her hesitation became any more obvious but Lizzie could feel a blush of gigantic proportions blooming. She felt somehow exposed. Vulnerable. Backed into a corner simply because she'd done a tiny thing for her own pleasure.

There was only one thing for it. She needed to come out fighting. Her chin rose sharply and she met those dark eyes directly.

'Where's Dr Kingsley?' she demanded.

As if to answer her sharp query, the door of the consulting room burst open.

'I'm so sorry, Lizzie,' Dave Kingsley said. 'I wanted to be here to introduce you to Jack myself.' He sent an apologetic smile to the younger man as he pulled another chair to that side of the desk. 'Didn't mean to abandon you for so long either.'

'Couldn't be helped,' Jack Rousseau said graciously. 'Emergencies happen.'

'Car accident to a patient of mine who had a transplant five years ago,' Dave explained to Lizzie, before turning back to his new colleague. 'Looks like he's damaged the kidney, unfortunately, along with messing up his spleen and liver.'

'He'll be on his way to Theatre, then?'

'Yes. I might get a call. I said I wanted to have a look

before any call was made about removing the transplant. Now…' The surgeon's smile signalled his change of focus to Lizzie. 'You've obviously met Jack already.'

'Mmm…' Lizzie kept her gaze firmly on Dr Kingsley.

'And he's explained why he's here?'

'We were about to get to that, I think,' Jack said.

Lizzie didn't have to look to know that he was smiling. She could hear it in his voice. He was finding this amusing in some way? She could feel the skin on her forehead tightening as she frowned.

'Let me do the honours, then,' Dave said. 'Mr Rousseau…Jack…is very well known for his expertise in abdominal transplant surgery, Lizzie. Westbridge Park has been trying to lure him away from his Paris base for some time but the best we've been able to manage is to persuade him to spend a month or so giving a series of lectures and working with other surgeons in some individualised training programmes. I'm one of them, I'm delighted to say.'

It would have been impolite not to shift her gaze to acknowledge the apparently famous expert. To nod, at least, as a sign of respect. Wiping the frown from her face was a bit more of an ask. Having their paths cross again like this still seemed a rather unfortunate twist of fate given her enthusiastic foray into the world of fantasy last night.

Her frown was noted.

'I'm not really as young as I look,' Jack Rousseau said kindly. 'I'm thirty-six and I can assure you that I've had considerable experience in cases such as yours.'

Was he planning to take over her surgery? *Misty's* surgery?

'I'm more than happy with Dr Kingsley's experience, thank you,' she announced. 'For myself *and* for my daughter.'

'Heavens above, Lizzie,' Dave put in. 'I'm not about to hand you over. Though I have invited Jack to supervise and possibly assist in the surgery if that's acceptable to you. Never hurts to have an extra set of eyes and hands, particularly if they happen to be regarded as the best in the world.'

The sound from the other man in the room was a protest of modesty. 'The real reason I want to be there,' Jack told her, 'is that I'd like your permission to film the surgeries for use in my upcoming lectures.'

Lizzie stared at him. So he was thirty-six? Yes, she could see the fine lines that life had etched around his eyes and the first hint of the odd silver hair in those dark waves. He had the aura that only came with a combination of intelligence and power and she could imagine how skilled those hands must be. Oddly, the memory of those hands made a sudden heat bloom in her belly. It was disconcertingly difficult to drag her gaze away.

'I can assure you that it won't compromise your care in any way,' Jack continued. 'I have a highly skilled cameraman who's worked with me in many major hospitals across Europe and in the States.'

Lizzie blinked at that. He must be famous and to be that famous at such a relatively young age must mean that he was seriously good at what he did.

And this was on top of being by far the most attractive man she'd ever been this close to. Certainly the first chance encounter she'd ever indulged in fantasising about.

That initial embarrassment had faded but did she really want him to be involved in any way with her medical procedures? Being in Theatre while she was lying there with her abdomen exposed?

The very idea made her squirm uncomfortably.

Jack could see that Lizzie wasn't exactly thrilled by the idea.

He sat back, toying with the stethoscope hanging around his neck, listening to Dave Kingsley explain how her case had been chosen out of all the ones they'd reviewed yesterday afternoon for just this purpose.

He could understand why she was uncomfortable with having to deal with an unexpected new development. This morning's appointment was a crucial point in the journey she was on and lives were at stake on this journey. Specifically, the life of a six-year-old girl. What he could see in front of him was a mother who was prepared to do whatever it would take to keep her family safe.

She didn't need a father for her children because she loved them so much she didn't need anybody else. Because they were the best little girls in the whole world.

He'd been right, of course. Her eyes were as blue as her daughter's.

'I don't care about myself,' she was saying, 'but I'm not having Misty turned into some kind of reality TV show.'

'It's nothing like that,' Dave assured her. 'She won't be identified and it's purely for the purpose of training other surgeons.'

Lizzie shot a suspicious glance in his own direction and Jack tried to look suitably serious. She was a fighter, this one. Determination like that, especially on behalf of someone else, was admirable. It was hard not to give her an encouraging smile.

She was also…*absolument magnifique.*

Quite possibly, the most attractive woman Jack had ever seen. So soft and feminine with those curves and the shining waves of her hair. It was her eyes that really caught him, though. They were utterly compelling. The urge to win her trust and thereby win permission to be part of the team that could remove some of the sadness from those eyes was so powerful it made him tighten his grip on the stethoscope he was fiddling with. The plastic cover on the disc popped off and provided him with a momentary and probably very timely distraction.

He shouldn't be so aware of Lizzie like this. It was unprecedented. Unprofessional. Jack took a steadying breath as he clicked the clear plastic circle back into place. It was only then that he noticed Dave getting out of his chair. He was reading his pager.

'Have a chat to Jack about it before you make a decision,' he was saying to Lizzie. 'We certainly won't do anything you're not happy with. Excuse me for a few minutes. They want a decision made about this kidney. It shouldn't take long.'

And then he was gone and Jack was again alone with Lizzie. He smiled at her.

'Do you have any questions you'd like to ask, Mrs Matthews?'

'Yes, I do, Dr Rousseau.'

Jack raised his eyebrows to encourage her.

'Dr Kingsley said you chose this case as being perfect for filming.'

'This is true.'

'He said you spent all afternoon reviewing every case available.'

'Also true.'

Her gaze was accusing. 'So how come I saw you in town, then? In Bennett's?'

She remembered him. Jack tried to ignore the pulse of something pleasant that was warming his gut. 'I was trying to fit in a bit of Christmas shopping.' Any further personal-type conversation was entirely unnecessary but Jack found himself continuing nonetheless. 'Unsuccessful, unfortunately. Partly due to those crowds but mainly thanks to my interlude of impersonating a nelf.'

Lizzie gave her head a small shake that send a wayward curl onto her cheek. She pushed it back. 'An *elf*? Holly said something about elves when she saw you but I had no idea what she was talking about.'

She was staring at Jack, clearly puzzled. There was a question in her eyes, too. One that carried an expectation. He had something she wanted.

An explanation? He could give her that, no problem. He could give her a lot more than that, if she would let him. He could potentially make a real contribution to giving her what she wanted more than anything—her child's health.

For some reason, this case was special. So special there was a distinct niggle at the back of his mind that it was unprofessional to want to be involved *this* much. Was it because the consultant surgeon he was working with felt the same way? Maybe the concern expressed when they had been discussing it yesterday had been contagious. Whatever the cause was, it had certainly never happened to Jack before and the pull was too powerful to resist. Maybe the 'nelf' was his ace card.

'An elderly woman became unwell after climbing the stairs. I needed somewhere to look after her and one of the saleswomen showed us a private space that happened to be Santa's rest area. Curtained off behind where he was sitting. Holly saw me through the gap in the curtain and wanted to know who I was and I said I was a helper.'

'Oh-h...' Lizzie was smiling now. Just a small smile but it was encouraging. 'I suppose it was her that decided you were an elf.'

'I got demerit points because I didn't have a hat.'

The smile widened. Then it faded and Lizzie's eyes widened. 'You were right there?'

'Yes.'

'So you heard what Holly was saying to Santa?'

'Ah...' The truth was probably obvious in his face. Or the way he diverted his gaze hurriedly. He couldn't tell her what he'd overheard, could he? Apart from the potential for mutual embarrassment, he was just getting further and further away from what needed to be discussed, which was Lizzie and Misty's surgeries and the permission for him to be involved.

In an effort to cover his discomfort, he pulled an impressive set of patient notes from the side of his desk to sit right in front of him. He even opened it to the latest sheaf of notes and test results, knowing that consent forms for both the surgery and the filming rights had been tucked behind them. When he glanced up, however, he could see that Lizzie was having none of the change of direction. It reminded him very strongly of the way Holly had refused to budge from Santa's knee.

'You're smiling,' Lizzie said accusingly. 'You *do* know.'

Jack sighed. He was probably blowing his chance of persuading Lizzie to trust him here and welcome his involvement in her case but Holly deserved respect for her determination and courage. So did Lizzie. He wasn't about to betray a small girl but Lizzie deserved nothing less than the truth.

'Yes, I do know,' he acknowledged reluctantly.

She leaned forward a fraction, clearly expecting to hear more. Her lips parted slightly in anticipation and she even moistened the lower one with the tip of a very pink tongue.

Jack felt a groan somewhere deep inside his body. One that could not be allowed to form properly, never mind escape.

'But I can't reveal anything,' he added firmly.

Lizzie's eyebrows shot up. 'Why not?'

'Nelf law, I'm afraid. We're expressly forbidden to reveal Christmas wishes. If we do, they lose any power they have to come true.'

Lizzie's lips twitched. She was silent for a moment and then it was her turn to sigh. 'Are you at least allowed to give an opinion on whether or not this wish might be granted?'

Jack rubbed his chin thoughtfully. 'I think that's permissible. And, yes, I think the odds on that wish being granted are quite high. Possibly not before Christmas, though.'

Lizzie's face fell.

'But it *will* happen,' he added hurriedly. 'I'm sure of it.'

How could it not happen when this woman was, quite simply, adorable?

If *he* could see that, as a man who had no interest whatsoever in finding a wife, surely she would be able to pick and choose from any available male that happened to come into her orbit? Not that it was any of his business, of course, and it was far too personal a topic to allow himself to even think about it for a moment longer.

He cleared his throat and tore his gaze away, looking down at the notes. 'Dave should be back soon. It's going to be a busy day for you with your final run of tests like the final cross-match and ECG and so on. I don't want to hold things up, so if you're really not happy about having me in Theatre, I'll leave you to it.'

He risked another glance to see her looking torn. Small, white teeth were worrying that full bottom lip and huge, blue eyes were fixed on him with a very searching gaze. 'So it's abdominal transplants you specialise in, Dr Rousseau?'

'Please, call me Jack. I dislike too much formality. May I call you Lizzie?'

She nodded. The pink flush on her cheeks was appealing.

He made his tone friendly but nodded in what he hoped was a serious, professional manner. 'Indeed I do specialise in abdominal transplants. Kidneys, livers, the occasional whole bowel, in fact.' He spoilt the serious effect a little by smiling at her. 'I think kidneys are my favourite. The results of a successful transplant are so rewarding, particularly when it's from a living donor. A case like yours in not uncommon because there are many parents who are willing to donate an organ or part of one for their child but it's not something I've documented for lecture purposes yet.'

'And you want to document my case?'

'I think so. I'd like to run through it quickly with you now, if you are agreeable. Just while we're waiting for Dr Kingsley to return?'

* * *

He was a stranger, this man, and yet Lizzie's faith in him was growing by the minute.

Trust had been won.

Because of 'nelf law'? How absurd was that? Except it had nothing to do with his sense of humour or ability to get out of a tight corner. It was to do with the kind of man who would stop and help an elderly woman who wasn't well. Even more convincingly, one who was prepared to keep the secret of a six-year-old child. Holly might not realise it but her secret was obviously safe.

It was also because of his obvious integrity. They only employed the best here and if Dave Kingsley trusted him on a professional level then she wasn't about to question his judgement. There was a more tangible level to his professionalism, however. One that made her feel like he genuinely cared about his patients.

Here he was, reviewing her file and reading personal information that she wouldn't have dreamed of sharing with a stranger on first acquaintance, but it didn't feel intrusive.

'So...normal pregnancy and delivery when you were...twenty-four?'

'That's right.'

'And the twins' development seemed normal for the first two to three years.'

'Yes.'

He read on in silence for a moment and then he looked up. 'Two toddlers, one of whom was sick, and you're a single mother? That must have been a tough time.'

She could see sympathy in his eyes. And a gentleness that made her want to cry. She pressed her lips together and looked away with a simple nod of response. She had learned to cope alone. She didn't need this man's sympathy.

The silence lingered a moment longer and then she heard Jack clear his throat again.

'The diagnosis of hypoplastic and dysplastic kidneys was made when Misty was three…but she didn't go into end-stage renal failure until earlier this year. And she's been on dialysis for the last three months?'

'Yes.'

'But not peritoneal.'

'No. I…didn't want her to have the catheter inserted in her tummy and do home dialysis and have to worry about infection and things. I'd already passed the first compatibility tests and there was no question about not doing a transplant. We hoped that it could be done before the need for dialysis but…what with shifting in with my mother to be closer to the hospital and Misty getting sick and then I caught that bug and…'

Her litany of woes ended as the door opened and her surgeon came back into the room. He looked at both of them and then at the opened case notes.

'Another review?'

Jack nodded. 'Just in case Lizzie is agreeable to the filming.'

She could still see the sympathy in his face. The gentleness. And something else. He looked as though he really wanted to be a part of this. As though he genuinely cared.

'I'm agreeable,' she said quietly.

'Excellent.' Dave Kingsley sounded delighted. He leaned across his desk to pull pads of requisition forms from a plastic tray. 'You'll need a chest X-ray and an ECG to sign off your fitness for surgery. We'll also do an ultrasound of your kidney and bladder and run off the final blood tests for kidney function and cross-match.'

'But we've done that so many times already. I'm as close a match as could be hoped for from a parent.' Lizzie found herself smiling at Jack. 'Holly wanted to give Misty one of her kidneys. She was really cross when we told her you had to be eighteen years old.'

He smiled back at her. 'They're identical twins, yes?'

'Yes. They…don't look exactly the same any more, though. Holly's taller and…' And so much healthier.

'She might well catch up after the transplant,' Dr Kingsley said. 'And it's good to know there might be a perfect match down the track if things don't go perfectly this time. You do understand there's no guarantee of success, don't you?'

Lizzie nodded. 'I know the statistics are better for live donations and the treatment for any episodes of rejection are getting better all the time. The odds are in our favour.'

'Very true,' Jack put in. 'But that's why we do a last-minute cross-match to check compatibility again. Just in case any antibodies have sneaked in as a result of the illnesses you've both had recently.'

Lizzie nodded again. She crossed the fingers of one hand in her lap, covering them with her other hand so that neither of these highly trained surgeons would see such a childish action.

'I'd prefer to run the standard checks again for Hep B and C and HIV as well, even though I see that your last results were fine.' Jack was smiling at her again. 'I like to tick all these boxes myself for cases I'm involved with.' He glanced at his colleague. 'If you don't see it as interference?'

'Heavens, no. Sounds like a good quality control

measure to me. Feel free to keep ticking boxes in Theatre as well,' Dave said.

Lizzie could swear that Jack gave her the ghost of a wink. 'There are so many boxes to tick in there, they need a supply of extra pens. Sterilised, of course.'

Dave was pulling sheets of loose paper from the case notes. 'I have the consent forms here if you're ready to sign them?'

Lizzie nodded.

Jack frowned slightly. 'You've discussed this already?'

'I know about the possible complications,' Lizzie said.

'Lizzie's a nurse,' Dave explained. 'She worked in Theatre for quite a while before moving to a job in the emergency department.'

'I'm not going to change my mind,' she added firmly.

Jack raised a single eyebrow that told them both this was one of his boxes and her breath huffed out in a resigned sigh.

'OK. Go ahead. I've only worked part time in a general practice since the twins were born so I guess I'm pretty rusty.'

There was an appreciative gleam in Jack's eyes now that suggested, rather flatteringly, that he thought it would take more than some time away from the front line for her mental wheels to collect rust. Clearly it wasn't enough to persuade him to make an exception, however. And that was good. A careful surgeon was a good surgeon. Even if he was only there in a supervisory capacity she wouldn't be impressed by someone who wanted to cut corners.

'The first thing I'll say is that death from a kidney

donation is exceptionally rare—approximately 0.03 per cent—but it has happened so I have to mention it.'

Lizzie nodded. It was a risk she was more than prepared to take. The alternative of staying alive and watching her precious child die was unthinkable.

'Other complications might include you needing a blood transfusion during surgery, a small degree of lung collapse, blood clots in your legs or lungs, pneumonia and a UTI or wound infection.'

Lizzie was reaching for the consent form.

Dave pointed to a line on the document. 'This states that I'll do the procedure laparoscopically, which should give you a much faster recovery rate, but if it's difficult for any reason, it gives me permission to go for an open procedure. That would give you a bigger scar and mean that you were in hospital for about a week instead of three to four days.'

'And Misty? How long will she need to be in hospital for?'

'Probably at least two weeks. She'll still need dialysis until the new kidney settles in and we'll want to make sure everything's fine before she goes home.'

'But it's possible she could be home for Christmas?' Lizzie asked anxiously.

'Absolutely.'

Oh…yes… Dr Jack Rousseau's smile was gorgeous, all right. It wrapped itself around Lizzie like a hug as she signed the necessary permissions for both her own surgery and Misty's.

Dave Kingsley's voice sounded oddly distant for a few seconds.

'Sorry, what was that?' she said.

'I said we'll send you out to see the nurse. She'll give you a gown and pop you in an examination room. We'll give you a bit of a once-over and then send you off for the rest of your tests.'

The warm glow that the visiting surgeon's smile had given her faded so fast Lizzie was left with a faint chill that trickled down her spine. A physical examination? With this Dr Rousseau watching or…worse….doing it himself? She wasn't bothered by the thought of him seeing parts of her she'd never see herself when she was being operated on. She'd be asleep after all. But to be awake and so aware of him? To have him maybe pressing his hand on her bare stomach?

Oh, Lord! Why did he have to be so young?

So impossibly good looking? And…*nice*, damn it.

And why, oh, why had she let herself step into fantasyland in the dead of night and imagine just what it would be like to be touched by him?

Maybe her reaction was obvious in the way Lizzie was prising herself off her chair to follow Dr Kingsley's instructions.

'I'll leave you to it,' she heard Jack say. 'I'll catch up with the test results later today before we go and visit Misty.'

'Misty Matthews? She's in Room 3. You must be Dr Rousseau.' The nurse's tone was awed. 'Welcome to Westbridge.'

'Thank you. I'm due to meet Dave Kingsley to review this patient. Is he here already?'

'He was but he got a call up to the ICU. He said to look after you until he got back. Would you like a coffee?'

Jack shook his head. 'My time is a little limited. I'll go and see Misty now, if I may.'

'Of course. This way.'

The whole family was in the small room.

'This is Dr Rousseau,' Lizzie told the child in the bed. 'He's the doctor who's going to help Dr Kingsley take Mummy's kidney out and give it to you.'

'Hi, there.' Jack took a step closer to the bed. His shirt collar felt inexplicably tight and he found himself loosening his tie.

He never felt comfortable around small people. They could see too much and had no hesitation in saying whatever came into their heads and sometimes he had no idea how to respond. Or he didn't understand what on earth they were talking about. Or, worse, they'd cry. A lot.

Misty wasn't crying. She wasn't saying anything either. Lizzie was sitting in a chair beside the bed and Holly was right beside the pillow, tilted in as if she wanted to be as close as possible to her twin. The resemblance between the twins was striking. Or maybe it was the difference between them that was making Jack feel like there wasn't quite enough oxygen in this private room.

Or it could be due to the way Lizzie was sitting, with her arms on Misty's bed as she leaned forward to talk to the little girl. The way it was making her cleavage so obvious, pushing mounds of skin that looked incredibly smooth and soft into a line of sight he couldn't avoid to save himself.

Well, he could, but that would mean meeting the intense stares that were coming from both Holly and the older woman in the armchair by the window.

'You're going to help with *both* operations?' The older woman sounded as wary as she looked.

'Not at the same time.' Jack tried his most charming smile. 'Lizzie's first and then we go next door to Misty.'

The sniff wasn't impressed. 'Doesn't Misty need a paediatric specialist for her surgery?'

'Mum…' Lizzie sounded embarrassed. 'We talked about this. And you heard what the nurses said about… Jack.' Her quick glance in his direction was appealingly shy. 'It wasn't that I was checking up on you or anything. They were all talking about how famous you are in your field and how lucky we are to have you involved in our case.'

Lizzie's mother was giving her a stern look. 'Oh… *Jack*, now, is it?'

'We got to know each other this morning,' Jack said. 'Didn't we, Lizzie?'

Her head bobbed. A touch of pink bloomed on her cheeks and she could only meet his gaze for a heartbeat. Jack turned his head back to her mother and extended his hand.

'Jack Rousseau,' he said, with another smile. 'I'm delighted to meet you, Mrs…'

'Donaldson.' Her gaze took a moment to meet his. She had been watching Lizzie rather carefully and she clearly hadn't missed any undercurrent. It was definitely too hot in this room. 'Maggie,' she continued. 'Excuse me if I don't get up.'

'Mum's got a bad hip,' Lizzie said.

'I'm sorry to hear that.' Jack leaned down to make it easy to shake hands. Maggie's grip was surprisingly firm.

'I'm on the waiting list for a replacement.' The tone was matter-of-fact. Her own physical impairment was an inconvenience that was being dealt with. 'Next year some time. Perhaps.'

The implications were not lost on Jack. This was Lizzie's mother. The grandmother of the two fatherless girls. Lizzie had moved in with her mother to keep Misty closer to this hospital and must be relying on her heavily for help. Being in hospital herself for at least the next few days would make Maggie's role even more vital. There were pressures going on here that were huge. Important. Maybe he could have a word with someone in Orthopaedics and see if there was any way of getting a priority sticker put on Maggie's case.

A warning bell sounded somewhere in his head. Just how involved was he trying to get here? Maggie's hip was well outside the orbit of what he should be concentrating on. He was here because of Misty. And Lizzie and their complementary surgeries that he was going to document. Whatever else was going on in his patients' worlds had absolutely nothing to do with *him*.

'It's Dr Kingsley that is actually doing the surgeries,' he told Maggie. 'Lizzie has kindly agreed to let me document them on film so that I can use them for the purpose of giving lectures. The reason for the same surgeon doing both of the operations is to have things matched up perfectly. Think of it like a jigsaw puzzle. If I cut a piece out myself, I can put it back in exactly the right place. That is something I want to be able to demonstrate to other surgeons.'

'He likes to tick all the boxes.' Lizzie nodded. 'For himself.'

'I'm not a jigsaw puzzle,' Misty said. 'I'm…me.'

Jack moved back to the bed. He loosened his tie a little more. He even undid the top button of his shirt. 'You are, indeed,' he told Misty. 'And I'm Dr Jack. How are you feeling?'

Misty said nothing. Was it too general a question for a child? The look he was receiving made him feel as though it had been a stupid question. And maybe it was.

Misty's arm was heavily bandaged and plastic tubes snaked from under the covers to the dialysis machine that was whirring quietly as it did its job to make sure her blood was as clean as possible before tomorrow's surgery. She was pale and thin and was probably quite used to feeling a lot less than well.

He tried again. 'Does anything hurt?'

'No.'

'Are you worried about the operation?'

'No. The nurse showed me all about it with the teddy bear. And Mummy says you and Dr Dave are going to take the best care of me.'

'Did she?' Jack couldn't help shifting his gaze to Lizzie. He met a very steady look. One that said she was trusting him but he'd better not let her down.

Fair enough. He didn't intend to.

'I'm going to read your chart,' he told Misty. 'And see what they tell me about all the tests you had today. Dr...Dave will be here soon so that we can talk about you and Mummy and make sure we're all set for tomorrow morning.'

'Are you going to read Mummy's chart too?' It was Holly who asked the question.

Jack smiled at her. 'I've already done that.'

'Did I pass?' Lizzie's tone was carefully casual.

'With flying colours.' The atmosphere in the room lightened just a little. 'And when I've read Misty's I'm going to give her a quick check-up. Unless Dr Dave is back here by then.'

It took a few minutes to get himself up to speed with the chart and the latest results in Misty's notes. He was aware of Lizzie moving around the room, straightening things up, and of the twins having a whispered conversation that nobody else could hear.

When he finished, he nodded in satisfaction and unhooked the stethoscope from around his neck. 'Can I have a listen to your heart and lungs?' he asked Misty.

He had to push aside the memory of how he had avoided doing that for Lizzie this morning. Because he knew it would be unprofessional to be so aware of the warmth that would come from that amazing skin if he got too close? He'd been right to keep his distance. When she'd moved away from the bed, she'd been forced to brush past him rather closely due to the size of the room and he couldn't help noticing a compelling scent that had nothing to do with any perfume she was wearing. He was still trying to bury the memory of it.

Good grief. The look he found being bestowed on him by both the twins was identical. If he didn't know better, he could swear they knew exactly what he'd been trying so hard not to think about. And children *could* sense things, couldn't they? Like animals could sense fear.

In perfect unison, the twins stopped staring at him and looked at each other. For a moment there was a silent communication going on and Jack could feel the intensity. Then they both nodded and looked back at him.

And smiled.

CHAPTER THREE

THERE was no real reason for Jack to go and visit Lizzie the next afternoon.

Her surgery had been completed this morning and he had been nothing more than an observer. Dave Kingsley's work on both Lizzie and Misty had been of excellent quality and had needed no intervention of any kind on his part.

The filming had gone without hitch for both surgeries as well and now all Jack needed to do was edit the footage and write up the notes he would need to accompany the lectures due to start next week. He needed follow-up details for how the patients progressed after surgery, of course, but he could easily get that from talking to Dave. Or reviewing the medical notes.

He wanted to thank Lizzie again for giving her permission to film but it was hardly appropriate to do it when she was in her immediate post-surgical recuperation. He should wait until a later date. In a few days, perhaps, when she would be on the point of being discharged. Or even later, when he would probably find her visiting Misty and helping to care for the small girl until she, too, was well enough to go home.

So why had he abandoned the video equipment and half-written notes in the temporary office he'd been assigned in Dave Kingsley's department? Why hadn't he paged Kingsley and asked how his patients were doing or made arrangements to accompany the other surgeon when he did his evening rounds?

He told himself he didn't want to interrupt anything important. That he might well come across Dave or one of his registrars if he wandered in the direction of the ward. He even convinced himself that, seeing as he was in the vicinity, he might as well pop his head around the door and say hello to Lizzie.

She was in a small, private room near the nurses' station. And she was awake. She saw him the moment he came into view and the look on her face suggested that seeing a surgeon associated with Misty's case might be due to bad news arriving. It had been several hours since her surgery but not so long since Misty had been taken to Recovery and then the paediatric intensive care unit. Had Lizzie been awake long enough to be told the good news? Or, if she had, had her head been clear enough to remember the details?

He couldn't very well just stand in the doorway. He had to move closer and find something to say that would take away the flash of fear darkening her eyes and making her lips tremble.

Jack tried to smile but, weirdly, his lips refused to cooperate. 'Mission accomplished,' he said quietly.

Lizzie burst into tears.

Oh…God. What was he supposed to do now?

He didn't do tears. He could understand them, of course, and even sympathise with the grief or sadness they represented. Unthinkable to indulge in such an outward sign of weakness himself, however, and if he was honest, it was probably the key thing that put him off babies and children so resoundingly. Crying was such a messy process. And noisy. And…and…*needy*. And crying women always wanted something from him that he couldn't give them.

Jack looked hopefully over his shoulder but no nurse materialised to help him out. Where was Lizzie's mother? Stepping closer to reach for the call bell, he spotted the box of tissues on the bedside cabinet. OK, maybe he couldn't give Lizzie what she might need emotionally but there was no excuse not to do something practical that might help. He snatched a couple from the box and pressed them into Lizzie's closest hand. Carefully, because she still had an IV port taped to the back of it.

'It's *good* news,' he reassured her. 'Couldn't be better.'

Lizzie nodded. And sobbed as though her heart was breaking. She blew her nose on the tissues but the tears continued to flow.

Jack pulled out more tissues. A huge handful. Lizzie pressed them to her face and made some hiccupping sounds. A muffled word emerged between the hiccups.

'S-s-sorry.'

'Don't be daft.' Shifting from one foot to the other, Jack was feeling increasingly uncomfortable. Needing to move but knowing he couldn't possibly leave her alone like this, he perched himself on one hip on the edge of her bed. He would wait it out.

Lizzie's leg was under the covers, a solid bar that would be pressed against his hip if he leaned back even slightly. The almost contact seemed to flick a switch inside him and suddenly it was easy to know what to do. He reached over her legs for the hand that wasn't clutching tissues. Small, delicate fingers curled around his and held on, warm and strong.

Any moment now Lizzie's mother would probably come in. Maybe Dave would arrive to check on his patient. Or a nurse would bustle in to check on her patient's vital signs and he'd be able to hand over this somewhat unorthodox semi-professional interaction.

Until then, however, he might as well give it his best shot. Without thinking, he stroked the back of Lizzie's hand with his thumb to get her attention.

'Misty came through like a little trouper,' he told her. 'She's in the paediatric intensive care unit now and still asleep but she's looking comfortable. And everything's looking just as I would hope. Dave did a brilliant job. Textbook stuff, perfect for filming and, believe me, I had a lot of boxes that needed ticking.'

There was a new sound from Lizzie. Still distinctly damp but definitely happier. A kind of gurgle that sounded like laughter. Her face appeared from behind the tissues, sporting a wobbly smile.

'I'm *so* happy,' she informed Jack.

His own smile came back from wherever he'd lost it. 'I can tell.'

He might be making light of her reaction but there was no doubting the very real joy in that smile. It lit up her face. No, actually, it lit up the entire room and the joy was astonishingly contagious. Jack couldn't remember when he'd last felt this happy himself. It was far more than the satisfaction of a job well done. This went deeper, tapping into long-lost memories or something.

You'd never get sick of seeing a smile like that, he thought. You'd be stupid not to do everything in your power to make sure you saw it as often as possible.

It began to dawn on him just how long they'd been doing nothing but smiling at each other. It was also only then that Jack realised he was still holding Lizzie's hand. He gave it a tiny squeeze, let it go and cleared his throat.

'How are *you* feeling?'

'I'm fine. Is Misty really doing well?'

'Absolutely. I would never be less than honest with you, Lizzie.'

Her gaze searched his and, finally, she gave a slow nod. She believed him.

'Thank God,' she whispered, her eyes drifting shut. Then they snapped open. 'And you, of course. Oh, help…have I even said thank you properly? I can't remember…'

Her smile had been thanks enough for anybody. Undeserved, in his case. 'You've got nothing to thank me for,' he assured her. 'And Dave will be back to see you before long, I'm sure. I might go and find out where he is for myself. Can I really tell him you're feeling all right?'

'I'm fine,' Lizzie repeated, but then she sighed and a furrow appeared on her forehead. 'A bit sore. Kind of tired.'

'Having a kidney removed is major surgery even when it's done via laparoscope. I'd be very surprised if you weren't feeling pretty wobbly right now.' On this occasion, he was quite prepared to forgive and forget the crying jag.

Judging by the way she caught her bottom lip between her teeth, he would have been better not to have said anything. Shame he wasn't still holding her hand so that he could give it another reassuring squeeze.

'I do apologise for the waterworks. You're not going to believe this but I hardly ever cry. I have no idea where that all came from.'

'From being bottled up for a very long time, I expect.' Again, Jack experienced a strong regret that he'd let go of her hand already. 'I do believe you, Lizzie. I think you're very strong and you've had more than any mother should have had to deal with. Years of it now. No wonder it's come flooding out with a bit of good news. Especially in the aftermath of a general anaesthetic.'

'Flooding's the word for it,' Lizzie muttered. She closed her eyes again, sinking a little further back on her pillows. 'Maybe you're right. I have tried to be strong. For the girls. And Mum. She's been a total rock for me ever since Jon died.'

This was none of his business. It had nothing to do with any kind of patient care. It didn't even have anything to do with the kind of background detail Jack liked to sprinkle his lectures with to make things more personal and interesting but he ignored the warning bell and asked anyway.

'How old were the twins when they lost their dad?'

'He didn't even get to celebrate their first birthday.' A huge tear came from beneath a closed eyelid and trickled down the side of Lizzie's nose. 'They won't have any memories of him except for photographs. And news clippings.'

'News clippings?'

'He was a hero.' Lizzie gave a huge sniff. 'A fireman who died in the line of duty. He went back into a house because some kids said their father was inside. The roof collapsed on top of him. Turned out the father was down the road in the pub and it had been his cigarette that fell down the back of the couch and started the fire.' Her eyes opened and Jack was struck by the incredible depth of colour. And the sadness. 'He *was* a hero but you know what? I'd rather my girls had a dad.'

Jack could hear the echo of a small girl's voice in the back of his mind. Telling Santa that she and her sister wanted a daddy for Christmas. That she thought it would make Mummy feel better too.

The shoes of a man who'd gone into a burning building to save a stranger would be hard to fill. Jack could almost feel sorry for any man who tried. But if he succeeded, he would win Lizzie. He couldn't feel sorry for him now. He could almost feel...envious?

Good grief. He looked at his watch. Surely there was somewhere else he needed to be by now? He had those lecture notes to write up. Phone calls to make to arrange to meet the other surgeons he was expecting to mentor over the next couple of months. Probably more than a hundred emails that would need attention.

'How's the pain level? I can check whether Dave has charted additional pain relief for you, if you like.'

'No...I don't want to be too fuzzy when I go and see Misty.'

'That won't be till tomorrow morning at the earliest. I'm sure that complete bed rest has been ordered overnight. That's certainly what my patients would be getting.'

'But—'

'Misty's asleep, Lizzie. Being extremely well cared for. She'll be on sedation overnight. You can be there when she wakes up.'

'But—'

A nurse bustled into the room. 'Oh...Mr Rousseau! I didn't know *you* were here. We're short-staffed and flat out at the moment.'

Her tone suggested she would have been in the room a lot sooner if she had known he was there. Was it unprofessional to be glad she hadn't known?

Quite likely, but it paled in comparison to sitting on a patient's bed, holding her hand and grinning at her like an idiot for goodness knew how long. Or even worse, feeling envious of some non-existent man who might become Lizzie's partner and a father figure to her daughters at some point in the future. The sooner he got things back on track the better. His career was his life and always would be. There was no room for anyone or anything else. His choice. End of story.

'I actually came by to try and catch up with Dr Kingsley. Is he around?'

'Just down the corridor, in Room 1. As far as I know, Lizzie's next on the list for a check-up. Shall I tell him you're here?'

Whatever drugs were in her system from the pain control or as an aftermath from the anaesthetic were doing strange things to Lizzie. Or maybe it was the sheer exhaustion that followed in the wake of her emotional release that was responsible for this peculiar, out-of-body experience.

The flash of anger at having her request to see Misty denied was long gone. She was too tired to feel angry and, in any case, she wasn't about to let anyone stop her from seeing her daughter. They could wheel her down in her bed if necessary, for heaven's sake. None of the medical staff around here seemed to understand how important it was. Dr Kingsley had been just as horrified as Jack had been at the idea of her being moved anywhere just yet.

She couldn't really be angry with either of them, could she? Dave Kingsley had apparently done a brilliant job with the surgeries. And Jack...well, he'd been nice enough to sit there and hold her hand while she'd bawled her eyes out.

There was a cringe factor there, with him having seen her looking her absolute worst. She might have to come up with a new fantasy to exorcise it. One in which Jack would see her in a pretty, floaty dress with her make-up and hair looking perfect. Where there was soft music playing in the background and he was taking her hand to lead her onto the dance floor.

The feel of his hand wouldn't be fantasy. She knew now how it felt to have him holding her hand. She would never forget the strength that had flowed from his touch. That had been what had enabled her to pull herself together finally.

There was a warning bell sounding there. Trying to remind her that she'd once been totally dependent on someone else for that kind of strength and how hard it had been when it had been ripped away. But she didn't need to take heed, did she? She knew she had learned to rely on herself. A moment to take strength from someone else was excusable given that she had just come through major surgery and it wasn't as if Jack's intentions had been anything other than professional.

Even if there'd been the faintest possibility of there being anything else, seeing her looking such a mess would certainly have killed it. Not only that, he'd probably thought she was about to dissolve again at any moment. No wonder he'd been so pleased when Dr Kingsley had come into the room and they had been able to discuss purely medical matters. And that had been fine by her. She'd got to lie back with her eyes shut and let her mind drift on a wave of drug-induced peace with the added comfort of knowing she would be independent and brave again as soon as she had healed.

If she took a deep breath and let herself relax just a tiny bit more, she could slip into that new and improved fantasy that Jack would be starring in. Now that she knew who he was, the knowledge of how unwise that would be was perfectly clear despite the fuzziness of her thought processes but, somehow, it didn't seem to matter. The pull towards the fantasy was way too powerful, thanks to the sound of his voice, so close to her bed.

Of course it was Dr Kingsley who was pressing gently on her abdomen, but Lizzie didn't mind a bit that her skin was exposed to the other man present. She liked having Jack in the room. When this consultation was finished he would disappear, along with Dr Kingsley, and she might never see him again.

'Did that hurt?'

Lizzie forced her eyelids open as the words finally penetrated. From somewhere in the fuzziness in her head she caught the echo of the tiny groan she must have uttered aloud at the thought of never seeing Jack Rousseau again. Oh…*God*…

'Um…no. I don't think so.'

'Hmm.' Dave's voice faded as he turned to speak to someone else. The nurse, perhaps. 'We'll bump up the morphine in the IV. She's on PCA?'

'Yes,' the nurse confirmed.

Patient-controlled analgesia. She had a small remote and she could press the button if she wanted to increase the dose. With just a click, she could probably retreat into that very pleasant land of fantasy for hours to come. But if she did that, she wouldn't be seeing Misty until the drugs wore off. Lizzie curled her hands gently into fists.

Maybe someone else pushed the button. The voices

faded completely and when she opened her eyes again, her room was empty of medical staff. To her joy, there were visitors she was desperate to see.

'Mum… Holly…hello, darling.'

'Hello, Mummy. Is your tummy sore?' Holly climbed carefully onto the end of the bed and hugged Lizzie's feet.

'No, it's fine.' Lizzie smiled at her daughter but instantly raised her gaze to her mother. 'How's Misty?'

'She's fine, too. Doing really well, they tell us.'

'They let me sit in the chair with Nanna,' Holly said proudly. 'Cos I told them I'd be really, really quiet. Like a little Christmas mouse.'

Lizzie was astonished. She gaped at her mother. 'They let Holly into the intensive care unit? I thought they'd be looking after her in the relatives' area while you were in there.'

'I think they made an exception because of the twin thing. Don't worry.' Maggie bent and gave Lizzie a kiss. 'She's so used to seeing Misty on dialysis, I don't think the equipment fazed her in the least.'

'Misty's asleep,' Holly told her. 'She won't wake up till tomorrow. And she's got this special bag on her bed. The nurse told me that when her new kidney starts working, that's where her wee is going to go.'

Lizzie's question was silent but Maggie shook her head. 'Not yet,' she said quietly. 'But the doctors are happy. They've both been up there, checking on every tiny detail. He's a nice young man, that Dr Jack of yours.'

'He's not *my* Dr Jack, Mum. He's not even my surgeon. He's just working with Dr Kingsley and making a film for his lectures. I'm sure we'll be delighted that he's here if anything goes wrong but he doesn't need to be nice. He just needs to be very, very good at his job.'

'Never hurts to be nice,' Maggie murmured.

Holly's eyes were wide as she listened to the exchange. 'Is Dr Jack being nice to you, too, Mummy?'

It was sweet how important it seemed to be. Lizzie smiled reassuringly. Dr Jack had given her fistfuls of tissues. He'd held her hand and made her smile. He'd taken very good care of Misty.

'Oh, yes,' she murmured. 'Very nice.'

But Holly wasn't listening any longer. She was leaning over the edge of Lizzie's bed.

'Ooh… You've got one of those special bags, too, and it's all full of yellow stuff. Is that your wee?'

'Mmm. I've got a thing called a catheter so I don't have to get up to go to the loo. They're going to take it out later.'

'When?'

'Soon, I hope. I want to go and visit Misty.'

Maggie looked horrified. 'You're not planning on getting out of that bed and walking for miles, I hope.'

Lizzie sighed. 'No, Mum. I thought they could wheel my bed over to the ICU.' Her voice wobbled and she pressed her lips together, willing the tears not to return. She would frighten Holly if she started crying again. She didn't want to upset her mother either. Maggie was looking very anxious. But why couldn't anybody understand?

'I just want to *see* her,' she whispered.

Her mother reached out to stroke her hair. 'I know, love. And it's hard but you've got to take care of yourself, too…for Misty's sake as well as the rest of us. She's fast asleep. She wouldn't even know if you were there.'

But *I'd* know, Lizzie thought stubbornly.

'Are you sure you're all right?' Maggie was looking close to tears herself. 'I could call your nurse. Or Dr Kingsley. Or that nice Dr Jack.'

Lizzie shook her head as firmly as she could. 'I'm fine, Mum. I feel a bit like I've been run over by a steamroller, that's all.' She gave her mother the best smile she could summon. Maggie had more than enough on her plate without having to worry about *her* state of mind. 'A good rest and I'll bounce back. I'll be able to go home by the end of the week.'

Maggie sniffed softly but nodded. 'That's what we want to hear,' she said brightly. 'That's where we're going now, isn't it, Holly? Home to have a bit of tea and feed Dougal. And then we'll pop back to say goodnight to you and Misty.'

Lizzie closed her eyes as she drew in a careful breath. 'Thanks, Mum. I really don't know what I'd do without you.'

'It's what mums are for.'

Lizzie opened her eyes. Her smile wobbled. 'You're the best of the lot. Not only are you taking care of me and the girls and all this hospital stuff, you've even found room for a hairy, smelly dog in your apartment.'

'Dougal doesn't smell.' Holly sounded offended.

'He might by now,' Maggie said dryly. 'He might have been shut inside all day if Kerry didn't get off work early. Come on, sweetheart. Let's go and see what he found to chew up today. You can choose the prettiest Christmas tree from all the ones we can see in the shop windows on the way home.'

Lizzie watched them leave, her mother limping more than usual, with a small girl clutching her hand. She couldn't keep the tears away then and they were still rolling down her cheeks when her nurse came back into the room.

'Oh, dear...what's happened?'

Lizzie shook her head, saying nothing. How could she begin to explain how hard life was at the moment? How much she loved her mother? How incredibly precious her children were?

How desperately she wanted to see for herself that Misty was all right?

The nurse's smile was sympathetic. 'It's a bit rough after surgery, isn't it? It's amazing how quickly people get over donating a kidney, though. A bit like a Caesarean, I guess. When there's a positive motive for doing something, it seems to make it easier somehow. Now...let's get that catheter out and when you feel like you need the loo, we'll see how you go on your feet.'

The urge to slip into sleep and forget about everything filled the room after the nurse had gone again and for quite some time Lizzie dozed. She couldn't fall into a really deep sleep, however, because something important was floating around her brain, being elusive.

Something her nurse had said.

But all she'd chatted about had been how busy they were. Two nurses had gone home sick with a bug that was doing the rounds and there was more than one patient who needed a lot of care. It was just as well she was doing so well. If she needed someone, she could just ring her bell, but otherwise it might be a while before anyone popped back to check on her.

Yes...that was it. She was on her own. She didn't have any real idea how much time had passed while she'd been drifting in and out of sleep and trying to remember what was important but surely her mother and Holly would still be away for some time?

The PICU wasn't that far away. Along the corridor and up two floors in the lift. If she took it very carefully, she could go and have a look and then come back to her bed and nobody would even know she'd been missing.

She could just imagine the look on Maggie's face. She could also see a disapproving frown on the remarkably clear image of Jack's face that appeared. There would be a box that needed the tick erased, wouldn't there? But they weren't here. And she wouldn't do it if it felt like it was going to do any real damage. She could just test out what she'd be like on her feet, couldn't she? After all, the nurse had said that's what they'd do later.

Moving very slowly and cautiously, Lizzie let her legs dangle over the side of the bed as she sat up. She held onto the bedside cabinet very carefully when she lowered herself to the floor. The flash of pain in her tummy subsided quite quickly and, surprisingly, Lizzie didn't feel as faint as she had expected. In fact, she felt quite strong.

It was easy enough to disconnect her IV. Lizzie smiled. She might not be able to work as a nurse any more but her training came in useful in all sorts of ways these days.

Taking a step was a bit more of a mission. Lizzie eyed the door of her room, which looked further away than it had when she'd been lying in bed. It was only a few steps, though. If she could manage that, then she'd know whether she had any chance of getting to the elevator at the end of the corridor. At least there was a rail that ran down the walls out there. That would help quite a lot.

Very slowly, she edged her way to the door. Bent over a little, with her hands supporting her stomach. It became easier rather than harder, which was a good sign. By the time Lizzie could look out and see if the corridor was clear, it wasn't hurting very much at all.

She looked towards the nurses' station first. The area was bright with red and green crepe paper streamers and the occasional huge paper bell but it was reassuringly empty of people. The staff was obviously all busy with other patients. She turned her head to scan the other end of the corridor.

And found herself looking at the solid figure of a man wearing theatre scrubs.

Her imagination had got it a bit wrong. The look on Jack Rousseau's face wasn't disapproving. It was more like he'd seen a whole herd of flying pigs.

'Where the *hell* do you think *you're* going?'

CHAPTER FOUR

HER face was a picture.

A mix of guilty child and determined rebel. There was something else in her eyes as well. A longing that was bordering on desperation. A plea that no man could have resisted.

Jack could feel it touching something very deep in his chest.

It made him want to gather her close and hold her. To protect her. It made him want to stand and fight by her side, whatever the threat might be. It certainly made him suck in a good lungful of air. He felt it escape in a resigned kind of sigh.

'You were planning to walk all the way to the PICU, weren't you?'

Eyebrows lifted so that they disappeared under the soft curls on her forehead. Small, white teeth captured a lower lip. Half of it, anyway. Lizzie had amazing lips. Full and soft and clearly designed for smiling.

Or kissing…

Jack shook his head, trying to disrupt the errant thought before it got caught irretrievably in his memory. 'Why didn't you ask a nurse to take you in a wheelchair?'

'They're awfully busy,' Lizzie said quickly. 'I didn't want to add to the pressure for anyone.'

'Nothing to do with the fact that they would probably have said no?' Jack asked dryly.

She caught his gaze and couldn't quite control the twitch of her lips.

'Mmm...'

How could anybody keep a stern face after that hint of mischief in the almost smile?

'Don't move,' he ordered. 'I'll be right back.'

He could have left a message for Dave that his patient needed a stern talking to. He could have taken her arm and marched her back to her bed himself. He could have found a nurse to help with the ill-advised excursion. Instead, Jack found himself propelling a wheelchair down the corridor a couple of minutes later, with Lizzie comfortably seated and now wrapped in a warm dressing gown.

'Are you sure you've got time for this?'

'Dave's still in Theatre, closing up on a liver transplant patient. We were both going to have another look in on Misty before going home. I said I'd go and check on her after I'd checked that *you* were obeying instructions so that you would recuperate as fast as possible.'

He could only see the top of Lizzie's head but he could swear she was smiling. And why wouldn't she be? She was on her way to see her daughter. She was getting exactly what she'd wanted.

And deserved, too, damn it. That fighting spirit took his breath away. Not only was she prepared to give up a body part with all the pain and fear that had to accompany the gesture, she had been ready to push herself to the nth degree just so she could get close enough to see for herself that her child was all right.

It took very little time to get Lizzie to where she wanted to be. Beside Misty's bed. Jack got the nurses to adjust the position of some of the monitoring equipment so that he could park the wheelchair at the head of the bed. As close to the unconscious child as possible.

'Oh….' Lizzie's hand traced the shape of the small head on the pillow with infinite tenderness. 'I'm here, darling. Mummy's here.'

Her hand trailed down, staying in contact with Misty's arm until it reached a small, still hand that peeped out from the bandaging that covered IV lines. Very carefully, Lizzie took hold of Misty's hand. She lifted it just a little, bending gingerly forward until she could touch the small fingers with her lips.

The air in this space felt curiously thick all of a sudden. Full of…

Love.

A kind of love that was outside anything Jack had ever experienced. As an adult or a child.

Pure.

So powerful it blew everything else away. It even sucked the oxygen out of the air. That would explain why it felt hard to take a decent breath. And why there was a curious ache behind his ribs.

If he hadn't failed in his marriage, would he have had children of his own by now? Could he have experienced a touch of what he was feeling around him? He'd never know. And while it was his choice and perfectly acceptable, it was also…very sad.

'I'll leave you to it,' he said, his voice oddly gruff. 'One of the nurses will take you back to your room when you get tired.'

Lizzie looked up.

'Thank you *so* much, Jack,' she whispered.

The smile that accompanied the soft words was astonishing. It matched the glow in her eyes. Soft and tender and still full of the overflow of the love she was giving her child. Instead of feeling as if he was looking at a scene that he was in no way a part of, Jack could feel himself being drawn in.

He could almost imagine what it would be like to be one of the people Lizzie loved.

It was…utterly compelling.

Disturbingly so.

Jack turned away, only to find Lizzie's mother on her way into the unit, leading Holly by the hand. The older woman was looking very tired and she was limping badly but the smile that Jack received was very like her daughter's. This had to be where Lizzie had inherited her determination and grit and the ability to love with such generosity.

What an amazing little family. How lucky were these two little girls?

Maggie had spotted Lizzie beside Misty's bed. She clicked her tongue in dismay but Jack smiled at her.

'She has permission to be here. But only until she's tired and then she'll be escorted back to her room.'

'Mummy!' Holly's cry was joyous.

'*Shhh,*' Maggie warned.

'*Mummy.*'

The word was a whisper but still loud enough to make the nursing staff smile. Holly let go of her grandmother's hand and ran to the wheelchair. Lizzie gathered her under her free arm. She was still holding Misty's hand on the other side. Maggie went towards them and touched the top of Lizzie's head in a gentle caress.

This time, Jack made it out of the unit but that last picture of the small family was imprinted on his brain.

Linked physically by touch but far more significantly by a love that left him feeling strangely left out.

Bereft, even.

Worse, it was making him revisit aspects of his own life he had considered dealt with and buried. If he dwelled on it, he might even start having doubts and that could only lead to the possibility of his life seeming less satisfying. He'd spent years getting his life exactly the way he wanted it. He'd made the choice between his career and his marriage. Or rather the choice had been made for him.

Maybe all he needed to do was remember that it was his commitment to his work that had made his marriage such a miserable failure. His wife, Celine, had told him in no uncertain terms the extent to which he had failed as a husband because of that. Just before she'd hurled the Christmas roast turkey through the window as he was picking up his car keys to answer the call that he simply couldn't delay responding to.

Bad enough to fail as a husband. How much harder would it have been if children had been involved? To fail as a father?

Yes. This was definitely the right direction to take in getting his head together again.

A hot shower in the locker rooms helped as well. So did changing out of the scrubs. Getting out of the hospital was the next logical step. Right away from any potential source of these disturbing thoughts and unwelcome memories he was getting. The paperwork and writing and emails could all wait until the morning.

But where to go? It was only 6:00 p.m. and he wasn't on call even though he'd told Dave to get in touch if he wanted to discuss any of his current patients, and all he needed for that was to have his phone within reach.

He'd stayed in his town apartment last night but if he really wanted to get away, maybe he should do the hour or so drive to his 'real' London home.

The property he had inherited in one of the prestigious green belts comprised several acres with its own woods and stream and a rambling old house. It was always available, thanks to his housekeeper, Mrs Benny, but he rarely stayed there. He really should rent it out if he was going to keep the place for investment purposes but somehow that decision had been put on the back burner.

Had he, subconsciously, wondered if there might be a time in the future when he would change his mind about having a family of his own? They went together, didn't they? The big house and the vast garden for children to have adventures in. And that was probably the real explanation of why he'd kept the place at all. The only really happy memories he had of his own childhood were rare jewels that had everything to do with this particular property.

Good grief, he should put it on the market and be done with it. In the meantime, it would certainly not be a good idea to be rattling around in it by himself given the current disturbances to his state of mind.

He would go and have dinner somewhere nice and head back to the inner-city apartment. His upmarket bachelor pad with its bedroom, bathroom, kitchenette and tiny balcony with the view that probably made it an even better investment than the country estate. Why was it that the prospect of a gourmet meal and then the modern comfort of the apartment was less than appealing right now?

Maybe it was the seasonal vibe that would permeate

anywhere he chose to go in the city. Decorations everywhere and, worse, Christmas delicacies on every menu.

Or was it because he would be alone?

Well, that was easily remedied. In fact, the solution was right in front of Jack as he stepped out of the theatre locker rooms to leave the hospital. Fate decreed that one of the more attractive scrub nurses who had been present during Lizzie's surgery that morning happened to be coming out of the door of the female locker rooms at precisely the same moment.

What was her name again?

Ah…yes. 'Tania…' Jack turned on his best smile. 'Heading home?'

'Unless I get a better offer.'

Tania had an exceptionally pretty smile. She was young, in her mid-twenties maybe and she was in civvies now, which were a pair of well-fitting jeans and a T-shirt kind of top that advertised her generous curves.

Curves that would probably look fantastic in a red and black striped bustier. The glimmer of interest in finding out was welcome. This was the distraction he needed. His downward glance at Tania's outfit had been discreet and he raised his gaze before his smile had begun to fade.

She had the colouring that went with her Irish accent. Dark hair, pale skin and blue eyes.

And in the second that Jack registered the colour of her eyes, he knew that he wasn't about to provide the better offer.

The blue was just wrong. Not dark enough or warm enough or…*something* enough. The hair was too dark and too straight and Tania was too young.

You want *company* for the *night*, a small voice mut-

tered in the back of his mind, you're not looking for a
life partner.

But it was too late. The comparison was simply there
and instead of being a distraction, Tania might only
make things worse.

'Good luck with that,' he heard himself saying aloud.
'Me—I've got a mountain of paperwork that needs
some attention.'

It was true. It would be an excellent idea to get a
decent head start on those lecture notes to accompany
the video footage and thanks to any appetite for food or
women being effectively squashed, that was what Jack
decided to do. He shut himself in his new office space,
spent thirty minutes attending to his most urgent emails,
left phone messages for three surgeons in other London
hospitals he was to visit and did some last-minute edit-
ing on a paper on whole-bowel transplantation that was
due for publication in *The Lancet*.

He put off reviewing the video footage of today's surgeries. It was fourteen hours since he'd arrived at this
hospital today and he was weary enough to feel quite…
normal. If he put off watching and thinking about Lizzie
and/or Misty's surgical procedures, he might even manage to keep feeling like that.

It seemed to work, so he put it off the next day as
well, which was easy to do because he had to spend a
lot of time away from Westbridge Park visiting other
London hospitals. He checked up on Misty's progress
late that evening to find the little girl still in the paediatric intensive care unit and still well sedated. The
new kidney hadn't started functioning yet but she was
stable and there was nothing to set off any alarm bells.

He popped in on Lizzie as well. Just to update his

records on both his patients. It added a nice, personal note to his lectures when he could deliver a detailed summary of post-surgical progress on the patients. She would probably be asleep, anyway.

She wasn't. Lizzie was propped up on her pillows, the reading light a soft glow beside her.

'I'm behaving,' she assured him. 'I'm in bed, see? I'll be asleep soon, honestly.'

He believed her. She looked as if he had already been asleep. Comfortable and a bit…rumpled. Her hair was a cloud of curls on the pillows and the sheet wasn't pulled up far enough to hide the lace on the top of her night-gown.

He really shouldn't have come to visit. Except, now that he was here, the thought was more like how could he have stayed away?

'Did you have a good day?'

'Excellent, thank you.' Lizzie's smile was joyous. 'I had a shower by myself this morning and I walked as far as the elevators and back and I've been to see Misty three times.' It seemed like a cloud crossed her face as her smile faded. 'She's…doing fine, isn't she?'

'Yes.' Jack smiled, hoping that it would bring the glow back to Lizzie's face. It didn't. 'She's doing very well,' he added.

Lizzie's voice had a small wobble. 'Why isn't my kidney working for her yet?'

'It can take time for things to settle down. Be patient, Lizzie.'

She was hanging onto his every word. He had the power to make life that little bit better for her right now and it was a good feeling.

No. Make that a *great* feeling.

'Sleep well.' Disconcertingly, he had to clear his

throat because his words had a rough edge to them. 'You might be pleasantly surprised by what tomorrow will bring.'

Jack was in Dave Kingsley's company the next day when they made a visit to the PICU. It was no surprise to find the three generations of Misty's family clustered quietly around her bed.

His own pleasant surprise at seeing Lizzie again so early in the day was easy to disguise because everybody here was delighted. The bag hanging beneath Misty's bed had a small quantity of liquid in it.

Liquid gold.

The kidney was starting to function.

Lizzie was well on the way to her own recovery. She had walked all the way here herself, she informed her surgeon.

'And I can go home tomorrow, can't I, Dr Kingsley?'

'Indeed you can, my dear.'

'But when Misty gets shifted to the ward, I'll be able to come in and stay with her?'

'We'll see about that.'

It was Maggie who spoke up. Lizzie's mother was looking very weary, Jack noticed. And no wonder. How often had she been back and forth to the hospital in the last three days? Coping with the pain of that bad hip? Looking after a lively six-year-old and worrying about her other granddaughter and her daughter?

It wasn't his problem.

Having to be absent from Westbridge Park and in an operating theatre on the other side of the city for the rest of that day was a good thing.

Passing Lizzie and her mother and Holly by chance the next day when Lizzie was clearly leaving the hospital was also a good thing. She was well enough to be discharged. She was heading back out into the world to get on with her own life.

Just as he was doing.

There was no real reason to keep tabs on Misty's progress now that she had been transferred to the paediatric ward and was doing well so there was every chance that this was the last time Jack would see Lizzie.

This was how it should be.

How it needed to be.

So why did he feel this odd sense of loss that was enough of a kick in the guts to make him unable to find any words to say in the first moments when he'd stopped with the intention of saying *au revoir* and wishing her well?

CHAPTER FIVE

THIS was it.

The moment to say goodbye to the man who'd sparked a fantasy she would have in her head for ever. Who had won her trust by keeping her daughter's secret and had won her heart by helping her through her lowest moment and making it possible for her to see and touch her precious child when she'd needed to so desperately.

Dr Jack Rousseau. The world-famous transplant surgeon she'd been lucky enough to have had involved in her life for a whole week.

She'd probably never see him again.

Because of hospital protocol, Lizzie was being ferried to the front door in a wheelchair. Her mother had stopped pushing the moment Jack had paused with the clear intention of saying something.

Except that he wasn't saying anything.

It was Maggie who spoke first, breaking what was on the point of becoming an awkward moment.

'Come on, Holly. Let's take the bag and make sure the taxi is waiting near the door. We don't want Mummy to have to stand outside and get cold.'

Lizzie suddenly felt embarrassed by the wheelchair. Or maybe it was the fact that she was having to look so far up to see Jack's face, as if she were only Holly's age and just as vulnerable.

'I don't need this thing any more,' she declared. 'Thank goodness.'

She took her feet off the metal plates and bent to fold them out of the way so that she could stand up.

'Here, let me.' Jack bent and flipped them up.

For a moment, their heads were very close together. It wouldn't have mattered except that Jack chose that moment to glance sideways and catch Lizzie's gaze.

She should have been watching his hands, not his face, but, for a heartbeat and then two, she was caught. Was she imagining an unspoken message? That it was a shame that this was goodbye but it was the way things had to be?

When he extended his hand to offer her assistance to get out of the wheelchair, Lizzie took it without hesitation. But the touch was brief. It felt brisk and professional.

No whisper there of any missed opportunities. She must have imagined what she'd thought she'd seen in his eyes.

'So...' Jack let go of her hand as soon as she was on her feet. 'You're going home.'

'Yes. I'll be back every day, though, to see Misty.'

'I hear she's doing very well.'

'Yes.' Lizzie's smile came easily. 'She is. Another week and we'll have her home. In time for Christmas.'

Jack was giving her a smile that she would be happy to see every day of her life. It was gorgeous. 'I hope it's the best Christmas ever. For all of you.'

'It will be.' The words were a vow. 'I...hope you have a wonderful Christmas, too, Jack.'

His smile faded. The warmth in his face seemed to

fade as well and Lizzie had the odd impression that she'd said something wrong. Stepped over a boundary, perhaps, by saying something a little too personal to a member of staff?

He knew so much about her but what did she know about him? Virtually nothing. Why would she?

This moment could have become even more awkward than when he'd stopped in the first place but Maggie came back through the electronic doors.

'Taxi's here, love. We're all ready for you.' She smiled brightly at Jack. 'Thank you so much for everything you've done, Dr Rousseau.'

Still he seemed to hesitate.

'Will you be all right?' he asked. He gave Maggie a quick sideways glance and then straightened his stance. Even his tone was stiff. 'To get out to the taxi, I mean?'

It was Maggie who answered. 'We'll be fine,' she assured him. 'Thank you again, but we've taken up enough of your time. You must be a very busy man.'

'Indeed.' Jack merely raised a hand in farewell as Maggie took Lizzie's arm and walked with her to the doors.

Lizzie couldn't help a final, backward glance when was settled into the back seat of the taxi and they were pulling away from the hospital entrance.

Jack can't have been that busy, she thought, if he was only just moving away now.

Maggie insisted that Lizzie stayed at home and rest the next day but the day after that there was no stopping her from spending time with Misty. They all went in the afternoon and stayed until the evening, when Lizzie had to admit she was sore and tired and needed to go home.

The weather had turned bleak over the last couple

of days. It was cold and wet with intermittent sleet and taxis were getting harder to find. That was probably why Maggie raced ahead of Lizzie as they came out of the hospital entrance that night. And why she slipped on the puddle of sleet and went crashing to the pavement.

'Oh, my God!' Lizzie ignored the stab of pain in her side as she rushed to where her mother had fallen and crouched beside her.

'*Mum*. Can you hear me?'

'Of course I can. I'm not deaf. Don't shout, love. Help me up.'

Lizzie started to but even in the artificial light muffled by another shower of sleet she could see the way the colour drained from Maggie's face. She could hear the stifled cry of pain. Holly burst into tears beside her.

Help arrived. A taxi driver leapt from his vehicle and then took off into the hospital. Staff from the emergency department arrived a commendably short time after that.

'Look at that,' a young doctor said. 'External rotation on her left foot. Visible shortening, too.'

'Fractured neck of femur?' someone else asked.

'I'd say so. Bring that stretcher over here. Let's get her inside.'

All Lizzie could do was to comfort Holly and wait after Maggie was taken to the emergency department. There was a wait for X-rays to be taken and an even longer wait for an orthopaedic surgeon to arrive for a consultation.

The surgeon was only in the department for a matter of minutes and he was a very cheerful man.

'No more waiting list for you, Mrs Donaldson. You'll get your new hip first thing tomorrow morning.'

After that, things became rather surreal for Lizzie. Her mother was transferred to the orthopaedic ward and had enough pain relief on board to be remarkably comfortable. Having promised to be back to see her before she got taken to Theatre in the morning, Lizzie made her way slowly down to the front door again with Holly.

Having reached the hospital foyer, she was intercepted by a young woman who turned out to be a social worker from the emergency department.

'I got sent to find you, Mrs Matthews. Thank goodness you hadn't left yet. I've heard that you're only just out of hospital yourself. Do you need help?'

Lizzie blinked at her. She still hadn't quite got her head around this new development. Her own exhaustion had been compounded by fear for her mother and the need to reassure Holly that the world wasn't really falling apart around them. All she'd been doing since the moment Maggie had fallen had been to cope with each moment as it came. Going home was the logical thing to do next and she'd been on her way until this perky young woman with a clipboard had stopped them.

'All I need is a taxi,' she said. 'So that we can get home.'

'Are you sure? How are you going to cope on your own with a child? We have foster-families available for just this kind of situation, you know.'

Lizzie tightened her grip around Holly's hand. 'That won't be necessary.'

'If you don't mind me saying so, Mrs Matthews, you don't look very well. What was it that you were in hospital for?'

'That really isn't any of your business.' Lizzie started moving again.

'Oh…I'm sorry, but it kind of is.' The social worker

was following her. 'There's quite a difference in being able to look after yourself and having to look after someone else as well.'

Lizzie was almost at the door now. The social worker actually caught hold of her arm.

'And what about when your mother gets discharged? You're certainly going to need some help then, aren't you? We have all sorts of agencies that we can call on. We just need to fill in a few forms.'

'We'll be fine,' Lizzie said wearily. Aware of someone behind her, she stepped to one side so she wasn't blocking someone's exit. Except that the person didn't take the invitation to pass. He stopped. And stared.

'Lizzie…is everything all right?' Jack Rousseau asked. 'You know Mrs Matthews?' There was a look of relief on the face of the earnest young woman with the clipboard.

'Yes.' The response was cautious. It didn't take a genius to see that there was something very wrong here. Lizzie's face was pale and tight and Holly looked just as miserable.

It had been two days since he'd said goodbye to her. He'd stood almost in the same place he was now and watched her exit from his life, with an echo of the feeling he'd had that day in the intensive care unit when he'd felt himself being drawn in to something he wasn't entitled to.

Finally forcing himself to turn and walk back into his own life, Jack could have sworn he'd felt something tear deep inside but the momentary pain had been quickly followed by a wave of…relief. He didn't have to even think about disturbing, personal issues any more. He'd thrown himself into the series of lectures that had kept him fully occupied for these two days and it had been exactly what he'd needed.

The harder he worked, the better. That way, he didn't have time to think about anything else.

Or anyone else.

That was why he hadn't hesitated in responding to that late call from Dave for a consult on his MVA patient with the kidney they were still trying to save. Which was why he was only just getting away from the hospital now, at 8:00 p.m.

'Nanna fell over.' It was Holly who spoke up. 'She has to have a hopper-shun.'

'Operation,' Lizzie murmured. She met Jack's gaze. 'Mum slipped on an icy patch outside and broke her hip. The surgery's scheduled for tomorrow morning.'

'And Mrs Matthews is only just out of hospital herself,' the social worker put in. 'There's some concern about her being able to manage.'

'I'm not about to let Holly go and stay with strangers.' Lizzie's tone was clipped. 'Thanks, anyway, but we'll manage just fine.'

Would they? Lizzie's independence was admirable but was she overestimating her capabilities? He couldn't simply take her word for it and walk away feeling relieved that he didn't need to get involved again. He couldn't let some social worker try and take Holly away from her mother either.

'Do you have anyone else that could help? A relative or friend?'

Lizzie nodded. 'There's Kerry. She lives in the flat next door and she's been helping out with Dougal.'

'Dougal?' Jack could feel his eyes widen. There was a man involved here as well? And what if there was?

It shouldn't make him feel… Good grief…it couldn't possibly be a touch of jealousy, could it?

'Dougal's our puppy.' Holly's voice was muffled because her face was pressed against her mother's leg.

'A two-year-old bearded collie,' Lizzie amended. Her smile was wry. 'Puppy is a more accurate description, though. He still bounces and chews everything.'

'And this Kerry is looking after him?' This sounded hopeful. Anyone who could care for a dog would probably be good with small children.

'She lets him out if we're away for a long time. But…'

'Kerry's fat,' Holly informed Jack. 'She's going to have a baby.'

'And she's still working,' Lizzie said. 'She's a barmaid at the pub down the road. But I don't *think* she's working tonight. She'll be happy to help. *If* it's needed.'

The young social worker was looking doubtful.

Jack knew he shouldn't look at Lizzie. This was none of his business. He should excuse himself and let the system do what it was there to do. But he couldn't help himself.

'All we need is a taxi,' Lizzie was saying.

She sounded calm enough but Jack could see she was almost at breaking point. Close to tears, probably, because there was an odd sheen to her eyes that made them appear even bluer than ever.

How many blue-eyed women had he known or had yet to meet? How could he possibly be this certain that only one pair of eyes could ever be this perfect colour? Or could make him feel like he could bend or break any rules and get away with it? That he wanted to, because if he did, somehow it would make the world a better place.

For Lizzie.

And for himself.

'There's no need for a taxi,' he heard himself saying. 'I'm heading home myself. I'll give you both a lift.'

CHAPTER SIX

'IF YOU park here, your car should be safe for a while.'

Lizzie crossed her fingers in her lap. How bizarre was it to be rolling up to a housing estate like this, cushioned on the leather upholstery of a sleek, late-model BMW?

'That light isn't broken again yet,' she added, 'and Mr Stubbs lives in a ground-floor apartment and spends his life watching what happens outside his window. It's that one, with the reindeer, see?'

Nobody could miss spotting that window. The reindeer were made of lurid red and green lights that flashed on and off. Two standing reindeer and a leaping one in the middle, all pulling sleighs. They flashed in sequence to give the impression of movement.

Illuminated by the deer, a curtain twitched reassuringly as Jack killed the engine and got out of the driver's seat. She waved in the direction of the window and then turned to see Jack looking upwards. She could understand where that grim expression was coming from. She'd been shocked herself at the first sight of this tenement block but that had been long ago, before she'd got to know some of the people who lived on her mother's floor. Good people lived here, amongst a few less desirable neighbours, and they made up for the tough living conditions.

One day, maybe, when they'd got through this rough patch of their lives and she could return to a full-time job, she'd be able to afford to move her little family somewhere else. Something semi-detached in a suburb would be perfect. Kerry was trying to talk her into emigrating to New Zealand but that was a bit too much of a fantasy for now.

In the meantime, Lizzie had to get past the embarrassment of the rubbish littering the grey, tiled flooring and the dim glow from unadorned light bulbs in the entranceway. She had to introduce Jack to Kerry, convince him that she could manage and then send him back to the world of being a famous surgeon and driving the kind of car that was probably worth at least two years of the rent she would have to pay to live in her dream house.

Please be home, Kerry, she prayed, waiting for what seemed an interminable length of time for the lift to come down.

'What floor are you on?' Jack's voice was so controlled it was devoid of expression.

'Ten,' Holly piped up. 'I can reach the button.' She stood on tiptoe and stretched. 'See?'

'Good girl.'

Holly beamed but Jack was staring straight ahead. Watching the doors slide shut and no doubt reading some of the obscenities scratched deeply into the metal or inked with indelible pen. Machinery screeched and clanged and the ancient lift jerked its way up.

'We usually take the stairs,' Lizzie muttered into the uncomfortable silence. 'It's good exercise.'

'Nanna doesn't, though,' Holly said. ''Cos she's got a

funny leg.' She pressed against her mother. 'But they're going to fix it now, aren't they, Mummy? That's why she has to stay in the host-hostible, isn't it?'

'Hospital,' Lizzie murmured automatically. 'Mmm.'

She stroked Holly's curls. That's where she should be at the moment, by her mother's side, keeping her company and providing reassurance about tomorrow's surgery.

Or with her other daughter, speeding her recovery with her willpower and sheer determination that life was going to get better for them all.

But she needed to be here with Holly as well.

It felt like she was pulled in different directions with so much force it was threatening to tear her apart.

She was sore. And tired.

Thank goodness Kerry was home.

'Gidday.' Her neighbour was wearing a Santa hat and she grinned down at Holly, who had insisted on being the one to knock on the door that led to the shared balcony on the edge of the tenement building. Kerry held her arms out instantly, looking up as Holly gladly accepted the hug, her small arms only getting part of way around an impressively swollen belly. Then she looked up and saw Lizzie's face.

'Lizzie! What's wrong? Where's Maggie?'

Her gaze shifted and her jaw visibly dropped as she caught sight of Jack, standing back a little and looking tall and dark and more than a little dangerous in the shadows.

The sideways glance from Lizzie showed her that he was returning the gobsmacked stare. Some people couldn't get past their first impression of Kerry with the numerous bits of silverware adorning her ears and eyebrows and nostrils and even underneath her bottom lip. At least the hat was hiding the startling fluorescent pink streaks she had in her hair but if you added the fact that she was only eighteen, single and about to produce her own child to the initial impression, Jack would probably be inclined to call in social services himself.

'Slight complication,' Lizzie said to Kerry, gathering her strength. 'Nothing we can't handle, though, with a bit of help from you.'

'You've got it, mate.' Kerry spoke without hesitation. 'What can I do?'

This was beyond belief.

Jack actually winced as the door to Maggie's apartment was opened and a large, hairy creature bounded out joyously and leapt at him.

'Dougal!' Holly was trying to sound authoritative. '*Bad* dog.'

He could swear the dog was laughing. A claw dug painfully into his thigh as the animal pushed off to launch itself towards the small girl. Holly was unperturbed. She was hugging Dougal as she lost her balance and tumbled into a sitting position.

Good grief! As if it wasn't unhygienic enough to be having her face licked by a dog, the floor of this shared balcony was probably indescribably filthy. Lizzie was flicking on a light now and he got another glimpse of her neighbour's extraordinary hair and the glimmer of all the hardware of her facial piercings.

This place was a circus.

Housed in a high-rise slum.

No way should Lizzie be allowed to stay here in her condition. She'd pick up some ghastly infection and probably die and then what would happen to her

mother and those two little girls who wanted a daddy
for Christmas?

'Thank you very much for the lift home,' Lizzie said,
standing back to let Kerry past. 'We'll be fine now.'

Jack's doubts must have been written all over his
face because Lizzie bit her lip.

'Come in for a bit,' she invited. 'And see for yourself. I'll make a cup of tea.'

'In your dreams,' Kerry said cheerfully. 'You're
going to be putting your feet up. The kitchen's out of
bounds except for me and Prickles, here.'

'Prickles?' Jack echoed faintly.

Holly was scrambling to her feet using one of the
dog's ears for balance. 'That's *me*,' she informed him.
'Cos Kerry says that holly has prickles.'

'Like a hedgehog.' Kerry grinned over her shoulder.
'And everybody knows that I *love* hedgehogs.'

Jack followed the small procession into the apartment and pushed the front door closed behind him.

Something odd happened as the door clicked shut.
Almost instantly, the grim, grey world outside seemed
to vanish. This apartment was as clean and bright as a
brand-new penny. There was a fresh scent of something
flowery that was only faintly dampened by a more canine odour. And it was full of colour. Bright rugs on
the floor and cushions like big, fat jewels on the couch
and chairs. Children's artwork was proudly displayed
on the walls, along with dozens of photographs, and
there was even a jam jar with fresh flowers in it on the
table. The contrast to what lay on the other side of the
door made these small rooms feel warm and cosy and
welcoming.

'Park yourself there,' Kerry ordered Lizzie, waving
at the couch. 'Dougal...cut it *out*.'

The dog dropped to the floor with his nose on his front paws. A contrite, doggy pancake with a tail that obviously couldn't stay still.

Lizzie lowered herself slowly onto the couch. 'Please sit down,' she invited Jack. 'Kerry won't let you go until you've had a cup of tea and a bikkie.'

Kerry was moving with surprising speed for someone in the late stages of pregnancy. She disappeared into another room and came back seconds later with her arms full of pillows and a patchwork quilt, insisting that Lizzie get tucked up on the couch like a pampered invalid. Then she busied herself in the tiny, adjoining kitchen. It couldn't be easy manoeuvring herself in that space with both Holly and the dog in the way but the strange-looking girl seemed to be blessed with endless patience.

'Don't climb on the bench, Prickles. Use the stool to get into the cupboard... Here...I'll help.'

At the same time as supervising her helper, Kerry was chatting to Lizzie and finding out about Maggie's accident.

'I'll take the day off work tomorrow,' she announced as soon as she was satisfied Maggie was being well looked after. 'I can look after Holly while you're with your mum. Yeah...OK, Prickles. I reckon we'll go for the chocolate bikkies but only cos we've got a visitor.'

He was the visitor. He didn't belong here and Jack had the uncomfortable feeling that he was spying on something that was none of his business. Looking for reasons why it wasn't a suitable space for a patient who should rightly be still safely tucked up in a hospital bed.

It would be easy to find something to criticise. The place wasn't that tidy. There were toys strewn about and a dog bed in the corner that harboured some disgusting, well-chewed items. But it was just as easy to ignore such details. This was so far away from anything Jack had ever been familiar with and yet he recognised it.

This was what a home was like.

Lizzie would be fine. She was in the place she belonged and with the people she loved. People that loved her and would care for her.

He could leave.

Except that now he had a mug of tea in his hand and Holly was offering him a plate of chocolate biscuits with palpable pride.

'They're *squiggle tops*,' she whispered loudly.

Kerry saw the way he eyed the slightly lurid decorations on the biscuits. 'My mum sends them from New Zealand,' she told him. 'They're not half-bad, though.'

'They're the best bikkies in the world,' Holly assured him. 'Kerry's going to send them to me when she goes home.'

'You're going home?' It was crazy, but Jack couldn't help honing in on a potential reason to continue worrying about Lizzie. 'When?'

'After bubs here makes an appearance. I left it a bit late to book a flight.'

'Lucky for us.' Lizzie shook her head, refusing anything to eat. She looked pale and very tired. 'Holly, it's time you were in bed, hon.'

'Sure is,' Kerry agreed. 'Come on, let's get those jim-jams on. And you'll have to go to sleep really fast.'

'Why?' Both Holly and Dougal were following Kerry from the room.

'Because I'm going to sleep in Misty's bed and that way you won't hear me snoring.'

Jack caught Lizzie's gaze as they heard Holly's giggle. They both smiled and suddenly it was hard to look away. The joy in that sound was enough to make his throat feel oddly tight. These people might have very little in terms of material wealth but they had something that was priceless. This atmosphere of a home and family, however different, meant that moments of happiness could be conjured up like magic.

It seemed like an extension of that magic that Lizzie knew exactly what he was feeling. He could see it reflected in those amazing blue eyes and it took an astonishing effort to break the contact. He ate his odd biscuit hurriedly, washing it down with tea that was hot enough to scald his throat.

'I'd better be going.' He shook his head as Lizzie started pushing back the quilt covering her. 'No, don't get up. If you're planning on being back at Westbridge tomorrow, you need all the rest you can get.'

'I'll rest.'

'She absolutely will,' Kerry assured him, appearing again with Holly holding her hand and looking smaller, somehow, in her pink pyjamas. 'Here, I'll see you out.'

She opened the door and Jack stepped out into the greyness he'd virtually forgotten about. For an insane moment, he wanted to turn around and go back into that bright apartment. Maybe it was just as well the door was shutting behind him. He needed to take a deep breath before he moved, though, and in that momentary hesitation there came a loud sound like a muffled explosion from somewhere on a lower floor. The door behind him flew open again.

'What on earth was that?' Kerry marched to the edge of the balcony and peered down.

Jack was beside her. They could see people running

away from the building they were in. Moments later they heard the first sirens.

'Holy cow...' Kerry breathed. 'I can see smoke!'

The explosion had been enough to rock the couch Lizzie was lying on.

Her eyes had been drifting shut, her mind still full of the extraordinary reality of Dr Jack Rousseau sitting here in this apartment only a minute ago. Of that moment he'd looked at her when they'd heard the delicious sound of Holly's giggle. Of seeing something almost like yearning in that dark gaze that had captured her heart and squeezed it hard.

She came completely awake with painful swiftness to hear Kerry's shocked cry about the smoke. And then alarms began ringing throughout the building. Her heart started thumping wildly and she pushed herself up so fast her head spun. She could see stars and hear buzzing sounds around her that were receding and then coming back like waves.

'Just relax,' came a clearer voice. 'I've got you.'

Lizzie could feel the quilt tighten around her body like a cocoon. She could feel the immense strength in the arms that were picking her up as if she were no more than Holly's size. The desire to simply relax into that hold and lay her head on a broad shoulder was overwhelming but she fought back.

'Holly...'

'Kerry's got her. And Dougal.'

'Is there a fire?'

'We don't know. We're getting out just in case.'

The alarms were louder now and there were many other voices. Frightened adults asking what was going on. Crying children. Jack's voice rumbled in his chest so that Lizzie could feel as well as hear it.

'Nobody use the lifts. Take the stairs.'

Ten floors of concrete stairs with a press of semi-panicked people. The jolts were painful but it was far worse not to be able to see and hold Holly.

'Hang onto me,' she heard Jack say. 'Holly, don't let go of Kerry's hand, OK?'

'OK, Dr Jack.'

The courage in that small voice brought a lump to Lizzie's throat that made it hard to drag in her next breath. Even harder not to let it go in a sob. To her disbelief, she felt the press of Jack's cheek against her hair and his voice was close enough to tickle her ear.

'We're almost there, Lizzie. Hang on. Everything's under control.'

For a blissful moment, Lizzie let herself believe that. She could let herself feel protected.

Safe.

And then she felt the curl of smoke in her nostrils and the bite of the icy night air on her face. She could see the flash of beacons from emergency vehicles and hear the sounds of shouted directions and the hum of an increasingly anxious crowd.

Under control? Her life seemed to be one disaster after another.

'That's your car?' she heard someone yell.

'Yes.'

'Move it now. We need more space for emergency vehicles.'

'Sure.'

Lizzie found herself gently lowered into the front passenger seat. She heard a back door open.

'Hop in, Holly,' Kerry ordered.

'But what about Dougal?'

Turning her head, Lizzie could see that Holly had a firm hold on Dougal's lead. Dougal had his favourite possession—a well-chewed stuffed toy duck—clamped in his jaws. For once, the dog's tail wasn't wagging.

'Get this car moved,' someone yelled. *'Now.'*

'Get in.' Jack sounded resigned. 'Dougal too.'

The car bounced as the back seat filled up. Jack slid into the driver's seat, started the engine and drove to where a police officer was signalling. He parked the car, leaving the engine going to run the heater, and for a long while they sat there watching the activity around the tenement building. Holly fell asleep on Kerry's lap. Dougal's anxious huffing steamed up the windows.

'I can't see any flames,' Kerry ventured. 'I'll bet it was only a small fire. Maybe Mr Stubbs blew something up in his microwave. They'll probably let us back in soon.'

'I'll go and find out.' Jack got out of the car, turning his coat collar up against the flurries of sleet. He got as far as the bright tape that was preventing anyone from going back inside. They could see him having a conversation with a senior-looking policeman.

When he came back, he simply sat, with his hands on the steering-wheel, staring through the windscreen.

Lizzie's heart sank. 'What?' she whispered. 'What's wrong?'

'There was methamphetamine in the building,' Jack said slowly. 'It blew up. Apparently nobody's been hurt but they're worried about contamination. Nobody's going to be allowed back in tonight. Maybe not for several days. They're setting up some kind of emergency accommodation in a church hall around here somewhere.'

The silence when he'd finished speaking grew as the implications sank in. Lizzie was in no condition to be in a temporary shelter with hundreds of other people.

'We could go to the pub where I work,' Kerry offered into the silence. 'They might be able to give us a room of our own.'

'Good idea.' Lizzie tried hard to sound enthusiastic but a wobble in her voice betrayed her. Jack turned his head.

'No,' he said. 'It's not a good idea.'

Another silence fell and then Jack spoke again. Decisively.

'Put your safety belts on,' he ordered. He waited until they complied and then eased the car through a gap between a fire engine and a police car.

'Is Holly properly buckled in?'

'Yes.' Kerry sounded unusually subdued.

'Where are we going?' Lizzie ventured.

'Somewhere you'll all be safe,' was all Jack said.

It was the logical thing to do.

For heaven's sake, he had this barn of a house that he rarely even visited but that his housekeeper, Mrs Benny, took pride in keeping ready for instant use. There would be fresh linen in at least eight bedrooms and clean towels in the bathrooms. The fridge and larder would be well stocked and if they weren't, that could be easily remedied in the morning.

Mrs Benny was astounded by the late-night phone call.

'Visitors? At this time of night? How many visitors?'

'Three,' Jack said, and then thought of what might happen when Maggie was released from hospital. 'At the moment,' he added.

He heard a sniff on the other end of the line.

'And a dog,' he said.

The appalled silence was annoying. He could see the problem, of course. His housekeeper had had the house virtually to herself for years now and it was always the same. Perfectly polished and nothing even an inch out of place. Sterile.

His housekeeper probably thought he was out of his mind. She could be correct but the fact that somebody else might think so was galvanising somehow. Right from the moment he'd seen Maggie lying on the ground outside the hospital he'd had a gnawing anxiety about how Lizzie was going to cope. Now that he'd been handed the opportunity to assist in a practical way, that knot of tension was going away.

And it felt…good.

'Never mind, Mrs Benny,' he said crisply. 'We can manage without you tonight. Sorry to have disturbed you.'

It meant the house was dark and chilly when they finally arrived but Jack could deal with that. He flicked every light switch he went past and cranked up the central heating to maximum.

'Whose house is this?' Lizzie asked in a dazed voice.

'Mine.'

'You…you *live* here?'

'No. It's empty. And available. Come upstairs and you can choose the rooms you'd like to use. Kerry, do you think you can find your way around the kitchen and look after the others?'

'No worries, Dr Rousseau.'

They put Lizzie in a spacious bedroom that had an en suite bathroom. Holly chose the room next door and Kerry would be on the other side of the hallway. Kerry's eyes had been getting steadily wider as Jack showed them around the house.

'This is a palace,' she said in awed tones.

'What's a palace?' Holly's words were distorted by a huge yawn.

'Where a princess lives,' Kerry told her.

'Am I a princess?'

'For tonight you are. Princess Prickles.'

Holly yawned again.

'Bedtime,' Kerry decreed. 'Come on, we'll go and give Mummy a kiss and then you can go to sleep.'

There was no reason for Jack to follow them on the mission but he found himself doing so, with Dougal plodding beside him.

'Ni' night Mummy,' Holly said. 'Sleep tight. Don't let the bed bugs bite.'

Jack's lips twitched. Imagine if Mrs Benny had heard that?

He left them to get settled and went back downstairs, heading for the drawing room and the crystal decanter that would be full to the brim with a vintage bourbon. It wasn't until he'd poured himself a glass and was standing beside the multi-paned French doors looking into a garden that was too dark to see that he realised he wasn't alone.

For some obscure reason, Dougal had followed him downstairs. He was sitting there quietly, the toy duck lying on the floor in front of him, and when Jack looked at him, he lifted his ears and wagged his tail.

'Oh… I guess you need to go outside?'

The tail wagged harder. It took a few moments to figure out how to unlock the French doors and Jack felt obliged to step outside himself as well. It would be a disaster if the beloved family pet took off and disappeared, wouldn't it?

There was a thin covering of snow on the expanse of lawn that Dougal seemed to find incredibly exciting. He put his nose into the snow and ran in circles, ploughing up flakes that were soon stuck all over his shaggy coat.

Jack took another swallow of his bourbon to try and keep the cold at bay. He'd never owned a dog but he remembered wanting one desperately when he'd been a boy.

Especially when he'd stayed here with his mother. The upper-floor apartment he'd shared with his father in Paris most of the time had been no more suitable for keeping pets than the tenement block Dougal was currently living in. But here...there were acres of garden and a small forest and a stream and even as a child he'd known that paradise could have been enhanced by having the faithful companionship of a dog.

Memories of this place were bitter-sweet. The visits had been few and far between. Random acts of duty from a mother who had been too busy living her glamorous life. A break from the greyness of the life he'd had with a father who had never recovered from the blow of his wife leaving and had buried himself in his work ever since.

He would have felt important if he'd owned a dog. Needed, maybe.

Wanted.

Jack drained the last of his bourbon. 'Come on,' he ordered the dog. 'Inside.'

Kerry came into the drawing room as he fastened the doors again.

'Can I make you a coffee or anything?' she asked.

'No, thanks. I'll head back into the city. If you think you can manage?'

'We'll manage fine.' Kerry's serious expression made her look older than her years. 'Why are you doing this for us, Dr Rousseau?'

'It's nearly Christmas,' was the best he could come up with. 'And...um...call me Jack.' He rattled his car keys in his pocket and started for the door.

Kerry followed him. 'Where are we exactly? Only I'll need to send for a taxi or something in the morning so that Lizzie can get in to see her mum.'

'No need. I'll have a car and driver sent out. Will you be all right here with Holly for the day?'

'Are you kidding? This is like winning some luxury holiday or something.'

'Good.' Jack was at the front door. 'I've left my card by the phone. Call me on my mobile if you're worried about anything.'

'OK.' Kerry was silent as he went outside but then she called out softly. 'Hey...Jack?'

He turned around. 'Yes?'

'I guess people tell you all the time but you're a really nice guy.'

No. Jack thought about that as he walked to his car. Nobody had ever told him that exactly.

It brought a disturbing echo of a small girl's voice into his mind.

He has to be nice...and kind...and he has to be really, really nice to Mummy so she'll like him too...

Oh...*mon Dieu*...what *was* he doing?

CHAPTER SEVEN

'IT WAS like something out of a movie, Mum. A car and a *chauffeur*. Can you believe it?'

'He's such a *nice* man, your Jack.'

'He's not my Jack, Mum.'

But Lizzie let her eyes drift shut for a heartbeat's wishful thinking. Jack Rousseau was, without doubt, the most astonishing man she'd ever met and he had been unbelievably kind in the face of her family's adversity, but what man in his right mind would be interested in *her*?

Not only was she minus a kidney and pathetically weak herself right now, she had a sick child and a mother who was about to be taken to Theatre to get a new hip.

Crazy.

Her whole world was crazy at the moment.

'I'm sorry about the apartment, Mum. I have no idea what's going to happen. I'll make some enquiries today and at least see if I get can some clothes and things out for us.'

'I'll be here for a few days anyway, darling. I'm sure things will be sorted by then.' Maggie's eyes were drifting shut thanks to the level of pain relief she'd been given. 'How's Misty?'

'I'm going to go and see her while you're in Theatre.'

'I'm sorry…' Maggie's voice trembled. 'I've caused you extra worry.'

Lizzie squeezed her hand. 'It's a blessing in disguise, if you ask me. OK, the timing wasn't the best but you're getting a new hip. You won't be languishing on a waiting list for goodness knows how long. It's the best Christmas present you could ask for, really.'

'But how are *you*?'

'Fine. Just…tired.'

More like she'd had the stuffing completely knocked out of her but Maggie didn't need to hear that. Fortunately she was too drowsy to notice how much of an effort it was for Lizzie to walk alongside the bed as she was taken away for surgery. Or that she got horribly dizzy when she bent to kiss her mother.

'Are you OK?' the orderly asked.

Lizzie nodded, giving Maggie's hand a final squeeze. 'I'll be in to see you as soon as they let me. I love you.'

Maggie's words were a little slurred. 'Give Misty a kiss from Nanna.'

'I will.'

To her joy, Misty was awake enough to return the kiss. And she was smiling. The PICU nurse told Lizzie that permission might be given to transfer her to the children's ward today. Dr Kingsley was going to decide when he did his rounds.

Dr Kingsley had more than the company of his junior doctors on his rounds. Lizzie felt her heart rate pick up and the bone-numbing fatigue ebb noticeably when Jack smiled at her. Good grief…the man only had to be breathing the same air as she was and the world seemed a much brighter place. She was dangerously close to falling head over heels in love with him.

Dave was more than happy with Misty's progress but he frowned noticeably when he took a second look at Lizzie.

'You need to be properly checked out. Don't you think, Jack?'

'I do indeed.'

The concern in that rich voice nearly undid Lizzie. It curled inside her, creating a melting warmth and a yearning that was overwhelming. It whispered the heady suggestion that he really did care about her.

And how on earth was she going to convince herself that he had no interest in being more than a good Christmas elf when he sounded like that? And looked at her like that? When she was now staying in his house, for heaven's sake?

'You haven't exactly been following orders and getting the rest you need, have you?' Dave asked.

'I haven't really had a choice.'

Her doctor sighed. 'So I heard. Jack filled me in on what happened to your mother. How's she doing?'

'I'm about to go and find out.' Had Jack not said anything about her apartment crisis? About putting them up in his house for the night? Why not? Was he embarrassed about a less than professional involvement with a colleague's patient? Or was he simply doing a good deed that meant nothing more and wasn't worth mentioning? Yes, that was probably it.

Lizzie hitched in a breath. 'She should be out of Theatre by now.'

'Don't you walk up there,' Dave commanded. 'And I want to see you in the ward as soon as you've made your visit. I'm going to run a few tests on you, my dear, and if you don't pass, you might find yourself back in here overnight.'

'But—' It was only that she was tired. Worrying about her mother had meant she hadn't slept at all last night.

'No buts.' Dave Kingsley was looking stern. 'And I meant what I said about not walking around the hospital at the moment. You look like a breath of wind would blow you over. We'll find a wheelchair and someone to push it.'

'Someone who'll make sure you get delivered to the surgical ward afterwards for that check-up,' Jack added.

Dave smiled. 'Good thinking. Needs to be someone she won't be able to wrap around her little finger as well. You want to volunteer?'

Jack's expression was unreadable. 'It would be my pleasure.'

Some of the expressions on the faces of the other medical staff waiting for Dr Kingsley to finish his patient's visit were far more readable. A junior female doctor nudged her friend and sent a ghost of a wink in Lizzie's direction.

She hoped, fervently, that Jack hadn't seen it.

The first opportunity to say anything at all to him didn't come until she found herself being propelled along a hospital corridor, minutes later.

'This is getting to be a habit,' she muttered. 'Sorry for taking up so much of your time.'

'Not a problem.' Jack's voice was well above her head level and sounded kind of distant. 'There was no real reason for me to finish rounds with Dave and I've got a lecture at Hammersmith to deliver this afternoon so I have a bit of free time.'

Lizzie was silent. It was frustrating enough not to be able to do this by herself. Feeling like Jack was picking up after her all the time was mortifying. Trying to distract herself, she looked around. There were staff members wearing Christmas accessories now. Reindeer antler headbands and flashing earrings. Two nurses were using a ladder to hang a string of bright silver baubles across the corridor. Jack had to manoeuvre the wheelchair carefully between them.

'It'll be the first time I'll be showing video footage of Misty's surgery,' he said into the silence between them. 'And yours.'

'Oh, help…Hollywood will be knocking on my door soon, then?'

His chuckle was delicious. 'I wouldn't hold your breath.'

'No.' She didn't even have a door anyone could knock on at the moment. The reminder of what lengths Jack had gone to for her made her take a deep breath. 'Seriously, Jack…I don't know how I can possibly thank you for everything.'

'There's no need,' Jack said quickly. 'No…honestly,' he added, having waited until two orderlies carrying overflowing boxes of Christmas decorations went past. 'New experiences are valuable and this is definitely a first for me.'

'You've pushed a wheelchair before,' she teased.

'That's not what I meant.' He stopped by the lift, angling the wheelchair so his face was visible. 'I was talking about getting rather more involved in the life of a patient I'm connected with.'

Was that how he saw her? And Misty? Simply two patients? The knot that was trying to form in Lizzie's gut made her side hurt.

'It's a bit of a no-no, isn't it? Getting involved with patients?'

Jack looked away. 'Officially, Misty isn't my patient.

She's a starring model for my video documentary. And you're certainly not my patient. You're my…ah…'

'House guest?' Lizzie suggested wryly.

'No.' The head shake was decisive. 'You'd only be my house guest if I was living there as well.' He shrugged. 'It's an empty house. You needed a place to stay. End of story.'

Jack pushed the button to summon the lift, making it a punctuation mark. Someone had stencilled snowflakes onto the stainless-steel doors with spray-on snow.

It wasn't the whole story, though, was it?

With the kind of wealth that made hiring a car and chauffeur merely the inconvenience of making a phone call, Jack could probably have put them all up in a hotel to do his good deed. Why take them back to his own house?

'It's a very beautiful place to stay,' she said quietly. 'When I saw it in the daylight this morning, I couldn't believe the gardens. You've got a lake!'

'More a big pond,' he corrected.

'It's frozen over. You could probably skate on it.'

'I wouldn't advise trying. It used to be quite deep in the middle and the ice won't be that thick.'

Lizzie was smiling as the lift arrived. 'Don't worry. I'll make sure Holly doesn't go near it and I'm probably not up to skating just yet.'

She waited until the doors had shut before voicing a new fear.

'You don't think Dave Kingsley would really try and make me stay in hospital tonight, do you?'

'I think if you have a good rest for the afternoon, it might not come to anything. But if Dave still thinks it's a good idea, you'd be well advised to follow orders.'

'But—'

'It wouldn't be a problem. Kerry's taking the best care of Holly and I'll get my housekeeper to make sure they have everything they need for a day or two.'

'It's too much to ask,' Lizzie said firmly, shaking her head.

'You're not asking. I'm offering. And it's nothing... really. Consider it a Christmas gift.' She could hear the smile in his voice and had to look up to see it. 'I'm making up for being somewhat lax in my nelf duties lately.'

Oh...dear Lord...that *smile*.

He's just being kind, she told herself very firmly.

Because of Christmas.

Because he'd become interested in Misty's case and she had a twin sister, maybe. Funny how people were captured so easily by the twin thing. They found it intriguing and then, when they got to know her girls, they were captured even more. Of course they were. They were amazing children and she owed it to them to accept this kindness she was being offered on their behalf.

It was just for a little while. A gift because it was Christmas.

A gift she would feel thankful for and be able to remember for the rest of her life. A gift that would give her a connection to Jack Rousseau, maybe also for the rest of her life. Having that length of time to consider was good. It meant that when she felt better, she would be able to think of some way to repay him.

Maggie was just awake but still very sleepy.

'I'm still in the land of the living,' she murmured. 'And you're here, Lizzie...and Jack. How *very* nice.'

Jack stayed at the end of the bed, reading the medical chart, while Lizzie held her mother's hand.

'You're doing well, Mrs Donaldson. You came through with flying colours by the look of this.'

'Mum's as tough as they come.' Lizzie voice wobbled but she was smiling.

'Look who's talking,' Maggie mumbled. 'You have the lion's share of courage, love. And a heart as big as Texas.'

She did. Mother and daughter were smiling at each other so they couldn't see the way Jack let his gaze rest on Lizzie.

She was special, all right.

Amazing…

It was disconcertingly difficult to stop looking at her. And it was impossible to ignore that curl in his gut that only the most desirable of women could account for.

He went to find a staff member in the recovery room to talk to, then came back.

'You can stay for ten minutes,' he told Lizzie. 'I've found a nurse who's going to make sure you get delivered for your check-up downstairs. I'll give Dave a call and let him know when to expect you. I'd better get myself over to Hammersmith.'

It was a relief to step back into normality. To give himself time to sort his slide presentation and negotiate city traffic to get to an important engagement on time. This was what his life was all about. Delivering his skills to the expected level of competence. Professional interactions and enough pressure on both his skills and available time to make anything outside work hours almost irrelevant.

Taking even moments of time to be aware of fuzzy, emotional things like family bonds or the pleasure of a dog's company was an aberration. One that, disturbingly, seemed to be happening with increasing regularity. Throw in even the stirrings of physical desire and the combination was becoming downright dangerous.

Delivering this lecture to a packed auditorium in one of London's most prestigious hospitals was a very good thing. A dose of welcome reality.

The lecture was extremely well-received and led to an interesting question and answer session at the end about the advantages and disadvantages of peritoneal versus haemodialysis for young children.

'Is peritoneal still the preferred treatment for children?' someone queried.

'Yes, it is,' Jack responded. 'It can be done at home during the day or with the aid of a cycler machine at night. It causes less disruption to a daily routine and makes attendance at school much easier.'

'Why do haemodialysis at all, then?'

'The disadvantage of peritoneal dialysis is the heavy responsibility that is put on the carer, usually a parent. Stress levels can be elevated, which can have a detrimental effect on family dynamics.'

Jack was astonished at how easily the picture of a family coping with a child in end-stage renal failure came to his mind. In front of hundreds of eager students and respectful colleagues, all he could think of for several heartbeats was Lizzie and her twin daughters.

'And family,' he added slowly, 'to any child, is the whole world. To a sick child, it's something that has to be part of any holistic care.'

When he felt his mobile phone vibrating in his pocket at that point, his first thought was also Lizzie and the thought that something might have happened to her was chilling.

It was far more likely that Dave was calling him about one of his more complicated cases, but a quick glance at the caller ID showed him that the call was coming from his country house. No way could he ignore it and he'd already gone over the allocated lecture time. He excused himself from the lecture theatre and called back.

'I'm so sorry to bother you, Jack, but you said to call if I was worried about anything...'

'Kerry?' She sounded breathless. 'What's wrong?'

'Um...nothing *bad*, exactly...'

Jack thought of the iced-over pond he'd been talking to Lizzie about and felt another chill run down his spine. 'Is Holly all right?'

'She's great. We've been making gingerbread men and...'

He heard the catch in her voice. And the unnerving silence that followed.

'Kerry?'

'Phew...I think it's stopped.'

'What's stopped?'

'The contraction.'

Oh...*no*... Jack squeezed his eyes shut as he took in a very deep breath. He rubbed his forehead with his knuckles for good measure.

'How often are you getting contractions, Kerry?'

'Um...it was about five minutes between the last two.'

'OK. Listen to me.' Jack pulled in another breath. 'I'm going to call an ambulance. Lock Dougal in the house when they get there and you'll need to take Holly with you. I'll meet you at the hospital. They'll probably take you to St Bethel's Hospital, which is a lot closer than Westbridge. I'll meet you there. Ask the paramedics to call me if they take you anywhere else. Got it?'

'Got it...and...Jack?'

'Yes?' He really didn't want to be told how nice he was.

'Sorry.'

'Don't be. Can't be helped.' But Jack found himself staring at his phone as he snapped it shut.

This was turning into some kind of nightmare and he was trapped in it.

After directing an ambulance to the young woman in labour, he put in a call to Dave Kingsley.

'Lizzie's fine. All she needed was a few hours' sleep. I've told her she's fine to go home but they've put her mother into the coronary care unit for a few hours. She had a bit of an arrhythmia when they were about to transfer her from Recovery to the ward and they want to monitor her cardiac activity carefully for a while. Lizzie's decided to stay with her but has promised to try and get some more sleep. She said she had someone she trusted completely to look after Holly.'

Did she need the extra worry of knowing that the person she trusted to care for her daughter was about to be collected by an ambulance and that she would have Holly in tow as she travelled to a strange hospital to give birth?

No, of course she didn't. She certainly wouldn't get any rest if she knew.

'Tell her everything else is completely under control,' he told Dave. 'She doesn't need to worry.'

He could do that much for her. Just for tonight and that would be it. His level of involvement here was becoming absurd.

Kerry was in a cubicle in the A and E department of St Bethel's, a small hospital on the outskirts of London.

'Wouldn't you know it?' she groaned. 'The contractions stopped the minute I got in here.'

'We're going to admit her overnight just to keep an eye on her,' the consultant told Jack.

'No!' Kerry looked as alarmed as Jack was feeling. 'I have to go home.'

'Those contractions could start again.' The consultant was scanning notes a registrar had already made. 'And from the looks of this, your antenatal care has been a bit…patchy. It would be prudent to have a good check-up.'

'Indeed it would.' Jack knew his voice sounded hollow. He tried to smile. 'I'm no obstetrician. You don't want me having to try and remember med school training at 3:00 a.m.'

The consultant was looking curious. 'You're a doctor?'

'Transplant specialist. Jack Rousseau.'

'I've heard the name.' They shook hands and the emergency department consultant raised an eyebrow. 'And you and Kerry are…ah…'

'No.' Kerry spoke up swiftly. 'Jack's being kind enough to let us stay in his house, that's all. We had an explosion in our apartment block last night.'

'Oh?' The consultant blinked. 'And the little girl who came in with you?'

'She's my neighbour's granddaughter. I'm friends with her mum. So's Jack.'

It was getting too confusing for the St Bethel's doctor, who shook his head in bemusement. Jack was very tempted to mirror the action. Instead, he turned to Kerry.

'Where is Holly?'

'A nurse said she was taking her to the relatives' room.'

'I'll take her home. My housekeeper, Mrs Benny, will look after her. You need to do what the doctors here advise.'

He didn't give Kerry any time to argue. He got directions to the relatives' room but paused on the way to ring his housekeeper.

'I'll be bringing a child home for the night,' he informed her. 'I'd like you to take care of her.'

The voice on the other end of the line was tight. 'You can manage without me, you said. As far as I'm concerned, Dr Rousseau, my employment with you has been terminated.'

Mrs Benny hung up on him.

Jack would have laughed aloud at this new twist in his personal nightmare but he had turned his head for some reason and now he could see into the relatives' room he'd been heading towards.

Whatever staff member had taken Holly there hadn't stayed with her. The small girl was sitting alone in an empty room.

Just sitting, with her hands clasped in her lap and an expression on her face that made Jack's throat tighten so much it was too hard to take a breath.

He *knew* that look.

This was why he avoided children. Why he'd put off the thought of ever getting involved enough to consider getting married or having a family of his own. It wasn't that children, or women for that matter, were so inclined to cry.

It was that *neediness*.

His memory was so accurate he could feel, deep inside himself, what it was like to be a child like that. So vulnerable and desperate. Or rather he knew what it felt to be like that and to not receive what was so desperately needed.

The misery of wanting something that wasn't there.

The responsibility of being the one expected to provide it. *That* was what was terrifying about marriage and children.

How could he ever give something that he'd never been given himself? He didn't know how.

Jack still hadn't moved. Not one step closer to Holly.

He didn't have to give this little girl what she needed most, though, did he?

She had it in spades. She had the most amazing mother. A grandmother. A sister. A neighbour who was more like a family member. She even had a dog that loved her.

A home she would be able to return to soon enough. People to love and be loved by.

This space of time was an anomaly. A crevasse in a normally emotionally secure life. He'd seen what the connection was like in this little family, that day when they'd been clustered around Misty's bed. Maybe fate had decreed that he would be in the right place at the right time, to make a bridge across that crevasse for Holly.

Just for now.

For Christmas?

She had begged Santa for a daddy for Christmas, hadn't she?

Not for ever.

Just for Christmas.

That was only a matter of days away and by the time Christmas was over, everything would be sorted. Lizzie would be well on the road to complete recovery. Maggie would be close to being back on her feet. Their home would be safe.

A bridge. That was all he needed to be.

A temporary daddy?

As if she'd finally sensed his presence in the corridor, Holly looked up. The fear and loneliness and need was still etched on her face but there was something different in the way she looked now. Or the way she was sitting, maybe.

Jack could actually feel the ripple of hope coming out to wash over *him*.

He held out his hand. 'Come on, Holly. It's time to go home.'

CHAPTER EIGHT

THERE was a supermarket on the route from St Bethel's to Jack's house.

'Dog food,' Jack muttered to himself. 'And milk.' He glanced over his shoulder. 'What do you want for your dinner, Holly?'

How bizarre was this? He'd never had to think about feeding a dog, let alone cooking for a child. Up till now, the most difficult meal decisions he'd ever had to make had been which gourmet restaurant to take someone like Danielle to and whether he could secure the most impressive table.

It seemed like a different life now. Right now, it should seem as alluring as, say, a tropical island holiday. Very odd that it seemed surreal and...meaningless.

'Sketti,' Holly said decisively.

'Sketti?' Jack's English was close to perfect after the years of boarding and then medical school but this was a new word for him. 'What's that?' Some kind of fish, maybe?

'*You* know.' Holly's tone was very patient. 'It goes on toast. Me and Misty call it worms sometimes but only when Mummy can't hear us.'

'Oh...' Comprehension came with a clunk. *Spaghetti.*

'Mmm. Sketti.'

'And what does Dougal eat?'

'Crunchy brown things. They don't taste very nice. He likes sketti better.'

Jack found an empty slot in the supermarket car park. He was still shaking his head as he went round to open the back door. 'How do you know that Dougal's food doesn't taste very nice? Do *you* eat dog food, too?'

Holly's eyes went very wide. She pressed her lips together firmly.

'Never mind.' Jack led the way into the supermarket. He was taken by surprise when Holly's hand slipped into his but maybe it was a good idea to keep a hold of it. He wouldn't want to lose her in the crowd.

Holly wanted to sit in the trolley. 'Cos my legs are sleepy,' she said.

She sat at the far end, with her knees drawn up to make room for the grocery items, including several cans of spaghetti and a loaf of bread. Halfway down the dairy aisle on their way to find butter, Jack suddenly realised he was actually enjoying himself. This was definitely a new experience. He'd never pushed a supermarket trolley before, let alone one that had a very cute, small girl directing proceedings. She was pointing imperiously now.

'*That* butter. Kerry says it's the bestest.'

New Zealand butter. That figured. Jack made a mental note to call St Bethel's later and check up on how Kerry was doing. He'd have to contact Lizzie somehow, too, but that was a little more problematic. With a sigh, Jack pushed the issue aside and went in search of the dog food aisle.

The supermarket was busy and the shoppers were predominantly women. By the time they got to the checkout, Jack was aware of how many looks he was getting, along with some rather impressed-looking smiles. The girl at the till provided a clue to the puzzle.

'Ooh, aren't you lucky,' she said to Holly. 'You get to go shopping with your *daddy*.'

Jack's heart skipped a beat. Any second now and Holly would say that he wasn't her daddy. He'd get a rather different kind of look then and goodness knows what kind of trouble he might find himself in.

The thought was alarming to say the least. The alarm almost, but not quite, obliterated that odd buzz he'd got from someone assuming he was Holly's father.

To his surprise, Holly said nothing at all. She gave Jack the oddest look and then simply smiled, picking up a can of spaghetti to put onto the conveyor belt.

'Quiet little thing, aren't you?' The checkout girl winked at Jack. 'My favourite kind of kid.'

Jack smiled at her. 'Mine, too.'

Dougal was overjoyed to have company and seemed thrilled by Jack's choice of kibbled dog food. He saw Holly eyeing the dog's enthusiasm for the new food.

'No,' he said, sternly. 'Don't even think about it. We've got sketti, remember?'

At least toasting and buttering bread and heating canned spaghetti were well within Jack's culinary skill level. Strangely, it didn't even taste that bad.

Holly finally pushed her plate away 'I'm as full as a bull,' she announced.

Her face was covered with tomato sauce.

'You need a wash,' Jack told her. A worrying thought occurred to him. 'Are you old enough to have a bath by yourself?'

Holly nodded. 'I'm *six*.' She screwed her face into

deeply thoughtful lines. 'The taps are hard, though. I've just got little fingers.'

'I'll run it for you.'

He stayed within shouting distance, too, sitting on the top stair with Dougal beside him while Holly was in the bath. He'd go in, he decided, if the singing and splashing sounds diminished into silence.

It was a good time to ring St Bethel's and he learned that Kerry was sound asleep. The contractions, probably Braxton Hicks', had stopped completely and she'd be able to go home in the morning.

The worry of what to say to Lizzie sorted itself with remarkable ease when *his* phone rang.

'Oh…Jack…I was expecting it to be Kerry.'

'She's having a bit of a rest.'

'Is she all right?'

'Yes.' He was telling the truth. Some of it, anyway. 'She had a few Braxon Hicks' contractions today but they've stopped now.'

'And Holly? Is she all right?'

From the corner of his eye, Jack could see a small, naked figure, trailing a towel by one corner and moving purposefully into the bedroom.

'She's getting her pyjamas on. Do you want to talk to her?'

'Please.'

Holly had her pyjamas on inside out. 'Mummy…we had *sketti* for tea.'

She listened for a while, nodding vigorously and then her face lit up with a joyous smile. 'I love you too, Mummy. Ni' night.'

The phone was handed back to Jack. 'How are *you*?' he asked.

'I'm fine. All I needed was a bit of sleep. And Mum's

fine, too. They've shifted her back to the ward and she's actually been up on her feet just to see how she went. I could leave but it's getting late and it would nice to be able to check up on Mum *and* Misty first thing in the morning.'

'Of course it would.' Jack brushed aside the desire to send a car to collect her immediately to bring her back here. 'Try and get some sleep, won't you? I'll get Kerry to call you in the morning.'

'Thanks.'

Lizzie sounded tired, which was hardly surprising given such an emotional day. Was he wrong in not telling her about Kerry? Or that he was alone in the house with Holly, pretending to be her daddy?

Probably. But it had seemed the right thing to do.

So was making sure that Holly got into bed and snuggled up. The child's eyes were drooping enough to suggest that sleep was not far away.

She was an astonishing kid, Jack decided. She hadn't been any trouble at all, really. Except that, when he said good night and turned to leave, her little jaw wobbled ominously.

'It'll be all right,' Jack assured her. 'Kerry *and* Mummy will most likely be home tomorrow to look after you. And it'll *be* tomorrow as soon as you've had a sleep.'

'But I can't go to sleep.'

'Why not?'

'Cos Mummy always gives me a love. And if she's not there, Nanna gives me a love. Or Kerry does. Sometimes Dougal does, too.'

Jack eyed the dog hopefully. Dougal stayed where he was at the end of the bed and thumped his tail.

Holly sniffed loudly.

'Um…' Surely Holly could sense how far out of his depth he was? Apparently not. Big blue eyes were fixed on him. 'I'm not sure I know about giving loves,' Jack muttered.

'It's easy.' Holly was out from under the covers like a shot. She stood on the bed and held her arms out. 'You just have to do this.'

He simply couldn't *not* do it. Jack opened his own arms and found himself hugging a small girl whose arms clung tightly around his neck.

She was so small. So fragile. He could feel her heart beating rapidly against his chest and hear her snuffling against his neck. He could smell soap and warmth and… something that reminded him of summer.

The neediness was certainly there but he seemed to be doing enough with nothing more than holding her. Or being there for her to hold. The fierce tension ebbed from the tight grip and Holly's sigh a short time later was contented. Jack bent down and the little girl obligingly slithered free and buried her face in the pillows. By the time Jack pulled up the covers to keep her warm, she appeared to be soundly asleep.

The dog gave him an approving look and padded after Jack but they both stopped at the bedroom door and turned back for a final glance.

Jack could still feel those small arms around him and the incredible softness of the hair that had tickled his skin. He could see the stain of tomato sauce that hadn't quite been vanquished by the bath. Most of all, he could see the echo of this child's smile when her mother must have told her she was loved and hear the sound of that contented little sigh after his hug.

It was doing something very strange, deep inside his gut. He could feel an odd, almost melting sensation. A liquid feeling that puddled around something very solid that he recognised as a desire to protect this small person.

Bemused at the overpowering strength of this new sensation, Jack went slowly downstairs and from out of nowhere he remembered something else he'd heard Holly telling Father Christmas.

Mummy looks after everybody. Me and Misty and Nanna. But there's nobody to take care of Mummy, is there? I'm still too little.

She wanted to, though, didn't she? This child had the same kind of heart as her mother. As big as Texas.

Jack could feel that sensation tightening inside him. Squeezing his heart.

Holly deserved something special. For herself. Something she could remember for the rest of her life.

But what?

Jack thought about it as sipped his vintage bourbon. He discussed it with Dougal when he took the dog out into the garden for a spell before closing up the house for the night.

And then it occurred to him. Christmas was important in this family for an extra reason. It was also the twins' birthday. What if—*this* year—it was really, really special? A combination Christmas birthday celebration that had everything two little girls could wish for?

A day that they would remember for ever.

So would he, because he would play at least a small part in it—*be* there—so that he could make their Christmas wish come true. And that really would be the end of it. He could cut short this consultancy stint by pleading pressure from his Paris base or something and then he would be gone. He could put this property on

the market and never come back. It might take months
to sell and Lizzie and her family could stay here until
it did and that would give them plenty of time to get
their own lives back in order.

The solution seemed neat. He could help, give them
all something nice to remember and tuck it into the past
and move on. The question now was how on earth could
he make it happen? Research was called for and, at this
time of night, the internet was the only place to start.

A Christmas tree shouldn't be a problem. His gar-
dener, Jimmy, could no doubt source one out in the
woods but this needed to make more of a statement
than a small branch of a spruce tree. He'd seen thousands of those impressive kinds of trees very recently,
though, hadn't he? The day he'd happened to eavesdrop
on Holly talking to Father Christmas, in fact, which
made it perfectly logical to go looking for an online
branch of Bennett's department store.

The array of goods available was mind-boggling.
The variety of the usual trappings of Christmas-like
trees and decorations and even food for a special meal
seemed limitless but Jack kept scrolling through page
after page, searching for an X factor of some kind.

He needed something…

Ah…the word in the sidebar said it all.

Personal.

He clicked on the 'Personal Shopper' tab and eyed
a screen full of photographs and profiles. These were
people who were specialist shoppers who promised they
could do whatever it took to make Christmas magic for
that special someone. They could take care of any decorations and catering and personal gifts. All they needed
was a link that would provide enough background information.

One of the photos caught Jack's eye. A young man by the name of Barnaby who stood out as being a bit different, with his flop of black hair covering one eye, a ring in the visible eyebrow and a distinctly mischievous smile. It made him think of Kerry and she would know far more than he did about the twins and other members of the Matthews family. He could engage the services of this Barnaby with some general information to grab his attention and then make Kerry the link to the family and the two of them could go to town. All he would have to do was to provide the details of his credit card and give them a very generous budget.

Perfect.

Jack clicked on Barnaby's profile and scrolled to the box to tell him who he'd be shopping for. He wrote about twin six-year-old girls, one of whom was due home for both Christmas and her birthday following a kidney transplant. He added a bit about their mother who had donated a kidney and the grandmother who was in need of some special care herself. He even put in a bit about Dougal. Nobody could read this little story without being moved, he decided. Hopefully, it would present a challenge that a personal shopper could rise to with the utmost determination to shine.

The sense of satisfaction in putting his plan into action so effectively was only equalled by the astonishment of realising how much time he had spent on this. And if it was 2:00 a.m., why on earth was his phone ringing?

'Sorry to wake you, Jack.'

'I wasn't asleep, Dave. What's happening?'

'I've got a kidney on the way down from Edinburgh. It's a good match for our MVA guy you know about but, given the complications we've got with his other abdominal injuries, I could really use your input on this surgery. Any chance you could get here in an hour or so?'

'Of course.' The response was automatic. It wasn't until Jack ended the call and went to pick up his car keys that he realised what he'd done.

He had a child asleep upstairs.

A child he was responsible for.

A groan escaped his lips. Had he really thought he could play at being a temporary daddy? Just for Christmas? Good grief…he couldn't even manage it for a single night.

He couldn't leave her.

But he couldn't not respond to the call. This was what he did. Who he *was*.

He could sort this, he decided, his mind working at the speed of light. If he took Holly in to the hospital with him, there would be a staff member who could care for her. An on-call room, probably, where she could be tucked up and continue sleeping with minimal disruption. It was far from ideal but it was, at least, a solution to the awful conflict he was still grappling with as he moved swiftly up the stairs. When he got to Holly's room, he stood for a moment, looking down at the perfect picture of a peacefully sleeping child.

This was *exactly* why it had been so unwise to allow himself any kind of involvement with Holly and her family. But he hadn't listened to the warning bells, had he? He'd allowed himself to get sucked in. Right from the moment his attention had been caught by the conversation Holly had been having with Father Christmas. Bit by bit, despite resisting, he'd been drawn closer and now here he was, facing the wake-up call.

It wasn't pleasant. His career meant that other people ended up being neglected and hurt. It had been bad enough to fail an adult partner who'd chosen to be with him knowing how he felt about his career but this time, he was failing an innocent child and it was, quite simply, unacceptable.

Holly whimpered but didn't wake up completely as he picked her up and wrapped her in the quilt.

'It's all right,' he murmured, 'We just need to go for a ride in the car.'

He carried the warm, sleepy bundle that was Holly downstairs and out into an icy night. She made another, distressed sound as he tucked her into the car seat and fastened the safety belt.

He leaned closer. *'Je suis vraiment désolé, ma chérie,'* he whispered. 'This won't happen again, I promise.'

CHAPTER NINE

'I DON'T *believe* this.'

Lizzie stared at Kerry in horror as she sucked in a new breath. '*Any* of it. He didn't even tell me you were in hospital, let alone…'

Her voice trailed off. The enormity of what had happened overnight, which she had known nothing about, was too much.

'He was being nice,' Kerry assured her. 'And it all worked out fine, didn't it? He sent the car to get me this morning and we collected Holly and went back home to get clothes and the dolls and stuff. Hey…you should have seen old Stubby's face when we turned up with a *chauffeur.*'

Lizzie didn't care how gobsmacked Mr Stubbs had been. Or that Holly was triumphantly carrying the bag of well-worn dolls and their paraphernalia that Misty was desperate to play with now that she was feeling so much better.

'He had no right taking over like that. I didn't have to stay here. I certainly wouldn't have if I'd known where you were. Or that Jack was looking after Holly by himself. Heavens…*Mum* would have had a fit if she'd known about that.'

'We had sketti for tea,' Holly piped up, sending a worried frown in her mother's direction.

'Lucky you.' Kerry grinned. She sent Lizzie a glance that suggested she might want to tone things down in front of Holly. 'It's all fine now,' she said calmly. 'I was in the place I needed to be and so were you. Jack didn't want to worry you any more, that's all. It's not that big a deal. He didn't want you *or* your mum having any kind of fit. How's Maggie doing, anyway?'

'She's great. Determined to finish making those felt stockings for the girls before she gets home.' Lizzie managed a tight smile for Holly's benefit but she could feel the knot of tension inside her continuing to expand.

What was Jack Rousseau's deal?

Being interested in the lives of particular patients was one thing. Being so kind to people in trouble at Christmastime was another. Slightly harder to accept but understandable. That he thought he could assume control of her family affairs without even consulting her was definitely a step too far. It wasn't acceptable at all.

'We'll go and visit Misty,' she announced. 'And Nanna. And then we're going to go and collect Dougal and go home.'

Holly's frown was puzzled now. 'But Dougal *is* at home.'

'He's at Jack's home.' Lizzie knew she sounded grim but she couldn't help it. The time had come to pull the plug on this fantasy they had all been caught up in. 'We have to go back to our own home.'

She shouldn't have let Jack become involved at all. She could have prevented it. Right back at the start when she'd had the chance to deny his involvement with Misty and herself in making that documentary video.

Nelf law had been her undoing. Not to mention that ill-advised fantasy about the man with the sexy accent and the dark, chocolate eyes. God help her, but she only had to see those eyes or that smile of his to get drawn back to that fantasy every time.

This was her doing, all of it. And it had led to her child being dragged from her bed in the middle of the night because the man looking after her had had bigger responsibilities.

Well, she didn't have. From now on, it was the welfare of her family that would take precedence and any personal inclination to spend more time in Jack's presence would have to be ruthlessly crushed.

It was probably just as well that her path didn't cross that of Jack's during the hours they were at the hospital that day. Misty and Holly had a happy time playing dollies and some of her anger faded as she and Kerry watched them and simply enjoyed the progress Misty was clearly making in getting back to being a normal, healthy little girl.

Time with her mother was just as rewarding. A volunteer choir was doing the rounds, singing traditional Christmas songs and carols and handing out warm mince pies. A physiotherapist was also there, giving Maggie her first lesson in using elbow crutches.

'I'll be back tomorrow and we'll get you taking a step or two,' she said to Maggie. 'You'll be moving properly within a day or two and when you can manage stairs, you'll be allowed to go home.'

She wouldn't be able to manage ten flights of stairs, Lizzie thought with dismay. She would have to keep her fingers firmly crossed that the lifts in the tenement block didn't have one of their all–too-regular periods of being out of action. In the new year, she vowed, she would start looking for somewhere else for them all to live. Somehow, she would make it happen.

By mid-afternoon, they were ready to go and collect Dougal and Lizzie was faced with a new dilemma. The car and chauffeur would be waiting nearby but maybe this was the moment to assert her independence and call a taxi. To hire a taxi to go all the way out to Jack's country house and then take them back again would be prohibitively expensive, however, and she wasn't even sure she had the funds available on her card.

It was Jack's fault that they were so far out of the city, though, wasn't it?

Or was it all her fault for allowing their rescue the other night instead of joining her neighbours at whatever shelter had been provided?

A compromise was the best option, she decided. She would use the car to get out there and then tell the driver his services would no longer be needed. They would get a taxi home.

An hour or so later, the wheels of the luxury car crunched over the thin layer of snow on the pebbled driveway of the country estate. The vehicle couldn't get close to the front steps, however, because an enormous truck was parked there.

A Bennett's truck.

Lounging near the rear of the truck was a young man with floppy, black hair and a gold ring glinting in his eyebrow.

Kerry was as transfixed by the apparition as Lizzie was but clearly for a very different reason.

'Who *is* that?' she breathed. 'Oh, my God…he's… *gorgeous.*'

'What's in the truck?' Holly sounded just as excited as Kerry.

'Why is it here?' Lizzie muttered, perplexed. 'What on earth is going on here?'

Despite her advanced state of pregnancy, Kerry was first out of the car. Holly bounced after her. By the time Lizzie joined them, Kerry and the young man were busy grinning at each other.

'This is Barnaby,' Kerry informed her.

'I think you might have the wrong address,' Lizzie told him.

'Don't think so.' Barnaby flicked his glossy hair so that, briefly, both his eyes were visible. 'You're Lizzie Matthews, aren't you?'

'Yes.'

Barnaby gaze slid away again instantly. 'And you're Kerry, aren't you?'

'Oh, my God…you're psychic, aren't you?'

They grinned at each other again.

'I'm Holly,' Holly said, standing on tiptoe and tugging at Barnaby's sleeve.

'I know that, princess.' He tore his gaze away from Kerry and ruffled Holly's curls. 'And you have a twin sister called Misty who's in hospital and a grandma who's in hospital too.'

Lizzie's jaw dropped. 'How do you know that?'

She knew, though, didn't she? Not only was Jack taking over control in her life, he was broadcasting personal information to all and sundry.

Barnaby had the cheek to wink at her. 'Cos I'm psychic?'

Holly tugged at his sleeve again. 'Why are *you* sick?'

But Barnaby just grinned. He held out his arms like a conjuror about to dazzle them all with a magic trick. 'I'm your personal shopper,' he told them.

Lizzie's breath left her in an incredulous huff. Barnaby's grin faded. 'Maybe I should explain?'

'I think you'd better.' Lizzie folded her arms tightly in front of her as though she needed to give herself a hug. 'Kerry? Do you think you and Holly could go and let Dougal out or something?'

'Sure...' Kerry cast a final glance in Barnaby's direction. 'I guess. Come on, Prickles.'

Lizzie glared at Barnaby as soon as the others were out of earshot but before he could even open his mouth to start talking, another vehicle came racing down the driveway. She could see Jack staring at the Bennett's truck as he came to halt but it was Lizzie who had his full attention when he came to join them.

'I need to explain,' he said.

Dougal came barrelling out of the house at full speed and went straight to Jack, planting already grubby paws on his immaculate merino coat.

'Down,' Jack commanded, moving away. He turned towards the open area of the garden and issued another command. 'Come with me.'

Lizzie thought he was talking to the dog but then he touched her arm. 'Please?' he added.

Without thinking, she obeyed the direction.

'Um...I'll go and have a chat with Kerry, shall I?' Barnaby called after them.

'Good idea,' Jack said, without turning back.

They walked to the edge of the lawn and watched Dougal ploughing furrows and then rolling in the snow, stopping only to lift his leg on a tree here and there. It was cold but Lizzie just rubbed at her arms. She had things to say to Jack that would be better said in privacy. Angry things about assuming control and putting her child at risk.

But Jack was shedding his coat. He draped it over Lizzie's shoulders.

'This is all my fault,' he said. 'I'm so sorry, Lizzie.'

The apology was so unexpected, Lizzie searched his face. 'What for?'

'I shouldn't have brought Holly here last night. I wasn't on call but, in my line of work, I'm never completely *off* call, I didn't think.'

'No. You didn't.' Lizzie was amazed to hear sadness rather than anger in her own voice.

Jack pushed his fingers through his hair. He was standing in his shirtsleeves but he didn't seem to be cold yet. Lizzie wasn't cold at all. She was wrapped in warmth that smelt like Jack and it was...delicious.

They walked a little further, through the archway of a beautifully clipped, round yew hedge that sheltered a water feature.

'I don't know quite how it happened,' Jack said. 'It certainly wasn't intentional. That's why I'm single, you know. Why I'll always be single, because I would never set out to let anybody down like that.'

Suddenly, berating Jack for what had happened seemed wrong.

Part of her brain was trying to replay his words. Trying to hammer home the message that Jack was choosing to be single. That he intended to remain single. Unattached. Unencumbered.

'There was no harm done,' Lizzie said slowly. 'And I do understand that you were only trying to help.'

'I shouldn't have. I'm not in a position to give that kind of help. I shouldn't have tried.'

Dougal did a circuit of the round garden room and then vanished again, barking to share his joy at being free to run.

Lizzie wanted to change the subject. Or not. Why was Jack beating himself up so much over this? OK, he'd taken a sleeping child from her bed in the middle of the night but he hadn't abandoned her, had he? And he hadn't told her about any of it because he'd known she'd had enough on her plate last night, worrying about her mother.

'You've been incredibly helpful,' she told him now. 'I can never thank you enough. But what I don't understand is…'

He was watching her face carefully. Listening to every word she said. Lizzie could feel the pull between them. Something that was powerful and real but they were both ignoring it. Why?

That was what she didn't understand. Why it was there. What it really was and whether it meant anything like what it felt like it *could* mean.

Was it simply humanitarian interest on Jack's part? A series of coincidences that was pulling them closer? Was it gratitude on her part? Loneliness maybe and feeling more vulnerable because she wasn't a hundred per cent healthy yet? All this with a bit of physical attraction thrown in?

No.

Lizzie's gaze hadn't left Jack's face. She knew every line of it now, she realised. The crinkles at the corners of his eyes, the aristocratic shape of his nose, the furrows that defined the edges of his cheeks and led to lips that were capable of giving the most beautiful smiles on earth.

He might not want it—in fact, he obviously didn't, having made his declaration that he would be single for ever—and she might not want to give it, having vowed to nurture her independence—but this man had Lizzie's heart.

For better or worse, she *loved* him.

Oh…God. He was still waiting for her to finish her sentence. Watching her face as if he could read her thoughts.

'The truck,' she croaked, a trifle desperately. 'I don't understand what the truck is doing here.'

'Ah…' Jack's eyes told her that he knew that wasn't what she'd been thinking about at all. His tone suggested relief that this was something he could deal with. 'It's here because of…Holly.'

'Holly?'

'Mmm.' Jack's gaze still hadn't left hers. There was an unspoken message going on but Lizzie couldn't figure out what it was. Neither could she look away. She watched the way the corners of Jack's mouth tilted up a little. A close enough reminder of one of his smiles to make her aware of a melting sensation in her chest.

'It's to do with what I heard Holly asking Father Christmas for that day.'

Lizzie's inward breath was almost a gasp. Was he going to tell her? Was he going to make her daughters' wish come true?

'It's in the truck? What they wished for?'

'Not…exactly.'

It was childish, but Lizzie was tempted to stamp her foot.

'Tell me…*please*, Jack. This is really important. If there's something they really want for Christmas and I can provide it for them, I really want to be able to do that. I'll do anything to make a wish come true for them at the moment.'

'Anything?'

There was a low note in Jack's voice. Perhaps amusement was part of it but it came across as a rumble that had purely sexual connotations. Lizzie could feel a wash of heat rising from her belly towards her face and, for a heartbeat, the world seemed to hold its breath.

Rather like the way Jack was holding Lizzie's gaze.

What would he want from her if she said yes?

Perhaps a more relevant question would be what *wasn't* she prepared to give him?

Dear Lord… Lizzie had to close her eyes and remind herself to breathe. And then she had to look away because it was simply too dangerous to let that astonishingly intimate gaze continue for even a moment longer.

Jack cleared his throat but his voice still sounded curiously hoarse.

'I can't tell you,' he said apologetically.

Lizzie gave a resigned huff. 'Nelf law again?'

'I'm afraid so.'

She risked a quick glance. He was still looking down at her. He still had a hint of a smile playing with his lips.

'But I can provide it,' he added.

'You mean…*buy* it?' Perhaps he had already and whatever it was was stowed in the Bennett's truck. 'Jack, I can't let you—'

His head shake was subtle but enough to stop her talking. 'It's a bit more complicated than that. It's all about a…setting as much as anything else.'

'What kind of setting?'

'A Christmas kind. A tree with decorations. Presents. Food and people. Particular people.'

'Like who?' Lizzie could see that Jack was finally feeling the cold. He was rubbing his hands together and she could see goose-bumps where the cuffs of his shirt ended.

'You, of course. And your mother. Kerry, too. Me, even.' The last words were added casually but to Lizzie they resonated with a particular significance.

Had Holly wished for a special Christmas Day? The kind that was idealised in children's stories? With a snow-covered garden and a big house full of warmth and light and the joys of an extended family?

Was it part of the twins' wish that Jack be included?

No. How could it have been when the wish had been made before they'd even known he existed?

As unlikely as it might seem, it was a possibility that it was Jack's wish to be a part of it.

He was single. Did he even have a family of his own to be with?

He might be dedicated to his high-profile career to the degree of allowing nothing personal to compromise that dedication, but there had to be times when he felt like he was missing out.

When he felt lonely, even.

Lizzie had the odd sensation that something was breaking inside her. A tiny piece of her heart, maybe.

'Oh…Jack,' she whispered. 'Is that what the truck is all about? Are you trying to make Christmas for us all?'

He didn't say anything. He just stood there, looking down at Lizzie with an appeal in his eyes that she couldn't possibly resist.

All her earlier resolve melted into oblivion. How on earth could she pack up and take Holly and Dougal and Kerry back to their tenement housing? It wasn't that it would ruin their own Christmas. She could manage to make a special day for them all but, if she did that, she would be taking away the opportunity Jack had to have a real, family kind of Christmas.

With songs and laughter and the kind of magic that only small children could bring to a family celebration. If she left, she would be leaving Jack alone in an empty house. She could imagine him coming out into this garden, in the snow, alone and...cold.

Impetuously, Lizzie opened her arms and slipped them around Jack to hug him. To offer him some warmth. To accept this incredibly generous offer. She couldn't reject it because, if she did, she would be rejecting *him*. Most of all, she wanted the hug to say thank you. To say that she understood.

For a moment, Lizzie could feel his surprise at her gesture but then his body softened a little and his arms came around her. He pulled the coat back over her shoulders to keep her warm but then they stayed around her. Pulling her closer, even.

Had she really thought he looked cold? His body was so warm. Alive. She could feel the thump of his heart and the strength of his chest as it rose and fell with each breath.

The pull that had been there between them all along was a liquid thing now and Lizzie was drowning in it. She looked up, intending to smile before pushing herself away so that she could breathe again.

But Jack's arms still held her and when she raised her face, it was to find him still looking down at her, with something like amazement in his eyes. Was he feeling the same, overwhelming pull?

Lizzie couldn't be sure who moved first. Did she stand on tiptoe, like Holly did when she really wanted to be noticed? Or did Jack dip his head and she had been powerless to resist meeting him halfway?

The moment their lips touched, it ceased to matter.
The world didn't just hold its breath this time.
It stopped turning.

CHAPTER TEN

JACK ROUSSEAU had kissed many women in his life.

He'd always been attracted to those he chose to kiss. He had been in love with the woman he'd chosen as his wife so many years ago.

So many women. So many kisses.

But not one of those kisses had been remotely like this one.

He wasn't sure how it had happened. He'd only intended to talk to Lizzie. To explain the emergency situation that had led to him dragging poor Holly from her bed last night and to apologise for it. He'd also needed to explain the presence of that Bennett's truck, which had meant telling her about his late-night internet activity and his desire to make Christmas special, for Holly in particular.

But something had happened. Some kind of connection had occurred when that joke about nelf law had been resurrected. As if it was a key of some kind that had taken them back to their first conversation, when Lizzie had chosen to honour him with her trust.

He had seen her passion for her children in the determination to discover their Christmas wish and make it come true. And then he'd seen something he remembered from that scene when he'd been with the whole

family just after Misty's surgery. It was that same kind
of warmth in Lizzie's eyes that drew him in and made
him feel a part of something. Made him feel...wanted.

To have her looking at him like that and then feel
her arms around his body. To have her face tilted up, so
close to his own, and see those soft, inviting lips parted
just a little.

Well...what was a man to do? Resisting the urge to
touch those lips with his own was inconceivable.

Just a touch. A mere brush.

But something else had happened then, hadn't it?
Like the way he'd felt them connect with that eye contact minutes ago. Except that where the earlier connection had been like the glow of comforting embers, this
one that came with the touch of their lips was a blazing
inferno.

Mon Dieu.

He'd never felt such desire that wrangled with such
tenderness. He wanted to make love to this woman, of
course, but it was more than that. He wanted to wor-
ship every inch of her body. With his hands, his lips...
his heart...

The sound of a dog barking was distant.

An irate voice with a heavy Scottish accent was not.

'Ye blithering mongrel. Away wi' you.'

Jack let go of Lizzie and stepped back just in time.

'Jack! What in heaven's name are you doing out here
in the snow and ice, lad?'

'Jimmy.' He had to smile at a man who never seemed
to change, except that he had become far less frighten-
ing than he'd seemed when Jack had been a child. 'How
are you?'

But Jimmy was scowling at Lizzie, who was looking completely stunned. Her lips were pink and plump

from his attention and they were still parted, but she wasn't looking at Jack. She was staring at the giant of a man who'd come through the hedge archway.

'This is Jimmy,' Jack explained. 'My groundsman.'

'I just came to check on the boiler and see if any snow needed shovelling,' Jimmy growled. 'And I find there's a blithering great lorry parked in the way. And this…*dog*.' He glared at Dougal who was sitting, gazing adoringly up at him, his tail sweeping arcs of snow from the neatly mown grass.

'The *truck*,' Lizzie murmured, as though she'd completely forgotten what they'd been talking about prior to that kiss.

She wasn't the only one. With a sigh, Jack realised he had rather a lot to sort out.

'I'll get it sorted,' he told Jimmy. 'It's getting a bit dark to shovel snow anyway, isn't it? Perhaps you could leave it until tomorrow?'

'Aye…' Jimmy's bushy black eyebrows were lowered as he stared at Lizzie again. 'This is *your* dog?'

'Um…yes…'

'He was digging a hole in the rose garden.'

'Oh…I'm sorry. I'll keep a better eye on him.'

'Lizzie's staying here at the moment, Jimmy,' Jack said. 'With her family.'

The eyebrows rose sharply and Jimmy seemed lost for words. Then he gave Lizzie another glower. Finally his mouth curved in a reluctant half-smile.

'Aye…well…I'll make sure I keep on top of the snow, then.'

With that, he turned and stomped away, leaving Dougal sitting remarkably still and straight, gazing longingly after the departing figure. Jack was standing close enough to Lizzie to feel her shiver and his fingers were beginning to tingle painfully with the cold.

'We'd better go inside,' he said.

'Mmm.' Lizzie gave her head a tiny shake. Returning to reality, perhaps? 'I think we should.'

It was utterly confusing.

Dougal followed them into the house and was leaving a trail of muddy pawprints on the flagged floor of the kitchen. Holly was bouncing up and down and trying to tell her something. Barnaby and Kerry were sitting at the kitchen table with Bennett's catalogues spread out in front of them and they both seemed to be laughing and talking at the same time.

Lizzie couldn't make head or tail of any of it.

All she could think about was that kiss.

The *heat* of it.

The sheer desire that had curled her toes and made her forget about…well, everything.

All the stress that had been steadily accumulating over the last months and weeks and days of her life.

The hurdles her future still presented.

Even the weight of responsibility she had to keep her family safe and happy.

Good grief…it had only been a matter of hours ago that she had made the firm resolution not to let her own desire to be near Jack interfere with those responsibilities to her family, and look what one kiss had done.

Jack looked as bemused as she was by the scene in the kitchen. Dougal's pawprints led all the way to his bed in the corner now. He picked up his bedraggled duck toy and trotted back to drop the offering at Jack's feet. She saw him slowly close his eyes as if he needed to find strength.

'I'll put the kettle on, shall I?' she heard herself ask faintly.

Somehow, over the time it took to give everybody a hot drink, a semblance of order returned.

'How are you feeling?' Jack asked Kerry. 'No more contractions?'

'Not yet.'

'Contractions?' Barnaby looked awestruck. 'You're not…I mean…when is your baby due?'

'I almost had it yesterday,' Kerry told him.

'No-o-o…'

'Could be any time, I guess,' she continued cheerfully. 'You've probably got a better idea than me, what with you being so psychic and everything.'

'I'm not sick,' Holly announced. 'I'm *hungry*.'

'Ooh…food.' Barnaby riffled through the catalogues. 'That's something else we need to think about for Christmas.'

'We might need something a little sooner than that.' It was a relief for Lizzie to have something practical to focus on but why hadn't she thought to drop in at a supermarket on the way here?

Oh…yes… She hadn't intended for them to still be here at dinnertime, had she?

'Let me take care of that.' Jack stood up quickly. 'We've got a few good shops in the village. Anyone got any objections to fish and chips?'

'Are you kidding?' Kerry beamed at him. 'I come from New Zealand. That's our national dish, mate.'

'My favourite, too,' Barnaby sighed. 'But I'll be in deep strife if I go AWOL with the shop's truck any longer.' He turned from Kerry to Jack. 'Do you want me to unload the tree and stuff?'

Jack looked at Lizzie and she saw a flash of, what…
apology? Hope?

'I ordered some decorations and things online,' he
explained belatedly. 'I thought that you might all…like
to spend your Christmas here.'

'I picked the best,' Barnaby assured Jack. 'I got the
biggest, most realistic tree there is and there's *eight*
different programmes on how you can make the lights
twinkle. Sparkling, chasing, my personal favourite
slow-glow…' He trailed off, his gaze going from Lizzie
to Jack and back again.

'I think that's the nicest thing anybody's ever done,'
Kerry said mistily. 'Christmas in a truck.'

'For me, too?' Holly's whisper could be heard because the room had gone so quiet. 'And…and Misty?'

Jack crouched to her level. 'Especially for you,' he
said softly. He looked up at Lizzie. 'If it's OK with
Mummy?'

Lizzie couldn't find any words. She couldn't even
find a coherent thought. She heard the softness in Jack's
voice and watched his lips move and all she could do
was relive the way his kiss had made her feel.

Helpless to do anything else, she nodded her head
and managed a rather wobbly smile.

Jack didn't want to go home.

There was no real reason t stay any longer, however.
He'd provided food and stayed to share it. Holly had
gone to bed and so had Kerry.

'They told me at St Bethel's to get lots of rest,' she'd
excused herself. 'See you tomorrow, Jack.'

Except she wouldn't if he went back to his apartment.
As he should do.

As he *was* doing.

Lizzie was seeing him out. 'Dougal could do with some fresh air,' she said. 'And I'd better made sure he stays off that rose garden.'

The boxes from the Bennett's truck were stacked in the front entranceway. Boxes of all shapes and sizes, including an extraordinarily long one.

'That tree…' Jack stopped to look at the box. 'I should help you unpack it.' He saw Lizzie open her mouth to protest but he was already shrugging his coat off again. 'You're still recuperating from surgery,' he reminded Lizzie. 'And Kerry could go into proper labour any time soon. This thing looks like it weighs a ton.'

In actual fact, it was remarkably light. The tree came in sections that fitted together, with a sturdy base to keep it upright and stable. The branches were folded against the trunk and there were smaller branches and then twigs that had wire inside so that they could be straightened and fluffed out into a real tree shape. Jack had to go out into snow that was falling quite heavily and unearth a ladder from the barn to fit the top sections in place. Lizzie was allowed to unfurl branches and twigs.

'It's huge,' she said. 'And so real looking. It even *smells* like a spruce.'

'I'm just glad it's green and not blue,' Jack said. 'Let's find those lights Barnaby was raving about. And some decorations. This tree is rather high and I can't let you or Kerry climb around on ladders.'

The lights came on netting and it took a while to lay it out and then it drape around the tree. And then, of course, they had to plug it in and test it. Jack turned out the main lights in the room and picked up the remote control, scrolling through the options.

'"Sparkling" is a bit frenetic, isn't it?'

Hundreds—possibly thousands—of fairy-lights were flashing on and off at speed and having a kind of strobe effect.

'Chasing' was better but still busy.

'Slow glow' made the tree black and then pinpricks of light slowly brightened until it glowed steadily all over and then they faded away again. As the light returned, Jack found himself watching Lizzie's face instead of the tree. Her eyes were as bright as the lights and she was smiling. What if he waited for the glow to start dimming and then leaned over and kissed her again?

'Nice,' Lizzie murmured appreciatively.

Oh…it would be. More than nice. But would they stop with a kiss? How could he even be thinking of anything more with a woman who was still recovering from some fairly major abdominal surgery?

A woman who was, first and foremost, a mother?

A woman who had a heart as big as Texas, who could love easily and completely. Who could have her heart broken.

Jack hurriedly clicked the remote. 'This is "Twinkle".'

'Twinkle' was perfect. Less romantic. Pretty and quintessentially Christmas, but Jack turned it off.

'I'll put the main lights on again,' he said, 'so I can do the decorations for the top of the tree at least. You and Holly can do the bottom tomorrow, maybe.'

He brought in box after box of the ornaments Barnaby had chosen. There were stars and balls and icicles in bright, primary colours as well as gold and silver. There were small Santas and wooden soldiers and angels and reindeer. Fruit of every kind and even tiny teddy bears and gingerbread men. And long, long garlands of gold stars and silver beads.

Lizzie unpacked and sorted things and passed them to Jack who threaded loops over twigs and branches.

'Just as well I trained as a surgeon,' he said. 'This requires a surprising amount of finesse.'

'It's looking wonderful,' Lizzie assured him. 'This room is just made for a tree like this.'

They had chosen the large drawing room of the house with its vast fireplace that could be lit on the day. The French doors would offer a view of the garden which, given the current weather conditions, would probably be like a winter picture postcard.

'It is, isn't it? Not that I've ever seen one in here before. My mother hated the cold. She always went to spend winter somewhere tropical.'

'So you had sunny Christmases? Like Kerry usually does?'

'No. I stayed in Paris with my father. Sometimes we didn't celebrate it at all. He was a very busy man and often on call on holidays.'

The reminder of how lonely a Christmas could be for a child was poignant. It wouldn't be like that for Holly and Misty. Not this year.

'He was a doctor?'

'An orthopaedic surgeon who specialised in hands.'

He could hear both hesitation and curiosity in Lizzie's voice. 'And your mother?'

'She was a model. She met my father when she was in Paris just starting her career. She left him when I was three years old, to live with her photographer. This was *her* parents' home that she inherited and they used it as a base. She sent for me occasionally, until they were both killed in an accident in South America when I was about fourteen.'

What was he doing, spilling information about his less than happy childhood? He'd never told anybody about it, even Celine. But Lizzie's warmth invited confidence. More than that. It was as if she deserved to know why he was so drawn to her and why he couldn't allow himself to act on his attraction to her.

He hung a shiny, green apple on the tree top.

'I brought my wife here once,' he said quietly. 'She hated the place.'

There was a long silence. Long enough for him to wrap the wires of half a dozen red cherries, scattering them around the smallest section of the tree.

'You're still married?'

'No. Long since divorced.' Jack didn't look down from his task. 'I learned my lesson. My job and marriage are not compatible. I'm sure you can understand. You were married to a man who served others. Heroically. It can't have been easy at times.'

'No.' The word wobbled and suddenly Jack had no desire to pursue this conversation. He'd said as much as he needed to. He didn't want to hear about how happy her marriage had been or how much she missed the twins' father.

Knowing that Jack had been married was a shock.

A piece of the puzzle that was Jack fell into place, however. On some level, she'd known there had to be a very good reason for the way he'd beaten himself up over what had happened when Holly had been in his care. Had he had to leave his wife, perhaps? Too often or on too important an occasion?

She'd been on the verge of telling him the real story

of her marriage. Of saying that a job that involved being on call for when others needed you might be an inconvenience but it was never enough on its own to destroy a marriage. Hers hadn't been easy for other reasons. She'd married a man who had lived only for the thrill of his job. A wife and especially children had been an inconvenience. But maybe that was how Jack felt about his work? Did she really want to go there?

There were other thoughts pushing into her head. What Jack had said, or rather what he hadn't said, about his childhood. Had he ever had a real, family Christmas? Was that need what this was really all about? Deep in thought, she reached into a new box.

'There's the most gorgeous star here.' She held it up. 'Do you think it should go on the top of the tree?'

It was huge, with long points. Snowy white with an intricate pattern of silver and gold glitter.

'I think it should,' Jack said gravely. He came down the ladder a couple of rungs to take it from her. 'And then we'll be finished decorating the top of the tree and we'll be done for the night.'

Would they?

Lizzie was caught by Jack's gaze. By the way his hand was touching hers as he took the star.

Had they stepped over some kind of barrier just now? Taken steps towards understanding each other?

Loving each other, maybe?

Jack attached the star to the very top of the tree and then came down off the ladder so that he was standing beside Lizzie. For a moment, they both admired the work in progress. And then they turned to look at each other.

'It's getting late,' Jack said. 'And by the look of the

weather out there, I might be stuck until Jimmy gets here with the shovel in the morning.'

'You could stay here,' Lizzie said. 'There are any number of bedrooms.'

'I could.' But Jack looked doubtful.

'You'll be here for Christmas, won't you?' It was more of a plea than a query.

She could see the way Jack drew in a deep breath. 'Do you want me to be?'

'Oh…yes.' Of course she wanted him to be here.

She wanted *him*. So much that it hurt.

'Then I will be here,' Jack said. His gaze held hers. 'Just for Christmas, Lizzie.' Bending his head, he kissed her softly.

Was he saying they could have this time together? As a gift?

It wasn't enough. It could never be enough but it was infinitely preferable to not having any of Jack at all.

It would have to be enough. Lizzie stood on tiptoe to return the kiss with one of her own.

'We'll just have to make the most of every moment of Christmas, then, won't we?'

Starting tonight. She was more than recovered enough to be close to a man she knew would be capable of being very gentle. She hoped she could convey that message with the look they were sharing. With another kiss.

It seemed to work. Jack took hold of her hand and led her upstairs.

CHAPTER ELEVEN

Two days later, Maggie came out of hospital.

Not only was the tree completely decorated by then, but there was mile after mile of tinsel throughout the house. Every doorknob was adorned and the banister rails entwined. A huge wreath, bright with holly berries, was attached to the big front door.

Jimmy, the groundsman, had been co-opted into moving a bed downstairs, into a smaller living area near the kitchen and an old, but perfectly serviceable guest bathroom. He drew the line at weaving fairy lights through the bare branches of the trees in the garden, however.

'Ne'er heard such nonsense in m' life,' he grumbled.

Lizzie simply smiled at him. It was quite clear by now that Jimmy had a heart of gold beneath his gruff exterior. He'd been a frequent presence since the day he'd discovered her with Jack in the garden. He found an endless list of jobs that needed doing, like shovelling snow and chopping and hauling firewood. Even burning hedge clippings out behind the barn. Whatever he was doing outside, Dougal was now his faithful companion. The Matthews' exuberant dog had never been so well behaved in his life, desperately eager for the tiniest hint of approval from the giant man who had arrived in their lives. Right now, he was sitting, ramrod straight, beside Jimmy as the older man watched Maggie climb gingerly from the car.

Lizzie was ready with the crutches.

'Not too many stairs, Mum. Not like at home, when the lifts aren't working, that's for sure.'

Funny how it sounded odd referring to their apartment as 'home'. While Lizzie knew all too well that it would cause her considerable grief in the not-too-distant future, her heart was here. In this wonderful old country house that was beginning to sparkle with Christmas joy. *Jack's* house...

Maggie took the crutches and positioned her hands. 'I don't know about this at all,' she muttered. 'Having Christmas in someone else's house. A *stranger's* house.'

'Jack's not a stranger, Mum. He's...'

The most wonderful man she could ever meet. Clever, kind, generous to a fault. *Passionate*...

'He's a friend,' she finished hurriedly, feeling her mother's keen gaze.

'Oh-h...*friends*, now, is it?' But Maggie's attention was suddenly diverted as she caught sight of Jimmy and Dougal standing nearby. She suddenly seemed to have a moment of difficulty keeping her balance with the crutches.

'This is Jimmy, Mum. He looks after this place for Jack. He lives in the old gamekeeper's cottage on the other side of the lake.'

'James McDuff,' Jimmy said formally. 'Pleasure, ma'am.'

'Heavens above.' Maggie blinked. 'You make me sound like royalty.'

She gripped her crutches firmly and moved care-

fully to the wide stone steps that Jimmy had shovelled
and swept snow from more than once today.

He was watching as Maggie got the first step and
paused, clearly going over the instructions from the
physiotherapist about how to tackle such an obstacle.

Jimmy stepped closer. 'I dinna think you should be
doing that, lass,' he said. 'I canna guarantee these blithering steps aren't as slippery as a sheet o' ice. Here…'
Without asking for any kind of permission, he took the
crutches from Maggie and handed them to a startled
Lizzie. Then he gently scooped Maggie into his arms
and carried her into the house.

'Oh, my goodness…' Maggie's voice was rather faint.
'Where are you taking me?'

'Bed,' Jimmy growled, obviously uncomfortable
being inside the house. 'I'm taking you to bed, woman.'

Lizzie could only follow behind, stifling a giggle
and carrying the crutches and Maggie's small bag. She
indulged in a small fantasy of being scooped up in a
similar fashion by Jack and having him say something
very similar, preferably in French.

That was the language he preferred, she'd discovered, when it came to the bedroom.

Such a beautiful language. She might not understand
the words but the gentle touches and searingly hot kisses
that came with them made the sounds more exciting
than anything she'd ever heard.

Jack had been *so* gentle that first night but she'd been
fine. The night after that she had spent in the hospital
with Misty but last night she'd been treated to a glimpse
of what his love-making could be like when she was
completely healed again and the whisper of barely contained passion had taken her breath away.

Would he be around long enough for her to discover the full depth of where that passion could take them?

Would he be around tonight, even, with her mother now in the house as well?

Jimmy certainly wasn't going to hang around inside for a moment longer than he had to. He was an outside man, through and through.

Maggie settled back against the pillows on her bed, staring at the door Jimmy had disappeared through. She was blinking like an owl.

'He called me *lass*,' she said to Lizzie. 'For heaven's sake, he can't be any older than I am and he made me feel like...like a girl.'

'It's a Scottish thing.' Lizzie smiled. 'And don't take any notice of his grumpiness. Jack said he was terrified of him when he was Holly's age but he's a lovely man, really. Apparently he adored his wife. She died about twenty years ago but he's never got over it.'

'That's sad,' was all Maggie said. 'Where *is* Holly? And Kerry, for that matter?'

'Holly's in the kitchen, trying to finish her "welcome home" card for you. I'll go and get her. Kerry's at Bennett's. Shopping.'

'Again? I hope you're keeping an eye on how much that girl is spending.'

'I suspect part of the lure is the supervision she's getting from young Barnaby. And I don't think I've got much to say about how much is being spent, Mum. This is Jack's doing. He's making Christmas, for all of us.'

Maggie gave her daughter a long look. 'I hope you know what *you're* doing, love.'

Lizzie nodded with more confidence than she felt. 'It's just for Christmas,' she said quietly. 'We're all going to make the most of it for as long as it lasts.' She lifted her chin. 'And then normal life will resume but... but we'll all have something wonderful to remember.'

'Hmm...' Maggie's eyes might be troubled but her smile was full of love. 'I could do with a cup of tea,' she said. 'And a cuddle from that granddaughter of mine.'

Kerry didn't finish all the shopping and wrapping that had to happen at Bennett's department store until three days before Christmas. Then Lizzie got a phone call on her mobile.

'Are you at home?' Kerry asked.

Lizzie was in the kitchen of Jack's house. There was a delicious smell of roasting chickens and vegetables coming from the Aga's oven.

Holly was in the 'Christmas room' as the living area with the tree was now known, happily showing her grandmother—yet again—the decorations *she* had attached to the tree all by herself.

Dougal was stretched out on the stone flags that were warmed by the stove, his paws twitching and his tail thumping occasionally, deep in a canine dream and utterly content.

Jack was on the other side of the kitchen table, pulling the cork from a chilled bottle of a very nice-looking white wine.

Lizzie closed her eyes for a heartbeat. 'Yes,' she said aloud. 'I'm at home.'

'Cool. I thought you might be in with Misty still.'

'I came home for dinner. I'm going back in later. She's got some very particular ideas about what clothes she wants to come home in tomorrow. I thought I'd spend the night in with her again. She's so excited she won't get a wink of sleep otherwise. Where are you?'

'Deep in the bowels of Bennett's. You wouldn't believe what it looks like down here. I'm absolutely sure that Santa and about a million elves are somewhere around here.'

Nelfs, Lizzie thought mistily. A smile tugged at her lips as her gaze flew to Jack.

He chose that moment to look up and it felt like he knew exactly what she was thinking.

It was all there, encapsulated in that tiny, non-existent word.

The way they'd met. The connection a small, sick girl and her twin sister had provided. The trust. The rescues that had made Jack the rock in a very traumatic period of her life. The overwhelming generosity of this man.

The overwhelming love Lizzie had for him.

Jack smiled back and, in that moment, Lizzie thought her life could never be more perfect than this.

Except that Kerry's excited voice was distracting her.

'Barney's sorting chains for the truck. Have you ever *seen* so much snow?'

Barney? Lizzie had to give herself a mental shake. 'It's amazing, isn't it? Jack's hired a four-wheel-drive thing that looks like a tank so he can make sure he can get to work. He's going to bring me and Misty home in it tomorrow.'

'Cool… Oh, hang on…'

Lizzie could hear a muffled conversation going on. Then some giggling. And then a long moment of silence. Kerry sounded distinctly breathless when she came back on the line.

'OK. We're good to go. I just needed to ring to make sure that you kept Holly somewhere she won't see the barn out the windows. We're going to stash all the presents in there and then we can put them under the tree on Christmas Eve when the girls are sound asleep. Do you happen to know if the barn door is unlocked?'

'I'll check.' Lizzie relayed the plan to Jack. 'The door will be open by the time you get here,' she informed Kerry a minute later. 'And I'll keep your dinner warm. There's enough if…um…Barney wants to stay.'

If they ate around the kitchen table, Lizzie decided, Holly would be well away from seeing the unusual arrival of a delivery truck in the dark. The ancient day-bed in the corner of this farmhouse-style room would be perfect to give her mother a comfortable place to eat.

'I had to get the key for the barn from Jimmy,' Jack said when he returned. 'I asked him if he wanted some dinner but he said he'd better supervise that delivery.' Jack was grinning. 'He muttered something about "bairns with bits of silverware stuck all over their faces" and not trusting them to lock up again.'

'I'll save him some dinner too,' Lizzie said. 'There's heaps.'

Dougal heard the arrival of the truck as they were sitting down to eat. Lizzie casually let him out the back door. She knew he would go no further than where Jimmy happened to be and that his newfound hero would bring him back to the house. Dougal had followed Jimmy home to his cottage only yesterday and Lizzie had been informed that her 'blithering dog' was a pest.

Sure enough, Jimmy turned up at the back door with Dougal in tow, some time later, when Holly was attacking a bowl of chocolate ice cream for dessert.

Jack went to the door. Lizzie was rinsing dishes in the sink and couldn't hear what was being said but the agitated tone of Jimmy's voice carried all too clearly. She was drying her hands on a tea towel as she moved swiftly towards the two men. She had the horrible feeling that Dougal might be in trouble again.

But it wasn't Dougal who was in trouble.

'Call an ambulance,' Jack told her quietly. 'And then bring some towels and a blanket or two out to the barn. Sounds like Kerry's in labour for real this time.'

The barn was a building even older than the house. It stood, tucked between some centuries-old oak trees on the other side of a sympathetically built but far more modern garaging complex. Beams, blackened by time, held a slate roof at an enormous height above a cobbled floor. Ancient farm machinery and dusty hay bales lined the walls.

It was amongst these bales of hay that Barnaby and Kerry had been stowing a vast pile of brightly wrapped Christmas gifts. It was now where Kerry was lying on blankets, clutching Barnaby's hands and groaning loudly as another contraction took hold of her body.

'This isn't supposed to be happening,' she gasped when she could speak again.

'Not entirely true,' Jack said calmly from his position between Kerry's knees. 'It was always going to happen at some point in the not-too-distant future.'

'Not *now*.' Kerry's upper back and head were being supported by Barnaby's body as he knelt behind her. His arms were around the young woman, giving her both of his hands to grip. He was looking very pale. 'Not *here*,' Kerry groaned. 'In a *barn*.'

'Hey, it's almost a stable.' Lizzie was beside Jack, ready with clean towels and anything else he might need from the medical kit he'd snatched from the boot of his car. She could see the baby's head beginning to crown. 'It's very Christmas.'

'Ooh...' Kerry screwed up her face and bore down. Barnaby looked like he was bearing down in sympathy.

Moments later, it seemed, the baby emerged into Jack's hands. Kerry's arms were outstretched now, reaching for her infant, but Jack held it for just a moment longer, watching as the tiny boy took his first breath and moved those miniature limbs.

Lizzie could see how gently he held the baby. She unfolded a soft towel so they could cover the baby to place it on Kerry's skin and for just a matter of seconds they were connected. Herself and Jack and the newborn.

Only the briefest snatch of time but it was long enough to remember what it had been like to see her daughters for the first time. To remember that all-consuming love that time had only served to make stronger. Long enough to imagine what it would be like if *this* child was her own. If Jack was the father.

Such a short space of time but Lizzie knew that yearning sensation would probably be with her for ever.

Thank God the delivery had been so straightforward. Jack hadn't had any part in delivering a baby since medical school but this infant hadn't been about to wait for some more experienced assistance. At least he'd had a medical kit available, even if he had only used the gloves and something to cut the cord with later.

He stripped off the gloves as Lizzie tucked the baby against Kerry's skin and covered them both with blankets while they waited for the paramedics to arrive.

He couldn't strip off the feeling of holding that newborn baby in his hands, though. He couldn't shut his ears to the wobbly cries or his eyes to the expression on Kerry's face. Or Barnaby's or Lizzie's for that matter.

Birth *was* a miracle. A new life. This baby had an

adoring, albeit very young mother. It potentially had a
father figure as well, if that look of pride on Barnaby's
face and the way he was staying in physical contact
with Kerry was anything to go by.

What would he look like if he really was the father?

What would feel like to see your own child come
into the world?

Jack had learned long ago that fatherhood would
not be a part of his own future but that didn't neces-
sarily mean that he wouldn't *want* to be a father. It just
wasn't possible. Echoes of Celine's voice were readily
available if he needed any reminders of why that was
the case. Vicious words of how inadequate he was as a
husband and how it was lucky they'd never had a child.
How it was just as well his job was so important to him
because it was all he'd ever have in his life and all he
would be remembered for.

It was the way it had to be, Jack reminded himself.

The recent happenings in his life had disturbed the
rhythm of his existence but this…this sensation of being
a witness to something he could never experience himself held a note of something as dark as grief.

Something powerful, anyway. Something even more
disturbing than anything else he'd had to contend with
in the last days and weeks.

Jack turned away. He went to where Jimmy was outside the barn, stamping his feet against the bone chilling cold, waiting to direct the ambulance to where it
was needed.

'It's a boy,' he told Jimmy. 'All's well.'

True enough, for Kerry and the baby, especially
when the ambulance arrived and whisked her off to
St Bethel's for a proper check-up. Also true for Lizzie
and her family. Maggie was rapidly recovering from

her surgery. Misty would be home tomorrow and they would all have a special, family Christmas.

But for himself?

All *would* be well, Jack told himself firmly. Christmas was only days away and then he would step back into his real life and leave these unsettling doubts and odd yearnings behind.

He could make a start even before then.

'Do you still want to go into Westbridge tonight?' he asked Lizzie as Jimmy locked the barn doors a while later, with the empty Bennett's truck now garaged inside. Barnaby had gone in the ambulance with Kerry.

She nodded. 'I promised Misty and Mum says she'll be fine to look after things here. Holly's going to sleep downstairs with her. Mum said Jimmy had given her his phone number if she needed any help.'

An odd sound came from Jimmy, as if he was clearing his throat and growling at the same time, as he walked off into the night.

Jack merely nodded. 'I'll drive you in. I may stay in there myself. Dave's got a young patient he's got me involved with and he's getting to crisis point, I think.'

'Oh, no…a child?'

'Four-year-old boy. Liam, his name is. He's already had a whole bowel transplant but it's been failing for some time. He's been back in Intensive Care since just after Misty got out. There's very little chance of him getting a new transplant in time.'

'Oh-h…' Lizzie looked stricken. 'That poor family. They're going to lose their little boy? At Christmastime?'

'Quite likely.' Again, Jack had to turn away from something overpoweringly emotional. 'Are you ready to leave?'

Lizzie was very quiet on the long drive into the city that night. They went their separate ways as they reached the foyer of the hospital. Lizzie was clutching the bag that contained Misty's clothes for the next day but she stood on tiptoe and planted a soft kiss on Jack's cheek. He could see tears in her eyes.

'I'm so lucky,' she whispered. 'Aren't I?'

Jack watched as she walked away to be with her child who was no longer sick, knowing that she could be content in the knowledge that the rest of her family, including Kerry and the new baby, were all safe. That they would all be together again very soon. In time to celebrate Christmas.

She was indeed lucky. Blessed, in fact.

If Jack could choose the family he would most want to have as his own, it would be this one.

But even he couldn't really belong, it didn't have to stop him caring about them, did it?

This way, he was getting to show them how much he did care. About all of them, but especially Lizzie.

And this way, they would never be let down by him. He would never have to see disappointment or the anger of betrayal in Lizzie's eyes when she learned how impossible it was for him to be more than a friend.

It had to be this way. For all their sakes. For himself, for Lizzie and for two little girls who needed a devoted, full-time father.

The thought was supposed to be comforting him that he was doing the right thing by everybody but the heavy feeling in Jack's chest wouldn't go away. It got worse, if anything, as he made his way towards the paediatric intensive care unit. To spend his night with a small patient he knew he was most unlikely to be able to save.

* * *

That weight was still there the next day. Caught up with the surgery Liam needed to remove another piece of his failing bowel, Jack had to arrange a car to take Lizzie and Misty home. He stayed in the city that night as well, after it became likely that Liam could be rushed back to Theatre at any time. The young boy's condition had stabilised overnight, however.

'Take a break,' Dave Kingsley advised, later that morning. 'It's Christmas Eve. Go home, Jack. I'll call you if anything changes.'

A change couldn't possibly be good. Unless...

It *was* Christmas. Maybe there was a miracle waiting to happen for Liam. Except that if it did happen, it would mean tragedy for a different family.

Life was a curious balance, Jack decided as he drove away from the hospital. Life and death. Joy and sadness. You could only do the best you could for the people you had the chance to care about.

And maybe that was why he automatically took the route away from the central city. Towards the place where he knew some Christmas magic was already happening.

The blanket of snow got thicker and softer as Jack got closer to the villages on the outskirts of London. Someone on the radio was telling him that the weather this year was breaking all manner of records. The whole of the British Isles would be having their whitest Christmas in decades.

The main roads were being kept reasonably clear and he knew that Jimmy was making sure the long driveway of the country estate was passable.

Lizzie had told him that, last night, when he'd rung to apologise for not being able to drive her home, as promised. He'd been listening for a note of disappointment in her voice because he'd let her down but she brushed off the apology.

'It was brilliant having the car again. Kerry and the baby were both given glowing reports and allowed to come home so, I hope you don't mind, I sent the car to fetch them.'

Of course he didn't mind but he was only half listening as Lizzie went on to tell him that Barnaby had arrived with a bassinet and baby supplies when he'd come back to retrieve the truck. He was too busy trying to analyse his strange reaction to Lizzie's acceptance of his inability to keep a promise.

Had she been prepared for it?

Did it not really matter to her?

Maybe he needed it to matter. For Lizzie to understand why the rules in his life couldn't be broken.

Even for her...

He hadn't come any closer to figuring it out when he finally reached the house in the early hours of the afternoon. The snow had stopped falling some time back during his journey and between the vast, cotton-wool balls of cloud a weak sun was making an appearance. It was still a surprise, however, to see so many people outside the house.

The twins were on the lawn, the snow almost level with the tops of their gumboots. They were buttoned up in anoraks and had mittens on their hands. Their heads were covered with woollen hats that left only their wide eyes and joyous smiles exposed.

Identical faces. With astonishment, Jack realised that this was the first time he'd seen the twins standing side by side. A complete set.

'We're going to make a *snowman*,' Holly shouted gleefully as Jack stepped out of the car.

'Just a small one.' Lizzie was also wrapped up well against the cold. She had a cherry-red knitted hat over her curls and her cheeks were almost the same colour. 'Misty's been cooped up in hospital rooms for so long, I didn't think a bit of fresh air would do her any harm.'

Her smile was as joyous as the ones on her daughters' faces and no wonder... Here she was, with two healthy, happy little girls, about to embark on a such a traditional, family activity.

The longing to be a part of it was too strong to resist. Letting his gaze hold Lizzie's for long enough to be far more than merely a greeting was just as irresistible.

This was a moment of joy, Jack realised. Part of the balance of life and exactly what he needed after the gruelling time talking to Liam's family this morning.

He didn't even need to ask. Lizzie's eyes were smiling. 'We could use some help. I don't want Misty out here for too long.'

Jack pulled his leather gloves from the pocket of his coat. A peal of laughter from the girls made him look up to see that Dougal was trying to run in the garden but the snow was so deep in places that he was having to bound along like a small kangaroo. He was staying within range of Jimmy, who had a very long ladder tucked under one arm.

'I canna believe I let Margaret talk me into this,' he grumbled as he marched past Jack towards where Maggie was standing beneath a tree, her crutches looking out of place on either side of snow-encrusted gumboots.. 'Lights in trees. Ne'er heard such nonsense.'

Jack and Lizzie shared a grin and the bubble of joy got bigger. Jack scooped up a handful of snow and patted it into a ball.

'Help me roll this,' he invited the twins. 'We can use it to make the snowman's tummy.'

Only Misty was paying attention as Jack demonstrated how to enlarge the snowball quickly. Holly was lying on her back, waving her arms and legs to make a snow angel.

'Look at me, Mummy. *Oof...* Dougal—get off. *Bad* dog.'

Jimmy looked down from the top of the ladder, a long string of coloured lights in his hands.

'Get out of it, dog,' he commanded.

Dougal leapt up, shook snow off his coat and slunk away, looking suitably chastened. Holly also got up and went to help Misty roll the snowball.

The snowman took on an odd shape as the twins scooped more and more snow and patted it around the base of the main ball. The middle ball became far too small and when Jack tried to position the head, it slipped off and broke.

'He's got no *head*,' Holly wailed.

Misty's eyes were huge. And sad. 'It doesn't look like a real snowman,' she said.

'Hmm.' Jack's tone was thoughtful. 'You know what? It looks like a snow *dog*.'

Lizzie's smile was all the encouragement he needed. 'Look...we can give him paws here...and ears there...' His gloves were soggy with melted snow and his hands were cold but it didn't matter in the least. 'All he needs now are some eyes and a nose. Can you find some stones on the driveway?'

But neither of the twins was listening.

'Where *is* Dougal?' Misty asked anxiously.

Lizzie sounded equally worried. 'I haven't seen him

since Jimmy told him off for wrecking Holly's snow angel.'

Jimmy was still up the ladder, onto his third tree now.

'James?' Maggie was keeping the base of the ladder steady. 'Can you see where Dougal is?'

The string of lights stopped moving. A moment later, Jimmy's voice floated down from the tree, heavy with disapproval.

'Idiot dog's out on the pond.' His voice rose to a roar. '*Dog...Come here.*'

Looking in the right direction now, Jack could see Dougal across the smooth expanse of snow covering the small lake. He must have made his way around the edge to get there but, in his eagerness to obey Jimmy's command, he was now bounding straight across the middle.

'Oh...*no...*'

Lizzie's head swivelled at his tone. So did Maggie's and the little girls'. They all heard the crack of thin ice and saw the moment that Dougal vanished. They all heard the dog's terrified yelp.

Jack looked at the fear in their faces. Dougal was a much-loved pet.

He had to *do* something. He had to fix this for them.

Aware of nothing but the need to protect every member of this family—*his* family—Jack walked out onto the ice. He ignored the shout that came from Jimmy as the older man descended from the tree at speed.

He wasn't being a 'blithering idiot'. He was testing each footfall and listening for the warning sound of ice that was too thin to take his weight. He'd even grabbed a long branch of dead wood, although he wasn't sure how helpful it was going to be.

He could see Dougal floundering in the icy water, desperately trying to haul himself out, but the edges of the ice were breaking away in chunks. The dog's heavy coat was waterlogged and he had to be getting very cold very fast. It would only be a matter of a minute or two until any energy he had to save himself would be gone.

Jack was closer now. Almost close enough to touch Dougal with the branch.

That was when he heard the ice starting to crack.

When he heard the fear in Lizzie's voice behind him.

'Jack...'

CHAPTER TWELVE

THE horror of hearing that ice cracking would haunt Lizzie for ever.

Two small girls were clutching at her and she had to crouch down and draw them both closer. Had to bow her head as the fear hit her that she might be about to lose Jack in a way she wasn't the tiniest bit prepared for.

In a way there would be no going back from.

'It's all right, love.' Her mother's voice came with a touch of her hands on Lizzie's shoulders. 'James has the ladder down. Jack's safe. He's using the ladder to reach Dougal.'

The twins sobbed more loudly at the mention of their pet's name. They were still sobbing when Dougal was brought back to them, a sodden, violently shivering and utterly miserable bundle in Jimmy's arms.

'He's a stupid dog,' Jimmy informed them, but his tone lacked any rancour. 'And he needs a hot bath. I'm going to take him to my house.'

'I'll come and help,' Maggie offered instantly.

'We want to help, too,' Holly sobbed. Misty grabbed her sister's hand and nodded, tears still streaming down her cheeks.

Jimmy looked at the twins. Then he looked at Maggie

and his face softened into the first real smile Lizzie had ever seen him give.

'Aye…come on, then, the lot o' you.'

Lizzie had to go with them, of course. Misty, especially, needed to be watched that she wasn't overdoing things and she could swear there'd been an unspoken conversation going on between her mother and Jack's burly groundsman that was both startling and a bit… wonderful.

Not that she was capable of feeling anything joyful right now. She was still shaking herself and it had nothing at all to do with the cold. She hung back as the small procession set off towards Jimmy's cottage.

'Why?' she had to ask. 'Why did you *do* that, Jack?'

He looked taken aback by the vehemence in her voice.

'I wanted to rescue Dougal,' he said. 'For the girls. For *you*. What sort of Christmas would if have been if anything had happened to the pet they love?'

Lizzie shook her head sharply, struggling to keep tears at bay.

'You wanted to be a hero,' she choked out accusingly. 'I know about heroes, remember? I was married to one.'

Jack's face emptied of any expression. 'Yes…you were.'

'You put *yourself* in danger,' Lizzie continued brokenly. 'Did you stop to think about what Christmas would have been like if something had happened to you? How would Holly and Misty have felt about that? And Jimmy, for that matter. And Maggie and Kerry and Barney and…and me.' She had to turn away. 'The people that *love* you?'

Jack wasn't saying anything and Lizzie couldn't turn

back to look at him. She'd just confessed her love to a man who'd made it very clear he could be nothing more than a friend. That whatever they had here—all of them—was only for Christmas.

'*Mummy.*' Holly's call was urgent. 'Hurry up. Dougal's *wet.*'

Lizzie's face was also wet. She couldn't let Jack she how broken she felt right now. Not after all he'd done for them. She couldn't let her family see either.

Scrubbing at her face, she hurried.

For the longest time, Jack simply stood there, watching the small knot of people disappear into the trees on the path that led to the cottage.

They didn't need his help. Jimmy would run a bath and warm Dougal and then dry him in front of the fire, probably with the help of the three generations of Lizzie's family and a lot of old towels.

Not being needed was disappointing but it wasn't what was creating this churning in his gut.

Lizzie thought he'd been trying to be some kind of hero. Like the twins' father had been. And she was upset. Because she was reminded of how she'd lost the man she'd loved?

But she'd said she loved *him.*

That they *all* loved him.

There was a very strange prickling sensation happening behind his eyes and his throat felt too tight to swallow.

A sense of loss, that's what it was.

That he was facing the loss of something so important it was turning his whole life inside out. Something just as important—maybe *more* important—than the career he loved with such a passion.

Mon Dieu.

Even his marriage to Celine had never presented a conflict like this.

Maybe he'd always known, deep down, that loving anybody like this would create this tearing feeling of divided loyalty. Maybe that was why he'd never loved anybody this much.

Or perhaps it was simply because he'd never met Lizzie Matthews.

It was a hopeless situation. He couldn't compromise his work because that was who he *was*.

Lizzie had been married to someone who'd felt the same way about his career and she'd suffered heartbreak because of it. She was strong and independent now. She didn't need him in her life any more than they'd needed him to help look after Dougal.

Jack felt curiously lost.

If he went inside the house, he would be with Kerry and her new baby and that could only make him more aware of what he was missing in his own life.

He needed dry clothes. The chill was rapidly closing in on his bones. Heating his vehicle would keep him comfortable until he got to his apartment. There were other things he could do today as well. He could check up on Liam's condition and remind himself of the career that was waiting to enfold and comfort him in the near future.

As he drove away, leaving the house and cottage and all the people they contained well behind, another idea began to take shape in Jack's mind.

Shops would be open until late tonight with it being Christmas Eve. Bennett's was probably open until midnight. Kerry had been tasked with finding presents for Lizzie and Maggie but the emphasis had been on Holly and Misty. And it hadn't occurred to him to try and find a gift that he could give Lizzie himself.

What if he could find something that would let her know how much he cared? Something that she could keep and treasure for ever?

Diamonds were for ever. Yes…that would be perfect. A beautiful necklace, maybe. Or a bracelet.

Something with diamonds and a sapphire.

Because he'd never see a sapphire again himself, without being reminded of the colour of Lizzie's eyes.

Lizzie had to draw on every ounce of courage and independence she possessed when she discovered that Jack had simply disappeared when they returned to the house with a still subdued but dry Dougal.

'He probably got called into the hospital,' Maggie said. 'He'll be back tomorrow. He said he wouldn't want to miss my Christmas dinner.'

It was a long evening, waiting for a phone call that didn't happen. Even the twins' excitement at putting out a glass of milk and a gingerbread cookie for Father Christmas couldn't melt the heaviness in Lizzie's heart. She finally got the twins settled, but only after giving in to the pleas that Dougal could be allowed to sleep on the floor between their beds as a special treat after his ordeal.

Lizzie had an ordeal of her own to deal with. One that she knew was very likely to keep her awake all night. She'd told Jack she loved him and he'd vanished. Part of her dreaded seeing him again.

A bigger part of her desperately wanted to.

Late that night, when they were sure the twins were soundly asleep, Maggie took charge of watching the still-nameless baby while Kerry and Lizzie ferried beautifully wrapped parcels from the barn to put under the Christmas tree.

Most of the gifts were labelled for Holly and Misty but Lizzie saw one labelled for herself. There was one for Maggie as well. Even some for Dougal, the size of one suggesting it had to be a new bed.

'I know nothing,' Kerry insisted, with a broad grin. 'I'm an elf who can keep a secret.'

She wasn't the only one, Lizzie mused as she stuffed the felt stockings Maggie had made with the small items she'd found in the hospital gift shop and then hung them over the fireplace. Would she ever find out what Holly had asked Father Christmas for, that day?

The Christmas room was now out of bounds until tomorrow afternoon because the tradition in the Matthews household was that the morning was for birthdays and the afternoon for Christmas.

There was always a bit of mixing up in the celebrations and that had become traditional, too. Like singing 'Merry birthday to you' as they shared a breakfast of Maggie's famous pancakes and a birthday cake. The gifts for the birthdays had been sorted well before any of the recent dramas in their lives and Lizzie was grateful she'd kept it simple, with pretty new dresses and shoes and cardigans that had been knitted by their nanna, with love. There was always a danger of overdoing things with a combined Christmas and birthday and the huge pile of gifts under the tree worried her that this year was setting a precedent that she would never be able to live up to.

Along with Jack, Jimmy had been invited to join the family for Christmas dinner. Barnaby had invited himself.

'Professional development,' he'd cited. 'I need to gauge customer satisfaction.'

Maggie insisted on being in charge of the kitchen. She was as fit as a fiddle, she claimed, down to using only one crutch and that would be gone in a week or two.

The turkey and vegetables were roasting and the bread sauce had been made. Brussel sprouts were waiting in their pot, much to twins' disgust. Plum pudding and the pavlova Kerry insisted was essential were ready for later and the beautifully decorated ham was resplendent on the formal dining table that had been set with the antique silverware and crystal glasses they'd found in the sideboard. The table had a lovely centrepiece Maggie had created from branches of holly and some real mistletoe.

'James found the mistletoe for me,' she said.

'Did he kiss you?' Kerry laughed.

Maggie smiled. 'Maybe.'

'Mum…' But Lizzie didn't get the chance to interrogate her mother. Their guests were arriving.

Jimmy came up the drive at the same time as Jack was pulling in to park, with Barnaby in his passenger seat. Jimmy cut an impressive figure in his Sunday-best kilt, his hair sleekly combed and his knee high white socks a blinding white, but Lizzie only had eyes for Jack. He was also well dressed but what he was wearing didn't matter at all, it was the expression on his face that caught Lizzie.

It was tender. A bit sad, maybe. But his smile was as gorgeous as it had ever been and it had a warmth that had Lizzie flying down the steps to hug him. Jack bent his head and brushed her lips with his.

'You look…*absolument magnifique, ma chérie.*'

The words were so soft. Intimate. Nobody else could hear them but Maggie had emerged from the house in time to see how close together they were standing.

'Oh, my goodness,' she murmured. 'Like that now, is it?' And then she caught sight of Jimmy and was rendered speechless.

Jimmy seemed to be equally lost for words and Jack smiled.

'Give us a hand with this box,' he requested. 'Barney helped me get it into the car last night. It's not that heavy. Just a bit awkward.'

The seats in the back of the four-wheel-drive vehicle had been laid flat to accommodate an enormous box, wrapped in Christmas paper with an oversized bow attached to the top.

Lizzie's jaw dropped. There was already way too much waiting for her children. Jack saw her expression.

'It's for the girls,' he said. 'I just happened to come across it and I thought...'

He didn't get time to finish. The girls had come to the door to see what was happening. They rushed down the steps like two butterflies in their new party dresses and shoes.

'Father Christmas came,' they chorused, each grabbing one of Jack's hands. 'Come and *see*.'

It was left to Jimmy and Barnaby to manoeuvre the giant box. They got it as far as the hallway and then, somehow, the whole family got drawn into the Christmas room and it was forgotten.

Kerry and Barnaby had made brilliant choices for gifts. There were bright backpacks and pencil cases and lunch boxes that let the girls know they would soon be back at school. Together. There were books and DVDs to share and games that needed more than one player. For Lizzie, there was a beautiful photo frame.

'For a *family* photo.' Kerry beamed.

There was a sewing kit for Maggie. And lots of Bennett's shortbread.

There was a stuffed hedgehog toy for Kerry. 'Holly told me how much you love hedgehogs,' Barnaby said shyly. 'I sneaked it in when you weren't looking.'

Dougal wasn't at all interested in his new bed but the replacement duck toy that still had a squeaker was a great hit. He squeaked, everybody laughed and the sound blended perfectly with the Christmas carols playing in the background.

It was Barnaby who came up with the most innovative gift.

'Noel,' he said loudly, after the long chorus of one of the carols.

'*Oui*,' Jack nodded. '*Joyeux Noel*. Happy Christmas.'

'No…' Barnaby looked down to where Kerry was feeding her baby as she sat beside him. 'I meant as a name.'

'Noel?' Kerry blinked. 'That's different.'

'Very Christmas,' Lizzie grinned. 'Goes with being born in almost a stable.'

'I like it,' Kerry declared. 'I really like it. Barney, you're a genius.'

'Goes with being psychic,' Barnaby said modestly.

'Yes,' Holly shouted. 'A Christmas name like me and Misty.'

'For misty-toe,' Jack murmured.

Lizzie's gaze flew to his. Where had he heard that? He leaned close. 'It's what Holly told Father Christmas,' he whispered.

'Are you going to tell me what else she said to him?'

'Maybe.' His eyes held hers. 'I believe there could be some dispensations for nelf law when it's actually Christmas Day.'

Maggie warned them that dinner would be ready very soon and that was when the box in the hallway got remembered. The twins were too overcome to unwrap it, so Lizzie did it for them. Very carefully. The flaps of the box were on the side so they could be opened like doors.

Inside, was the most beautiful dolls' house Lizzie had ever seen.

'They don't have one already, do they?' Jack whispered anxiously.

Lizzie could only shake her head. Even if they did, it would be nothing like this. A three-storied house that even had a slate roof and chimneys.

The men eased the house from the box and carried it into the Christmas room to place it near the softly crackling fire.

'You can have a peek,' Maggie said, 'but you can't play with it until after dinner.'

The back of the house opened like shutters. Some of the furniture had been displaced by movement and after the first, tentative touch, the girls were totally enthralled.

'Look, Misty...there's little cups and plates for the table.'

'There's a baby and it's got a pram.'

'Oh....*look!* There's two little girl dolls and they look just the same.'

The adults were all gathered nearby, watching. Lizzie could feel tears gathering. 'There are *twin* dolls?' she whispered to Jack.

'That's what caught *my* eye.'

There was a moment of worry when the smiles faded from the girls' faces. When they both reached into the house and picked up more of the dolls'-house family.

'This is the mummy,' Holly said to Misty.

'And this is the daddy,' Misty whispered.

For a long moment, the children stared at each other, doing that silent twin communication thing that Lizzie was well used to.

Then they both turned to look at Jack.

And they both smiled.

Maggie cleared her throat. 'Come on,' she ordered the children. 'The sooner you eat, the sooner you can come back and play. James, can I get you to come and carve the ham, please?'

Kerry, carrying little Noel, and Barnaby trailed after the others. Even Dougal left with the duck toy clamped in his jaws but Lizzie couldn't move.

Not when Jack was still standing beside her.

'That was the most amazing gift you could ever have given them,' she said. 'Did you see that they've taken all the dolls with them?'

He had seen. They'd taken the whole family, including the daddy, and he hadn't missed the significance of the look they'd given him. Suddenly, that look they'd both bestowed on him the first day he'd met them made perfect sense.

They wanted a daddy for their own family.

They had chosen *him*.

Jack's heart rate picked up. His mouth felt curiously dry. 'I have a gift for you, Lizzie.'

'You've already given me far too much. I don't...' Lizzie's voice trailed into silence as she saw him taking the small box from the pocket of his jacket.

'I went into Bennett's yesterday,' he told her. 'I

wanted to find a gift that was special enough to let you know how much I care about you. About *all* of you, of course, but *especially* you.'

His eyes held Lizzie's. He could see the sparkle of tears that made them as blue as the sapphire he knew was inside this tiny box.

'I looked at necklaces,' he continued. 'And bracelets, because I wanted something with diamonds on it. Diamonds are for ever,' he added. 'And that's how long I will care about you. How long I will love you.'

Lizzie's indrawn breath was audibly shaky. A tear escaped and rolled slowly down the side of her nose. Jack caught it with the pad of his thumb.

'I'm not sure I'm good husband material,' he said. 'My ex-wife would tell you that I'm not. I'm not sure I'm good father material either but there *is* one thing that I'm absolutely sure of.'

'What's that?' Lizzie whispered when he paused to take a slow breath.

'That my life without you would always be hollow. It would be missing a heart.' Jack wanted to smile but the moment was too big. Too important. 'In the end, there was only one gift I could find that could show you how much I love you.'

He opened the box. The ring was a work of art with tiny diamonds surrounding a heart-shaped, blazingly blue sapphire.

Lizzie had her fingers pressed to her lips. Her gaze lifted from the ring nestling in its velvet cushion to meet Jack's eyes.

'Is that…? Are you…?'

'Asking you to marry me? *Oui.*' Jack didn't even notice he was slipping into French to speak words of love. *Je t'aime, ma chérie. Pour toujours et toujours.*'

Lizzie seemed to understand him perfectly. 'I love you, too,' she whispered. '*So* much. Oh, Jack…of course I'll marry you.'

She threw her arms around his neck and Jack bent his head and kissed her, vowing that he *would* make this work. That he would make her happy. For ever.

He could have kept kissing her for ever but the sound of his phone ringing broke the spell. The unease he felt listening to what Dave Kingsley had to say to him vaporised it completely. A transplant bowel had suddenly become available for Liam.

Why had he done this? Today, of all days?

The anniversary of the day that had marked the end of his marriage to Celine. The Christmas dinner when the call that had taken him back to his hospital had been the final straw.

'I don't have to go,' he told Lizzie. 'Dave can do this surgery himself. He might want my expertise but it isn't essential.'

'But it is,' Lizzie said quietly. 'For Liam. This is the miracle his family has been praying for. You have to go.'

'But it's Christmas Day. Everybody's waiting for us in the dining room. You…and the girls… You are just as important to me as my job, you have to understand that.'

'I do.' Lizzie's smile was misty. 'But I understand what Liam's family are going through as well. It could have been me, Jack. Hoping against hope that a kidney would become available for my precious daughter and that someone—*you*—would be noble enough to postpone your Christmas dinner to make it happen.'

She cradled his face with her hands. 'We'll cope without you for a while. You know why? Because we'll know that you're coming back. That will give us the strength to cope with anything. Any time.'

'You're incredible,' Jack murmured.

She was. She was strong and independent enough to manage alone if she had to but he knew she would draw on the strength he could give her and *would* give her, at every opportunity he had.

She not only understood his career, she applauded his commitment to it. Loved him for it.

'We'll be here,' Lizzie added softly. 'When you get back. Wherever you are, Jack, we will always be here for you.'

She came to the door with him and he paused long enough for one more kiss.

'I can tell you now,' he said. 'Nelf law definitely does not apply between engaged couples.'

'Oh…' Lizzie caught her bottom lip between her teeth. 'Please…*tell* me what the twins wanted for Christmas.'

Jack bent his head and whispered in her ear.

It was well past the twins' bedtime when Jack returned to the house. They were almost asleep, worn out by the excitement of the day, when Lizzie poked her head around their door.

'Come with me,' she whispered. 'I've found one last present for you.'

Sleepily, holding each other's hands, the girls followed her downstairs in their pyjamas and trailing dressing gowns. Dougal padded in their wake, his new duck toy still in his mouth.

'There.' Lizzie pointed.

Holly looked puzzled. 'Did you put the dolls' house back in its box?'

'Open it,' Lizzie invited. 'And you'll find out.'

Together, the twins pulled the wrapping paper clear of the flaps and they pulled the box open.

Their mouths also fell open.

Jack was sitting inside the huge box.

Lizzie bent down, putting an arm around each of her daughters. 'What was it you asked Father Christmas for, Holly?'

'A daddy,' she whispered.

'That's what Jack's going to be. I'm going to marry him and he will be your daddy. Is that OK?'

'Not just for Christmas?' Misty checked. 'For ever and ever?'

'For ever and ever.' Jack spoke at the same time as Lizzie and they smiled at each other.

Holly climbed into the box with Jack. 'I guess you *are* really a nelf,' she told him kindly. 'Because you can make wishes come true, even if you don't have a green hat.'

Misty squeezed into the box, too.

'Is there room for me?' Lizzie smiled.

'Always.' Jack's smile was all the invitation she would ever need. He held out his hand.

'For ever and *ever*,' the twins shouted.

The noise brought Maggie out from her bedroom. She looked at the members of her family squashed into the box still festooned with strips of Christmas paper.

Her smile was a final gift for the most wonderful Christmas ever.

'Oh, my goodness…it's like *that* now, is it?'

* * * * *

ONCE A GOOD GIRL…

BY
WENDY S. MARCUS

MILLS & BOON

First published in Great Britain 2011
by Mills & Boon, an imprint of Harlequin (UK) Limited.
Harlequin (UK) Limited, Eton House, 18-24 Paradise Road,
Richmond, Surrey TW9 1SR

© Wendy S. Marcus 2011

ISBN: 978 0 263 88617 7

Harlequin (UK) policy is to use papers that are natural, renewable and recyclable products and made from wood grown in sustainable forests. The logging and manufacturing process conform to the legal environmental regulations of the country of origin.

Printed and bound in Spain
by Blackprint CPI, Barcelona

Dear Reader

People often ask me how I come up with my characters. Are they based on any one person? Should they fear winding up in one of my books? I laugh and answer, 'You never know.' But the truth is my characters are a conglomeration of traits and habits from lots of different people.

As for Victoria, the heroine in the book you are about to read, I'd say she has a bit of me in her. I am a perfectionist, a hard worker, and I am determined to achieve whatever goals I set for myself. While I didn't have to overcome the obstacles Victoria did, I attended night school to earn my Masters in Health Care Administration while working full time. At the age of twenty-eight I took over as Director of Patient Services for a large licensed home healthcare services agency—a job I absolutely loved.

But with the birth of my second child the measurement of my success changed from a red BMW and a pay-cheque with six figures to being the kind of mom I'd always hoped to be—one who attended school parties and arrived home in time to get her children off the bus. So I left my then dream job and created new opportunities for myself.

I wonder if Victoria would choose the same path. Probably not.

If you're new to my books, I introduced Victoria in my debut Medical™ Romance, WHEN ONE NIGHT ISN'T ENOUGH—the first book in my *Madrin Memorial Hospital* series. Roxie's story is up next. I hope you'll take the time to read them all.

I love to hear from readers. Please visit me at: www.WendySMarcus.com

Wishing you all good things

Wendy S. Marcus

This book is dedicated to Harold Glassberg. A knowledge-able advisor. A staunch supporter. A dear friend. (And the only man gutsy enough to join my mailing list!) For giving me a reason to write and the chance to find out how much I enjoy it.

With special thanks to:

My editor, Flo Nicoll, for your wonderful suggestions and fast turnaround times.

My agent, Michelle Grajkowski, for your fierce negotiating skills and answering my many questions.

My friend, Nas Dean, for helping me with promotion and all things requiring computer savvy,

Some special writing friends, Christine Glover, Joanne Coles, and Lacey Devlin, for your supportive e-mails and blog comments.

And, as always, to my family, for putting up with all the time I spend on the computer and accepting, without complaint, that I didn't cook dinner. Again.

Praise for Wendy S. Marcus

"Readers are bound to feel empathy
for both the hero and heroine. Each has a uniquely
disastrous past and these complications help to make the
moment when Jared and Allison are able to give their
hearts to the other all the more touching."
—*RT Book Reviews* on *When One Night Isn't Enough*
4 Stars

CHAPTER ONE

WITH a few adept keystrokes, 5E Head Nurse Victoria Forley shot next week's schedule off to the nursing office and closed down her computer. Today she would leave on time. She straightened her already neat desk then scanned her tiny utilitarian office to make sure everything was in its place. The memory of her son's tear-filled eyes made her heart ache. "Why am I always the last kid picked up from afterschool program?" Jake had asked last night at dinner. "My teacher gets so mad when you're late."

Mad enough to put Victoria on parental probation. Three more late pick-ups and Jake would be kicked out of the program. Then what would she do?

Victoria hated that the promotion she'd fought so hard for, a bullet-point in her ten-year plan to provide her son a future filled with opportunities rather than financial constraints, significantly impacted the wide-awake hours they spent together. Although, to be honest, it wasn't actually the job that was the problem; it was her obsessive compulsive need to achieve perfection at it. To show everyone at Madrin Memorial Hospital who thought a twenty-five-year-old wasn't experienced enough to be the hospital's newest head nurse that she was up to the task.

She grabbed her lab coat from the hanger hooked to the back of her door and slipped it on. A final check of her H-shaped unit and she'd be ready to go. Exiting her office, Victoria inhaled the familiar, disinfectant fresh odor of pine and scanned the white walls and floors to assure they were in pristine condition. She closed the lid on a laundry hamper and rolled two unused IV pumps into the clean utility room.

When she crossed over to the hallway of odd-numbered rooms she saw it, sitting quietly outside room 517. A shedding, allergy-inducing, pee-whenever-the-urge-hits golden retriever with a bright red bandana tied around its neck.

So, the elusive Dr. K., oncology rehabilitation specialist extraordinaire, finally deigned to put in an appearance on 5E, two hours late for their scheduled meeting. Well, now *he'd* have to wait for *her* to make herself available. And she was in no hurry to listen to him spout the merits of his program and, she was sure, begin lobbying for her support to make his dog's position permanent.

Not likely.

While she was all for an in-house staff member coordinating a multidisciplinary approach to the rehabilitation of cancer patients and administering daily bedside physical therapy to chemo patients too exhausted or too immunosuppressed to attend PT down in the department, she didn't see why Dr. K. needed a four-legged companion to do it. Victoria walked past the animal, who didn't budge from his position, the slight wag of his tail the only indication he'd noticed her. Okay. So it obviously wasn't a threat to visitors. Still. She was not a fan of unsanitary animals besmirching her unit. Unless it benefited her patients, which was why she'd agreed to hold off on casting her negative vote until after the four-week trial.

"We'll swing by tomorrow morning," a male voice said from inside the room. The rich, deep timbre and his words "swing by" caused a jolt of recognition.

Unease sauntered up her spine. It couldn't be. She looked into the room anyway, had to catch a glimpse to be sure.

A man stood at the foot of bed two. The blinds closed and the lights off, she could just make out was his height: Tall. Shoulders: Full. Arms: Big. Longish, dark hair curled haphazardly over the tops of his ears, reaching the collar of his lab coat in the back. As if he felt her eyes on him, he turned to face her. An unruly swag of bangs hung at an angle, obscuring part of his forehead. Despite his unkempt appearance he was handsome in a rugged, untamed sort of way.

Great. He'd caught her staring.

"Victoria?" the man asked, and started to walk toward her.

That voice. His stride. Please, God. Not him. Victoria felt flash frozen in place. When he emerged from the darkened room into the well-lit hallway, her eyes, the only body part capable of movement, met his. A blue so pale they'd look almost colorless if not for an outer ring of deep ocean blue. Eyes she'd loved and hated in equal measure, familiar eyes in an unfamiliar face, a man's face with a slightly crooked nose, obviously broken at some point, and strong cheek bones. A scar bisected his right eyebrow, another spliced the center of his chin.

But she'd know him anywhere.

Kyle Karlinsky.

Before she could stop it, concern flitted across her mind. What'd happened to him in the nine years he'd been gone? She mentally slapped it back. It didn't matter, couldn't have been worse than what she'd been through because of his irresponsible carelessness. "Victoria?" he asked. "What are you doing here?" He scanned the nametag clipped to the breast pocket of her lab coat. "You're a nurse?" He hesitated, digested his discovery and with narrowed, taunting eyes asked, "What happened? Couldn't hack it at Harvard?"

He'd happened. She resisted the urge to lunge for his throat and squeeze until his lifeless body collapsed to the floor. Instead, she stood tall, well, as tall as a woman of five feet two inches could, threw back her shoulders and lifted her chin. "I'm a head nurse. 5E is my floor."

"You're the 5E bitc—?" He held up both hands. "Sorry."

He didn't look sorry.

She knew what some members of the staff called her. She'd been the victim of name-calling since high school. Snob. Suck-up. It no longer bothered her. "Just because a woman is motivated to succeed and has high expectations for herself and those around her, people feel it necessary to call her demeaning names." She waved it off. "There's nothing I can do about it. But I'll thank you to keep your profanity to yourself while in my presence."

He looked her up and down. "Still dressing for success, I see."

For as long as she could remember, up until the time he'd turned his back on her, her father had impressed, "If you want respect, dress and act like you deserve it." Which was why, when she'd had little money to spare, she'd scoured consignment shops and tag sales to find quality designer pieces to complement the carefully selected clothing she'd been forced to purchase at a discount store.

Victoria took notice of Kyle's black pocket T, faded blue jeans, and black leather biker boots. "Still dressing for a monster truck rally, I see." Except his clothes were covered by a lab coat. Dr. Kyle Karlinsky's lab coat.

Kyle was Dr. K.? No way! Not possible. Before she'd started tutoring him, she a tenth-grade honor student, him an unmotivated junior, his highest aspiration had been to snag a third-shift job at the frozen pizza manufacturing plant outside town, because the night shift received a $2.00 per hour pay differential.

"You're a few months late for Halloween. What's with the costume?" Victoria asked, trying to control her breathing. While she'd been stuck in the anti-metropolis of Madrin Falls, getting tormented by people more than happy to witness the demise of her seemingly perfect life and raising their child, he'd left town to pursue *her* dream, to steal *her* future.

"Calm down, honey. It's not as big a deal as you're making it out to be" had been the last words he'd spoken to her until today. And they'd been incorrect. To a sheltered, motherless teenager raised to believe sex before marriage was a sin, giving up her virginity to the boy she'd fallen in love with, the absolute wrong sort

of boy who, just a few hours previously her father *had* forbidden her to see, *had* been a big deal.

Life as she'd known it changed that night. And two weeks before his high-school graduation, Kyle Karlinsky had abandoned her to deal with the consequences on her own.

"Not bad." He nodded in approval. "Marginally funny. Delivered with just the right amount of sneer. Looks like someone's developed herself a sense of humor."

"Is that what this is, some kind of prank?" He'd been famous for them back in high school. She glanced at the credentials sewn onto his lab coat beside his name. DPT. Okay, so he wasn't a medical doctor. But still. A doctorate in physical therapy? "No way you made it to PhD." The thought of him staying focused long enough to write a doctoral thesis was ludicrous. "And impersonating a physician is reprehensible."

"Pulling out the big words, huh? Let's see. Reprehensible. R-e-p-r-e-h-e-n-s-i-b-l-e." He spelled it out like he was in a spelling bee. "Reprehensible. Deserving of blame or censure." His smile widened at Victoria's surprise. "Maybe I wasn't as dumb as you thought. Maybe I only pretended so I could..."

Steal her virginity, as so eloquently bellowed by her enraged father.

"I never thought you were dumb, Kyle." An underachiever? Yes. A slacker? Most definitely. Stupid? Absolutely not. "I tutored you. I knew what you were capable of if only you'd have put forth a little effort. But you wouldn't."

"Now that's not entirely true. With the right incentive I was an excellent student." He mocked her, his eyes dark.

"I promise to study for my trigonometry test if you kiss me. Slip me some tongue, I'll get a B." Okay. So it wasn't an approved method of teaching. But, at the time, it'd been the only thing that'd worked.

"I seem to remember," he said, leaning close, invading her personal space. "I did a bit of tutoring myself."

He sure had, with a hand under her skirt in their private study room, up against the cinderblock wall behind the gym, and in a secluded spot down by the lake. At the memory, an unwanted, excited tingle crept out of hiding deep in her core. She slammed it back, refused to acknowledge it, would not let him get to her. Not again.

"Help," a woman cried out.

Victoria jerked her head in the direction of the panicked voice. A pale, middle-aged woman with dark hair ran into the hallway. "My father. He's choking."

Without hesitation, she ran to help. The morbidly obese patient she recognized as Mr. Schultz sat in an extra-wide chair beside his bed. Mentally she cued the information she'd obtained during morning rounds. Age seventy-two. Status post-CVA six days ago with residual right-sided hemiplegia, speech deficit, and difficulty swallowing.

"Are you able to breathe at all, Mr. Schultz?"

He slapped at his neck with his left hand and strained to inhale, a high-pitched wheezing sound the result.

Quick assessment: Face flushed. Diaphoretic. Eyes pleading. Inefficient air exchange. Victoria pushed his over-the-bed table out of the way, noticing an open bag of colorful hard sucking candies as she did. His daughter was going to get a stern talking to when this was all over. She inserted her hand behind his back and pushed him forward, giving four rapid blows between his shoulder blades.

Nothing.

"Papa. Don't die, Papa," the hysterical woman cried. "You have to save him."

Victoria moved in front of the patient. "Open your mouth, Mr. Schultz."

She could not see the obstruction. "What can I do to help?" Kyle asked.

"I need this bed out of the way." So she could reach the suction apparatus on the wall behind the patient. "Then please accompany Mr. Schultz's daughter and his roommate to the lounge." As stressful as this situation was for her, a trained practitioner, it was worse for a family member/roommate to experience, especially if things didn't turn out well.

"I'm going to help you, Mr. Schultz," she said, surprised at how calm her voice sounded, knowing the man was probably past listening or understanding but needing to say it just in case.

"I don't want to go. I want to stay with him," the daughter yelled.

Kyle spoke to her in soothing yet persuasive tones.

Victoria focused on her task. She reached for the disposable suction container and snapped it into the plastic wall receptacle, thankful her exemplary staff made sure each room was fully stocked with all necessary equipment at all times. Her hands shook. It'd been a while since she'd been in any life-or-death situations. They were not her favorite part of nursing, too many variables outside her control.

"Almost done, Mr. Schultz."

Kyle rushed back into the room. "Should I try the Heimlich?"

"Can you get your arms around him?"

"I think so." Unable to squeeze behind the patient since she was back there setting up suction, Kyle moved the chair like Mr. Schultz was the size of a child rather than the three-hundred-plus-pounder he was.

"I think his belly is too large for your thrusts to be effective," Victoria said. "Position your hands over his sternum instead. Pull straight back. Hard and fast."

Kyle did as instructed with excellent technique but no positive result.

The patient's skin took on a purplish reddish hue. They were running out of time.

Leaving Kyle to continue his attempts on his own, Victoria returned to the suction equipment, hooking the red vacuum tube to the container. She ripped open two sets of tubing, unraveled both. One she connected between the collection container and the wall gauge. The other she attached to the nozzle labeled "Patient", then pulled apart the ends of the wrapper on the curved oral suctioning catheter, and, attaching it to the suction cable, was finally ready to proceed.

"Any luck?" Victoria pulled on a pair of latex gloves and turned back to the patient.

"No. He looks about to pass out."

Yes, he did. If one attempt at suction didn't work she'd call for the code team. Victoria removed the suction catheter from its packaging, turned on the suction device and cranked the knob to high. When she reached for Mr. Schultz's chin, preparing to open his mouth, he grabbed her wrist. Hard.

Kyle intervened, prying the patient's fingers off her. "She's trying to help you, sir. Let her do her thing."

Victoria placed her finger on the patient's lower jaw to open it. "Open up for me, Mr. Schultz. I'm going to clear your airway." *Please, please, please let this work.*

He allowed her to open his mouth.

Pressing down on his tongue with her thumb, Victoria slid the catheter deep until it tapped something hard that did not feel at all like the walls of the mouth or throat. She pressed her finger over the hole in the neck of the hard plastic catheter to concentrate the suction into the tip, pressed against the hard object very carefully, and gave a little tug. Like a cork had been released, Mr. Schultz sucked in a huge, gasping breath. Then another and another. A coarse but wonderful sound.

Relief made Victoria's legs weak.

Tears streamed from Mr. Schultz's eyes.

Careful to maintain full suction so the obstructing object did not loosen from the tip and fall back into the patient's throat, Victoria eased back on the catheter. A bright red ball of candy stuck to the end.

Victoria blew out a breath.

"You did good," Kyle said.

Mr. Schultz took her hand and held it to his cheek. She patted his shoulder with her other hand. "You're very welcome."

Victoria hit the button for the intercom to contact the unit secretary. "Nora, is Ali back on the floor?"

"She's heading my way right now."

"Tell her Mr. Schultz just choked on a hard candy. He's okay. We're going to get him into bed. She needs to call his physician and come take a set of vitals.

"Would you help me…?" When Victoria turned back to the patient Kyle already had him sitting on the side of the bed. She rushed over to lift his swollen feet and together they pulled him up in bed, although Kyle did most of the work. Then she raised the head of the bed.

"I'm going to talk to your daughter, Mr. Schultz." She put up all four side rails and put the patient's call-bell in his left hand. "Push this button…" she demonstrated "…if you need anything before I get back."

He nodded and gave her a small half-smile using the facial muscles not affected by his stroke.

"Thank you for your help, Kyle." He followed her to the door.

"Still perfect in everything you do, huh?"

"Hardly."

He took her by the arm. She turned to face him. He leaned in until his mouth grazed her ear. "For the record, my thrusts are always effective. And hard and fast suits me just fine."

Typical. He'd taken her Heimlich instruction and turned it into something sexual. She didn't respond, would not be provoked. She simply looked down at his hand on her arm. He released her and she walked out of the room.

After discussing the prescribed dietary restrictions with Mr. Schultz's daughter and supervising the removal of all the remaining hard candies, Victoria left the patient in her best friend and Mr. Schultz's nurse Ali's capable hands, surprised to see Kyle waiting for her in the hallway.

His eyes seemed softer somehow, not as antagonistic as they'd been. But she refused to let down her guard until she found out why he'd come back to town.

"Nothing better to do with your time?" she asked.

"He okay?" Kyle tossed his chin in the direction of Mr. Schultz's room.

"Much better."

"You?"

"Fine." For a split second she appreciated his concern. Until a suspicion he was up to something pushed its way in. Why was he being so nice all of a sudden?

Nora called down the hallway, "Victoria, if you don't leave in the next five minutes, you'll be late to pick up Jake."

She cringed at the sound of her son's name blurted out in Kyle's presence. The less he knew about Jake the better. She glanced at her watch. "Fudge."

"Still can't say what's really on your mind," Kyle taunted.

"Lucky for you," Victoria replied, then yelled to Nora, "Thanks."

"I'll walk you out," Kyle offered, falling into step beside her, his dog beside him.

"Don't bother." She hurried up the hallway. "I've been walking since I was a child and am perfectly capable of doing it on my own." Apparently that didn't matter. She ducked into her office, grabbed her purse, briefcase, already packed with work she needed to do at home, and coat. Kyle stood propped up against the wall beside her door. She ignored him and headed for the stairs.

"I think I'm allergic to your dog." She pushed out what she hoped were a few convincing coughs. "Would you mind keeping your distance?" Why was he back now, after all these years, when she'd finally regained control of her life? Dread balled in her gut.

She yanked open the heavy metal door, his hand landed a few feet above hers and suddenly the door weighed nothing.

"Since we're going to be working together I think there're a few things we need to work through," he said.

Victoria hurried down the first flight of metal stairs, each pounding step echoing in the empty stairwell. She did not want to work through anything with him, could not get away from him quick enough…or fast enough.

He jogged a few steps behind her.

"To start with," he proceeded despite her silence, "why did you tell that crooked sheriff I raped you?"

Raped her? She stumbled, glanced over her shoulder. "Are you insane? I never…" The words died in her throat as she missed a step. Maybe two. Her right foot hit hard. Her ankle twisted at an awkward angle, her knee buckled. She grabbed for the railing, missed, screamed out as her forward momentum sent her diving toward the fourth-floor landing.

Tori barked in warning.

Kyle lunged forward, caught Victoria by the back of her lab coat and, thank you, God, slowed her fall just enough so he could hook an arm around her waist milliseconds before she face-planted onto cement. Sitting on the bottom step, breathing heavily, part exertion, part fear, she could have been seriously injured. He cradled her on his lap and rested his chin on her silky curls, giving his pulse a chance to slow. As much as she deserved to pay for what she'd done, Kyle had no desire to see her physically hurt.

"You're okay," he said to reassure himself as much as to reassure her.

There were names for men like him, and they weren't ones Victoria would want uttered within her hearing. Why, after that terrifying choking incident and when she was obviously in a rush, did he have to lob the question that'd been dragging down his subconscious for nine long years at her back, where she couldn't see it coming? And within minutes of their meeting up again.

She tried to scoot off his lap.

"Sit for a minute," he said, inhaling the scent of melon, sweet cantaloupe grown in the warm sun, picked from the vine at peak ripeness. She'd always smelled good. Clean. Fresh. Different from the beer-drinking, cigarette-smoking, heavy-perfume-wearing girls he'd been used to.

The feel of her, light and soft, brought back memories of innocent times, holding hands, walks in the woods, the sheer pleasure of having her close, of touching her to confirm she was real and not a dream. Because girls like Victoria didn't fall for guys like him. And yet, in some fluke blip of altered reality, she had.

For a time, Victoria had been the only good thing in his life. She'd made him believe in hope and possibility, until she'd betrayed him in the worst possible way.

She'd been destined for great things, had been all but formally accepted into Harvard, the alma mater of her father and brother. Pre-med. She'd talked of specializing in neurosurgery or maybe going into research to find cures for cancer, multiple sclerosis, diabetes, and a dozen other medical conditions. With her tenacity, he'd had no doubt, if there were cures to be found, Victoria would have been the one to find them. So what was she doing still in Madrin Falls, working as a nurse?

She tried to wriggle out of his arms again. He tightened his hold, not ready to give her up. And what was that all about? He despised her. But damn if she didn't have him thinking about working off his mad in a few rounds of angry sex.

Because she looked good, better than he remembered. Hotter. Pixie cute, but with class. Her black hair short and perfectly mussed. Minimal makeup. Slender figure. Her fashionable tan slacks and cream-colored blouse covered by an immaculate, wrinkle-free lab coat, high-end shoes on her tiny feet. She liked her fancy clothes, that's for sure.

"You're squeezing me too tight." She started to struggle in earnest. "I don't like being restrained."

He let her go.

She slid off his lap to the other side of the step. "You are a jinx." She fluffed her hair. "Bad things happen to me when you're around." Using the railing to pull herself up, she stood and winced when she attempted to bear weight on her right foot.

He reached out to support her.

"Don't touch me." She swatted his hand away and tried to take a step, quickly relieving the pressure on her right foot. She looked up to the ceiling. "I don't need this right now." Her frustrated yell echoed off the walls.

Kyle thought he may have seen a tear form in the corner of her eye, which sent him flashing back nine years to the last time he'd seen her. Hysterical crying as the sheriff had helped her into the front passenger seat of his patrol car. To spare her the embarrassment of anyone knowing exactly what'd transpired between them, Kyle picked up her panties, used them to clean up the small smear of blood from the loss of her virginity, and stuffed them in his pocket, where the deputy had found them a short time later.

Spending the night in jail had given him plenty of time to think about what they'd done. And she'd come to him willingly with her little moans of pleasure, her desperate pleas for more. Anger worked its way in as he pondered the other possibility that'd plagued him. Had she made the accusation to escape her father's wrath, to save herself from punishment and penance with a total disregard for what may happen to him as a result?

He emerged from his memories, the residual mix of guilt and lingering animosity not quite abated. "You know I didn't force you into doing anything you didn't want to do." So why the hysterics afterwards? It didn't make sense.

"I can't believe we're even having this conversation." She put her hand up to the juncture of her left lateral neck and shoulder, swiveled her head, trying to work out a kink, and locked eyes with him. "I never told anyone you raped me. Look, we had sex. It was my first time. You're huge. I'm not. I panicked. So what? No permanent harm done."

He didn't like the way she turned away when she said, "No permanent harm done."

Aside from the euphoria of experiencing the best sex of his young life with a girl he'd managed to fall in love with, and the rage of having to choose between standing trial and possibly spending years in prison or leaving town for good and never contacting her again, he held little recollection of the specific details of that fateful night. Except for the sublime feel of her, which he'd never managed to duplicate with any other woman.

"Did I hurt you, Tori?" The thought he might have made him sick.

"Don't call me that," she snapped. "Any physical discomfort went away a lot sooner than the pain of you leaving me without a word as to why."

She had no idea what he'd gone through after she'd been taken home? "The sheriff told me you accused me of rape. He dragged me off to jail, let me sit in that stinking cell for hours." While he'd summarized the evidence against him and recounted stories of what prison inmates did to rapists.

To her credit, Victoria looked genuinely surprised.

"It scared the hell out of me."

Her eyes narrowed.

"Well, it did."

"If you'd known me at all," she said. "If you'd loved me as much as you said you did, if you'd trusted me at all, you should have known in your heart I'd never have done such a thing."

But she'd been inconsolable, wouldn't talk to him. She'd pushed him away when he'd tried to hold her and comfort her, fought her way out of the car—just as the sheriff had pulled up beside them. He'd had no idea what was going through her mind.

"At the very least," she added, "I deserved the benefit of the doubt and a phone call to clue me in to what was happening."

"How was I supposed to call you?" Didn't she get it? "I was in jail. And a seventeen-year-old boy with no parents to stand up for him and a twenty-year-old sister too busy partying to care what happened to him didn't get the proverbial one phone call in this town. I was given two choices. Take my chances with a trial or leave town." A kid like him with a bad reputation and no one reputable to stand up for him would never have won a court battle against a family from the upper echelon of Madrin Falls. "I didn't see any way out but to leave. When I was released from custody, a deputy followed me home. I had ten minutes to pack and he escorted me out of town." And followed him another hour after that.

"You haven't been near a phone any time since?" Victoria asked. "Weren't you at all interested in how my father reacted to finding out his only daughter had tumbled, half-dressed, from the back seat of your car when she was supposed to be studying at the library?"

Honestly, as angry as he'd been, he'd still suffered twinges of guilt, wondering. Her uber-strict father was not a nice man. Kyle had thought about calling her. But never had, lowlife loser that he'd been, too busy, working to survive by day, boozing it up and releasing his rage in bar fights at night. Too intent on cultivating his hatred of the establishment, the haves who controlled the have nots, to realize until now that if the sheriff truly believed him guilty there's no way he would have let him leave town. *Idiot.*

"I loved you," she said. "I believed you when you said you loved me."

"I did."

"You did not. Or you would have found a way to get in touch with me to make sure I was okay." The hurt in her eyes coaxed him forward. The familiar urge to soothe her and make her smile kicked in. She held up a hand between them. "Don't. It doesn't matter anymore. I'm over it. So there's nothing more to discuss."

She looked at her watch, inhaled deeply, exhaled,

then pulled her cellphone out of her pocket and dialed. Keeping her eyes closed, she pinched the bridge of her nose.

"Hello, it's—" she said into the phone.

A woman yelled back at her.

She held the phone away from her ear. "I know. Strike one. I'm sorry."

More yelling.

"I'll get there as soon as I can." With a press of a button she cut off the irate voice in mid-rant.

"I've got to go," she said to Kyle. Balancing on her left foot, with one hand on the railing, she bent to pick up her purse and briefcase with the other. She looked so sad he actually felt bad for her. "Let me help you," he offered, reaching for her briefcase.

She clutched the strap to her shoulder. "I don't need your help." She mumbled something under her breath that sounded like "Not anymore."

"At least let me examine your ankle. You may need an X-ray."

"I don't."

He watched her limp to the door leading to the fourth floor. "It's unsafe for you to drive."

"Go back to work, Kyle."

"I'm done for the day. How are you going to press on the gas and brake pedals? Let me take you where you need to go." Give him a chance to make amends.

The little color that remained in her cheeks drained out. "No." Her voice cracked. "Really, I'm fine."

They entered the half-full elevator.

Looking straight ahead, Victoria asked, "Shouldn't your dog be wearing a vest or something to make him look...more...?"

"Service dogs wear vests," Kyle explained. "*She's...*" he reached down to pat Tori's head "...a therapy dog. Therapy dogs are meant to be petted and cuddled. A vest interferes with that."

When the doors opened, Kyle and Tori followed Victoria out. As she hobbled through the lobby, Kyle noticed she didn't acknowledge one person she passed, and no one went out of their way to acknowledge her.

In the parking lot she stopped next to an old black Camry that looked a lot like the one her Aunt Livi had bought a few weeks before he'd left town.

He made one last attempt to convince her not to drive. "So, who's this Jake and why's he so important you'd risk your life to pick him up rather than accept a ride from me?"

CHAPTER TWO

OKAY. That's it.

Victoria tossed her briefcase on the back seat of her car, slammed the door shut and waited to the count of five before turning on Kyle. She spoke slowly, fought to maintain an even tone. "Jake is none of your business. My life is not your concern and I'll thank you, in advance, to stay away from me for the short time you'll be in town."

"Like it or not, most of my patients are on your floor and, once my therapy dog program is approved, I plan to accept the full-time staff position I've been offered." He leaned toward her. Challenging. "The next time I leave town it will be on *my* terms."

"You make it sound like approval for you to bring your dog to work is a given. It's not. We're firm at three for and four against. I'm against." As was her mentor, the director of nursing.

"We have four weeks to change your mind." He patted his dog's head, looking unconcerned.

"No one can be as good as the two of you are touted to be. The patient outcomes and lengths of stay will speak for themselves."

"Oh, we are that good, honey," he said confidently.

"Don't call me..."

"Come on, Tori," he said as he turned to walk away. His dog trailed after him.

She sucked in an affronted breath. "You named your dog after me?" she called out.

He glanced over his shoulder. "She was a stubborn little thing when I started working with her. Reminded me of a girl I used to know."

Victoria resisted the urge to scream. Having Kyle Karlinsky around was going to be an exercise in self-control. And secrecy. At least until she decided whether to inform Jake that his father, who she'd promised to help him search for when he turned sixteen, had returned to town eight years ahead of schedule.

Using the utmost care not to bang her now throbbing foot, Victoria slid onto the cold leather driver's seat.

No doubt Jake would be thrilled to finally meet the man whose picture sat on his night table. He deserved a chance to get to know his dad. At some point. Was now, when he was so young and impressionable, the best time? Until she could learn a bit more about Kyle, where he'd been, why he was back, and maybe gauge his reaction to having a son, she would not risk Jake getting hurt.

Although the drive to school turned out to be a bit more difficult than anticipated, Victoria avoided any major problems. Thank the Lord two pedestrians crossing at Third Street saw her in time to jump out of the way.

The second she got out of the car and set her right foot on the ground for balance, pain exploded in her ankle, the intensity on a par with labor contractions. She eyed the distance from her parking spot to the door of the cafeteria. It may as well have been the length of a football field rather than the twenty or thirty feet it actually was.

Eleven minutes late, she couldn't afford to be any later. Clenching her teeth hard enough to crack a filling, she made a limping dash towards the school. Halfway there Jake exited the building, in the process of pulling on his hat, and without looking at her walked directly to the car.

The afterschool program teacher—Mrs. Smythe—followed.

The temperature dropped a few degrees.

"I had to take care of a choking patient. Then I twisted my ankle rushing to leave," Victoria explained.

"If it wasn't that it would have been something else," the evil woman replied. "I have a life outside my job, you know."

Was it common knowledge that, aside from Jake, Victoria didn't? "I'm sorry."

"Don't be sorry," she said as she, too, walked past Victoria without looking at her. "Be on time."

She would do better, Victoria decided when she climbed into the car, glimpsed into the back seat and saw the unhappy pout on her son's precious face. Jake, the most important thing in her world. "I love you," she said.

He stared out the window.

"I'm sorry I'm late." Victoria started the car and changed the radio to Jake's favorite station.

He lunged over the front seat and turned it off.

Except for the heat blasting from the vents, a tense silence filled the car.

She looked at him in the rearview mirror. "Put on your seat belt."

He didn't.

"Jake, I said I was sorry. You understand why Mommy has to work so hard, don't you?"

Nothing.

It was going to be a long night.

"I'm talking to you, Jake Forley. And we will not leave this parking lot until you answer my question."

"Because it's just the two of us," he said, still looking out the window. "And you need money to pay bills and send me to a good college."

"And so you can play baseball in the spring."

He jerked his head, his eyes went wide. "Really?" He scooted to the front edge of his seat. "You're going to let me play?"

An impromptu, anything-to-cheer-him-up decision she would likely live to regret but, "Yes. And you're going to need baseball pants, a bat and glove, and shoes."

"Cleats, Mom," he said with an eye roll and an air of eight-year-old disgust at her ignorance of sports lingo. "Baseball players wear cleats."

"After dinner we'll go online and do some research." To figure out what cleats were. "Sound good?"

"Sounds great! Thanks, Mom!" He leaned forward and kissed her cheek. "I love you, too."

"I know." But she'd never tire of hearing him say it.

The next morning, her purplish, swollen right ankle elevated on an overturned garbage can and propped up on a pile of folded towels, her neck stiff, and her right knee almost twice its normal size, Victoria felt like she'd been selectively beaten by one of the dozens of baseball bats she'd viewed on the Internet the night before. With everything she needed to consider—barrel, taper and grip size, length and weight, as well as material makeup: wood, aluminum, or composite—choosing the correct bat was more complicated than calculating a biochemical equation. On the plus side, she now knew baseball cleats were little more than fancy sneakers with molded rubber studs to increase traction on the field.

She smiled. After a difficult start, she and Jake had had a super-terrific—his words, not hers—evening together. He was now an officially registered little-leaguer assigned to a team in the Madrin Falls Baseball League, practices to start next week, the season opener three weeks after that.

It would require creative scheduling, but she'd find a way to squeeze in everything. Work. Jake's school. Her school. Religious school. And now baseball. Her stress level spiked up a notch just thinking about it.

"Knock, knock," a familiar male voice said from her office doorway. "How's the ankle?"

Victoria turned her head in that direction, forgetting her neck felt fine as long as she didn't try to move it. "Go away." She lifted her hand to the stabbing pain and tried to work out the cramp.

Kyle walked in, towered over her, filled her tiny office. He set two cups of coffee on the desk, and squeezed into the small space behind her. His body pressed against her back, pushing her ribs into the desk. She couldn't move. "Wait."

As if his fingers had the ability to shoot potent muscle-relaxer beams deep into her screaming elastic tissues, the spasm lessened with the contact of his big, warm hands on her skin. A pleasant tingle danced along her nerve endings, made her wish he'd branch out a bit. Lower.

Heaven help her, she still loved the feel of his hands on her. Strong. Knowing.

She forced her eyes open. This had to stop. But it felt so good. She let them drift closed, again. One more minute. Maybe two.

But, on the cusp of total relaxation, Victoria's memory kicked in and transported her back in time. Something had her wedged in place. Confined. Squished. She couldn't expand her chest. Couldn't breathe. Could not pull air into her lungs. Please. Not again. She needed to get away. Escape this place. She was an adult, refused to be imprisoned. Never again.

"What's wrong?" Kyle's concerned voice sounded far away. His face appeared in front of hers. Kind. Searching.

She returned to the present standing on both feet, the garbage pail lying on its side. She shifted her weight to relieve the pressure on her right ankle, the move so quick she lost her balance and grabbed on to the desk for support. Her chest constricted, floaters dotted her vision, a wave of dizziness threatened to tip her over.

"You're okay." A strong arm wrapped around her upper arms and basically held her up. "Come on. Breathe. In and out. Move my hand." Which he'd placed over her diaphragm. "That's it."

"I need..." She tried to push away from him.

"You need to sit down for a minute."

Not again. Not now. It'd been nine years, for heaven's sake. Why was his voice, his touch, sending her back in time?

He guided her into her chair. "Here." He handed her one of the cups of coffee he'd brought. "Drink this."

In a daze she lifted a cup to her mouth.

"Careful. It's hot." He removed the lid and blew on it like a parent cooling his child's hot cocoa. Like he would have done for Jake had he been around for the past eight years. Clarity returned.

"I'm fine." She took the cup from him, even though she didn't drink coffee. "Thank you."

He picked up the other cup, took a careful sip and watched her. "What just happened?"

Rather than answer, she countered with a question of her own. "Where's your dog?"

"In with a patient."

"Aren't you supposed to be with her at all times?" Per hospital protocol developed specifically for his and Tori's probationary period.

"Patients open up to Tori. Part of what makes me so good at my job is knowing when I'm in the way."

"Typical man," she said, feeling back to normal, "letting the woman do the work while you go for coffee."

"I brought the coffee up with us. Do you have panic attacks often?"

Not recently. She took a sip of coffee. "It wasn't a panic attack," she lied. "More like an allergic reaction to a new irritant in my life."

He smiled, unperturbed by her verbal jab. "Guess I'd better start carrying around some antihistamines in my pocket."

"I have things to do. Did you come here for a reason?"

"To check your ankle." He squatted down, picked up her right foot in his hand, and slid off her shoe.

"Impressive colors. But look at these." He pointed to depressions in her edema. "Your shoe is too tight."

"No, it's not." But, boy, it felt good to have it off.

He gently rotated her foot watching her face as he did. "Decent range of motion. Moderate discomfort. How'd you sleep?"

Woke up every time she'd changed position. "Like a baby."

"Keeping it elevated?"

She pointed to the garbage can. "As much as I can. I'm a nurse, I know how to treat a sprained ankle, Kyle."

"You're sure that's all it is?"

She hoped. "Yes."

A loud bang followed by frantic dog barking echoed through the hallway.

Without a word, Kyle placed her foot on the floor and ran from the office.

Victoria slipped on her shoe and followed.

Kyle slammed into room 514 where he'd left Tori with Mrs. Teeton, a fifty-four-year-old female, ten days post-op radical abdominal hysterectomy for treatment of stage II cervical cancer. Undergoing combination chemotherapy and radiation. Suffering from severe adjustment reaction to her diagnosis, debilitating fatigue, and deconditioning. Completely dependent for all ADLs— activities of daily living.

The balding woman sat with her bare legs on the cold hospital floor, her upper torso, arms, and head draped over Tori's back. "Mrs. Teeton. Are you okay?" he asked, dropping to the floor beside her.

"I'm so weak," she said quietly, her cheeks wet with tears. "Can't even sit up by myself."

Kyle handed her a tissue from the bedside table. "You

are going to get through this phase of treatment, and I'm going to show up every day, several times a day, to help."

"What happened?" Victoria asked as she half ran, half hopped into the room, and, ignoring the bits of food spattered on the floor from the overturned meal tray, got right down on her knees next to Kyle. "What hurts, Mrs. Teeton?"

The pale, sickly woman tried to lift her head, couldn't, and set it on Tori's fur. "My pride."

"Before we get you back into bed I want to check you for injury," Kyle said. "Can you move your arms and legs for me?"

"I'm crushing poor Tori," Mrs. Teeton worried.

"A dainty little thing like you?" Kyle asked. "I think she's mistaken you for a blanket. She looks about ready to fall asleep."

Victoria smiled, a bright, encouraging smile he remembered from the hours she'd spent tutoring him. The one that used to make him feel all warm inside. And you know what? Still did.

"He's right," Victoria said.

Kyle patted the dog's head. "Good girl." She opened a sleepy eye.

With his assistance, Mrs. Teeton moved her arms, legs, and head without a report of physical discomfort. "I'm going to lift you into bed." She felt like a child in his arms. A small woman, like Victoria, Mrs. Teeton had all but stopped eating since her diagnosis three weeks ago, losing an estimated eleven desperately needed pounds. Too weak to participate in her own care and refusing psychological counseling, she had the highest acuity ranking of any patient on Kyle's roster.

Once in bed, Victoria took over, checking the patient's abdominal incision and taking her blood pressure before tucking her into bed. "The incision looks good. Your blood pressure is low. Before I put a call in to your doctor, tell us what happened."

"I'm so tired."

"It's important." Kyle put his hand on her lower leg, touch a big part of his therapy.

"I wanted to give Tori a treat from my breakfast," Mrs. Teeton said, her eyes closed.

"That breakfast is for you to eat, not Tori. And I told you, she's trained not to accept food from patients."

A hint of a smile curved her lips. "Wanted to see. Sat up but so dizzy." She sounded about to drift off to sleep. "Started to roll forward. Tori caught me." She mumbled something ending with, "Good dog."

"That's the most I've heard her say since admission. And I visit her every day," Victoria said quietly, looking at Mrs. Teeton's sleeping form.

"Tori gets them talking."

"Don't sell yourself short." She looked up at him, her beautiful blue eyes soft and warm. "You were great with her. So gentle and kind."

The hint of disbelief he detected bothered him. Before he could call her on it she headed for the door. "I'll call Dr. Starzi. Would you please put up all four bedrails and make sure her call-bell is within reach?"

As he was in the process of raising the last bed rail, someone walked into the room. A nurse, dressed in what he'd recently learned were 5E's trademark lavender scrubs. Brown hair up in a messy knot, girl-next-door pretty. Even with the surprise of her pregnant belly, Kyle recognized her instantly. His friend Ali Forshay, who Victoria had befriended back in tenth grade, as unlikely a pair as he and Victoria had been. Some kids had accused Victoria of slumming, others had called Ali and Kyle her charity projects.

Maybe they had been.

Good, a friendly face. He clicked the railing into place. One of the two he'd hoped to see while back in town. At least he'd thought so until he noticed her scowl.

She observed the patient then pulled the cord to turn off the overhead light. With narrowed eyes and pursed lips she pointed at him and then the window.

Did she expect him to jump?

A second later she grabbed him by the lab coat and pulled him deeper into the room, yanking the curtain partition into place as she did. The second bed lay flat, empty and raised to the highest position with the covers folded down at the foot of the bed, likely waiting for the occupant to return from the OR.

"Why did you come back?" she whispered curtly.

Because Dr. Starzi was the best oncologist around and Kyle refused to pass up the opportunity to work with him simply because of where he had to do it. And what reformed degenerate wouldn't want to ride the success train back into his hometown? Show everyone who'd labeled him worthless and turned a blind eye in his direction except to blame him for things he hadn't done and threaten him away from their daughters that they'd made a mistake in writing him off.

"No hug?" he asked, half teasing. In anticipation of seeing Ali he'd visualized their happy reunion. They'd been pals, both with difficult home lives. They'd looked out for one another. It'd been Ali who'd suggested Victoria tutor him when the thought of failing out of high school hadn't bothered him all that much. He owed her, planned to help her out if she needed it. But from the looks of her, and the size of the diamond engagement ring on her finger, she'd turned out okay, too.

"You're lucky I don't scratch your eyes out after what you did," she said.

And she looked ready to do it. He took a step back, kind of glad to have Tori in the room. "Exactly what did I do?"

"You stay away from Victoria." Again the pointing, this time at his chest. "Better yet, go back to where you came from."

"Hey," he said quietly, cupping her bent elbow. "We were friends. What happened?"

She looked up at him, her expression a mixture of sadness and hurt. "You're not the person I thought you were. I'm sorry I ever encouraged Victoria to give you a chance."

Ali had been one of three people to see something good in him, something of value, at a time when he had been unable to see it himself. Victoria and her Aunt Livi had rounded out the triumvirate.

The intercom in the room sounded. "Recovery Room on line two, Ali."

"Be right there," she responded without taking her eyes off of him. "Do the right thing, Kyle. Leave. And don't come back. Victoria's worked so hard to put her life back together. She's interested in a man for the first time since you..."

What? Since he what?

"You are the last thing she needs right now."

With that parting shot, Ali, at one time his closest friend, turned and left.

Back in town for two days and Kyle had more questions than answers. If Victoria hadn't cried rape, where had the accusation come from? What was she doing in Madrin Falls, working as a nurse? A caring, competent nurse from what he'd heard and seen, but why hadn't she gone to Harvard to become a physician as planned? Why was Ali warning him off? Why did Victoria's life need putting back together? The most stable, together person he knew, why was she suffering panic attacks? Who was Jake and how serious was their relationship?

Sensitive to turmoil, Tori nuzzled his thigh. He petted her soft head. "We'll find out, girl." And since Victoria and Ali didn't seem eager to enlighten him, after work he'd visit Aunt Livi.

The small raised ranch-style home looked better than he could ever recall seeing it. Neater. Prettier. The white siding could have passed for new, the once-dingy black shutters gleamed and a bright red door matched what looked like a freshly painted version of the heavy, antique planters he'd lugged out of the garage every spring and back every fall, which sat at either side of the front porch steps.

The gravel driveway he'd shoveled every winter for years looked newly paved, and the grass he'd mowed summer after summer, while sodden from the winter thaw, seemed fuller, healthier.

Odds were Livi had finally snagged herself a man with an interest in home maintenance. Good for her. Only knowing she had a man inside made him feel a bit guilty showing up at dinnertime, with an apple pie and an empty stomach.

The woman knew how to cook, and had never passed up an opportunity to invite Kyle in for a meal. Something he used to thank his lucky stars for, daily.

A boy responded to his knock. That was unexpected. He looked familiar. Probably because he shared Livi's kinky red hair.

"I thought you were the UPS man," he said with disappointment. "Mom," he yelled over his shoulder. "There's a man at the door."

The kid looked up at him, got an odd look on his face. Kyle noticed his eyes, the same eyes that stared back at him every time he looked in the mirror.

"Jake Forley, you know better than to open the door when you don't know who it is," a familiar female voice said from the top of the stairs.

Over the kid's shoulder Kyle caught a glimpse of Victoria, heading toward the door, looking very at home in pink warm-up pants and a white V-neck T.

This was Jake? Kyle shifted so Victoria couldn't see him. "Is that your mom?" Kyle asked quietly.

The boy nodded.

"How old are you?"

"Eight."

Holy hell!

CHAPTER THREE

VICTORIA struggled down the steps to the front door to see who Jake was talking to, stopping short at the sight of Kyle, holding a pie box, his expression a disturbing mix of suspicion and loathing.

"Go downstairs, Jake," she said, needing a few minutes to talk to Kyle, to diffuse his anger before making any formal introductions. Although, based on the way they studied each other, Kyle had a pretty good idea who Jake was. And vice versa.

Her son turned to her, looking hopeful and excited. Of course he'd recognized his father, whose picture he spoke to every night before bed. "But it's…"

"I know. Go downstairs and give us a few minutes to talk."

"I don't—"

"Now." She flashed him the look that said she meant business then moved her gaze to Kyle. "What are you doing here?"

"Aren't you going to invite me in?" He glared at her, dared her to refuse him.

Every instinct she had screamed: Slam the door in his face, grab your son, and run. She needed time to talk to an attorney to find out Kyle's rights. Her rights.

To talk to Jake about his expectations and set limits on the time he'd spend with his dad, if any. To prepare her son for the possibility Kyle might not be in town long and might not be interested in playing an active role in his son's life. And most important, she needed time to figure out how to protect herself, both personally and professionally. He'd almost ruined her life once. She would not give him the chance to do it again.

"No," she answered, hoping he'd leave, sure he wouldn't.

"But, Mom..." Jake whined.

She pointed to the door of his playroom. "Down. Stairs."

"Can I take the dog?" Jake asked.

For the first time she noticed Tori sitting quietly, looking up at her, watching her life unravel. "No," she said.

At the same time Kyle said, "Yes."

Discord, two minutes into co-parenting.

Victoria tilted her head and shot Kyle her best evil eye, the one guaranteed to make most people squirm. Kyle was not most people. He simply shrugged. "Livi loves animals. I came to see *her*."

"Aunt Livi is dead," Jake said matter-of-factly, and walked downstairs into his playroom. With a flick of the wrist from Kyle, his dog followed.

"Close the door," she said to her son.

Jake did.

Except for pictures and the many stories Victoria had repeated through the years, Jake had little memory of his grandaunt who'd died a few weeks before his third birthday, leaving Victoria alone to care for her son. Not that Aunt Livi had been much help the last year of her life, but she'd tried.

Kyle paled, clutched the storm door, his knuckles white. "When?" The word came out hoarse.

His upset did not surprise her. Kyle and Aunt Livi had had a special bond. *"Despite his upbringing he's a good boy. There's something special inside him. We can't let it go to waste."*

She'd sure changed her tune when Victoria wound up pregnant, and Kyle wound up gone.

"Five years ago," she answered. "Heart attack." Victoria still harbored guilt that taking in her pregnant niece against her brother's wishes, dealing with his threats and harassment, and helping a distraught teenager care for her infant son had been too much for Aunt Livi's fragile heart. That Victoria had been at least partially responsible for the death of the woman who'd loved her like a daughter and, in return, she'd loved like a mother.

Tears threatened.

Not a day went by that she didn't think of Aunt Livi. "And you live here now."

"She left everything to me and Jake." The house and second mortgage. The car and car loan. Unpaid taxes. Credit-card debt.

The news about Aunt Livi seemed to neutralize Kyle's anger, leaving him weary. "May I please come in?" Even though he could have pushed right past her, he stood on the porch and waited for an invitation. "Looks like there's something more we need to discuss after all."

"Now that's where you're wrong," she said, ignoring the cold air chilling her exposed skin, not wanting him inside her home. "We needed to talk eight years and eight months ago, when I learned I was pregnant. Or maybe eight years and six months ago when my father figured it out and issued his ultimatum: 'Get an abortion or get out.'"

"That sanctimonious bastard wanted you to kill our baby?" The usually calm Kyle did a convincing impression of someone ready to do a little killing himself.

"Shhh. Keep your voice down. And watch your language." She glanced downstairs to make sure Jake wasn't eavesdropping. Then she pulled the front door to her back, partially closing it to give them some privacy. "In dad's mind," she said quietly, "it was preferable to people finding out his perfect daughter had succumbed to temptation and gotten herself knocked up by the town's teenage Lothario."

"I wasn't…"

He stopped before he spat out a lie.

"Okay. Maybe before I met you," he relented. "But for the year we were together I didn't touch another woman. I swear on my parents' graves."

"I know." She crossed her arms over her chest and shivered.

"This is ridiculous. You're freezing. Come on, Tori. Let me in."

Come on, Tori. One quick feel. Under your bra this time. I swear I'll be the perfect student for the rest of the hour... Come on, Tori. Live a little. Just strip down and jump in. I promise I won't look... Come on, Tori. I want to show you how much I love you. Let me love you...

She shook her head to clear it. This flip-flopping between past and present had to stop. "The girl you knew as Tori died the day you left town," she said.

"You make it sound like I suddenly decided, hey, let me run out on my girlfriend today. I've got nothing better to do. Why don't I pick up and leave everything I know behind? Oh, and while I'm at it, I can rip out my heart and smash hers to bits in the process." He leaned in, his eyes locked on hers. "If you'd known me at all," he said, "if you'd loved me as much as you said you did, if you'd trusted me at all, you should have known in your heart *I'd* never have done such a thing."

He threw her words back in her face. Maybe he was right. "But you did leave. And since I haven't heard from you for almost nine years, I had absolutely no idea why. You knew where I was. At any time you could have called me to explain why you left, to ask me what I'd said to the sheriff. If you couldn't reach me, you could have asked Aunt Livi or Ali to get me a message. But you chose not to."

Victoria inhaled deeply, tired from a long day at work, drained and ready to be finished with this conversation. "None of this matters anymore."

"It sure as hell does matter." The sound of the storm door banging into the side of the house made her jump. "I've had a son for eight years and no one thought it necessary to tell me?"

"How was I supposed to tell you? I had no idea where you were."

"You were a very resourceful girl who has no doubt grown into a very resourceful woman." His voice turned cold. "If you wanted to find me you could have."

She'd thought about trying, many times. Early on when she'd been so scared about the pregnancy and childbirth, then again, after Aunt Livi's death, when she'd been desperate for help, for a break from Jake's incessant crying, for protection from the creditors who'd called night and day. But she'd convinced herself if he didn't want her, then she didn't want him. And as much as it pained her to admit it, a part of her had been relieved to not have to deal with the issue of sex between them.

As if during her silence he'd come to some realization, he lifted his hand and ran a gentle finger down the side of her face. "We have a son."

She didn't want his tenderness. Not now. "I know we have a son," she snapped. "I carried him inside my body for nine months. I logged hundreds of miles walking him up and down these hallways when he suffered from colic. I stayed awake night after night because he'd only sleep propped up on my chest and I was scared to fall asleep with him in my bed. I've bathed him, bandaged his scrapes and cuddled him when he's had nightmares. I have taken care of him, loved him, and provided for him as best I could every single day since he was born."

"If I was here I would have—"

"What you would have done doesn't matter. It's what you actually did that matters. And you left. Without a care for me or Jake."

"If I'd known about Jake I never would have left."

"So I didn't matter but a son would have? My father was right about you all along." She took on a husky man-voice and repeated her father's harsh words. "A boy like that will ruin your life, Victoria. He'll find a way to latch onto you and drag you down." She glared at Kyle and asked the question that'd haunted her for years. "Did you even wear a condom that night? Or were you trying to get me pregnant?"

He recoiled like she'd taken a swing at him.

Years of suppressed hurt, anger, and resentment surged to the surface with a force she couldn't contain. "Don't pretend the thought never crossed your mind. My father told me about his visit to the garage to warn you to stay away from me, and his threat that if you didn't he'd see to it that you did. Is it pure coincidence that very evening you surprised me at the library, took me to a secluded spot, and made it impossible for me to say no?"

"This is insane. I never set out to get you pregnant. You're turning a beautiful memory into something tawdry."

"Beautiful memory? You're joking, right? We were crammed into the back seat of your car. I felt crushed beneath you. I couldn't move, could barely breathe."

He looked physically ill. "Why didn't you tell me?"

At first, she hadn't spoken up because he'd aroused her to the point she had to know what came next. She'd loved Kyle, had wanted to be with him, wanted him to find pleasure in her body. But as the car heated and the windows steamed up, as his passion increased and his body covered hers, panic had taken over, transporting her back to that terrifying day in the closet.

Not thinking clearly, she'd allowed her father's words to seep in and take hold. *If you don't keep quiet you'll have to endure it another half-hour.* Keep quiet, she'd instructed herself over and over, just like she'd done all those years before. And using the coping mechanism she'd mastered as a child, she'd imagined she was somewhere else.

After he'd left town, she couldn't help wondering if he'd been able to tell. If he'd found her so inadequate and disappointing that he couldn't bring himself to face her.

"Look. I knew your father meant business," he said. "I thought that night might be the last time we'd be together. I wanted to be your first. I wanted you to always remember it. I wanted you to remember me."

Oh, she remembered him all right, but not in the way he'd intended. "What about what I wanted? Did you give any thought to that? Because I sure didn't want to be pregnant at seventeen. I didn't want to be joked about and ostracized by the kids at school. I didn't want to miss out on my senior year, senior prom and giving my valedictorian speech. I didn't want to forego Harvard to get stuck in this small town, going to community college, and owing years of my life to the hospital that paid my tuition. I didn't want a baby. I didn't want to lose my father's love. I didn't want any of it!"

"You didn't want me?" a small voice said.

Her son's voice.

Victoria stiffened, her carefully constructed world crumbling under her feet. Slowly she turned to see Jake standing at the bottom of the stairs. "Honey, I..."

With hurt, wet eyes and a look of complete devastation and utter betrayal he turned and ran. The door to the garage slammed, followed by the side door leading outside. Victoria took off after him, the pain in her right ankle and knee nothing compared to the lacerated walls of her heart. The guilt and shame of her admission squeezed her chest. How could she have been so heartless, so careless and cruel?

On the third step down, Kyle grabbed her from behind. "Give him a few minutes."

"I can't. He'll run into the woods and get lost. He doesn't have his coat." *He's upset and alone and thinking his mother didn't want him, doesn't love him.*

"You're not wearing any shoes."

"I don't care." She fought against his hold, didn't care if he was bigger or stronger. Her son needed her and nothing would keep her away. "I have to find him. Explain. Oh, God. What have I done? Let go of me." She bit his arm.

"Hell." He yanked one arm away, but held her firmly around the ribs with the other. "Calm down. Tori's with him."

"He doesn't need a dog, he needs his mother," Victoria screamed.

"What he needs is time to blow off some emotion."

"You've been a father for all of, what, fifteen minutes? You don't know the first thing about being a parent."

"Maybe not," Kyle said calmly. "But I know plenty about being a hurt, angry eight-year-old boy." He turned her, lifted her chin, and forced her to look into his eyes, to see his concern, his caring. "Trust me. Five minutes and I'll go after him."

"I'll go with you. Let me get my—"

"No." Kyle stood firm between her and the coat tree. "I'll bring him back. It's past time he had his father to look out for him."

A father.

At twenty-six years of age, Kyle Karlinsky was father to an eight-year-old boy he'd had no idea existed until today. What the hell did he know about raising a kid? His father was certainly no one to emulate. Didn't matter. He had a son, who was currently trudging through the thick, dank woods behind his home in need of rescue. At least, according to Victoria.

Victoria, who dogged his psyche on a regular basis, his own personal super-ego, despite repeated attempts to purge her with booze and women. Victoria, who'd failed to tell him about his son, denied him the opportunity to know his child from birth, yet had stood up to her father, probably for the first time in her life, to keep their child safe, and had given up her dreams to raise him, virtually on her own.

How was a man supposed to react to all that? Rage wrestled remorse, each one holding their own, while hope and happiness waited on the mat to take on the winner. Which would prevail in the end? He pushed at a tree limb before it scratched his face.

He called out "Tori" again, and followed the dog's responding bark.

Close enough to hear Jake say, "Stop barking. He's going to find us." He smiled. Because that's what dads were supposed to do, look out for their kids, guide them, and bail them out when they got into trouble. If he focused on that, maybe he'd be okay.

On the other side of a wide old oak tree Kyle spotted Jake's red sweatshirt through the scrub, Tori walking beside him. "Your mom wants you to put on your winter jacket," Kyle said.

Jake stopped, turned around. Dirt smudged his damp cheeks, a twig stuck out of the side of his sweatshirt hood, and muck soaked his sneakers.

Kyle walked forward, holding out the jacket.

Jake slipped his arms into the sleeves without saying a word.

"And I'm supposed to tell you there are two juice boxes and two chewy granola bars in one pocket and your hat and gloves in the other. And just in case you need them, I have your boots." He held up the weighted-down plastic grocery bag hanging from his wrist. "She plan on you staying out here all night?"

That got a smile. "She worries."

"Because regardless of what you heard or how she may have felt when she first found out she was pregnant, she loves you."

Jake nodded.

"And that's the only thing that really matters."

A tear formed in the corner of Jake's left eye.

To alleviate his son's upset Kyle asked, "But she has absolutely no idea how tough an eight-year-old boy really is, does she?"

"No, Dad." Jake shook his head. "She doesn't."

Dad. The word hit him with the force of a category-five hurricane. Dad. And just like that Kyle fell in love, wanted to pull his son into his arms and hold him there, wanted to listen while he recounted every second of his life from birth to this very minute. But the last thing he wanted to do was come off like some touchy-feely freak. So he channeled the requisite calm of a cool dad. "You recognized me at the door," Kyle noted.

"I have your picture by my bed."

That surprised Kyle. Even though Victoria would probably rather gut him than invite him to dinner, she'd made him a daily presence in Jake's life and created an atmosphere where Jake readily accepted his sudden appearance.

"Mom promised to help me look for you when I turn sixteen. I didn't want to wait but she said I had to."

As much as it hurt to think if he hadn't come back to town he wouldn't have known about Jake for another eight years, he understood Victoria's thinking. She was cautious, protective of those she loved, had once been protective of him. She wouldn't expose her son to possible disappointment and disillusionment before he was mature enough to handle it. Kyle had been an apathetic teen with no direction, no goals or dreams of success, despite Victoria's repeated attempts to convince him of his potential. If not for the accident and meeting Fig, there's no telling how he would have turned out. "She was right."

Jake looked up in question. Not wanting to address it, Kyle asked, "So what has she told you about me?"

"You like soda, like me." Jake picked a leaf out of Tori's fur. "I have your smile." He tilted his head up to demonstrate and, sure enough, he did. "You're smart like me, you always did all your homework, and broccoli is your favorite vegetable."

He almost laughed out loud. Back in high school he hadn't worked hard enough in school for anyone to think he was even the tiniest bit smart, he'd only done his homework so he could spend time with Victoria, and he ate broccoli, max, twice a year as part of a Chinese chicken and broccoli combo meal.

"So where've you been, Dad? Mom said it must have been someplace important for you not to come visit me."

He'd been turning himself into the type of man a boy would be proud to call his father.

"And why'd you leave without telling Mom?"

Because he'd believed the insults and lies and threats

and had been too much of a coward to stay and fight for what he'd wanted.

But how do you explain all that to a little boy? He settled on, "It's complicated." Kyle couldn't withstand the urge to touch his son one minute longer. He reached out and put his hand on Jake's shoulder. "What's most important is I'm here now." He squeezed. "And I won't leave you again."

Jake lunged forward and threw his arms around Kyle's waist, smushed his cheek to Kyle's diaphragm. "I'm glad you're back, Dad."

He returned Jake's hug, wanting to make up for every hugging opportunity he'd missed over the years, yet careful not to squeeze his son so tight he busted a rib.

Tori barked.

Victoria appeared from behind the oak.

"You were supposed to wait at the house," Kyle pointed out. With her foot elevated. He released Jake.

She limped over to her son, and, with a hand on each of his upper arms, held him in place. "Honey, I need you to understand that when Mommy got pregnant I was very young. Daddy left. I was alone and scared. And for a short time I wished I wasn't pregnant. But then I felt your first kick."

"Like I was practicing karate," Jake inserted.

"Yeah." Victoria smiled. "And I couldn't wait to meet my little night-owl baby who made me crave strawberries dipped in dill pickle juice and dry roasted peanuts coated with vanilla yogurt."

"And beef jerky," Jake said proudly.

Victoria made a "blech," sound, and they both laughed.

Kyle's heart ached for all he'd missed, running to the

store to satisfy her crazy cravings, watching her grow large with his child, feeling his son's first movements. The memories and private jokes and unconditional love between parent and child.

She moved her palms to Jake's cheeks and bent a bit to put her face directly in front of his. "You have to know from the minute you were born I've loved you with every single cell in my body."

Jake wiped an eye and pushed away his mother's hands. "Don't go getting all mushy." He turned to Tori, who had occupied herself by rolling in some leaves. "Tori's gonna need a bath."

"Yeah," Kyle said.

"Can I help you give her one?" Jake asked.

"That dog is not coming into my house," Victoria answered. "She's filthy." She looked Jake up and down. "And look at your sneakers. I'll never get them clean."

"I'm sorry, Mom."

"I'll buy him a new pair," Kyle offered.

Victoria glared at him. "I can afford to buy my son new sneakers if he needs them."

"But we don't have money to waste," Jake recited, as if he'd heard the words a hundred times before, then turned to Kyle. "Can I go with you to pick them out?"

"Sure," Kyle said.

At the same time Victoria said, "No."

"Mommy and Daddy have some things we need to work out first," Victoria said.

Leave it to Victoria to make the situation more difficult than it needed to be. No matter. He knew how to handle her, how to scratch away at the thick protective layer she showed to the world. What lay beneath was worth even the most exhausting excavation.

"It's starting to get dark," Victoria said. "We'd better head back."

The second time she stopped to rest her ankle Kyle scooped her into his arms. "I don't know why you're being so obstinate. You shouldn't be bearing weight on that ankle. I don't mind carrying you."

She squirmed in his hold. He tightened his arms around her and started to walk.

"Put me down," she insisted.

He didn't.

She started to kick and twist. Her "I mean it," sounded panicked.

He set her on her feet. She stumbled away from him, breathing heavily, her eyes wild, the same as when she'd been desperate to get away from him in her office.

Oblivious to his mother's distress, Jake asked, "Mom. Do you remember when you said you loved Daddy and he loved you and that's why you made me?"

Either Victoria had developed some sudden onset gastrointestinal distress or she seriously regretted her explanation.

She choked out a "Yes."

"Now that he's back, does that mean you're gonna get married?"

The appalled expression on her face would have been comical if the question hadn't been asked so seriously.

Victoria swallowed, wrapped a hand around the back of her neck, and rolled her head from side to side. "No, honey," she said, looking at Kyle. "Mommy and Daddy will never get married. Don't think about it. Don't wish for it. And don't waste your time trying to change my mind. You won't."

* * *

Later that night Kyle pondered the events of the day over a few beers at O'Halloran's, one of the three bars in Madrin Falls. The subdued lighting and dark wood suited his mood. A few guys hung around the pool tables. A couple threw darts in the corner. A college basketball game played on the big-screen TV beside the bar. No one bothered him except the bartender, who showed up with a refill each time Kyle emptied his mug.

Unfortunately, his increasing intoxication did not facilitate him finding clarity in his situation. He wasn't looking to get married, so why did Victoria's vehement statement, *Mommy and Daddy will never get married*, bother him so much? Why did she get to decide? What if him being back in town was a chance for them to right the wrongs of the past? What if they were truly meant to be together and divine intervention put them both in the same place at the same time?

He laughed at the sentimental scat polluting his brain.

Damn, he needed a diversion.

As if summoned by wishful thinking, a very female body pressed up behind him and a voice made for phone sex cooed into his left ear. "Hey, baby. I heard you were back in town."

CHAPTER FOUR

VICTORIA did not like elevators, the confined space, the cloying scent of an older woman's perfume, being forced to listen to the babble of two just-out-of-college nurses when she had important things to think about. Like the new transfer from ICU whose arrival on 5E, within the hour, was destined to cause chaos. As much as she didn't like elevators, Victoria abhorred chaos even more. She unzipped her jacket and adjusted the strap of her briefcase over her shoulder.

Second floor.

"I finally met Dr. K. yesterday," the tall blonde nurse, who'd pressed the button for the fourth floor with an inappropriately long red fingernail, said. "In the cafeteria. Your description did not do him justice. He is a major-league hottie."

"And maple syrup sweet," said the brunette with the gorgeous curls, that should be pulled back into at least a ponytail for any hint of a professional appearance. "I'm going to marry that man. Imagine me, a doctor's wife."

He's not a medical doctor, you shallow twit. A little ankle pain and some increased knee discomfort would have been a small price to pay for a peaceful climb up the stairs.

Third floor.

"We all know it's why you went to nursing school," the blonde said.

"If you want to catch a big fish you need to be where they swim."

Big fish indeed.

A third nurse, also blonde but practically and professionally dressed in the green scrubs of the OR, said, "You may want to hold off on ordering your invitations. I heard he got wasted at O'Halloran's last night and went home with Leanne, the secretary in the case management office."

"She's such a tramp," the tall blonde said.

"Why can't she settle in on one man?" the brunette added.

Realization hit. The reason Kyle had returned to town. Leanne. The elevator floor shifted beneath her feet like it'd been jerked to a stop. Only it hadn't.

Fourth floor.

She leaned against the back wall for stability. Pretty, flirty and fun. Leanne, Kyle's on-again off-again girlfriend from eighth to eleventh grade. Leanne, who somehow found out about Victoria's secret relationship with Kyle and never passed up an opportunity to offer her opinion that Victoria wasn't skilled enough or woman enough to fulfill the desires of a guy like Kyle. Turns out she'd been right.

Fifth floor.

On shaky legs, Victoria exited the elevator. The glimpses of a new Kyle, a competent medical professional who showed caring and compassion for his patients, affection and kindness to his son, was a façade. Kyle Karlinsky was the same hound dog he'd been before they'd dated, and she most assuredly would not allow a man like him unsupervised access to her child.

She turned into the 5E corridor and glanced at her watch. Fifteen minutes after eight. At precisely nine a.m. she would place a call to her attorney.

But first, as soon as she walked into her office she called Nora at the nurses' station. "Please have Ali and Roxie come to my office ASAP."

After hanging her coat on the hook behind her door she turned back to her desk to see Kyle, his hair more unruly than usual, his clothes rumpled and his eyes glassy.

"There's something I need to—" he said, looking guilty.

"Shhh. Come here." She motioned for him to move closer. "Bend down," she whispered. He did. She moved her mouth close to his ear and yelled as loud as she could, "Rough night?"

"Jeez." He gripped his temples as if trying to contain the vibration of a gargantuan gong. "Sadist."

"I'm working. Go away." She tried to move past him to get to her desk.

He blocked her path. "I forgot how fast news travels here in Madrin Falls. Victoria, nothing happened."

"That love bite on your neck tells a different story." It shouldn't matter, but it did. Hearing about Kyle and Leanne together was hard enough, but seeing evidence of their tryst made her want to strike out and hurt someone. And since Kyle just happened to be handy... "I don't care what you do or who you do it with. But if *my* job was probationary and *I* was hoping to turn it into a full-time gig, I wouldn't want my proclivity for unsavory woman to overshadow my work."

"Proclivity. Now there's a word you don't hear very often. Here's one for you. Unctuous. It means—"

"I know what it means. And I am not pious or moralistic." Not really.

"Leave it to you to have a working knowledge of a word like unctuous."

"Where'd *you* pick it up?" she asked.

"I read," he said. "A lot. Always have."

News to her. "Well, good for you. Are we done playing vocabulary volleyball? Can I get to work now?"

"Based on how ornery you are this morning, one might think you care about what I do a little more than you let on." He reached for her chin, tilted it up and looked directly into her eyes. "Nothing. Happened. When you're ready to hear the details I'm happy to tell you everything. I've got nothing to hide."

"Except for Leanne's brand. I may have some concealer in my purse." She studied the offensive discolored blotch on the left side of Kyle's neck, tilted her head, pursed her lips, and tapped her index finger on her cheek, pretending deep consideration. "On second thoughts, flaunt it. It marks you as an easy lay. Maybe you can parlay it into a few more drunken encounters with loose women."

Kyle's response wasn't at all what she'd expected.

He smiled then laughed. "God, I've missed you." And he swooped down and kissed her.

Only their lips touched. His soft and supple, sensual as he pressed them to hers. Familiar. He didn't demand, he offered, exerted the perfect amount of pressure to draw her in. Exquisite. Each one of her protective instincts failed, her thought processes taken over, transported back to innocent times, consumed by rapture.

This was what she liked, the promise of more, not the actual more.

"Whooee. If it gets any hotter in here I'm going to start disrobing." The voice of Roxie—her friend and one of the 5E nurses—permeated her lust-clogged senses.

Oh, no. Victoria pulled away.

Kyle gawked down at her, stunned. "I'm sorry. I shouldn't have. I didn't expect…"

"Go," Victoria said. Half in a daze, her lips numb, her heart pounding, she turned away from her staff. How could she have let that happen, at work, in her office? Anyone could have walked in. Her face burned with embarrassment and anger. How dare he put his moves on her, place her in such an awkward position? And why, after everything she'd been through because of him, did she lack the willpower to resist his kiss?

"I told you to wait," Ali said, probably to Roxie. "I told you the dog sitting by the door meant Dr. K. was in here."

"When the boss says ASAP, I give her ASAP."

An arm came around her shoulders. "He's gone. You okay?" Ali asked.

Victoria nodded, but she wasn't. He'd circumvented her defenses. Again. Just like in high school. They were all wrong for each other. She couldn't be the type of woman Kyle needed. And he was the absolute opposite of the type of man she hoped to one day share her life with. Kyle thwarted the rules she followed implicitly. He dissed authority, would never understand or support her need to attain the director of nursing position when the present director retired.

Within five years. When I'm confident my replacement is ready.

Three candidates. All competent. Victoria the favorite. But the tiniest infraction could plummet her to the bottom of that short list in an instant. Something like getting caught kissing a co-worker in her office. And all her hard work to date would be wasted. The opportunity to achieve the top nursing spot, to prove to her critics, her father, and herself that one youthful indiscretion would not deter her from success, would be lost.

Victoria inhaled. Exhaled. Turned to her staff and couldn't contain her smile. Roxie, an extravagant dresser who towered over her by a good ten inches, wore a red, white, and blue polka-dot turtle-neck under her lavender scrub top. At least a dozen colorful cartoon character pins adorned her left chest area. Her rectangular red-framed glasses hung from a bright purple chain at her sternum, the yellow string cord attached to her fuchsia pen and the brightly patterned socks on her six or so inches of exposed ankle, since she had trouble finding pants that were long enough, all combined to make Roxie a walking hodgepodge of color.

Victoria hated to admit it, but if she hadn't worked with Roxie and witnessed her nursing expertise first-hand, she likely would not have hired her to work on 5E.

"Time's a-wasting," Roxie said. "I have a date with a colostomy bag that needs changing. What's up?"

Victoria spoke to Ali first. "You're getting a transfer from ICU. Into room 514 with Mrs. Teeton." Wait for it. "Melanie Madrin."

"Friggin' wonderful."

No need to explain who Melanie Madrin was. The mayor's daughter. State Senator Madrin's wife. And while no one knew much about her, Senator Madrin had a reputation as an elitist, condescending, just plain difficult person. And reports of his demanding and disrespectful behavior at his wife's bedside down in ICU continued to circulate throughout the hospital.

"ICU will call you with a report," Victoria said. "Are you familiar with her accident?"

"Out on Clover Hill. MVA. She was struck by a drunk driver and sustained multiple, major trauma. Her three-year-old daughter was killed," Ali said.

"Alleged drunk driver," Victoria clarified. "To my knowledge no charges were filed." But that didn't stop half the town from declaring him guilty based on the rantings of Mrs. Madrin's husband. "Regardless, guilt or innocence has no bearing on the care we provide our patients."

"And this involves me how?" Roxie asked, looking at her watch.

"501B. Your patient Mike Graker was the driver of the other car."

"No way," Roxie said, making her already bugged-out eyes even more pronounced.

Mike Graker, the most popular high-school teacher in the Madrin Falls school system, had the other half of their divided town fighting mad about what they saw as heinous, unsubstantiated attacks on his good name.

"How can they put both patients on the same floor? It's crazy," Ali said.

It was a test, Victoria was certain. Would she go running to the director of nursing to complain, allow the publicity and controversy and potential for confrontation to disrupt the smooth operation of her unit? Absolutely not. She would take charge of the situation, handle it proficiently and professionally.

"Each treating physician insisted their patient be admitted to 5E. We're the best." Victoria shrugged. And their superb reputation meant they rarely had an empty bed.

"So what's your plan?" Ali asked, assuming she had one. And, as always, she did.

"Sit," she directed Roxie so she didn't have to strain her sore neck to look up at her. "Please close the door," she instructed Ali while she assumed her position behind her desk.

Ali hesitated. "Are you sure?"

Victoria rarely closed the door to her tiny, windowless office, except when a situation required privacy. "Yes." Then, like a general in a high-stakes strategy meeting, she gave her troops their orders.

Three hours later, a short seventeen minutes after her last tour around her calm unit, Victoria received the call to battle. "Mr. Madrin has Mr. Graker pinned to the wall outside the patient kitchen," Nora whispered frantically through the intercom speaker in Victoria's office. "By the throat. Come quick."

"Come on, girl," Kyle said to Tori as he held open the ground-floor door to the stairwell. He started to climb, took the steps two at a time, welcoming the sting in his thighs, the chance to burn off some pent-up energy.

He'd kissed Victoria. The result, a mudslide of wants and needs he hadn't been able to satisfy with other women. And, boy, had he tried. Victoria look-alikes, polar opposites, dozens of in-betweens who lacked her spunk, determination and sarcastic wit, her innocence, fierce loyalty, and hidden vulnerabilities. In nine long years, no woman had challenged him as much, loved him as deeply, or filled the void inside him as perfectly as Victoria had.

And now, having her within reach, no substitute, not even Leanne, was good enough. Too bad he hadn't realized that before Leanne had leeched onto his neck, leaving what he now knew was referred to as her territorial tattoo.

Not good. Of course Victoria would think he hadn't changed. He had a damn hickey on his neck. And why should it matter what she thought? Why did her jealously fill him with satisfaction? And why the hell was he counting the minutes until he could kiss her again?

He jogged around the second floor landing.

You're not good enough for her, boy. The disgust and hate in Victoria's father's eyes remained vivid in his memory. *You were born to white trash, you live and think like white trash, and that's all you'll ever be. Stick to your own kind, or you'll live to regret it.* Kyle, working at Milt's Garage, dressed in his dirty work jeans, his T-shirt and hands stained with grease. Mr. Forley, impeccably dressed in some high-end designer suit, his shoes shiny like they'd been waxed and buffed that morning. Kyle had never felt more low class, worthless and undeserving.

After the third-floor landing he started to take the stairs three at a time.

Reality check. He wasn't that alone-in-the-world kid without resources anymore. He held a doctorate in physical therapy. And while he couldn't care less what people thought of him, they respected his work. Medical professionals sought him out for consults on patients not responding to therapy. He had a good job, money in the bank, and respectable, high-powered allies in Fig's parents and several of his professors.

He was more confident and secure. No one could run him out of town now. No one could keep him from what he wanted. But what exactly did he want?

By the time he reached the fifth floor, Kyle and Tori were panting. He stopped for a minute, squatted down to catch his breath, pretending to fix the bandana tied around Tori's neck.

The hospital's PA system sounded. "Security to 5E. Stat. Security to 5E. Stat."

With a thought only for Victoria's safety, Kyle made a dash down the empty corridor that connected the bank of elevators with the 5E hallway. He turned. Rage flooded his system at the sight of Victoria, wedged between two huge men, trying to separate them. Good thing the three were located more than halfway down the hall, which gave Kyle some time to reconsider his first inclination, to yank Victoria out of the fray and use his years of bar-fighting expertise to lay both men out for putting her at risk. This was Victoria and she was not the type of woman to appreciate a man's interference, no matter how noble his intentions.

So, hard as it was, he walked to within five feet of her, close enough to dive in if needed, far enough away to let her handle the situation, leaned against the wall, and waited.

"You chose to drive drunk. You should be dead, not my precious angel," the larger of the two men, the one holding the other by his neck, said. "You killed my little girl."

"I'm sorry. Don't…drink alcohol." The smaller man, who was by no means small, just smaller by comparison, struggled to get the words out while fighting against the grip constricting his airway. "I'm diabetic. My blood sugar…low." He broke the stranglehold on his neck. Gasped in a breath. "I didn't know. I wish I could…"

"Well, you can't. My daughter's dead because of you."

"Because of a terrible, horrific accident, Mr. Madrin," Victoria said calmly, and placed her palm on the aggressor's choking hand, easing it away from the neck it was intent on wrapping around. "Please, Mr. Madrin. The police will sort it out. This vigilante justice will only serve to get you into trouble. And your wife needs you. Think of your wife."

Kyle took heart at the relief that flashed across Victoria's face when she noticed him.

The larger man's aggressive stance deflated. "Melanie won't eat, can't stop crying." His head hung down, his shoulders slumped forward. He wiped at his eyes. "She says it's all her fault. But it's not." He lifted his head, glared at the other man, his anger regaining strength. "It's yours."

Tori barked, which she only did to alert him to trouble.

Kyle turned, noticed a thin, pale woman with remnants of bruising on her face, leaning heavily on an IV pole, standing in the doorway of Mrs. Teeton's room. She weaved unsteadily, on the verge of falling. "Warren, stop," she said weakly.

Kyle made it to her side just in time to catch her, and ease her down to the floor.

"Melanie," a man's worried voice called out.

Tori licked the woman's face.

"Get that mutt away from her," a male voice boomed.

Melanie reached a shaky hand up to pet Tori's head.

Ali appeared next to him. "Are you hurt, Mrs. Madrin?"

"No. So tired," she said.

"Dr. Karlinsky," Victoria said, all business. "Would you help Ali get Mrs. Madrin back to bed while her husband and I take a minute to speak in private?"

"Certainly." Kyle actually felt sorry for the man, until he said, "I'm not going anywhere."

Mistake #1: going after one of Victoria's patients. Mistake #2: not obeying a nicely worded direct order. There was no saving the man from the verbal lashing in his immediate future.

"Your physician wants your wife on this floor," Victoria started off diplomatically. "This is where she needs to be. And if you want to be allowed back up here to visit her, I suggest you accompany me to my office." She turned and walked in that direction. "If not, Security just arrived. They can escort you out."

"Is there anything I need to be careful of?" Kyle asked Ali, turning his attention to the woman on the floor before him, preparing to lift her and carry her back to bed.

"Healing rib fractures, right and left, and a healing chest-tube puncture site on the right. Maybe we'd better help her stand instead."

"I am a state senator, you can't…" Mr. Madrin blustered from behind them.

"Wait," the patient said to Ali.

Kyle, Ali, and Melanie looked up to see what would happen.

Victoria turned to face Mr. Madrin. "In this hospital you are a visitor who is disrupting the operation of my floor, posing a threat to a patient I am responsible for, and upsetting your wife to the point she put herself at risk by climbing out of bed, unsupervised and unassisted, to try to stop you."

Victoria Forley, shoulders back, head high, taking on a New York State senator. A force Mr. Madrin had not anticipated at the onset of his tirade.

Go, Tori! No. This was no girl. She was one impressive woman. Go, Victoria!

They stood at the front counter of the nursing station in an old-style standoff. Mr. Madrin staring her down. Victoria standing up to him, rigid, unflinching.

"If you don't like your choices, to come with me or go with Security," she clarified, "I'll offer you an option three. I can call the police and have you forcibly removed. Mr. Graker may not want to press charges, but I have no problem giving a statement about what occurred here."

"Please, Warren," Melanie said, her voice little more than a whisper. "Please."

"We need to get you back to bed, Mrs. Madrin," Ali said. Then she whispered, "Victoria can handle him, and I doubt she'll go as far as to call the police as long as he cooperates. Right now we need to focus on you."

Dr. Rafael Starzi was a big man, in every way but stature. Despite his size deficiency he commanded attention, respect and obedience through sheer volume, confidence, and authority, seeming perfectly at ease with his littleness. Kyle liked him.

"Seven days on the job and I have heard nothing but good things about you, Dr. Karlinsky," he said.

"Thank you." Kyle resisted the urge to follow his words with "sir".

"Sit down." Dr. Starzi pushed over a chair. "How tall are you, anyway? Now, I've reviewed your extensive plans of care for each of my patients and am in complete agreement."

Kyle couldn't help feeling a rush of pride. And, well, validation. Dr. Starzi, a renowned oncologist, not only in upstate New York but across the U.S., liked his work. His brusque disposition and businesslike bedside manner aside, people traveled hundreds of miles to be treated by him. A known perfectionist, he was very particular about who cared for his patients, preferring 5E to any other floor in the hospital, and now Kyle to any other physical therapist.

At the sound of Victoria's voice, Dr. Starzi looked to the other side of the nurses' station. Kyle peered around the lazy-Susan-style chart rack in front of him.

"Ah, the woman I plan to marry," Dr. Starzi said loud enough for anyone in a twenty-foot radius to hear.

He'd better be talking about the amazon nurse with the bugged-out eyes standing next to Victoria.

"If I ever decide to marry, you'll be the first candidate on my list," Victoria responded.

Like hell. Victoria was *his* first love, the mother of *his* child, and after the kiss they'd shared, feeling the attraction that still sizzled between them, if and when she decided to marry, there'd better only be one name on her list. Kyle Karlinsky.

The vehemence of that spontaneous thought surprised him because he was far from ready to settle down. He and Victoria barely knew each other. But now that he'd found her, available and unattached, he refused to entertain the possibility of her with any other man.

"Impeccable work habits," Dr. Starzi shared only with Kyle. "Commitment to excellence. Well spoken. Highly regarded by hospital management."

He made her sound like an appealing job applicant.

"And beautiful. Did you know she's being groomed for the director of nursing position?"

No. But the news didn't come as a surprise.

"In four or five years she and I will rule this hospital."

Dr. Starzi strutted out of the nurses' station to stand beside Victoria. Way closer than was acceptable in a purely professional relationship. Kyle's stomach tightened, acid crawled up the back of his throat. Both neatly pressed and stylishly dressed, Starzi topping her by maybe two inches and twenty pounds, they made a nice-looking couple.

"You all set for our lunch date?" Dr. Starzi asked. "We can get a jump on planning our future together."

Victoria didn't look at him, actually blushed.

She's interested in a man for the first time since you...

Victoria and Starzi? Not as long as blood circulated through Kyle's veins and air flowed into his lungs. Sure, they'd make a great Christmas-card photo. But both uber-smart perfectionists driven by a compulsion to advance in their fields, they'd burn each other out. And what would happen to Jake in the process? No. Victoria needed someone to slow her down, to remind her to have fun, to live in the moment rather than constantly planning for the future. Someone to make her laugh, to draw out her warmth and take care of her, even though she was more than capable of taking care of herself.

She needed *him*.

And *he* needed time, to get to know Victoria, to consider the possibility of putting the past behind them and trying again. For Jake. For the chance to be a part of a functional, traditional family like Fig's, like he'd dreamed of since childhood.

But Starzi was out of his league in professional status, pedigree, and personality. The only place Kyle could compete on his level was in bed. No man outperformed him there. Maybe Victoria needed a little reminder of the powerful chemistry between them.

"Something's come up," she said.

Good.

Dr. Starzi moved in close to Victoria's ear. "Next time I won't take no for an answer."

Kyle noticed she didn't shy away. He gripped his pen, envisioned hurling it, javelin style, toward one of Starzi's lust-filled eyes.

Victoria glanced at the oncologist, gave him an uncharacteristic flirty smile. "You always say that." Victoria I-don't-do-public-displays-of-affection Forley was flirting. With another man. While at work.

Kyle located the trashcan, ready to spit to get rid of the terrible taste of jealousy accumulating in his mouth.

"This time I mean it. We're not getting any younger." Dr. Starzi turned to the amazon. "Wha-da you say, Olive Oyl? You got time for some lunch?"

"Sure thing, Tiny Tim. Can you wait five minutes?"

"For you? No. Meet me down at the cafeteria."

"With those itty-bitty legs I guess it's only fair I give you a head start."

"Gigantor."

"Pipsqueak."

"See you in ten." Dr. Starzi turned to leave the floor. "And keep up the good work, Karlinsky," he said. "Glad to have you on board."

Victoria stiffened. Took a step to the left and saw him watching her.

Caught. He forced a pretend smile and waved.

She flashed a look so cold his balls contracted. Then she stormed off.

A few hours later, his rounds on 5E complete, Kyle ventured to Victoria's office. Almost to the door, he heard her talking to someone.

"Hi. Can you stay with Jake tomorrow night from five forty-five to nine-fifteen? My babysitter's sick." Silence. "Shoot. No. Have fun. I'll work something out."

Perfect. He peered into her office. "Is it safe to come in?"

"No."

"I'm free tomorrow night."

"Good for you. I'm sure all the single ladies in Madrin Falls will be thrilled. Shall I send out a mass e-mail?"

He ignored her taunt. "I can watch Jake."

She raised her eyebrows. "Nothing better to do than slink around outside my office? I'll let Dr. Starzi know you don't have enough work to keep you occupied."

"More like I was checking to make sure you weren't holding any sharp objects that could puncture my person."

"Hold on a second." She patted around the top of her desk and looked inside a drawer. "I'm sure I have a pair of scissors around here somewhere."

"Ha ha. What time do you need me?"

"I don't. I'll work it out."

"It's worked out. You need someone to watch Jake. I'm available and I'd like to spend some time with him, get to know him."

He waited for her to say, "That's a great idea."

She didn't.

Instead she said, "I haven't seen or heard from you in nine years. You're back in town for a week and a half. Jake has met you all of twice. You are a virtual stranger, Kyle. There is no way I'm going to leave you alone with my son tomorrow night."

"He's my son, too."

"Genetically speaking." She broke eye contact, gathered some papers and stapled them together.

Ouch. "How am I supposed to change that if you won't let me spend time with him?"

"We invited you to lunch over the weekend."

And it'd been nice. But... "At a crowded diner. How am I going to get to know my son at a diner?"

"I'm not saying you can't spend time with him alone. It's just... I don't know anything about you. Are you married? Living with someone? Do you have any other children? Addictions? Contagious diseases?"

"No. No. No. No. And, no. Do you want a copy of my pre-employment physical?" he joked.

"I'm serious."

"You know me, Victoria." Better than anyone. "A while back you loved me and trusted me."

"And look how that turned out."

Unwilling to challenge her point, he tried a different tack. "The way you handled Senator Madrin was amazing," he said, meaning it.

She lifted her eyes to his. "Thanks for not rushing in and taking over."

"I knew you had everything under control." He hesitated. "So, I'll swing by at five forty-five tomorrow. I can take Jake for a bite to eat then hang with him until you're done doing whatever it is you need to do." Hold on a minute. Maybe he should have thought this through a little better. Where exactly did she need to be at dinnertime on a Wednesday night? A date with Starzi? Some other doofus?

She smiled.

Damn. Even after all their time apart, she could still read him.

She put her elbow on the desk, rested her chin in her palm and looked up at him all innocent and playful. "You know what? Why don't you plan to come over at five-thirty, just in case I can't find anyone else? That'll give me time to get ready."

Get ready for what? Minx.

He forced a nonchalant expression. "Five-thirty it is."

CHAPTER FIVE

TREPIDATION flitted around Victoria's insides like a passel of hummingbirds, their wings creating a discomfiting, fluttery feeling as she steered her car onto her dark road. She shifted in the driver's seat and gripped the steering wheel with both hands. Bad decision asking Jake if he might like to spend Wednesday evening with his dad. What had she been thinking? And what kind of irresponsible mother gave in to her son's begging and allowed a man she hasn't seen in nine years to babysit?

One out of options.

If not for the presentation that counted for forty percent of her grade, she would have skipped class rather than deal with the angst of the past few hours. And after a busy workday cluttered with the media's attempts to gain information about the alleged altercation between NYS Senator Madrin and the man reportedly responsible for the death of his daughter, she was exhausted. Tack on an accident that closed the highway, lengthening her trip home by forty-five minutes, and Victoria's mind and body were in cahoots to shut down despite her need to remain sharp and in control around Kyle.

She covered her mouth with the backs of her fingertips and gave in to a very unladylike yawn.

Her nerves settled a bit at the sight of his old black pickup truck illuminated by her headlights. He hadn't taken her son and run off, after all. She blew out a relieved breath then took note of her dark house, not one light lit inside or out. Jake wouldn't go to sleep without the hall light on and it was well past his bedtime. She'd gone over Jake's routine, left written instructions. And where was Kyle if not watching television in her family room?

Her bedroom. The only room without a front-facing window.

A snippet of last night's hot, supposed-to-be erotic dream turned nightmare popped into her head. The scent of vanilla candles hovering in the air. Kyle, in her bed, propped up on an elbow, the muted lights from a dozen flickering flames dancing on his naked skin, her mauve sheet inconveniently draped between his thighs. She slammed on her brakes, shook her head. "Go away."

He didn't.

"Come on, Victoria," he'd said in that enticing tone she'd always found hard to refuse. At the same time he'd patted the mattress beside him. "Round two. You're in charge this time."

Dream Kyle didn't balk at the rope that magically appeared and anchored his hands and feet to unfamiliar bedposts. No sense taking chances he'd renege and she'd lose the opportunity to explore and experiment and finally work through her sexual issues and insecurities. On top. In control.

She sauntered toward the bed, swaying her hips. A sexy seductress.

"What's the matter?" he'd asked. "Trying out a thong again?"

Like she'd ever voluntarily repeat that unpleasant experience. Okay. Attempt at seduction, aborted. She'd let the silky, sex kitten robe she'd never seen before slip from her shoulders to the floor, climbed onto the bed and, while up on her knees, scanned his amazing, firm body, careful not to overlook one delectable detail. At least until she reached his massive erection and suffered a visual stutter, could not make her eyes move past it.

"You're going to have to do more than stare if we're going to have any fun at all tonight," he'd said.

So she'd taken him into her palm, gripped him loosely so as not to hurt him, and began a tentative slide up and down.

"Not like that," he'd said impatiently. "You're acting like you've never done this before."

Because she hadn't.

"Come on, honey." He'd tugged at his restraints, sounded frustrated. "When Leanne does it she..."

And so began the litany of sexual comparisons, highlighting all the areas Leanne triumphed and Victoria failed. For someone who prided herself on always being the best, it'd been profoundly humiliating.

Berated and belittled in her own dream. Her first sexual fantasy involving a real man, one with definite convert-to-reality potential, hijacked by insecurity. She'd awoken in a tangle of sheets, mortified and determined to remedy her sexual inexperience once and for all. As soon as she could muster up some lust and trust for a man whose size wouldn't intimidate her should things turn intimate.

Victoria yawned, again.

Too tired to think any more about it, she resumed her drive and pulled her car into the garage. No sense putting off the inevitable. Inside the basement, an eerie light came from Jake's play room—which also faced the back side of the house, she remembered with relief. She walked to the doorway.

The room was dark except for colorful patterns of changing light emitted from the television. Kyle sat cross-legged staring at the screen, some type of controller in his hand, playing a video game, which was odd since Jake wasn't allowed to play video games and she didn't own any. Rage started a slow simmer when she saw two empty bags of potato chips and a flattened box of cookies. In a flash it turned to a hard boil at the sight of her son asleep on the couch along the back wall.

"Why isn't Jake in bed?" she asked, too angry to worry about keeping her voice down.

"Hold on." Kyle jerked the controller and jammed his thumb repeatedly on a button. Something on the screen exploded then he looked up at her. "You're home early. What time is it?"

Actually, she was late. "Ten o'clock." She crossed her arms over her chest. "And I'll ask again. Why isn't Jake in bed?"

"He fell asleep down here."

He said it like it made perfect sense. "When?"

"When he got tired," he answered with a total disregard for the fact it was a school night and on school nights Jake's bedtime was eight-thirty. "It's no big deal. I'll carry him up." Kyle stood and stretched.

"No," Victoria snapped, seizing the opportunity to get rid of him. "Just go. I'll take care of him." She shook Jake's shoulder gently. "Wake up, honey. Time to get into bed." He'd passed the stage where she could safely carry him at age five. She removed the afghan covering him. Her boiling anger surged to pressure-cooker powerful. "He's still in his clothes. Didn't he take a shower?"

"One day without a shower isn't going to kill him."

Maybe not, but it was part of Jake's nightly routine, a routine she'd instructed Kyle in and expected him to follow. "Did he at least do his homework?"

"Yes. That he did. Homework before video games," Kyle said proudly, as if showcasing his good parenting skills.

Hardly.

"Come on." Victoria helped her sleepy son into a sitting position. "Up we go." She leaned in to help him stand.

"I don't feel good," Jake said, approximately ten seconds before he vomited down the front of her. If it were physically possible, steam would have shot from her ears.

"This is what happens when he eats too much junk food," Victoria forced out between clenched teeth, gesturing to the wrappers on the floor. "What were you thinking?" Jake slumped against her, half-asleep, mashing her saturated, stinky blouse into her chest.

"I'm sorry. I wanted us to have a fun time," Kyle said, jamming his hands in the front pockets of his jeans and looking down at the carpet. "Be buddies, our first guys' night." He kicked an empty potato-chips bag. "Junk food and video games are required."

Kyle looked so upset, so filled with remorse she actually felt sorry for him. And strangely enough, she understood. "But he's not your buddy," she said calmly.

"He's your son. He needs supervision, guidance and love. He needs responsible parenting and limits."

"You make it look so easy," he said.

"It's not." She smiled. "I've had years of trial and error to get where I am," Victoria said, widening her stance to support Jake's weight. "Don't be so hard on yourself. Give it time. You'll get the hang of it."

"That's easy for you to say. He already loves you. I've missed the first eight years of his life. I owe him so much. I want to make him happy, give him everything."

To get Jake to love him. His sincerity touched a place so deep she hadn't been aware it existed. "Jake already loves you, Kyle. You may not have known about him, but you've been a part of his life for as long as he can remember. You may not have heard him or felt him, but he's spoken to you about his day, kissed your picture and said, 'I love you, daddy,' every night before bed for years."

Kyle's emotion-filled eyes met hers. "Thank you for that." He stepped closer and placed his hand on Jake's head. "I love him, too. And I want, so much, to be a good dad." He moved his hand to Jake's forehead. "Do you think he needs to see a doctor?" Kyle asked, looking worried.

"No. I think he needs to shower and go to bed."

"Let me take him upstairs for you," Kyle offered.

"I'm already a mess," she said. "Come on, honey." She shook Jake gently to wake him and with an arm around his waist guided him out to the hallway. Just outside the door she looked over her shoulder at Kyle. "Please take the video games back to your place and lock the door behind you."

As Victoria walked Jake upstairs, the school's sickness policy ticker-taped across her mind. 'No child shall return to class until a minimum of twenty-four hours after their last bout of vomiting or diarrhea.' Technically Jake's stomachache shouldn't be classified under sickness. It was more gluttony secondary to ineffective parenting. At least, she hoped that's all it was.

Please let Jake feel better in the morning. Too much was happening at work, she needed to be there, absolutely could not miss a day.

An hour later, Jake showered and asleep in his bed, Victoria showered and her clothes soaking in the bathroom sink, she limped to the kitchen to check over Jake's homework and make both their lunches for the next day. Positive thinking yielded positive results. *Jake would feel better in the morning.* She opened the refrigerator door and took out some packages of deli meat. *Jake will go to school.* She grabbed the mayo. *The swelling in her knee and ankle would decrease tomorrow.* She took out four pieces of bread and placed them in the toaster. *The pain would go away.* She lined up their lunchboxes on the counter. *She did not need to see a doctor.*

A floorboard creaked in the family room, the sound unmistakable in the otherwise quiet house. Out of the corner of her eye she saw a shadowed movement. Victoria's chest tightened, her body went cold with fear. Frozen. Until she pictured Jake cozy in his room and lunged for the knife block.

Aunt Livi's favorite carving knife in one hand, a cleaver in the other, her back to the sink, she looked back and forth between both entrances to her kitchen, wishing she were taller, bigger, stronger. Wishing Kyle were there, not to protect her but to protect Jake if she wasn't successful in fending off her attacker.

But she was alone. Always alone.

Something brushed against the floor plant in the dining room. He was coming from the right. The wall phone caught her eye. 911 on speed dial #1. She dove for the receiver. A man's hand shot out and grabbed her wrist before she reached it. "Stop," a commanding male voice barked.

Like she had any intention of obeying a burglar/rapist/murderer.

She screamed, fought his hold, but he was too strong. The cleaver dropped from her hand. God willing, it would lodge in his foot. When he didn't cry out in pain and loosen his grip, Victoria slashed out with the carver, aiming for his gut. "Cut it out." He clamped his hand around her other wrist and easily took the knife. "It's me. Kyle."

Victoria yanked her hands away from him, clutched her fist to her heaving chest, her erratic, pounding heartbeat palpable through her sternum. "What were you thinking, sneaking up on me like that?" She fought to control her breathing, to keep from dissolving into tears of relief. "I thought you left."

"I stayed to make sure Jake's okay. I feel terrible I screwed up. It won't happen again."

Her mouth so dry she could hardly swallow, she limped to the cabinet by the sink, went up on her toes to reach past the lower shelf that held Jake's plastic cups, up to the next shelf, took out a grown-up glass, and filled it with water.

When she turned back, Kyle seemed entranced by the bottom hem of her nightshirt. She looked down at her legs, bare from the upper thighs to her pink fuzzy slippers. She shifted her stance, felt the brush of cotton on her butt and remembered. Heat crawled up her neck into her face and out of her hair follicles. Of all nights to eschew panties after her shower. Had she just given him an eyeful of her natural assets? From the look of wanting on Kyle's face, yes.

Not good.

"You have the most beautiful legs," he said with a satisfying amount of reverence in his tone.

She wanted to ask, "Nicer than, Leanne's?" but didn't. She refused to enter into a competition she had no chance of winning.

He stepped toward her.

She stepped back and bumped into the counter. "You should go."

"Look at your knee," he said.

Yes. Let's look at her knee. Pale. Swollen. Not at all attractive. A total turn-off.

"Is that from your fall?" he asked.

"Yes. But each day it feels better," she lied. "It's really no big deal."

Kyle must not have agreed because he closed the distance between them, dropped to his knees at her feet, and placed his thumbs where her kneecap should be.

Her nerve endings went I-just-won-the-lottery wild at the feel of his hands on her sensitive skin, until he pressed on a particularly sore spot. "Ow." Party over.

"You might have a meniscal tear. You need an MRI."

Definite downer. Nothing short of total sedation would get her inside one of those airless tubes of horror.

Like he'd tapped into her thoughts he said, "You get the prescription. I'll find you an open unit." He smiled.

"I'll even go with you and hold your hand if you're scared."

"I'm not scared."

His touch lightened, turned into more of a caress. He flattened a hand on each of her thighs. "So smooth."

So good, her touch receptors moaned at the feel of someone else's hands on her naked flesh, skilled hands capable of rapturous delight she'd been unable to duplicate on her own. She should push him away and demand that he leave. But a fierce need unfurled inside her, for intimacy and love, acceptance and understanding. And with him kneeling in front of her he didn't seem so big and capable of smothering her.

He slid his hands up further, slowly, sensually. Her body cried out for more. And he responded, continued up, over her hips, and around to her butt. He squeezed, pulled her toward him. "God help me, it's like I never left, like I'm back in high school. I can't stop thinking about you." He pressed his stubbled cheek to her thighs. "The feel of you. Your scent." He turned his head so his nose touched her skin and inhaled. "Fresh and clean with a hint of melon."

Cucumber melon.

She ran her fingers through his thick hair, held him to her, savored the closeness she'd shared with no one but him.

He went up on both knees, moved one foot to the floor and started to stand.

No!

He rose to his full height in front of her.

Back on your knees! Now!

He looked into her eyes with such longing she thought her legs would surely give out, and gently cradled the base of her skull in his large hand. "I have to kiss you." He leaned in and did just that.

It started off tender and sweet. Tender and sweet she liked. Slow was good. But with each passing second his ardor grew. The gentle pressure of his kiss, the tentative introduction of his tongue transformed. Arms tightened around her. A body towered over her, pressed against her. She couldn't move, couldn't breathe.

Victoria tried to break free. Couldn't. Her visual field narrowed, her chest tightened. Panic. She jerked her head to the side. "Get off of me. Now. I mean it." She gasped for breath. At the same time she fought for her life. Punching. Elbowing. Kneeing.

He jumped back. "Whoa. Calm down." He reached for her.

"Don't touch me." She pointed at him forcefully. "Do. Not. Touch. Me."

He looked at her, dumbfounded. Concerned.

Pitiful. She was absolutely pitiful. And weak. She hated weak. Why did she have to be like this? Tears welled in her eyes. "You should go." Her voice cracked.

"No," Kyle answered, watching her, a trapped animal desperate for escape. From him. Why? "What's going on?"

She shook out her hands in a nervous release of energy, wouldn't look at him. "Just go."

If she kept hyperventilating, she'd pass out within the next two minutes. "Here." He handed her the glass of water from the counter.

She took it, trembled. Water sloshed over the rim of the glass, splattering on her legs and slippers. Kyle grabbed a dishtowel and went to wipe her off. She reacted like he was coming at her with a knife. "Stay away from me." She held up her hand and backed away. "Go. Just, go. Please." The pleading in her tone was totally unexpected and out of character.

"I'm not leaving until I know what the hell is going on." Why his touch sent her into a panic. She used to love his touch. Welcome it.

She dropped her head into her hand. "I don't want you to see me like this."

Like what? Scared and vulnerable? He wanted to comfort her. But how? Taking her into his arms was definitely out. He settled on, "Let me help you. Tell me what I did to upset you."

From his perspective everything had been moving along splendidly.

"I don't want to talk about this. Not here. Not now." Her "not ever", while unspoken, came across loud and clear.

"Tough."

She squared her shoulders and glared at him. "I want you to leave."

Atta girl. He took a stand, crossed his arms over his chest and leaned toward her. "Make me." That got some of the blood to return to her face.

She tilted her head and quirked her left eyebrow. "You don't think I can?"

Welcome back. "Oh, I know you can. You are the smartest, most resourceful woman I've ever known, and you can do anything you put your mind to doing. I just don't think you will." He studied her. "Because for some reason you're scared of me. And I want to know why."

"I most certainly am not afraid of you." Her words,

while haughty, lacked their usual conviction. As if she knew he knew, she avoided eye contact and took a sip of water. At least her hands had stopped shaking and her breathing had slowed. "I'm going to get my bathrobe," she said, walking out of the kitchen. "Feel free to show yourself out."

Yeah, right.

A few minutes later she returned wearing a peach-colored fleece robe over a pair of gray sweatpants.

"I'm claustrophobic," she said matter-of-factly, walking over to the sink and placing her empty glass inside.

"Claustrophobic?" Exactly what did that have to do with anything?

She turned to face him. "I have a severe, irrational, panic-inducing fear of suffocation brought on by tight spaces and feeling restrained."

Restrained? "I never..."

"Maybe you don't intend to. But you're so big." She wrapped her arms around her chest but was unsuccessful in containing the shiver that ran through her. She walked over to the refrigerator and rested her back up against it. "And I'm, well, I'm not."

A horrible thought came to him. "Did I hurt you?"

"No." Her lips formed a tenuous smile. "It's more like a sense of impending doom."

Whoa. "Let me get his straight. My touch gives you a sense of impending doom?"

She nodded.

"Way to grind up my manhood."

She smiled.

"Does this happen with other guys?" As much as he didn't want to think about Victoria with other men, he had to know.

She developed a sudden interest in one of her cuticles.

"We used to talk about everything." Or so he'd thought. "Speaking of which, how come I didn't know about the claustrophobia?"

"It's not something I talk about." She tightened the sash on her robe. "Dad used to say never reveal a weakness as people will use it against you."

Her father would have made a good general in the armed forces.

"And to prove his point, whenever I was really bad, he used to put me into time out in the storage closet under the stairs." She rubbed her upper arms.

"You? Bad? I thought you were the perfect child."

She smiled but it didn't reach her eyes. "Perfection is in the eye of the beholder. And I'm afraid no matter how hard I tried he managed to find some deficiency or infraction that required punishment."

She stood quietly, staring into the darkened dining room, looking deep in thought.

"I hated that closet. So much junk in there. So dark and stuffy." She shivered. "When I was young I tried to fight him. But he was so much bigger than me. Stronger.'

Hell. Like Kyle.

"He'd simply pick me up or catch me in a bear-hug and squeeze until I stopped squirming." She swallowed and looked down at the floor. "The more I struggled the tighter he held me until I stopped. There was no escape. The end result always the same. A half-hour in the closet. And if I cried or carried on once in there, he'd calmly say through the door, 'If you don't keep quiet you'll have to endure another half-hour.' That shut me right up."

Was that why she hadn't spoken up that night in his car? Because she'd thought she needed to suffer in silence or he'd force her to "endure another half-hour"? Kyle felt sick, wanted to bash his head into a cabinet for not realizing, wanted find her father and lock *him* in that damn closet. And, boy, would he enjoy the battle it would no doubt take to shove him in there.

"When I was ten," Victoria went on, "I got punished for something my brother did. I couldn't keep myself from complaining about the unfairness of it. I cried and yelled and threw myself against the door. My dad didn't even acknowledge me. All my thrashing around must have dislodged some of the piles, because no sooner did I sit down, resigned to serve my sentence in quiet, than there was a cave-in. Old coats. Sports equipment. Boxes and bags of who knows what piled on top of me, covered me, pinned me down. I couldn't move, could barely breathe under the weight." She pulled at the collar of her nightshirt and inhaled a deep breath. "But I didn't cry or call out because I knew my dad would only make me stay in there longer. So I cried in silence while I waited for him to release me."

She looked up at him. "Little did I know Dad had fallen asleep in front of the television."

Bastard.

"When he finally unlocked the door I could tell he felt bad, but he didn't apologize. Dad never had to put me back into the closet after that. The threat was all I needed to keep quiet, work hard and follow the rules."

Until she'd met Kyle. He'd had no idea the risk she'd taken when sneaking around with him, felt his gorge churn and rise into the back of his throat at the thought of what she must have been subjected to after the sheriff had brought her home, at the mercy of her sadistic father.

She shook her head as if trying to clear the past and return to the present. "Anyway," she said, "that night in your car it was so stuffy and cramped. You were so heavy on top of me. I felt trapped. Squashed. It took me back to the closet." She palmed the back of her neck and stretched it out. "And now every time you touch me I feel on the brink of returning there and I panic. I don't want to revisit that place. I can't stand what it does to me."

While he'd been experiencing a sexual epiphany, she'd been gasping for breath beneath him, reliving a horrible experience. And he'd been oblivious. God help him. He deserved to have an ice pick shoved into his eye. "You should have told me." He would have done things differently, made it easier for her.

"It's getting late." She pushed off the refrigerator. "I need to get some sleep."

"You never answered my question. Do you get this panicky sense of impending doom with other men, or just me?"

Instead of answering, she walked over to the toaster and started to make sandwiches.

He waited, watched her economy of movements, like she performed the same motions night after night, week after week, month after month. Ever efficient.

After putting both lunchboxes in the refrigerator and wiping down the counter, she threw the sponge into the sink and blurted, "You're going to make me say it, aren't you?"

He leaned against a cabinet, crossed one foot over the other, prepared to wait as long as it took.

"Fine. There haven't been any other men."

That pleased him way more than it should have.

She flung her arms into the air. "Exactly when was I supposed to snag myself another boyfriend? When I was seventeen and heartbroken and pregnant? When I was taking care of an infant and trying to graduate high school? When I was eighteen, nineteen, or twenty, taking care of a baby and a sick aunt while working and going to college? Or any time after that while I was raising an impressionable young son, on my own, working to create a better life for us, struggling to pay off Aunt Livi's creditors, to keep my house, and maintain my sanity? Who on earth do you think would have wanted me?"

He would have. In the tick of a clock, the beat of a song, without one millisecond of hesitation.

"No one worthwhile," she snapped.

Or was that all just a huge rationalization for the real problem? She was scared.

"I needed to make something of myself. I needed to turn my life into something I'm proud to share with someone else."

"And now that you have, you want Dr. Starzi?"

"Don't say his name like that. We're the same type of people. We want the same things."

"Then answer me this," Kyle said. "If you like him so much, why didn't you tell me to stop when I kissed you in your office? Why did you kiss me back like you'd dreamed about it for years, like you needed it to sustain your very life?" She hadn't panicked then.

"Who knew you had such a flair for the dramatic?" she said. "You should try your hand at writing romance."

"You read a lot of romance books? Do you get all

hot and achy with want when the hero uses his tongue to make the heroine—?"

"Stop it."

Gotcha. He walked toward her. She didn't back away. Good. She stood with her hands balled into fists at her sides. Defiant.

He lifted a finger to tuck a soft curl behind her ear. "I'm not a randy seventeen-year-old kid anymore. I know how to take care of a woman, how to give her what she craves."

Victoria swallowed. "Well, good for you, because despite the rumored praise from your many high-school paramours, from my recollection, there was a lot of room for improvement."

And with that *whack* from her verbal mallet, the ground bits of his manhood were flattened into unrecognizable form. He'd disappointed the one girl who'd mattered, the one he'd wanted most to please. "Maybe you should give me an opportunity for a re-do," he suggested, wanting it more than just about anything. He leaned in close, careful not to touch her. "Let me show you how good it can be, how amazing I can make you feel."

She stared up at him, knowing Victoria, running every possible option with each responding outcome through her head. After what seemed like an hour she said, "I'd have to be on top."

Limiting, but doable. "Anything you want."

"What if I insisted on tying you to my bed and gagging you?"

A dominatrix? Not Victoria. Bossy, yes. A control freak. Most definitely. But into sexual bondage and domination? Absolutely not. There was something more going on. He called her bluff. "I'm always open to new experiences."

"Good." She surprised him. "I have some rope in the garage."

CHAPTER SIX

"THEN what?" Ali asked with eager anticipation after Victoria finished explaining the details of her previous night's encounter with Kyle.

"I went down to look for the rope." Which she'd found instantly thanks to being compulsively organized. Then she'd spent a good fifteen minutes pacing, trying to work up the courage to go back upstairs. Her problems had started with him, so he should be the one to help her work through them, right? "Is it hot in here?" Victoria picked up a manila folder from her desk and used it as a fan.

"You can open the door as soon as you tell me what happened next." Ali shifted to the edge of her seat.

"Oh, yes. How can I not share the best part? On my way upstairs..." Nervous about what she'd decided to do, excited to finally have the chance to test out her theory: She'd be fine with sex as long as she could be on top and in control. "I met Kyle heading downstairs. He said it'd occurred to him he didn't have any protection and unless I had some condoms around, which I'm sure he knew I didn't, he'd have to take a rain check."

"Didn't have any protection?"

"I know. Lame, with a capital L." Men like Kyle always had protection stashed somewhere on their person. She'd almost asked to see his wallet so she could check for herself, the sure sign of a desperate woman.

So what if he flirted and teased, that's what Kyle did. Give him some time to really consider her lack of experience coupled with her psychotic aversion to suffocation and he wanted no part of her, ran like her afflictions were contagious and further exposure would render him impotent.

"I'm sorry," Ali said.

Unable to tolerate the confines of her cell-like office for one more minute, Victoria stood and whipped open the door, to see Kyle.

"You're an idiot," Ali said to him as she squeezed past to exit the office.

"Ouch." Kyle flattened his palm over right nipple. "Don't you think it's about time you give up that annoying pinching habit?" he called after her.

With Kyle occupied, Victoria tried to slip out behind Ali. No such luck.

He stepped to the side, blocking her path to freedom. "No sense asking what you two ladies were talking about. Still no secrets between you?"

"Very few."

He leaned against the doorframe all relaxed and casual and in her way. "I came to see if you'd have lunch with me."

After last night? Not even if she were starving and he held the last sandwich within a hundred-mile radius. "I brought my lunch, sorry."

"What about dinner? You, me and Jake. You choose the restaurant. My treat."

A peace offering. Not interested. "Busy."

"How about Friday?"

"We already have plans." Not.

"I'd like to take Jake shopping for a baseball glove," he said.

Not happening. Victoria would be buying her son his first glove. "And what exactly do you know about baseball gloves?" He didn't play baseball. Did he think shopping for sports equipment required a set of testicles?

"They need to feel comfortable and catch baseballs."

A typical Kyle answer. "Can you tell the difference between a glove meant for baseball and one for softball? What about infielder and outfielder gloves? Leftie, righty, and catchers' gloves?"

"I'm guessing I can figure it out."

"Did you know glove size varies according to what position a child plays? That there's a certain measurement you need to…"

He held up a hand to stop her dissertation. "We'll all go. Bind up your research and bring it along. How about Saturday?"

"Busy." Taking her son shopping for his new baseball glove, followed by lunch at the mall, just the two of them.

Kyle narrowed his eyes, finally catching onto the trend. "So what day *is* Jake free?"

"Why don't you give me your attorney's name and he and my attorney can work out a visitation schedule?" Time to create some distance between them, to let him know he couldn't swing back into town on a whim and mess with her life.

"I get it." He crossed his arms over his chest. "You're mad. I changed my mind and decided I didn't want to be your trussed-up sex toy with a pulse. Sorry I disappointed you."

Of all the unprofessional, inappropriate, truly awful things to say. Victoria grabbed Kyle by the T-shirt, yanked him into her office, and after sticking her head out into the hallway to make sure no one overheard his crass remark, shut the door behind her. "Don't you ever talk to me like that at work." He made it sound so hideous and objectionable. She'd had every intention of satisfying him, or at least giving it her best attempt, multiple attempts if necessary.

"So at home it's okay?" He glared down at her.

He had no reason to be mad. She was the one who'd been rejected. "It's rude and base and never okay. What's the matter with you?"

"Maybe I'm a little pissed myself. Maybe I'm insulted that the only way you'll have me in your bed is tied down, like I present some sort of threat, like you don't trust I'll be careful with you."

So he'd figured her out. Give that man his pick from the wall of prizes. "Actually, I'm a wicked person, a staunch sexual deviant. And if being trussed up isn't something you're comfortable with…" she shook her head "…I'm afraid we're not at all compatible."

"Cut it out, Victoria."

Fine. "It was not my intention to insult you." She made it a point to look him in the eyes. "For that, I'm sorry." On most days, Victoria couldn't sit in her office for more than five minutes without someone needing something. Now, when she could really use an interruption, no one bothered her.

"I want to try something," he said, positioning himself in front of her, leaving a foot between them. "An experiment." He dipped his head and kissed her.

Victoria didn't have a lot of experience, but she doubted anyone kissed better than Kyle. Soap-bubble kisses, dotting along her lip line this time. Sweet. Benign. And surprisingly erotic. A scrumptious urge for more undulated inside her.

After way too short a time, he pulled back. Her lips followed his retreat, not quite finished with the data-gathering portion of his experiment. She met air. It took a few seconds for her lusty fog to evaporate and her eyes to focus enough to notice his smile.

"My hypothesis was correct," he teased. "We are absolutely compatible. You still like my kisses." He lifted his hand slowly and eased it behind her neck, slid his long fingers up the base of her scalp, into her hair. Before she could stop them, her head dropped back into his palm, and her lungs released a relaxing breath.

"You still like my touch," he said.

Oh, yeah. But innocent kissing and touching weren't the problem.

"And you want my body." He lifted her hand and placed it on his firm chest, the definition of his muscles evident through the soft cotton T. "Even if you only want it tied to your bed," he half joked.

"It was a silly idea, from a dream. I shouldn't have…"

"What did you do to me while you had me under your control in this dream of yours?"

"Nothing." She shoved him away.

At his look of surprise she explained, "You would not stop talking."

"Which explains the gag. Okay. Limit the verbal nasties while in bed with Victoria," he said with an air check. "Got it."

"You weren't talking dirty, you idiot. You wouldn't stop comparing me to…" Uh-oh. Too much information. "Don't you have someplace you need to be? Or is Tori doing all your work again?"

"Comparing you?"

"It's silly. No big deal. Just a dream."

"Who did I compare you to?"

Man, he could sure focus when he wanted to. "Leanne. Okay? It never took Leanne so long to blah, blah, blah," Victoria mimicked dream Kyle. "When Leanne does it she blah, blah, blah."

Real Kyle smiled.

"It's not funny. Leanne is perfect. Tall. Pretty. Voluptuous." Victoria was the antonym of voluptuous. "And she's good at sex while I'm…" Not. Might as well put it out there.

"She's also vain, manipulative, and self-centered," Kyle countered. "And to clarify, nothing happened between Leanne and me. She drove me home, tried to renew our *friendship*. But when I closed my eyes it was your face I saw. It was you I wanted kissing me, your hands I wanted touching me."

Victoria tried to stifle the thrill of hearing he wanted her more than Leanne.

"So I got out of there," Kyle continued. "But from what I remember and the rumors I've heard around the hospital, Leanne is not just good at sex, she's great at sex."

Thrill effectively stifled. "Thank you for all that unwanted information."

"Do you want to know what makes Leanne so great at sex?"

"Not really. No."

He told her anyway. "She does it with a lot of guys."

"Good to know," Victoria said, unable to look at him. "I'll get right on it."

"She practices." His voice dropped an octave and he reached out to turn her chin in his direction. He leaned in, putting his handsome face directly in front of hers. "And you can get right on it, with me. Any time. Anywhere."

Of course someone would choose that exact moment to knock.

"Think about it," Kyle whispered in her ear. "You don't have to tie me down to have your way with me."

How did one respond to an offer of that nature, while at work, with someone waiting, possibly listening, on the other side of the door?

"It will be so much better than those trashy books you read," he said seductively, his hot breath on her ear sending an ill-timed flush of arousing warmth through her.

So he *had* snooped in her bedroom. "I live vicariously."

"Not anymore." His words held equal parts of confidence and promise.

Victoria wished she'd replaced her oscillating fan when the motor had burned out.

Another knock, more insistent this time.

Kyle opened the door.

The director of nursing stood in the hallway.

Of all people, why her? Why now?

The dark gray suit she wore matched her hair and

was flatteringly fitted on her rotund shape. A tallish woman, the sensible pumps she wore, an outdated style Victoria would never be caught dead in, brought her forehead level with Kyle's nose. She shifted her eyes from Victoria to Kyle then back to Victoria. Knowing. Disapproving.

Not good. Victoria felt like a child about to be reprimanded, caught in a compromising situation by the woman who controlled her future.

"Thank you for your time," Kyle said to Victoria, using his professional voice. "If you have any further questions don't hesitate to ask. And I'll wait to hear back from you about the matter we discussed."

If she flicked water on her face it would surely sizzle.

"Where is your *pet*, Dr. Karlinsky?" The director asked, doing an impressive job of looking down her nose at Kyle, who stood a good six inches taller.

"If you're referring to my *therapy dog*, Tori, a patient requested a few minutes alone with her. And I'd best be getting back to them." The director watched Kyle walk away then shifted a condemning gaze to Victoria. "Don't ruin everything you've worked so hard to achieve by getting involved with a man like that," she warned, and entered Victoria's office, closing the door behind her.

One of the highly anticipated perks of becoming director of nursing was that Victoria would have a window in her office, allowing immediate access to fresh, breathable air whenever the need arose. What she wouldn't give for the ability to do that right then.

"He scoffs at authority," the director continued, "and does not follow the hospital dress code. Frankly, he is a blight on the wonderful staff of this institution."

"His patients love him, and Dr. Starzi seems to think very highly of him."

"Yes. Let's discuss Dr. Starzi." The older woman stuffed herself into the chair opposite Victoria's desk and motioned for her to sit as well. "As you are well aware, young lady, you are more to me than a talented colleague I've taken under my wing. You're the daughter I wish I'd had."

Victoria nodded. But knew full well her tenuous role as pseudo-offspring was contingent upon her working hard to meet the director's expectations, siding with her in all hospital matters, and following her 'suggestions' to the letter.

"And I envision you with a man who is smart and respected," the director went on, "above reproach. An exceptional conversationalist. Someone an ambitious, professional woman can be proud to have on her arm. The perfect asset when socializing with Administration and schmoozing the upper tier to court prospective benefactors. Play your cards right with a man like Dr. Starzi..." she wagged her index finger "...and you can be half of a major power couple."

One of the two reasons Victoria had encouraged his pursuit. The other being he'd make a wonderful role model and father figure for Jake.

The director clasped her hands in front of her buxom chest. "With his wealthy, thankful patients spanning the country, just think of the opportunities for fundraising."

"At this point," Victoria said, "neither gentleman is a candidate for my arm. If I may speak candidly?"

The director nodded. "Of course."

"You should know Dr. Karlinsky is the father of my

son." There'd been no need to identify Jake's paternity prior to this point.

Not one to make rash decisions or comments, the other woman sat quietly, introspective. After a short time she reached out and covered Victoria's hand with her own. "Many of us have a bad boy or two in our past. But I'm happy to report, as we mature and identify what course we'd like our lives to take, our taste in men becomes much more discriminating."

Kyle stared at Victoria, who sat on the other side of the sticky, white food-court table, sipping a diet cola, more interested in her straw wrapper than him. "Thank you for including me today," he said.

She spared him a glance, one of the few he'd been gifted with during their Saturday afternoon excursion. "Jake wanted you here, so here you are."

"I've never seen a kid so happy to shop for a baseball glove." And it made him feel a part of something special to be included in the excitement.

"He's been bugging me to play for a while." She dragged her eyes back up to his. "Thank you for treating him to the glove and the new sneakers. It wasn't necessary."

"It's the least I can do. By my calculation, I owe you a couple of thousand dollars in back child support." And so much more.

She concentrated on the long white paper strip, intent on folding it into accordion pleats. "You don't owe me anything."

"I knew you'd say that." Miss independent. "So I made this out to Jake." He handed her an envelope that contained a check for five thousand dollars. "Put it into his college fund." No doubt in his mind Victoria already had one started.

She looked at the envelope, didn't move to take it. For a few seconds he thought she might refuse. Then she said, "Thank you. That's very generous," and tucked it into her purse without opening it.

He hated the stilted conversation between them ever since the old bat who ruled the nurses had shown up and caught him and Victoria behind closed doors. "So what did the nursing director want?"

"Mr. Madrin stormed her office to make a formal complaint about me."

"That man deserves a—"

"She talked him out of it, and came to commend me, in person, for my handling of the situation."

The dictatorial woman moved up a few notches in Kyle's estimation. "That was nice of her." Victoria flattened out the straw wrapper and began winding it around her index finger.

"Are you going to tell me what's bothering you?" he asked.

"Nothing's bothering me."

Her words came out too fast and high-pitched to be true. "How long is Jake's party?"

She glanced over at the arcade where they'd dropped him off ten minutes earlier. "Two hours."

"You want to get out of here? We can go to my place, it's closer." If he could just get her alone he knew he could get her to relax.

"I don't even know where you're staying."

"I'm renting a one bedroom in the big condo complex a few minutes from the hospital." A functional unit, nothing fancy, which suited Kyle. "You want to take a look?" To sweeten the offer he added, "There's a pull-out couch if Jake ever wants to sleep over," knowing she'd want to check out his digs before allowing their son to visit.

She didn't respond to his invitation, just sat there looking up at him. "You know wearing jeans to work is against the hospital dress code, right?"

"That was random."

"So why do you do it? Acting the rebel in high school is one thing, but you're all grown up. Enough already."

So that's what was bothering her. "Answer me this. Does my wearing jeans impact my ability to do my job; does it affect my performance in any way?"

"No, but—"

"Have my patients, your staff, or Dr. Starzi complained I lack professionalism? Have any of them taken issue with the care I provide while in my jeans?"

"No, but—"

"Come on." He held out his hand. "I'm not going to waste the brief time we have together talking about work. Jake's safe, he's having fun. Let's do a lap around the mall."

"My knee's a little sore."

It'd been fine all morning, her gait even with no noticeable limp. Maybe it was the elastic support he'd given her, or the written home exercise plan, or the private PT he'd forced on her since seeing her swollen knee. Whichever, he didn't believe her knee was too sore for a slow, casual stroll. "I'll get you in for an MRI on Monday," he threatened. "I've already spoken with the tech. She said to call first thing in the morning and she'd give me an idea when she can squeeze you in."

Victoria actually blanched. "Fine." She smacked her

hand on the table, the breeze blowing the straw wrapper to the floor, where Kyle stepped on it so she couldn't pick it up. "Let's go."

After weaving through the weekend crowd they entered the flow of foot traffic behind a couple, walking hand in hand, a young boy perched up on the man's shoulders. Kyle felt a pang of regret that he'd missed out on moments like that with Victoria and Jake.

"So, tell me," Victoria said. "Where did you go after you left and how did you wind up with a PhD?"

Happy to get some real conversation going, Kyle answered, "The morning after everything went down I got in contact with Milt at the garage to tell him what'd happened." Aside from Ali, who would hear the news from Victoria, and his sister who would find the note he'd left for her when she finally returned to their trailer, Milt had been the only other person who might care what happened to him. "He called around and found me a job out in Habersville." Three short, or long depending on how you look at it, hours from Madrin Falls.

"You know, after that night he refused to service any of my father's cars."

Milt, who'd lived in a double-wide a few trailers down the row, had been more of a father to Kyle than his own father. "He looked out for me, even made me promise to take a high-school equivalency exam within one month or he'd have me fired."

"Good for him," Victoria said.

"Anyway, I spent my days working and my nights partying." Getting drunk, venting his anger by brawling with equally inebriated idiots, and screwing dozens of nameless, faceless women in a futile attempt to exorcize Victoria from his brain. "After a couple of months," during which his life spiraled out of control, "I got into a car driven by a guy drunker than me. He drove us into a cement overpass." And had almost killed them both.

Victoria stopped and reached up to trace the scar on his chin, her touch soft, caring. "That's where you got this."

The group of kids walking behind them split up and filtered past.

Kyle guided her to the railing overlooking the ground level.

"Concussion. Broke a few bones." Eight to be exact. Spent seven days in ICU, six weeks on a medical surgical floor, and three months in a physical rehab facility. "During rehab I had a roommate named Fig." Ryan Figelstein. Eighteen like Kyle. Also involved in an MVA, only he'd been the driver, and his "accident", Fig had confided one night, had actually been a suicide attempt. "We hit it off, made each other laugh through the pain. When his parents overheard I had no one to go home to, they arranged for Fig and me to be discharged together and took me in." It'd been the first time he'd felt a part of a real family.

"Come on, there's a chocolate store up ahead," he said and, with a gentle hand on her back steered her in that direction. "Anyway, Fig's father asked what I wanted to do with my life. After spending so much time in physical therapy I told him I might like to try being a physical therapist. Next thing I knew I was enrolled in the same college as Fig on a full scholarship." When he'd questioned the scholarship Fig's dad had told him, *"You keep an eye on Fig and get him to stay in college until he graduates, and we'll call it even."*

"I got in good with a few teachers who'd received a

research grant. They invited me to work with them. I qualified for financial support as long as I was working toward a PhD in physical therapy so I signed up. And here I am."

"I'm glad everything worked out for you." Her words sounded distant, almost sad.

Because while he'd been cruising through college, blessed by the generosity of others, she'd been giving up her dreams, struggling to survive and make a decent life for their son. Talk about trading places.

"I'm sorry," he said. "I didn't mean…" to carelessly recite how easy he'd had it for the past eight years.

"Don't be sorry."

But he was. Sorry he hadn't protected her well enough. Sorry he hadn't made any attempt to contact her or inquire about her. Sorry he'd unknowingly traumatized her their last night together and she still suffered from the after-effects.

At least that he could fix, without a doubt, but not as a training mannequin, at the disposal of a student. He wanted her to experience pleasure from his touch, not fear, to yearn for intimacy with him, not run from it. He wanted to drive her wild with passion, to give her the ultimate satisfaction, again and again, to make up for all the years she'd gone without. He wanted to make her crave him, the way he craved her. And once he accomplished that, he'd go after her heart.

Because, with each passing day, Kyle grew more convinced that Victoria was indeed, his "one". He looked forward to seeing her, talking to her, even fighting with her. He enjoyed discussing Jake and participating in family activities, like heading to the mall. She was a wonderful mother, had been a great girlfriend. He'd lost her once, would not let her go again.

"Oh, look," she said, and veered over to the window of the chocolate shop. As she stood, staring through the glass with a look of desire Kyle hoped to one day soon see directed at him, he ducked into the store.

He returned to find her right where he'd left her. He handed her a small white bag. "Here."

She gave a gasp of surprise, smiled, and peered inside. "Pecan turtles."

"Only two." If it were up to him he would have purchased a dozen, but back in high school whenever he'd treated her she'd always specified, *"Only two."*

She placed her hand on his arm. "You remembered."

He remembered lots of things. How she'd sat with him and Ali every day at lunch, walked right past the brainiacs and her snotty, rich peers, despite taunts she was headed to the wrong side of the cafeteria. How she'd fought with Mr. Strich when she'd thought Kyle had received an unfair grade on his trigonometry mid-term. (And got the grade changed from a C to a B.) And how she'd skipped school, for the first time ever, to sneak off to his trailer when he hadn't shown up to class for three straight days. His telephone had been disconnected for non-payment at the time. Upon finding him delirious with fever, she'd dragged him to her pediatrician, demanded an appointment, then carted him to Aunt Livi's house to recover from his pneumonia.

Sick as he'd been, with the two of them doting on him, it'd been the best two weeks of his life.

Victoria bit into one of the candies, inhaled, let her eyes drift closed, then exhaled. The expression on her face was one of such joy he couldn't help but wonder when she'd last indulged in her favorite treat. From this day forward it'd be a weekly event. When she slid the second half between her lips all Kyle could think about was making her replicate that look when they were alone and naked.

And to further his quest to make that happen, he needed more opportunities to entice her. "I want to show you something." He started to walk and she, licking her fingers, fell into step beside him. They'd passed the destination he'd had in mind earlier, but he didn't dare suggest they enter with Jake.

CHAPTER SEVEN

VICTORIA stopped short when she saw the store they were headed toward.

"I think I'll wait out here," she said. It'd make her the ultimate hypocrite to patronize a store she'd signed a petition to keep from opening.

"Don't go getting all prissy." He tugged her along. "Give it five minutes. If you don't like it, we'll leave."

Rock music blared through speakers almost unidentifiable in the dark-painted ceiling. Incense, at least she hoped that's all it was, permeated the air. Black T-shirts screen-printed with celebrities she didn't recognize lined the walls. Hundreds of novelties and gag gifts were displayed on huge shelving units. She walked past one display containing play handcuffs, fang tooth inserts, and fake blood, then another holding breast mugs with nipple spouts and realistic looking penis spoon rests, to stand in front of a display of colorful lava lamps. Out of the corner of her left eye she saw Kyle talking to a blonde-haired salesclerk. The girl smiled up at him, removed an elastic bracelet from her wrist, and handed it to him. She slid her eyes to the right to see a high-school-aged girl trying out an actual stripper pole. That's it. Probably only a minute had elapsed since she'd entered, but Victoria had seen enough. In the process of turning to leave, she halted when a synthesized cartoon voice sounded next to her left ear. "You're sexy."

She swung around to see Kyle holding a palm-sized, red gadget. He held it up and pressed a button. The voice said, "Are those real?"

People started to look in their direction. "Stop that." Victoria grabbed for it. Kyle held it up out of reach and pressed a different button. "Can I touch them?" A group of girls, standing close by, started to giggle.

Victoria couldn't help smiling. "You are going to pay for this." It felt fun to play. Frankly, she couldn't remember the last time she'd done it.

Seeming unconcerned with her threat, Kyle pressed another button.

"Pretty please?" the voice asked.

"Two can play at that game," she said, and grabbed for a similar-looking toy from the shelf beside Kyle. Holding it up, she pressed the top left button.

A different synthesized voice yelled out, "You're an asshole."

Victoria's jaw fell and her eyelids stretched so wide that if her eyeballs weren't anchored in her head, they would have dropped to the floor. "That's terrible." She threw the offensive voice box back into the basket with the others. "I'm out of here."

"Not yet." Kyle slid his arm around her shoulders and maneuvered her toward the back of the store. "All the good stuff is locked up." The moist heat of his breath singed her ear and sent a rush of arousing warmth surging through her.

"I've seen and heard enough, thank you very much." She tried to twist away.

"Two more minutes."

They stopped in front of a dark gray door. The red lettering on the sign that hung at eye level read: "Adult Amusements. Must be 18 or older to enter. See salesclerk for key."

"Ooh, no." She shook her head, stepped back and bumped into Kyle. "I'm not going in there." Yet at the same time she wondered what illicit items the secret room behind the door held. Some of the books she'd read had touched on sexy board games, sex toys, and other bedroom...paraphernalia. Could they be so easy to obtain? One quick trip to the mall?

Kyle used the key on the elastic bracelet to unlock the door. When he pushed it open the overhead lights flicked on.

Victoria hesitated in the doorway.

"Try something new," he whispered in her ear. "No more living vicariously."

Right-o. It's what she wanted. At twenty-five years of age, it was high time she allowed herself to actually experience life instead of just reading about it.

"It's so small," she said, tugging on the neck of her sweater, hoping doing so would allow more air to enter.

Kyle coaxed her inside. "There's plenty of air," he said in a soothing tone. "I won't let you suffocate."

He didn't joke or tease. He was completely serious. And she appreciated that, especially when he closed and locked the door behind them. Despite her fear of tight spaces and the narrow isles stocked full of merchandise that made the small room feel even smaller, her curiosity urged her forward. Past feathered ticklers and wooden helping hands? Flavored body mousses and lotions, and edible bikini underwear? She picked up the box to take a closer look.

"If you put them on I'll eat them off," Kyle whispered in her ear as he walked past.

Maybe another time. Victoria threw the box back onto the shelf.

"Look at these." He called her over to a display on the far wall. "I'm told every girl should have one. Personally, I don't get the appeal."

He stood in front of a wall of vibrators. Her face heated. "I already have one."

"No way." He turned to her and smiled. "I can't picture it." And he looked to be trying rather hard. "You don't seem the type."

She wasn't. "A few months ago the pathetic state of my non-existent sex life became the topic of conversation at a girls' night out." And hadn't that been a totally mortifying experience since the decibels of Roxie's speech had increased proportionately to the number of beers she'd consumed. "The next morning I found an electronic gal pal on my desk along with a book about the elusive female orgasm."

He slid in behind her, placed his hands on her shoulders, and positioned her dead center in front of the display. "It's not a myth," he said.

So far she hadn't been able to prove otherwise. "So you say."

"Which one?" He asked his voice low, intimate.

She pointed to the model tucked away in a box in her closet.

"Do you ever use it?" He ran his tongue over the

inner rim of her ear. It tickled, made the left side of her face tingle.

"Once." Sex with an inanimate object had turned out to be empty and unfulfilling and not at all for her.

He kissed down the side of her neck. Without considering the consequences, she tilted her head to give him better access. His hands slid down her arms, settling on her waist. He didn't crowd her, kept his touch gentle. His hands felt so good. "Did you like using it?"

She shook her head. He shifted his hands up her rib cage, stopping just below her breasts.

Darn it.

"You're going to like having me inside you."

But the last time...

"No. Don't stiffen up on me." He traced the outline of both her breasts at the same time, sliding up over sensitive nipples then back down again. "We'll take it slow. You'll be in charge." Up. Down. "Take only as much of me as you can handle." Up. Down.

It sounded perfect, but, "I don't know, Kyle. We're too different. We don't want the same things." And after giving it a lot of consideration she'd decided she wasn't the type of woman to engage in sex for the sake of sex. Once she found a suitable man who cared for her, whom she cared for in return, she'd share her issues and trust him to help her work through them.

"I want to explore your body," he said, his voice deep. "Learn what you like, what drives you wild. I want to give you pleasure, make you come." His palm grazed down her belly, the tips of his fingers sneaking beneath the waistband of her slacks. "I'd bet my life you want the same."

She wanted more.

He slid his hand further down, under the elastic of her panties.

Her mind knew she should stop him. Her mouth refused to convey the command, her hand wouldn't move to deter him.

"Do you want the same things?" His hand moved lower. "If you don't answer me I'll find out for myself."

A few inches and he'd find her wet and needy and ready to clamp down on his finger like a Venus fly trap to keep him from leaving her. She let her head fall back to his chest. "You have to stop, Kyle. We are at the *mall*."

He smiled against her cheek. "I tried to get you over to my place." Without warning he slid a finger to her opening and sighed. "I knew it."

A battle raged inside her sex-starved body. The urge to tilt her hips to facilitate him sliding inside vs. a moral scream of outrage. She tilted her hips. He accepted her offer, the sensation foreign. Spectacular.

Within seconds he had her on the verge of something wonderful. "You need to stop." She circled his forearm with both hands and tried to lift his hand from her pants. "Please. I can't. Not here."

"Let me come over tonight," he pleaded, his voice rough. "I can ease your ache. You need me, and I need you, so much." As if to support his claim he pulled her back against his hard body. "You have to. We'll both die if you don't, then what will happen to Jake?"

Since there was no way to deny her attraction and retain any semblance of credibility, she opted for a version of the truth. "I'm not on birth control."

"I have condoms." *Now* he had condoms, when she was thinking clearly and rationally. She lifted his hand out of her pants and moved away. Feeling on edge, she tucked in her blouse with damp, shaky hands. "The last time I left a man responsible for birth control it didn't work out so well for me."

"I know," he said quietly, sincerely. "And I am sorrier than I can put into words for all you've been through. But I'm not sorry to have Jake. He's a great kid."

"He is."

"So..." He shoved both hands into the front pockets of his jeans and did some rearranging. "Do you have any plans to go on birth control in the near future?"

Yes. She had a doctor's appointment scheduled for Monday. For a birth control shot, which, based on her cycle, should take effect immediately. But she told him, "No."

He cocked his head, studied her and smiled. "You know I could always tell when you lied."

"And what makes you think my going on birth control has anything to do with you? Are you so over-confident you can't fathom the possibility I made the appointment months ago?" She hadn't. Bottom line, Kyle's return and his effect on her body had compelled her to make the call. She simply did not trust herself around him.

His smile grew. "Go ahead and deny it, but we both know you want me," he teased.

"Sometimes I want to eat a pound of chocolate or skip a day of work," Victoria countered. "It doesn't mean I do."

"It's your call, sweetheart. Put off the inevitable if you must." He moved in close, set his lips to the outer rim of her ear, and whispered, "But know this, I am ready, willing, and, oh, so able, whenever you decide to give in to your urges."

The heat from his mouth sent tingles into her jaw and down the side of her neck. Her body, still aroused, fought the pull of attraction, the allure of all he offered. Gathering her restraint, she stepped back, not at all happy with his cocksure grin. Time to shut him down. "By the end of my date on Tuesday night I expect all my urges will be satisfied. But thanks for the offer."

No sooner did they clear the exit doors from the mall than Jake asked, "Can Dad come home with us?"

Victoria had had about all she could handle of Kyle for one day so she answered with an unequivocal, do-not-argue-with-me "No."

"But now that I have my mitt I need to get good at catching," Jake whined. "Daniel's been practicing with his dad for weeks. So has Jeremy. If I don't practice I'm gonna stink."

"And it will be all your fault," Kyle whispered to Victoria with a smirk.

"Okay," she growled. He could keep Jake occupied while she finished her homework.

Of course Kyle needed to stop by his condo to walk Tori and get his glove, which required even more time in his presence.

Jake was out of the truck and halfway to the stairs before Victoria even processed Kyle's invitation to check out his place. Tori met them at the door, happily rubbing up against each of them. "Hey, girl." Victoria massaged her behind the ears. After seeing the benefits of Tori's therapy, she'd grown to like the dog.

"Come on, Tor. Let us in." Kyle patted the dog on the butt and Tori ran back inside followed by Jake.

A discount motel room felt homier and more welcoming than Kyle's rental unit. It kind of reminded her of the neglected, downright dismal atmosphere of the trailer he'd once shared with his sister, which she'd only been inside the one time he had been too sick to deny her entry.

Most noticeably lacking were any personal items. Books. Pictures of family and friends. A favorite coffee mug or cookie jar. A colorful afghan knit by an aged aunt. At least it was neat. Orderly. And clean. "I love what you've done with the place," she teased.

"It has everything I need."

Perfect for the man who required no more than the most basic necessities. But sad. Who could possibly be happy living such an empty existence? Next chance she got she'd give him some of Jake's art projects to decorate the place, maybe a few pictures.

"That sofa pulls out into a bed," Kyle said. He glanced into the bedroom where Tori and Jake were busy playing. "In case Jake ever wants to sleep over," he added in a whisper.

She appreciated his discretion. Jake had mentioned sleeping at his dad's condo at least a dozen times in the past two weeks. But she wasn't ready to say yes. Not yet. The couch looked several decades old and well used since its manufacture. "We'll need to clean the mattress, dust the frame, and check for bedbugs," Victoria said.

Kyle smiled. "Of course we will."

Jake walked into the living room and asked, "Can we bring Tori home with us?"

"It's okay with me if it's okay with your mom," Kyle answered.

All three of them looked at her.

"Fine," she agreed. "But she stays downstairs."

"Goodie," Jake said. "Come on, girl." He ran to the door.

"Hold on," Kyle said, and walked over to grab a brand-new adult-sized baseball glove, complete with tags, from the dining room table. "Okay. Now I'm ready."

"That your glove?" Jake asked.

Kyle held it up. "When we went out to lunch last week you were so excited about playing baseball. On my way home I picked this up so we could have a catch together." He slipped it on and punched the palm area.

While Jake examined the glove and said "Cool" about six times, Victoria leaned against the wall, struck speechless by the thoughtful gesture, made after Kyle had spent a combined total of, at most, two hours with his son. It bespoke of him taking an active interest in Jake and wanting to be a part of his life.

"Come on, kid," Kyle said. "We're wasting daylight. You ready?" he asked Victoria.

"Sure." She followed them down to the parking lot. Jake chattered excitedly, holding onto Tori's leash. Kyle listened, squeezing in a response here and there when Jake took a breath. And Victoria walked behind them, all but forgotten. Until Jake asked Kyle, "Can I sit in the front seat on the way home?" And Kyle gave his standard answer, "It's okay with me if it's okay with your mom." And they both stopped and turned to her.

Well, of course it was not okay. Jake knew that. He was too small and barely out of his booster seat. "No."

"But, Mom, *Dad* says it's okay."

Call her naïve, but Victoria did not expect this play-one-parent-against-the-other routine, not from Jake. "You're not old enough or big enough to sit in the front seat, Jake, and you know it. I don't like you trying to take advantage of Daddy because he doesn't know all the rules yet. Now say you're sorry."

"Sorry, Dad," Jake said, looking adequately contrite, his expression changing to absolute jubilation when Kyle told him he'd be sharing the back seat with Tori.

Once home Jake and Tori ran off to play.

"I'm sorry about the front seat thing. I didn't know," Kyle said. "Give me a second to get over there. I'll help you down."

She opened the door and waited. "I can't expect you to know everything in two weeks." She tried to ignore the feeling of his strong hands on her waist and the enticing hint of cologne.

"Why don't you stay outside with us?" Kyle asked.

Victoria punched the code into the keypad by the garage door. "I've got work to do," she said. "And I don't have a glove anyway," she added with a shrug.

But knowing Kyle and Jake were outside, Victoria couldn't concentrate on her schoolwork. Instead she stood at her office window, watching them play in the yard. Envious. Kyle threw Jake the baseball, which bounced off the tip of his glove and rolled to Tori, who scooped it up in her mouth and ran. Jake dropped his glove and took off after her. Not far. Tori rolled onto her back, Jake rubbed her belly and she released the ball. Jake picked it up, said something and made a 'yuk' face. Kyle dropped his glove and chased Jake. Tori ran with them, jumping and barking, until all three wound up in a heap on the grass.

They wrestled around. Jake laughed and smiled with unrestrained joy. She hadn't seen him so happy since... never, could not recall him ever looking that happy with her. Because she always had so much to do, someplace to be, something to plan or worry about. And when they did play she tended toward educational games, always with his future in mind. Having Kyle around was good for Jake. For her? Not so much. He preoccupied her. Case in point—she looked down at the blank computer screen on her desk, her report guidelines and research papers still in her school folder. At the hospital she listened for him to arrive on the floor, waited with schoolgirl anticipation for him to visit her office. Why? So he could kiss her and proposition her and make her desire to act most improper? God help her. Yes.

Even at the risk of the promotion she needed to assure a stable economic future, Jake's attendance at the best colleges, and the chance for vindication. Validation. Which was why, from now on, she needed to be on guard to never wind up alone with him.

She sat down at her desk and fiddled with a pen. Then there were the niggling thoughts. Have sex with him. Get it out of the way. You'll stop thinking about it so much. If things turned out as awful as she feared, problem solved. He'd never bother her again and they could get on with co-parenting sans the underlying sexual tension between them.

But what if it wasn't awful? What if she managed to get through it without panicking and it turned out to be wonderful and loving and all she'd hoped for their first time? What would happen then? Could she incorporate

Kyle into her ten-year plan? Would he support her goals and ambitions? Or derail her life plan? Again?

The basement door slammed.

Victoria walked to the top of the stairs. "Did you have fun?" she called down.

"Can Daddy help me finish my puzzle?" Jake yelled in response.

The puzzle they'd worked on together for weeks? He wanted to share the thrill of placing that final piece and the fun of the job-well-done dance with Kyle? Not her? It was only a puzzle, she told herself. So why did Jake's defection hurt so much? Why did she feel like an outsider with her own son, in her own home?

Before she could answer she heard Kyle say, "Sorry, champ I've got to run. There's someplace Tori and I need to be."

Where? Victoria wondered, but didn't ask. Kyle's life was none of her business. He could do whatever he wanted. With whomever he wanted. Made no difference to her. After she said her goodbye Victoria went into her medicine cabinet to take an antacid, hoping it would sooth the burning in her chest.

"Good afternoon, Mrs. Teeton," Kyle said when he entered her hospital room on Monday afternoon. "I hear you gained two pounds. Congratulations." He set a tin of chocolate-covered mints, apparently her favorites, topped with a big red bow, on her over-the-bed table.

She met his gesture with a tired smile. "Never in my fifty-four years have I ever celebrated putting on weight."

"Today is a day of firsts, like getting out of this room, for instance. You promised me and Tori a promenade."

"Nice segue."

"I'm a smooth operator."

A laugh that closely resembled Victoria's sounded out in the hallway.

"Are you ready?" he asked his patient.

Tori went up on her hind legs and placed her front paws on the bed beside Mrs. Teeton's shoulder. She reached over to pet Tori's head.

"No. I'm sorry. I'm going to have to cancel," she said. "I don't feel up to it."

A typical complaint in his line of work, but it was his job to keep his patients moving. "Then there's one more thing you should know about me," Kyle said a little louder than necessary, just in case Victoria was still listening. "I rarely accept no as a final answer."

"It's the truth," Victoria said, hustling into the room, going straight to Mrs. Teeton's closet and taking out her red bathrobe. "And he can be a real pest about it. It's best to just give in and save yourself the aggravation of having to deal with him."

"If only all women followed that philosophy," Kyle said, "I would live in a state of perpetual happiness."

Victoria brushed past him. She bent to whisper something in Mrs. Teeton's ear. The woman nodded. "Maybe you'll feel better once you get out of this bed," she said and, as efficiently as she did everything else, she slid the patient's legs over the side and assisted her into a sitting position. "Just sit for a few minutes." She kept her hands on Mrs. Teeton's shoulders to steady her. "The dizziness will pass."

"I can take it from here," Kyle offered.

"Can you really?" Victoria asked. "And just what do you know about getting a woman ready for her hallway debut?" She winked at Mrs. Teeton. "Give us a few minutes." Her expression serious, she added, "Maybe you can bring Tori to visit with Mrs. Madrin while you're waiting?"

When Kyle hesitated she tilted her head and mouthed, "Please."

"Sure thing," he said, and crossed over to the other side of the drawn curtain to find Mrs. Madrin lying on her side in bed, staring out the window.

"Excuse me, Mrs. Madrin. Are you up for a visit?"

Vacant eyes met his. "Do I know you?"

"You may not remember me but—"

"Hi, there, boy," she said to Tori, a hint of life returning to her eyes.

"She's a girl," Kyle clarified. "Her name is Tori. She's a therapy dog."

"Growing up I had a golden retriever just like her. Come here, girl." She tapped her hand on the mattress.

Tori, a notorious attention-monger, didn't wait for the command to proceed.

"Can she come up on my bed?"

Victoria answered from the other side of the fabric partition. "On top of the blanket, no pressure above your hips."

"Up," Kyle said in conjunction with the hand signal instructing Tori to jump onto the bed. Once there she turned in a circle, plopped herself at the foot of the bed and cuddled up against Mrs. Madrin's bent legs, setting her head on the woman's thigh.

Mrs. Teeton peeked around the curtain. A colorful scarf tied in a fashionable knot covered her head. Light makeup brightened her lips and cheeks. Victoria held onto her arm.

"I think Tori's tired," Mrs. Teeton said with a pointed look at Kyle. "Maybe she can stay with you while we walk?" she asked her roommate.

"I'd like that." Mrs. Madrin showed no emotion but continued to pet Tori.

Kyle glanced at Victoria who nodded.

"She's a good listener," Mrs. Teeton said.

"You can tell her anything and she won't repeat it," Kyle added, reciting the speech he gave each new patient. "Sometimes you need to say something out loud to hear how it sounds, before you're ready to share it with someone else."

Mrs. Madrin's eyes filled with tears.

"We'll leave you with Tori," Victoria said. "If you need anything at all, press your call bell and Ali or I will be right in." Outside, Victoria partially closed the door behind her. "Thank you," she said to Mrs. Teeton. "Getting out of that room will do you as much good as it will do your roommate to have a few minutes to herself."

"And thank *you*..." Victoria placed her hand on Kyle's arm and looked up at him with appreciation "...for loaning out Tori. I wanted to ask you before you went in there but I didn't see you arrive on the floor."

Because instead of stopping by her office to say "Hi," like he'd gotten in the habit of doing, he'd come down the other corridor, still angry and not ready to face her after finding out her Tuesday-night date was real, and she'd be spending it with Starzi.

"Shoot," Victoria said.

Kyle followed her line of sight to see Mr. Madrin and one of his assistants walking down the hall.

Without hesitation, Victoria intercepted them. Kyle

listened, too far away to intervene, unable to leave Mrs. Teeton.

"Good afternoon, Mr. Madrin," Victoria said. "Your wife requires some privacy for the next ten or fifteen minutes. Feel free to wait in our patient lounge at the end of the hallway."

"Why? What's going on? What's happened?" Mr. Madrin made a move to walk around Victoria. She stepped to the side, effectively blocking the intimidating man's path on behalf of her patient.

She was one amazing woman.

"Please," she said to Mr. Madrin. "Your wife is in with our therapy dog."

Kyle liked her use of "our", like Victoria was comfortable with Tori being on her floor, confident in the service she provided.

"That's absurd. This is a hospital, not a petting zoo."

"Don't underestimate the power of animals to help in the recovery process," Kyle offered when he and Mrs. Teeton finally caught up to Victoria. "Animals are non-judgmental. They don't interrupt or voice their opinions or make suggestions. They simply listen when someone needs to talk."

"Tori helped me tremendously," Mrs. Teeton added.

"We've tried everything we can think of to get your wife to open up about the accident, to discuss her loss," Victoria said. "So far nothing has worked. She barely eats and lies in bed staring out the window when no one's visiting. I refuse to give up until we find a way to help her. Our therapy dog, Tori, has a wonderful disposition and is extremely well trained. She is an asset to our staff and our patients adore her."

Victoria's words of praise for Tori made Kyle feel like a proud papa.

"Your wife's doctor approved Tori's visit," she said. "Your wife welcomed her."

Typical Victoria, checked with the doctor beforehand.

"I'm sure I saw her smile," Mrs. Teeton said.

"She...?" Mr. Madrin couldn't finish, overcome with emotion he turned away.

You could say a lot of negative things about the man, but he loved his wife.

"Please." Victoria took his hand in between both of her own. "Go down to the cafeteria for a cup of coffee. Tori's handler, Dr. Karlinsky, is on the floor. And I will remain at the nurses' station in case your wife needs anything. If she asks for you I'll have you paged immediately."

Mr. Madrin placed his other hand on top of Victoria's. "I was wrong about you."

Most people were, mistaking her businesslike efficiency for a lack of caring, her superior intellect for a lack of compassion.

Victoria watched Mr. Madrin exit the floor then turned. "Whew. That went better than expected."

"Come on, handsome." Mrs. Teeton tugged on his arm. "I got all gussied up for our date. Are we going to spend it standing around doing nothing?"

"Absolutely not," Kyle said. "We're off."

A few hours later, almost finished with his chart documentation on 5E, Kyle watched Dr. Starzi strut onto the unit and cozy up next to Victoria outside the clean utility room. If this had been high school, Kyle would have been tempted to wedgie him up and leave him hanging from a hook on the door in the janitor's closet.

If there was any satisfying of Victoria's urges to be done, Kyle would be doing the satisfying.

"You're going to snap that pen in two and get ink all over the place if you don't lighten up," Roxie said, sitting down beside him.

"What's going on between the two of them?" Kyle asked, fighting the sick need to watch Victoria and Starzi together.

"He's shopping for a wife. Victoria caught his eye, meets his requirements."

"Does she have feelings for him?"

The pen did, in fact, snap, making a mess of Kyle's hand and the progress note he'd been writing. "Damn."

"Watch it." Roxie passed him a handful of tissues. "Or you'll have the profanity policewoman up your ass."

Kyle smiled.

So did Roxie.

"She's been alone a long time," Roxie said. "I think she likes Dr. Starzi, respects him as a physician. But she doesn't look at him the way she looks at you."

Hope surged inside him. "And how does she look at me?"

"Part puppy in a pet shop looking for someone to take her home and love her, part woman stranded on a deserted island, devoid of male companionship for nine long years."

He checked to make sure Victoria didn't look at Starzi the same way. She didn't.

"Don't play with her," Roxie warned. "She doesn't look it, but she's fragile." She leaned in close. "If you hurt her I'll insert scalding-hot pokers into every orifice in your body. If you pull another vanishing act, I will make it my sole purpose in life to hunt you down and make you suffer in ways you couldn't imagine in your worst nightmares."

"Did you give Dr. Starzi the same warning?"

She waved him off. "He's harmless. You, on the other hand, hold the potential to break her heart."

"I won't." Not again. "And thank you," Kyle said.

Roxie raised her over-plucked eyebrows.

"For caring enough to threaten me."

"Don't disappoint." Roxie slapped him on the back. "Go win back your girl."

Oh, he planned to.

Two hours later, on his way to have a little chat with Starzi, Kyle headed past Victoria's office. As he neared her closed door it began to open. The director's voice said, "I don't know what you're waiting for, my dear. If you'd rather he not accompany you, he's not the man to build your promising future around."

Rather *who* not accompany her *where?* And whether the dragon lady liked it or not, Kyle was the only man Victoria would be building her future around.

The door opened fully and the director of nursing walked out. "Oh, look," she said when she spotted Kyle. "What prodigious timing."

Victoria walked into the hallway, looking ready to hurl.

"We were just speaking of you," the director said. "Next Saturday night is a dinner honoring several of our employees of the month. It's black tie optional. I hope to see you there," she added with false sweetness, and waddled away.

After she'd gone Kyle asked Victoria, "You okay?"

She nodded, took a deep breath, and sipped from the bottle of water in her hand.

"Why would I care about an employee of the month dinner?" Kyle asked.

Victoria scrunched her face. "Because I'm Miss January."

Kyle smiled at the centerfold image that flashed across his mind, Victoria draped across the front of a snowmobile, wearing nothing but a red and white striped ski hat and matching mittens. He blinked to clear it and focused back in on their conversation. "Then I wouldn't miss it."

He chose to ignore what looked more like uncertainty than happiness at his willingness to attend.

In the cafeteria Kyle found an empty table in the corner and waited. When Starzi entered he watched the little man fill a cup with coffee, add a splash of creamer and two packets of regular sugar. After he paid the cashier, Starzi scanned the tables until he spotted Kyle.

"You needed to speak with me?" Dr. Starzi pulled out a chair and sat down. "What's so important we couldn't discuss it up on the floor?"

"It's about Victoria," Kyle said. "And your date tomorrow night."

CHAPTER EIGHT

"SORRY I'm late," Victoria yelled as soon as she entered the basement. She slipped out of her shoes and hurried up the stairs. "I'll get dinner started in a minute."

"Take your time," Kyle answered from the kitchen. "Super-chef and I have everything under control. Dinner's almost ready."

What? Victoria stopped at the entrance to the kitchen and took in the wondrous scene before her. Jake, in gray sweatpants, his Superman T, and a red cape, stood on a chair in front of the stove beside Kyle. He had a spatula in one hand, a soup ladle in the other, and a chef's hat fashioned from paper towels on his head.

A warm contentment bloomed in her heart, circulated throughout her body. She smiled. Father and son, working together. Both so handsome.

"Go away, Mom," Jake said, spreading out his arms, and trying to block the burners with his body. "You'll ruin the surprise."

"I'm not looking." She pretended to cover her eyes. "Thank you for picking him up," she said to Kyle.

"Anything I can do to help."

"Where's Tori?" she asked, hoping the dog wasn't curled up on a bed somewhere.

Through the spaces between her fingers she watched Kyle turn to face her. "In Jake's playroom. Go get changed."

Victoria had suffered a twinge of disappointment when Dr. Starzi had cancelled their dinner date earlier that morning. She'd been looking forward to getting to know the man behind the doctor, to seeing if she could rouse up an attraction to more than his high ambitions and outstanding work ethic. But seeing Kyle and Jake together, she realized there's no place she'd rather be than at home with the two of them.

After setting her briefcase in her office and changing into a jogging suit, Victoria returned to the kitchen. She knocked on the wall before entering. "May I come in now?"

Some urgent whispers and contagious giggles later Jake called out, "We're ready."

The small table in the kitchen empty, Victoria entered the dining room. "Very nice," she said, nodding in approval.

"I set the table myself," Jake boasted, and pulled out a chair. "You sit here."

He'd put Kyle in her seat at the head of the rectangular oak table and used Aunt Livi's good china, which she kept in the cabinet above the refrigerator. No way Jake had gotten to it without help.

She raised her eyebrows and slid a questioning glance to Kyle.

He shrugged. "The kid wanted tonight to be special." He placed his cloth napkin in his lap.

"Because it's our first family dinner," Jake said. "And me and Daddy cooked for you." He puffed out his chest proudly.

"Daddy and I," Victoria corrected automatically. "I love it." She kissed Jake on the cheek. "And I love, *you*."

"Kiss Daddy, too," Jake ordered. "He helped."

Kyle extended his cheek in her direction and with a smile she kissed him, too.

"Now let's eat before it gets cold," Kyle said.

In the midst of an excited child who happily discussed his day and his father who listened intently and offered a high five for an A on a spelling test, grilled cheese sandwiches, tomato soup, and baby carrots never tasted so good. "Absolutely perfect," Victoria said, alluding to more than the food.

Kyle and Jake bumped fists then made a show of flaring their fingers on the pull-back.

"After dinner we have man-work to do," Jake said seriously, then slurped his last spoonful of soup.

"Not until your homework's done," Victoria said.

At the same time Kyle said, "After you do your homework."

They shared a smile.

"What do you have planned?" Victoria asked.

"Remember the p-r-e-s-e-n-t we talked about?" Kyle spelled out "present".

"What'd you get me? What'd you get me?" Jake slid off his chair and jumped up and down next to Kyle.

Victoria shrugged. "He's spelling at a fifth-grade level."

"What is it?" Jake asked again. "What's the thing we have to put together?"

Kyle looked at her.

She nodded her permission to tell Jake.

"A pitchback."

"A what?" Jake asked, scrunching his eyebrows together.

"Something to help you practice baseball," Victoria clarified. "If you're done eating, go get your homework," she said.

Jake ran to grab his backpack.

When Victoria stood to clear the table, Kyle stacked his dishes and stood, too.

"Thank you for dinner," she said. "You cooked. I'll clean up."

"I don't mind helping," Kyle offered, and followed her into the kitchen. "You wash. I'll dry."

Sometimes, during the long hours she spent alone, Victoria wondered what it would be like to share her life with a man, to have adult conversation around the dinner table and help with parenting's day-to-day responsibilities. How Jake would respond to welcoming a father figure into their little family. Apparently, if that man were Kyle, there'd be no problem at all. She soaped up and rinsed the first plate and handed it to him.

Having Kyle in such close proximity zapped her recently reawakened libido into full alert mode. Various body parts associated with procreation hummed to life.

Any time. Anywhere. Kyle's words tempted her.

She handed him the second plate. His arm brushed against hers. An enjoyable tickle shot from wrist to elbow.

Then Jake walked into the kitchen and asked, "Can Daddy help me with my homework?"

Kyle. He wanted Kyle to help him. Not her. Helping Jake with his homework was one of her favorite times of the day, the two of them totally focused on one another. She loosened her grip on a delicate bowl for fear she'd break it in two. This was a good thing. She rinsed the suds. After years on her own she now had help. She should be thankful. Accept it. Embrace it. Kyle hesitated, seemed to sense her turmoil.

"Go on," she said with a smile, hoping she'd achieved an air of indifference meant to cover her inner unrest. And as she finished the dishes she listened intently to the sounds coming from the dining room, in awe that Kyle could make even homework fun.

After Jake called out, "We're all done," Kyle entered the kitchen and held out the worksheets they'd completed together. "You'll probably want to check these over." He smiled.

He knew her so well.

"While we're outside we'll replace your basketball net. I picked one up while I was at the store."

There were some definite pluses to having a man around. "Thanks."

"Can I wear my tool belt?" Jake asked.

"You know where it is," Victoria said. Then smiled when, despite Jake's complaints, Kyle insisted he needed to wear a coat. Like a father, not a buddy.

Progress.

"And grab your glove," Kyle said to Jake. "When we're done we can throw the baseball around." He turned to Victoria and said, "Come outside with us."

"But you're going to do man-work." She smiled. "Male bonding over tools is not really my thing."

"It'll take fifteen minutes. Twenty tops. Promise you'll come out then."

"I have work to do." Between her job and school and the house there was always something that needed her time and attention.

"It'll keep for an hour. Come on. Have some fun with us."

She wanted to but, "I don't have a glove."

Kyle held up his index finger. "Are you saying if you had a glove you'd come out and have a catch with us?"

No. "It's a moot point because I don't have one."

"Wait right there." Kyle turned, jogged down the stairs and out the front door. A minute later he came back the way he'd left, carrying a bag from the sporting goods store. At the top of the stairs he handed it to her.

"What's that?" Jake asked, walking down the hall with his kid-sized tool belt around his waist, carrying his baseball glove in one hand and his coat in the other.

"Open it," Kyle said to Victoria.

She looked inside the bag. He'd gotten her a baseball glove.

"It's one you tried on when we were shopping for Jake," Kyle said.

She looked up at him. "You went back to the store and bought it for me?"

"So you could play with us," Kyle said.

It was truly the nicest, most thoughtful gift she'd ever received. "Thank you."

"Twenty minutes," Kyle said with a pointed look. "Promise?"

Victoria nodded, actually looking forward to it.

"Don't worry I'll get them," Jake yelled to Victoria when she missed the last of their six balls and it rolled across the yard to join the others.

"I catch like a girl," Victoria said, frustrated by her lack of skill.

"To catch like a girl you'd actually have to *catch* the ball." Kyle shot her a wink.

Victoria took off her glove. "I'm ruining your fun."

"Nah." Kyle wandered over to stand beside her. "I think we're ready to do something else."

"How about hopscotch?" Jake asked, running toward them, his jacket pockets stuffed with balls.

Kyle grabbed for his chest dramatically. "Say it isn't so." He stumbled to the ground. "My son plays hop-scotch?"

"I'm good at it, too," Jake said undeterred. "I'll get the chalk." He ran into the garage.

"What's wrong with hopscotch?" Victoria asked. It helped Jake learn his numbers and improve his coordination. "It's not as easy as it looks."

"You're going to get the kid beat up playing that girly game."

"Don't be ridiculous." Victoria waved him off.

Jake came out of the garage carrying his bucket of multicolored chalk.

"Please tell me he doesn't play with pink chalk, too?" Kyle moaned.

"Knock it off." Victoria nudged his arm with the toe of her sneaker.

Kyle sat up. "I have a better game," he suggested. "Crime scene."

Victoria didn't like the sound of that one bit.

Jake did. "Cool!" He ran to Kyle. "How do we play?"

"Allow me to demonstrate." He flopped back on the driveway his arms and legs spread wide. "Now outline me with chalk. You do the top half," he said to Jake. "Your mom can do the bottom."

Oh, goodie. She reached into the bucket of chalk,

spotted one of her favorite colors and decided to have a little fun.

Unfortunately Kyle caught her. "No pink chalk." He rolled away. "What kind of television do you watch? The real cops outline the bodies in white chalk."

"Even I know that, Mom," Jake agreed.

And he did, in fact, have a white piece of chalk in his hand. "How on earth would you know something like that?" Victoria exchanged her chalk for a more acceptable color. Yellow. This time she hid it from view.

"When I go to Frankie's house," Jake said, "*his* mom lets us watch whatever we want on TV."

No more visits to Frankie's house.

"Stop yapping and start tracing," Kyle said. "It's cold down here."

Victoria started at his hip, moved the chalk down around his boot and up his inner thigh.

"You want to get in real close to the body," he said, challenging her, "so the drawing looks realistic."

She rounded the apex of his thighs, brushed the taut denim, saw movement beneath his zipper. She hesitated, watched, returned to his knee and started again. He shifted his pelvis.

"Come on, Mom," Jake said. "I'm done already."

She continued down the other side. "He's got long legs," she pointed out. Long, muscular, appealing legs. Stop it.

When it was her turn to play corpse, Kyle had no problem keeping tight to the curves of her body. So much so that she almost sent Jake inside to get her a drink so she could steal a kiss and feel his hands on her for real.

After each one had a turn, they traced each other in

contorted positions and before long the driveway really did look like a crime scene. Victoria hoped for rain to wash it away.

Kyle looked at his watch. "Almost eight o'clock," he called out to Jake, who'd lost interest in Crime Scene and was chasing Tori. "Time to clean up and go inside." To Victoria's surprise she'd been having so much fun she'd lost all track of time. When was the last time that had happened?

Kyle showed her how to collapse the pitchback and while he and Jake carried it into the garage Victoria headed upstairs.

Outside the kitchen Jake asked, "After my shower can Daddy read to me?"

Victoria clamped both hands around the wrought-iron railing, hesitated and tried not to let her hurt show. Reading to Jake before bed was their special time together, to cuddle and wind down from the day. Having Kyle here was a novelty, that's all, she tried to convince herself. It's not like Jake preferred Kyle. Tomorrow night would be back to normal. She forced a smile. "Sure, honey." She reached down to flatten a rogue curl. "If that's what you want."

Kyle watched her. Understanding dawned. "How about your mom and I both read to you tonight?"

"Even better." Jake bounced on his toes and clapped.

"Meet you in the bathroom," Victoria said. She waited for Jake to ask for his dad to help him and felt an irrational, profound relief when he didn't.

"Thank you," she said to Kyle.

He placed his hand on her shoulder. "I know this isn't easy."

No. It wasn't. For so many reasons.

Half an hour later Kyle followed her out of Jake's room.

"I know I've said it before but he really is a great kid," Kyle whispered. "Helpful, respectful and eager to please. You've done an awesome job raising him."

His words came as sweet music to her ears, confirmation she'd done well despite her concerns she didn't spend enough time with Jake, was too strict, too serious. For some reason, praise from Jake's father meant so much more than she'd imagined it would. Moisture accumulated at the base of her eyelashes.

Kyle loosely gripped her arm, stopping her. "Thank you," he said with heartfelt gratitude. "For not getting rid of him. For all you had to give up to keep him. For raising him better than I could have done on my own." He turned her, lifted her chin, and looked deeply into her eyes. "You are an amazing woman, Victoria Forley." And he kissed her.

A gentle, sensual, wonderful kiss.

He wrapped his arms around her and twirled them into the kitchen, landing with his back to the counter. She pushed up against him, relished the evidence of his arousal. For her. And decided it was time. Tonight. With Kyle. They may not love each other, may not have any future together aside from raising Jake, but she cared for him and could tell he cared for her. More importantly she trusted him, believed he would be careful with her, listen to her.

"Remember when you said I could practice? With you? Any time? Anywhere?"

Kyle held her close, rested his chin on top of her head and said, "Yeah."

"How about tonight? In my bedroom?"

She braced herself to be scooped up and carried off down the hall.

Instead Kyle placed a hand on each of her shoulders and eased her away. "Are you sure?" he asked, totally calm and in control.

At her nod, he reached for her hand and quietly led the way to her room.

There was no mad dash to the bed, no heated frenzy to tear off each other's clothes.

Kyle locked the door. "Do you want the light on or off?" he asked.

"On," she said. "I want to see you." To survey every beauty mark and muscle and hair follicle.

He smiled and walked toward her.

Surprisingly, she felt more excited than nervous. Eager. Ready.

"There's something I want to try. But first..." She reached for the hem of his T-shirt and asked, "May I?"

He tilted his head in agreeable fashion and like they were attending high tea and she'd asked for a taste of one of his sweet cakes he answered, "Please do."

His chest bare, she ran her fingers over the hills and valleys of his beautiful physique, set her cheek to his soft, warm skin and inhaled his scrumptious masculine scent.

He brought his arms around her and gently caressed her back.

"I like this," she said. This closeness with a man. With Kyle.

"Me, too," he agreed.

But she wanted to give him pleasure, needed to prove she could do it. With her hands leading the way, down his sides to his hips, she dropped to her knees, looked up, and smiled at his look of surprise. "Okay?"

"Sure, but…"

She unsnapped the button of his jeans, shutting him up, then eased the zipper down over his growing erection. Excitement fizzed inside her. She slipped a finger under the elastic waistband, freeing him, and lowered his underwear and pants together.

Kyle stood perfectly still, his magnificent erection pointing due north. As a nurse she'd seen hundreds of naked men over the years. But none had made her want like this one. She reached for him, suffered a moment's hesitation, remembering—*No, not like that. When Leanne does it she…*

Big hands surrounded hers, eased her on to his heated flesh. "Like this," he said, showing her what he liked.

For something so big and hard his skin felt remarkably smooth.

Kyle expelled a breath. "Damn."

She let the curse slide.

Remembering a scene from one of her favorite novels, Victoria took him deep into her mouth.

Kyle moaned.

Eyes closed, head tossed back, his look of absolute enjoyment thrilled Victoria. She retreated, relished the feel of him inside her mouth. When she reached the tip she swirled her tongue and took him deep a second time.

Again he moaned.

Victoria's confidence grew. She loved this power to control his pleasure, to go at her own pace, to make him come. And she set to work doing just that.

* * *

Kyle kept his eyes closed for fear the sight of Victoria on her knees at his feet would be too much. Lord help him, he couldn't remember any woman arousing him more.

He clasped his hands behind his butt to keep from coming on too strong, controlling her or scaring her. But, damn, if she kept it up he was in real danger of coming embarrassingly quick. He needed to think about something other than her moist lips and soft tongue and hot mouth.

Twenty-six bones in the foot.

She sucked him deeper. He fought the urge to thrust into her, his control growing fickle.

Calcaneus. Talus. Navicular.

She gripped him with both hands, moving them in tandem with her mouth.

Medial cuneiform. Intermediate cuneiform. Lateral cuneiform.

"Am I doing this right?" she asked, sounding frustrated. "Shouldn't you be gripping my head or telling me how good my mouth feels on you?" She looked up at him. "Maybe moving a little, like you're enjoying yourself?"

He almost laughed out loud, but didn't, although it was touch and go for a few seconds. "Is that what the men do in those trashy books you read?"

"They're not trashy." She pouted. "And yes. They do. If I'm doing something wrong, you need to tell me."

"Baby." He slid his fingers through her short hair. "You are doing everything right." Any more right and he'd be basking in post-orgasmic bliss. "I'm trying to be on my best behavior since you're new at this." Wait a minute. Could she possibly have developed such skill solely from reading romance novels? "You are new at this, aren't you?"

She nodded. "Pathetic, isn't it?"

"It is light years away from pathetic." It was exciting yet humbling at the same time. "And for the record, you've pushed me to the edge so quick I feel like a teenage newbie."

Still on her knees, she looked away. "It's not the same when I have to ask you to say it."

Leave it to Victoria to give him a hard time during a blowjob.

"I'm sorry. I've ruined the mood," she said. "Maybe you should go." She started to stand.

Nothing short of a five-alarm fire with flames posing a direct threat to them or Jake could make him leave her bedroom right now. He placed his hand on her shoulder, halting her movement. "Honey, I bet we can get it back in under a minute." Under fifteen seconds.

"You think so?"

"I'm certain."

Not one to back down from a challenge, Victoria took him back into her mouth. And yessiree, he'd been correct. "You see what you do to me?"

Cuboid. First metatarsal. Second metatarsal.

He cupped the back of her head, careful to not make her feel forced in any way. And, Oh. My. God. His vision went blurry. A delicious pressure started to build.

So good. Too good. But when Victoria set her mind to something there was no stopping her. And, frankly, he only half wanted to.

The urge to come was too powerful to stop. "I'm going to…" was all he could choke out before a deluge of frenzied lust took over. His hips moved of their own accord. His knees weak, his mind a haze of ecstasy, satiated perfection.

Heart pounding, lungs heaving, Kyle felt like he'd just finished a full marathon. Totally spent. Drained. He reached out a hand to steady himself against the wall,

"Wow," Victoria said as she stood and bent to brush off her knees. "I did it."

"Yes, you did. And I'd like to check out a few of those books you like to read." He pulled her against his chest and kissed the top of her head. "Give me a moment to rebound and I'll do *it* to you."

"Yeah. About that." She pushed away, looking suddenly nervous. "It's getting late." She faked a yawn. "Maybe another time."

Like he'd let her go that easy. "Give me fifteen minutes. Let me make you feel as good as you made me feel."

"Fifteen minutes. You are a fast one." She fidgeted with her watch. "But if it's all the same to you, I'd rather not rush." She looked everywhere but at him. "I'm thinking we'll need at least an hour. Maybe two."

In a perfect world.

He hated to see her distressed, but if he had any hope of helping her conquer her fears, of making her comfortable with his touch and rekindling an intimate relationship between them, he couldn't let her run from him any longer.

"Come here." He kept his voice quiet, held out his hand palm up. Inviting, not commanding. She needed to come to him on her own. And he was prepared to wait as long as it took.

"I may not be able to…"

"You will," he said, confident he could give her the ultimate satisfaction.

"What if I have a panic attack?"

"You won't."

She flung her hands to the sides and cried out, "How do you know?"

"Because we are going to take it slow, and you decide how far we go." He kept his voice calm. "We're going to talk the entire time I'm touching you. I'll tell you what I plan to do before I do it, and you'll tell me what you like and don't like." He wanted to step toward her, meet her halfway. He didn't. "You're going to tell me if anything I do makes you even the tiniest bit uncertain or uncomfortable, and I will stop immediately. I won't let you go back into that closet." He cheated and leaned, just a little. "I want you right here, with me, in the present, the entire time."

Kyle understood. He'd always had an uncanny ability to figure her out, to burrow to the root of her moods, identify the catalyst then soothe with affection or diffuse with distraction and humor. In their short time together he'd grown to know her better than anyone else, and it seemed he still did. He held out his hand to her. An offer from a caring friend, a boy she'd once loved, a man she trusted to help her through the next fifteen minutes.

She took it.

He blew out a relieved breath.

"I like it when you kiss me," she said.

He smiled and gave a little tug. "Then let's start with that."

Victoria walked forward, her head tilted, up her lips ready.

His kisses disarmed as much as they enchanted, made her want, no need, more. She looped her arms behind his neck and held him close.

"I need to sit," he said against her lips. "Come." He shifted them toward the bed. "Straddle my lap." A marvelous idea. But once settled into place she realized he'd be holding up their combined weights with nothing to support his back. "This can't be comfortable for you."

"Honey, I could be sitting with my bare butt on a block of ice and be perfectly content as long as I had your body right where it is."

Good. Because she liked their current position, she rocked her hips along his length. A lot.

"I want to see you," he whispered, and reached for the zipper of her jacket. He waited for her to nod her agreement before he proceeded to lower it.

Then with the care and skill of a seasoned artisan handling delicate gold leaf he divested her of her clothes until he had her naked from the waist up, giving her a play by play of everything he planned to do before he did it.

"You're beautiful," he said with the perfect amount of reverence. "I'm going to kiss you now," he said, then listed the spots he planned to show some attention. Her neck, collarbones, breasts and nipples tingled at their mention.

At the end of his titillating journey, Victoria ached for him to shift his focus to the empty, throbbing place inside her, to fill her and make her whole. As if he could sense her need, he slid his hands below the elastic of her sports pants, palmed her butt cheeks, and pulled her against him as he undulated beneath her.

"I can feel your heat through my jeans," he said, his breath coming in harsh pants. "Tell me you're ready. Tell me you want me." Keeping up his assault down below, he ducked his head and kissed her.

At that moment fear and uncertainty were distant emotions, a protective safety zone of arousal and desperate yearning keeping them at bay. "Please," she said. "Make love to me. Like this. Just like this."

"Take off your pants," he said. Not a command, a plea.

Done. She had her remaining clothes discarded before he'd fully unzipped his jeans. So she helped him.

"Hold on." He pulled out his wallet and took out two condoms.

"A-plus for positive thinking," Victoria said. "But one should be sufficient."

He smiled and pushed his briefs and pants to the floor. "We'll see." Her mouth watered at the glorious sight of him, as he rolled on a condom and returned to the bed.

"Come."

With that goal in mind, she climbed back onto his lap, the feel of him between her legs making her weak with desire.

He moved his hand, stroking and circling, around where she wanted him, closer, almost there, before moving away.

"Tease," she said.

Totally serious he told her, "I need to feel you. Please."

She nodded, fought the urge to clench around him

as his fingers slid in and out of her primed body easily. Spectacularly.

"My God." He dropped his head onto her shoulder and trembled. "You feel so unbelievably good." With that pronouncement he removed his hand, placed it on the bed behind him and leaned back. Waited.

Now it was her turn. *You feel so unbelievably good.* She could do this, would do this.

"Kiss me," Kyle said, leaning forward just enough for their lips to meet. She sank down on top of him, lifted then lowered herself again, each time taking a little more of him into her body. He stretched her, but where the first time there'd been discomfort, this time she simply felt a sublime fullness, the best possible kind of full.

He kissed down the side of her neck. "You okay?" he whispered.

Better than okay. "Yeah."

He groaned. "You have no idea what you're doing to me."

Then he pushed in the rest of the way, shifted beneath her, and she felt it. The connection she'd hoped for all those years ago, the melding of body and soul, the binding of two people in love. And part of her loved him still. His caring nature at work and with Jake, his commitment to being a good father, and his ability to spark her to life with the simple act of entering a room. They were different. She ambitious, he content. She stressed, he carefree. She serious, he fun. But they complemented each other. Was that enough to build a relationship on? To try again? Did she even want to? Did he? Or was this nothing more than sex between two old lovers? A one-time therapeutic, guilt-easing joining to absolve him of the past?

"What are you thinking about?" he asked.

"Nothing," she lied, picking up the pace, determined to finish.

Kyle groaned, the sound empowering.

She moved fast, liking the ability to control his pleasure.

"That's it," Kyle said. "Just like that. And if you care for me at all, you will not stop again."

Victoria settled into a rhythm that had Kyle's breath coming in pants. Before long her breathing matched his.

"Lean back and put your hands on my knees," Kyle said.

She did. And the next time he surged deep a solar flare of wonderfulness shot off inside her. "That was…" he hit the same spot again "…so…" The third time her cry of completion joined his and she would have collapsed to the floor if Kyle hadn't caught her.

Holding her against his chest, still inside her, Kyle fell back on the bed, bringing Victoria with him. He hugged her close and kissed the top of her head. "That was…amazing."

And the magnitude of the moment hit. She'd done it. Had sex. Amazingly great sex. Without panic or fear. She lifted her head and looked at Kyle through blurry eyes. "Thank you," she said, unable to control her emotions. "Thank you." She collapsed onto his chest and cried.

"Honey," Kyle said. "What's wrong? Shhh." He caressed her back. "Please, don't cry."

Relief and satisfaction and utter contentment at being in Kyle's arms sent her to a tranquil place. "I didn't think I could do it." She let her eyelids drift closed, completely relaxed for the first time. "Thank you for showing me I can."

"With me," he said, then tightened his hold on her. "Only with me."

At some point, Victoria couldn't pinpoint exactly when, Kyle must have tucked her into bed. She awoke to him snuggled in behind her, his hot, naked body pressed to hers, and for a few minutes imagined Jake was someplace else so she could spend the entire night in Kyle's arms, every night in Kyle's arms, every minute.

Good Lord, stop it. She opened her eyes. She was not some infatuated teenager. She was a woman with responsibilities and a ten-year plan, a woman who would not lose focus on her goals because of a man. No matter how yummy that man turned out to be or how right it felt to be cuddled up next to him.

CHAPTER NINE

KYLE never understood a woman's desire to cuddle after sex. He did it to make them happy, but got the heck out of there at the first opportunity. So why did he hold Victoria in his arms, her back molded to his front, worried if he let go they might never share this closeness again?

Because she'd been ripped away from him once.

"Are you awake?" she asked.

"Yeah."

"About the employee of the month dinner."

"That mind of your never shuts down, does it?"

"Not often. And not for long." She lifted the hand she held and kissed his palm. "You don't have to go if you don't want to."

If you'd rather he not accompany you, he's not the man to build your promising future around.

"If you're going to be there, of course I want to go." He hesitated. "Unless you'd rather I didn't."

A tense silence ensued.

"You know it's black tie?"

Was that all that was bothering her? "I seem to recall the nursing director mentioning that."

"You know what that means, right?"

"I don't live under a rock. Of course I know what it means." He kissed the back of her head. It wouldn't be the first penguin-themed affair he'd attended.

"I figured the last thing you'd want to do on a Saturday night is dress up in a tux."

"True." He cuddled her close and nibbled her ear. "I'd much rather be dressed in my birthday suit."

"Cut it out," she said, and smacked his arm playfully. "I'm worried you're going to have a terrible time."

Probably. "But you'll make it worth my while afterwards, won't you?"

"I'll do my best." She rubbed his thigh. "Shoot. I forgot. I'm on the planning committee so I'll have to be at the dinner two hours early. Would you mind meeting me there?"

"That'll give me some extra time to work on the little surprise I have planned for you." He'd been thinking about it since finding out about the upcoming affair.

"A surprise?" She partially turned onto her back to face him. "Will I like it?"

"That's the plan."

"What is it?"

"I'll never tell," he teased.

She turned to face him, well, his chest anyway, and reached her hand down between them. "I bet I can make you."

Damn, she was a fast learner. "Feeling confident?" He rolled onto his back. "Give it your best shot."

As successful as her attempt had been, it wasn't enough to get him to share his secret then, or any of the other times she'd tried over the next week. But he'd sure enjoyed her efforts.

* * *

Kyle looked in his rearview mirror, straightened his black bow tie and grabbed the corsage from the passenger seat.

He ignored the looks of disdain from a snobby older couple, the white-haired man dressed in a perfectly cut tuxedo and the white-haired woman wearing a full-length fur coat, and, head held high, pulled open the door to the hospital's catering hall and entered the den of vipers.

The first person he saw was Mr. Wheeton, owner of Wheeton's Pharmacy. Kyle fought the urge to confront the man, remembered the helpless anger of being accused of stealing condoms, being restrained and having to deal with the cops, when he'd done nothing wrong. Mr. Wheeton had said nothing to the well-dressed boys who'd actually stolen them and had laughed at Kyle's predicament on their way out of the store. Even though a humiliating search of Kyle's clothes and backpack had turned up nothing, Mr. Wheeton had not apologized, and he'd barred Kyle from the store anyway.

Mr. Wheeton, who had not aged well, looked Kyle over and nodded in approval, obviously not recognizing him. Teenage Kyle would have shot him the finger. Adult Kyle simply turned away without acknowledging him. This was going to be a long night.

He entered the ballroom and spotted Victoria right away, talking to a group of women beside the dance floor. Rather than approach her, he decided to take a few minutes to savor the beauty of the striking, knee-length red satin dress that showcased her fabulous figure and enjoy the anticipation of being the envy of every man in this room once he took her into his arms.

At least he'd thought so until she noticed him and

charged in his direction, looking ready to engage the enemy in battle. "How could you do this to me?" She glanced from side to side and dragged him into a quiet corner. "I specifically told you this is a black tie affair, and you show up in jeans? What were you thinking?"

He pointed to his brand-new black bow tie. "I am wearing a black tie." He waited for her to notice his snazzy new black suit jacket and $100.00 dress shoes.

If she did, she didn't mention them.

"You think this is a joke? Some sick joke?" Her eyes widened in horror. "Is that the same black T you wear to work every day?" She made it sound like he only had one and hadn't washed it. "You couldn't even buy a nice dress shirt? Why, Kyle? Why tonight of all nights?"

She sounded frantic. Her breathing sped up. She was really upset. "Whoa, honey." He reached for her. "Calm down."

She twisted away. "Calm down?" she asked loud enough to attract the attention of two couples standing nearby. "Calm down?" she asked, again, even louder. "My father is here," she snapped. "I haven't spoken to him in over eight years. I haven't seen him in over two. And he's here. Tonight. In this very room."

Kyle went on guard, scanned the crowd. "Did you know he was coming?"

She clutched her fist to her chest and inhaled deeply. "No, I didn't know he was coming. He's on the board of directors but he's never come to a dinner before." She looked Kyle up and down. "And you, my date, show up looking like the troublemaker you were in high school."

"This is not as big a deal as you're making it out to be."

She stiffened and narrowed her eyes into angry slits.

"It's a big deal to me. You have no idea how long and hard I've had to work to earn the respect of the people in this room," she said in a curt whisper. "And the first date I bring makes a mockery of the formal nature of the affair."

"You're joking, right? You were born into these people, you *are* these people."

Had her eyes been swords, he'd no doubt have two lengths of steel penetrating his brain. "You mistake me for the girl you knew in high school, before I got pregnant and had my previous life stripped from me," she said tightly. "Almost everyone in this room knows me as a nurses' aide who went to community college, someone who benefited from the hospital's scholarship program. I don't have a fancy degree from a prestigious university to recommend me. I have worked and networked and, yes, kissed butt, and I am on track to become the youngest director of nursing in the history of Madrin Falls Memorial Hospital. And how do you think my skeptics will view my ability to manage a three-hundred-bed facility when I can't even manage my date?" She glanced around. "Perfect. Everyone's staring at you."

Only a few people, and probably due to her carrying on more than his attire. "They're staring at you because you're the prettiest woman in the room," he said to pacify her. "Here." He handed her the corsage.

"You got me a wrist corsage? Made of daisies?"

"Your favorites." Apparently not anymore because she held the plastic carton like it contained a dead lizard.

He took advantage of her silence to explain. "You missed your senior prom because of me. I thought maybe we could pretend tonight is prom, you know, recreate the magic, and…" he held his hands out to the sides "…this is what I would have worn. I could have rented a tux and showed up like the rest of these yahoos, but then the night wouldn't have been special."

"It would have been special for me," she pointed out. "So this is your big surprise?" Well, yeah. Recreate prom. Show up with a corsage. Dance too close. Maybe sneak outside and steal a kiss beneath the stars. And right about now she was supposed to be in his arms, telling him what a wonderful idea it was and how much she appreciated the thoughtful gesture.

He waited.

The MC took the microphone and directed everyone to take their seats.

Victoria didn't move.

The director of nursing walked over and looked Kyle up and down in her usual disapproving way. "Is everything okay over here?"

Victoria held her corsage behind her hip, out of view. "Yes," she said. "Fine."

"Come," the director said. "Let's find our table."

Our table. Kyle had an ominous feeling the night, which started off teetering precariously close to the edge of disaster, had just been pushed into its depths.

"Kyle was just leaving," Victoria said. "He only came to drop off…"

What? He couldn't believe his ears. His outfit embarrassed her to the point she'd rather toss him aside than be seen with him? And without a crumb of appreciation for his attempt to make up for her missing prom? At that moment, Victoria epitomized everything he'd rebelled against. Fine. She wanted him gone, he'd go.

Unfortunately, before he could escape, the director threw a beefy arm around his waist and anchored him in place. "Nonsense," she said, then turned to Victoria. "You're an honoree, dear. You must be accompanied by a date."

Exactly where was that written?

When they reached their table the director said in her booming voice, "Ladies and gentlemen, may I present our lovely Victoria's date, Dr. Kyle Karlinsky."

A hush fell over the table and a few of the surrounding tables as men and women checked him over with disapproval. Unfazed, he plastered a fake smile on his face and pulled out Victoria's chair. She stood so stiffly he half expected to hear a crack when she sat down and bent to hide her purse and the corsage he and Jake had designed specially for her under the table.

As the MC droned on, his voice an irritating buzz in Kyle's head, he drifted to peruse the crowd, recognized his pain-in-the-butt high-school principal, the stodgy mayor, and Victoria's father, whose eyes shot poisoned darts of contempt in his direction.

Acting cool, while his body shifted into fight mode, Kyle slid his left arm around the back of Victoria's chair and lifted his beer in a toast to him. Intense hatred flared in the man's eyes.

The swallow of brew that followed did not go down easily.

Kyle's life had come full circle, landing him under the scrutiny of the societal elite who'd judged and condemned him in his youth, who despised him as much as he despised them. Only tonight Victoria stood among them. And while he couldn't care less what the others thought, Victoria's opinion mattered. He should have realized how important this night was to her and dressed the part, not focused on his need to make up for the past. Stupid. Stupid.

When Victoria took the small stage she looked radiant, poised and genuinely pleased. To her apparent surprise, before letting her sit down, the MC read three letters of praise for Victoria and her staff, the last from Senator Madrin, then handed her the microphone. In response she gave an impromptu speech that was both succinct and impressive, and held the audience rapt. Kyle watched, with pride, the ease with which she engaged the crowd and earned their adoration. She belonged up there, a polished speaker, a born leader. The director beamed as if she'd birthed Victoria herself. Victoria's father focused on his daughter. Proud. Bereft. He tossed back a shot of what looked like whisky.

After being ignored through the ceremony, Kyle leaned in to apologize over salad. "I'm sorry."

"It's okay." Victoria smiled politely.

But it wasn't, a fact she made all too clear each time she refused his request to dance.

As if their tablemates picked up on the discord between them and took it as a personal affront, they made little effort to include him in their conversations, which suited Kyle just fine. He hated judgmental idiots who formed opinions about a person based on their attire or where they lived. Screw them all. He had nothing in common with these people and could not wait to leave.

He took a swig of beer, open bar the only bright spot of the evening.

"Well, well, well. If it isn't the happy couple," a familiar voice slurred behind him.

Victoria went rigid.

"You did great up there, honey," her father said. "Then you sat down next to this hoodlum and lost all credibility."

"Please don't do this, Daddy," she pleaded, looking down at her plate.

Kyle calmly placed his napkin on the table and stood. "Why don't we take this outside, sir?" he suggested.

Victoria's father swayed on his feet as he turned his enraged eyes on Kyle's. "Back to claim the prize, huh, gutter rat?"

"Nothing can stand in the way of true love," he answered quietly, then leaned in and added, "Not even a bogus rape charge."

Victoria pushed back her chair and stood. "How could you?" she asked her father, the hurt in her voice provoking a physical pain in Kyle's gut.

"Figured that out, did you?" Her father laughed, the sound pure evil. "Well, it served its purpose well enough."

"And what purpose was that?" Kyle asked. A dangerous rage gathered strength. "Breaking your daughter's heart? Controlling her life?" A concentrated loathing oozed and boiled in his core. "And what kind of father disowns his child when she needs him most? Leaves his daughter and grandson to struggle?"

The old man still had some muscle on him because he pushed Kyle back into the table hard enough to send glasses flying. Something shattered. A woman shrieked in alarm. The chatter around them came to a halt. Kyle knew he should stop, walk away, but he couldn't, the opportunity to make her father pay for his heinous acts, for manipulating *him*, making him miss out on eight years of his son's life and separating him from the only woman he'd ever loved, too appealing to pass up.

"She'll always be too good for you," the other man spat. "Look in the mirror. You'll never measure up, never be man enough to deserve her."

"That's not true." Victoria stepped between them. "Kyle's a PhD. He's doing a fantastic job at the hospital. He's a wonderful father to Jake."

"His illegitimate son."

Victoria recoiled, glanced at her father then at the surrounding crowd in absolute horror and humiliation.

Kyle imagined how good the crunch of Mr. Forley's eye socket would feel against his knuckles. Fists up and ready to do damage, Kyle stepped forward. Time for Daddy to pay for his sins.

"He's an embarrassment." Mr. Forley moved his hand up and down as if displaying Kyle's faults. "A low-class nothing. Look at him, ready to brawl like a common street thug."

"I like it better when you ignore me, Dad," Victoria said, sounding tired. "You've had too much to drink. Let me find you a ride home."

Kyle tried to sidestep around her so he could wipe that smug—

"Stop it." She flung her arm out to stop him and glared up into his eyes, determined, her body trembling with anger. "If you don't walk away this instant I swear on my mother's grave I will take Jake in the middle of the night and you will never see either of us again."

They were almost at her house, without one word uttered between them, when Kyle pointed to Victoria's lap and said, "You should put that on. Jake helped me pick it out." Which made her feel even more terrible.

She opened the plastic container, the sound unexpectedly loud in the quiet car, and slipped the elastic band onto her wrist. "Thank you," she said quietly. "For the flowers and pretend prom. It was sweet." But she'd been too blinded by panic at seeing her dad for the first time in years and disappointment over Kyle's apparel choice on such an important evening to acknowledge it until now.

"Just not the right time or place," he conceded.

"No," she agreed.

"Jake and I thought daisies were your favorites."

She stared out at the shadows of the passing landscape. "Because he picks them for me." Like Kyle used to whenever they'd visited their special spot by the lake.

"Do you have a favorite flower?"

"Roses. Look, I'm sorry for giving you a hard time. When you said you had a surprise I assumed you'd rented a tux. I got all pumped up to show you off and introduce you around. Then Dad showed up and I thought, even better. Let him see firsthand how he'd misjudged you, how well you turned out."

"And the only way you could be proud to show me off, the only way to prove I turned out well, was if I showed up in a tux?"

He made her sound like a superficial snob. Maybe she was. "It shouldn't matter, I know," she said. "But it does." Especially now when she had so much riding on the professional reputation she'd spent years cultivating, which after tonight probably equaled the value of one pair of contaminated disposable gloves.

He drove down her driveway, parked next to Roxie's car, and turned off the ignition.

"Goodnight," she said, hoping to end it at that.

"I promised Jake I'd come in to tell him about our night."

"Fine." Victoria slipped out of the truck and jumped down without waiting for him to assist her. Five minutes, that's it. Then she needed to figure out how to salvage her career after the airing of her past in a room filled with people pivotal to her advancement at the hospital. And distance herself from Kyle.

It was going to be a long, sleepless night.

But evaluating, planning and strategizing got pushed to the back of her mind upon first glimpse of the mess that greeted her in the hallway outside Jake's playroom. Victoria felt on the verge of bursting into flame.

"What do you think, Mom?" Jake asked, bobbing on bare toes that peeked out from beneath his pajama pants, his fingers clasped together, an elated smile on his face.

"I think you should be in bed." She spoke to Jake but glared at Roxie, who held up both hands in surrender.

"You said you'd be home to kiss him goodnight," Roxie said. "He was concerned if he got into bed he'd fall asleep and miss it. You know I have trouble saying no to the tyke."

Victoria scanned the haphazard piles of toys and stacks of books lining the downstairs hallway. "Obviously."

"Ah, well," Roxie said with a swift swivel toward the stairs. "Gotta run. Work tomorrow. Want to get a good night's sleep so I'm ready to give it my all bright and early." In thirty seconds tops she collected her things and closed the front door behind her.

"Why?" Victoria asked, standing in the doorway of Jake's emptied-out playroom.

"Me and Roxie were talking," Jake said, cautious, his eyes wide, recognizing she was not as happy about his surprise as he'd been a moment earlier.

"Roxie and I," Victoria corrected automatically.

"That it didn't make sense for Dad to live all by himself when we have room for him to live here," Jake continued.

Roxie had better hope Victoria forgave her by Monday or she'd be assigned to narcotics count, crash-cart check and the night shift for a month.

"I said he could move into my room, but me and Roxie..." Jake stopped. "I mean, Roxie and I decided Dad was too big for bunk beds."

If she hadn't been so at odds with him, the thought of Kyle's big body hanging over a top bunk might have brought a smile to her lips.

"And you need your office to do your work, Mom."

"So you cleaned out your playroom to make a place for me to stay," Kyle said.

Would this nightmare of a night ever end?

Jake's excitement returned. "The couch turns into a bed, and we left you the TV and some movies."

Kyle knelt down and opened his arms, his sincere appreciation for Jake's thoughtfulness evident. "Come here."

With a great big smile Jake ran to his dad, jumped at his chest, and clamped his arms around Kyle's neck. "That's the nicest thing anyone has ever done for me." Kyle hugged him tightly and kissed his cheek.

"It's time for bed," Victoria said. Time to take back control of her life.

"Can Daddy tuck me in?"

Another toothpick to the heart. "Not tonight, honey," Victoria said.

"But we have to talk about guy stuff," Jake begged.

"Your mom said no, Jake." Kyle sounded stern. Fatherly. "We can talk tomorrow."

Jake cupped his hands around his mouth and asked in a stage whisper, "Did she like the flowers?"

"She loved them," Kyle answered.

Victoria looked down at the pretty white petals. "I did," she said. "I do. It was so nice of you and Daddy to buy them for me."

Jake stood in the hallway, the disappointed, argumentative face that usually preceded one of his infrequent meltdowns looking up at her. Victoria could not handle one more confrontation this evening so she gave in. "Oh, go ahead," she said to Kyle. "Five minutes," she stressed to Jake, holding up five fingers for emphasis.

"Yay! Come on, Dad," Jake said. And Kyle followed him up the stairs.

Victoria had just poured a cup of herbal tea when she heard Kyle emerge from Jake's room. She didn't move, had hoped to be safely locked away in her bedroom before he left.

"You okay?" he asked from the doorway.

Was she okay? Whoever said, "There is no such thing as a stupid question," had been wrong. "You mean for someone who's lost any chance at the promotion that was the foundation of her ten-year plan? Or someone who may find herself searching for a new job next week? Maybe someone who's going to have to explain to her son why he has to go to a state school because she can't afford a private college?" She dunked her tea bag so aggressively water splashed onto the counter.

"It's not as bad as all that," Kyle said from directly behind her.

"Oh, no?" She turned on him. "You have psychic powers?" She held out her palm. "Please. Give me a reading." Her anger started to escalate. How dare he minimize the magnitude of this evening's events? "Tell me when I can expect to be offered the director's job. Make sure to take into consideration the stigma of teenage pregnancy. Oh. And the fact my date to a major hospital function, the father of my son, a man who is already on the outs with the director of nursing—the woman who gets final say in her replacement and holds control of my future—for rebelling against the hospital dress code, showed up in jeans. Oh. And here's the best part. Are you ready? And then gets into a public altercation with the hospital's chairman of the board."

"Your father is chairman of the board? Hell."

"I couldn't have said it better myself." Victoria thrust her palm at him, purposely poking her fingers into his chest. "So go ahead. Give a look. Exactly when can I expect the promotion that will finally give me the financial security I need to ensure my son's future? My guess is one week after never," she yelled.

"Calm down," Kyle said. "You're going to wake Jake."

"I'll calm down after you leave." Hopefully. Maybe after a hard run on the treadmill for an hour.

"I'm not leaving until you calm down."

"You're the one making me crazy," she screamed.

Like an absolute lunatic. She dropped her head and let out a breath. "I'm sorry."

"Come, sit at the table," Kyle said, reaching around her to pick up her cup. "Talk to me. Tell me why this job is so important to you."

Thinking maybe it would help him understand why she needed to put the kibosh on their budding relationship, Victoria sat across from him at the tiny two-person table, looked into her tea, and began. "For the first seven years of Jake's life we struggled. After Aunt Livi died, no matter how many hours I worked or how much I economized, there were weeks all we had to eat was macaroni and cheese or peanut butter and jelly. I gave Jake terrible haircuts and limited him to the small box of crayons, which I made him use down to the nubs, and sent him to daycare with yard-sale finds because I couldn't afford the cool toys his friends had. And even though he never complained, I felt ashamed I couldn't do better."

Kyle reached out and touched her arm. "I know you said what I would have done doesn't matter," he said. "But I swear on everything I hold dear, if I'd known about the baby I would have worked two jobs, three if needed, to provide for you both. I would have gone to the labor classes and parenting classes and happily helped you take care of Jake. I most definitely would not have left you to deal with being pregnant and raising a child on your own." He reached for her hand and took it in his. "I wish I'd known. I wish I could have been here to help you."

"I appreciate that." She slid her hand from his. "But you weren't here. It's been just Jake and me for five years now, and he is the most important person in my world. Seeing to his needs, ensuring I can provide him the best possible opportunities for his future are my top priorities." She blew on her tea and took a sip. "I will never revisit that desperate time in my life. For as long as I live I will see to it he never has to go without another day in his life."

"You're not alone anymore." Kyle squeezed her forearm. "You can count on me to help you in any way I can, to share the financial load. You don't need to chase after some high-profile job that requires you to suck up to self-important, judgmental egomaniacs."

Victoria sat back in her chair she hoped out of reach. "When I was little I thought I could count on my mom to be there to take care of me and love me every day. And she died when I was five. I thought I could count on my dad to always be there for me, but he disowned me when I made a decision he didn't agree with. I thought I could count on Aunt Livi for a safe haven, but she died and left me worse off. And I'd thought I could count on you until you disappeared without a word for almost nine long years." She couldn't keep the bitterness from her voice. "The only person I know, without a doubt, I can depend on is me."

"I get it. You have no reason to believe me," Kyle said. "But I'm not going anywhere."

"Regardless of whether you're a part of our lives or not, I need to be financially independent, to know I can support myself and my son. That I'm prepared for him to enter the college of his choice and grad school or medical school, whatever he wants." She took a sip of tea.

"To do that I need a high-paying job," she continued. "The director of nursing job. And I will do whatever it takes to get it." Even carve the man she was starting to love out of her life because he didn't mesh with the image she needed to project to upper management and the board of directors.

"Tell me something," Kyle said. "What's so special about the director of nursing position at Madrin Memorial? Someone with your drive and determination could easily make more money doing any of a dozen managerial positions at a larger hospital."

But if she left town no one would see her success. Her father who'd given up on his pregnant daughter, convinced keeping Jake would ruin her life. All the kids at school who'd teased her, the valedictorian too stupid to use birth control. All the adults who'd criticized and lectured her, the wealthy girl, giving up a promising future to enter the ranks of unwed teenage moms.

"This is where I live, where my friends are," Victoria explained. "But I want that job for the financial security it will provide as much as for the chance to prove to the people of this town that I am smart and capable, not stupid for getting pregnant so young. I want the challenge and prestige and respect that comes with it. I enjoy getting dressed up to attend fancy dinners for fundraising and networking." Now for the kicker. "And I want the man in my life to accompany me as an asset. Not a liability."

Kyle showed no reaction. "So that's all I am? A liability?" he asked, calm as can be.

She swallowed. Hated to say it, but, "Tonight, at the dinner, yes. And as long as you buck hospital policy and loathe the very people I'm trying to impress, I can't be with you."

"Let me get this straight," Kyle said. "Getting that promotion is more important to you than me?"

It'd been her goal since she'd first stepped into the hospital as a nursing student eight years ago, something to strive for and look forward to and feel positive about.

Unable to look at him, she stared into her tea. "Over the years I've given up so much. I refuse to give up my goal to achieve the top nursing spot in the hospital." And for the final blow. "After Jake, it's the next most important thing to me."

"Then I guess that's it." Kyle placed his hands on the table, pushed back his chair and stood. "The last thing I want is for you to lose out on one more opportunity because of me. But I'm Jake's father, and I'd like to be able to spend time with him every day."

"We're adults. I'm certain we can figure out an arrangement that works for both of us."

Without another word, Kyle left, slamming the front door with a finality that brought on the terrible ache of loss, the emptiness of feeling totally alone and the tears that accompanied both.

CHAPTER TEN

KYLE spent a good part of his Sunday on the somewhat smelly green couch in his living room, with Tori, reflecting on his past, thinking about the future, and missing Victoria and Jake. The book he'd tried to start, one he'd been eagerly awaiting from the library, lay closed on the coffee table. It didn't hold his interest. The quiet emptiness of his condo taunted him, the stark contrast to the activity and warmth of Victoria's home, the grim reality of life devoid of family.

He'd done it again. Walked out on Victoria without so much as a thumb wrestle of resistance.

What was wrong with him? Why hadn't he pointed out that her getting the director's job and them being together didn't have to be mutually exclusive? That he loved her. And if he needed to dress different and try harder to impress her colleagues and business associates, he would do whatever it took to make her as proud to be with him as he was to be with her.

Not that any of it would have mattered. Because, after all Victoria had been through, she wouldn't believe his promises. He'd need to show her, to prove himself with actions rather than words. The realization had him sitting up so fast Tori jumped off the couch and started to bark.

"Quiet down, girl." Kyle rubbed her back. A plan started to take form. And after taking Tori outside for a quick walk, Kyle took a trip to the mall.

"Three more," Kyle said to Mrs. Teeton early Monday morning.

Lying on her back in her hospital bed, his patient tried to straighten her left leg while he supported her calf and applied a moderate level of resistance to the heel of her foot.

"Why do you insist on torturing me day after day?" she asked with a grunt of exertion.

"Resistance exercises are for muscle strengthening. When we first met, three weeks ago, you couldn't get out of bed by yourself, now you're able to walk the hall independently."

"The way you've been pushing makes me think you want to be rid of me."

"I want you safe and able to take care of yourself when you return home tomorrow. Now the other leg." He held out his hand and she bent her right leg and placed her heel against his palm. "Speaking of which, I sat in on your discharge planning meeting. Four more. Come on. You're almost done."

Mrs. Teeton finished her reps. Kyle lowered her leg to the bed and brought the covers up to her waist.

"Thank the Lord that's over with," she said, just as she did at the end of every bedside PT session.

"I hear your boyfriend wants to take you home and you're refusing him," Kyle said. "Like you've refused his visits since you've been in the hospital."

She wouldn't meet his eyes. "This is none of your business, Doc."

Kyle pulled a chair next to her bed and sat down. "I'm making it my business. The man obviously cares about you. According to the nurses, he calls in daily to check on you. He wants to take care of you and help you."

"That's the problem," Mrs. Teeton said tears forming in her eyes. "I don't want to be a burden." Kyle handed her a tissue. "He took care of his wife for two long years before she lost her battle with cancer. He's such a sweet man." She blotted at the inner corner of each eye. "I don't want him to have to go through that again."

"It's what people do when they love someone," Kyle said, realizing it's what he'd do for Victoria without a moment's hesitation.

"Not that it matters. One look at me…" she ran her hand over her bald head "…and he'll run in the opposite direction."

Kyle took a trifold paper out of the folder he carried with him. "Here's another pamphlet from a woman who sells wigs made from real hair. Call her this time, tell her what you want, and she'll stop by the hospital with some options first thing in the morning."

Mrs. Teeton opened the advertisement. "How do you think I'd look as a redhead, Melanie?" she asked her roommate.

Mrs. Madrin walked over to Mrs. Teeton's bed, Tori walking beside her. "I think you'd make a beautiful redhead. And I can call my husband's secretary to bring over an assortment of cosmetics that will get rid of those dark circles and play up your beautiful blue eyes."

Tori had bridged the gap between the two women, who had become very close over the past few weeks.

"A little blush on your cheeks," Melanie continued, "and some color on your lips and he won't be able to tell you're sick."

"But I am sick." Mrs. Teeton dropped the pamphlet to the floor and closed her eyes. "And I have months of outpatient chemotherapy before Dr. Starzi will know my fate."

"It's not about the time you have left," Kyle started.

"It's what you do with your time," Mrs. Teeton finished.

"Your boyfriend sounds like a nice man," Melanie said.

"He asked to meet up with me tomorrow morning so I can teach him your exercise plan." Kyle bent to pick up the pamphlet and placed it on the over-the-bed table.

"Don't you dare," Mrs. Teeton warned.

"It's that or I coordinate in-home physical therapy, where someone like me will visit you three times per week."

"Heaven help me. There's no escape, is there?"

"You've made so much progress. I won't take a chance on you backsliding after discharge," Kyle said.

"Let Dr. Karlinsky teach your boyfriend your exercises," Melanie coaxed. "And let that sweet man take you home. I've heard so much about him, I just have to meet him."

Mrs. Teeton lay there quietly with her eyes closed. Kyle and Melanie waited. After a few minutes she whispered, "Okay."

Kyle set his hand on the blanket covering his patient's thigh. "I know that wasn't easy, but I think you made the right decision." He'd had serious concerns about her not eating or exercising and winding up right back in the hospital within a month if she went home alone.

"Oh, she did, she definitely did," Melanie said, looking happier than he'd ever seen her.

"I hear you're going home tomorrow, too," Kyle said to Melanie.

"Well, they couldn't keep one of us here without the other," Mrs. Teeton said.

Melanie reached down to pet Tori. "Thank you for giving my husband the information for Tori's breeder. He promised to get me a dog just like her."

Kyle held out his hand to Melanie. "It's been a pleasure getting to know you. Good luck."

Melanie shook his hand, looking near tears. "Thank you. Tori has…"

"Yeah." Kyle leaned over and patted Tori's side. "She's a good girl."

"I'm off. I will see you…" he pointed to Mrs. Teeton "…tomorrow morning."

"Not too early," Melanie said. "Her boyfriend can't see her until after her wig arrives."

"I'll tell him eleven o'clock."

With a quick knock on Victoria's open door, Ali walked into her office. "Did you see Kyle? Dang, he cleans up good."

Like she always knew he would. But even she'd been shocked by his transformation. Charcoal-gray dress slacks, a white button-down shirt, and a tie. A tie.

Kyle's barber had sheered the swag of bang that partially obscured his handsome face, opening it to full view, while leaving plenty of short, thick waves in the back. Perfect for a woman to run her fingers through.

Victoria had come close to suggesting he wear a hat lest the site of him trigger a rash of gotta-catch-me-that-man hysteria among the available women at the hospital. Unless that's what he was going for now that he knew there was no chance for them to be together.

The burn in her chest worsened.

"For as good as he looks," Ali said, "he's walking around here with a big old storm cloud over his head. One that looks remarkably similar to yours."

"Leave it alone, Ali," she warned her friend.

Who didn't listen. "Is it because of what happened at the dinner? You know, your father deserves a good punch in the face, and after what you told me about that sham of a rape charge, I think it's fitting for Kyle to be the one to do it."

"I'm not talking about this," Victoria said, scanning a computer printout on her desk, pretending interest on some random page.

"He loves you. Any fool can see it."

The words blurred.

"And you love him, too, although you're too stubborn to admit it."

"Hello, ladies," the director of nursing said from the doorway. "I hope I'm not interrupting."

Victoria blinked to clear her vision before looking up. "Of course not." She stood. "Come in. Ali was just leaving."

"I see you've finally brought that man of yours up to snuff," she said, waiting for Ali to slip out before walking into Victoria's office. "I had no doubt, if it could be done, you'd be the one to do it."

Victoria did a double take. Had the director really just said what she thought she'd heard? Because to date, the woman had given no indication she thought Kyle was at all redeemable.

The director closed the door.

Would there ever come a time when she didn't feel the need to seal Victoria in her office to speak with her? "He's not my man," Victoria clarified, taking a sip of water from the bottle on her desk, in desperate need of an antacid. "And I'm sorry about Saturday night. I promise it will never—"

"Oh, pish-posh." The director waved her hand shoo-fly style. "That's the most excitement we've had at a hospital event in years. I bet our June dinner gets more interest because of it." Which would benefit the hospital since the quarterly dinners also served as fundraisers.

Glad her family problems were good for a boost in attendance.

"Don't look so conflicted, dear." The director handed her several letters. Some handwritten, the one on top typed. "On award night I highlighted excerpts from Senator Madrin's letter, focusing on the sections that pertained to you. But he also mentioned Dr. Karlinsky. It seems *your man* came in after hours to visit with his wife and give her time with Tori. Mr. Madrin credits that as a major facet of her recovery."

Why had no one on her staff mentioned his visits?

"In one short month, he's accumulated seven complimentary letters."

After seeing Kyle in action at work, it didn't surprise her. He didn't go about doing his job in a grandiose manner, like Dr. Starzi. He didn't seek praise or recognition. He simply did what needed to be done, and more, in his unassuming, low-key way, quietly earning the respect of his patients and co-workers. He got results. He made a positive impact on the lives of his patients and their families, and in the end that's what mattered. Not what he wore or what Administration or anyone else thought of him.

And she'd been too blinded by her need to succeed to recognize his true value.

"I wanted you to know," the director went on, "I will be nominating him for April employee of the month. Close your mouth, my dear. That look is most unappealing."

Victoria did as instructed.

"I hope it's enough to entice him to take the staff position he's been offered, because even with the positive response to his dog, I cannot abide that animal walking the halls of this hospital. At Friday's meeting to discuss the continued presence of his pet, my vote will remain a steadfast no." The director locked eyes with Victoria. "And I expect your allegiance."

"Of course," Victoria responded. She always sided with the director. But she'd never disagreed with her mentor's course of action.

Until now.

And since she had a personal stake in the outcome of this particular matter she would need to go out of her way to handle her decision on how to proceed delicately and objectively.

Someone knocked at the door. "I'm in a meeting," Victoria called out.

The door opened the slightest bit. "I'm sorry to bother you," Nora said, "but your 'do not disturb' button is on, and Jake's school is on line one. It's the principal. He says it's urgent."

* * *

When Victoria arrived home she went straight to the freezer to make Jake two fresh baggies of ice for his eye and lip. "I don't understand why you wouldn't tell the principal who did this to you," she said, swallowing down an intense urge to retch at the sight of her baby's battered face, the skin around his left eye an angry, swollen red, his upper lip cracked and puffy, and the rim of each nostril crusted with dried blood.

"It's over. I don't want to talk about it," Jake said, his words muffled behind an icepack.

"It most certainly is not over," Victoria said, handing him the fresh bags of ice, each wrapped in a paper towel, and tossing the melting ones into the sink. "Not until the person or persons responsible are punished. Now, come, sit down." She pulled out a kitchen chair for him. "Talk to me. Tell me what happened."

"No."

"No? You're telling me no?" She crossed her arms over her chest. "That is absolutely unacceptable, Jake Forley. If we don't give the principal at least one name, what's to stop any of them from hurting you again?"

"He won't."

"He? So it was one boy." Good. That was a start. "Was it someone from your class? Did anyone else see what happened? And where on earth was your teacher while you were being beaten?"

"Stop it, Mom."

"I will not stop it, young man. Not until you give me this boy's name. And his parents are notified and he is reprimanded."

"No," Jake yelled. Panicked.

"Honey." She sat down on the chair across from him. "Are you worried this boy will get angry and hurt you again? Because let me assure you, when I'm finished at that school he'll be lucky to be accepted back into class."

"You can't go down to school. I promised."

"Who did you promise?"

"Why do you make everything a big deal?" Jake jumped off his chair and threw his bags of ice on the table. "I hate you. I want Dad. Only Dad."

His verbal missile landed dead center in her chest. The result: catastrophic. The aftermath: complete devastation.

Jake ran down the hall. A door slammed.

All Victoria could do was breathe. Her sweet son, the most important person in her life, hated her for trying to protect him, for doing her job as a mother.

I hate you.

I want Dad.

Only Dad.

She inhaled. Exhaled. Moved her arms and legs to get the circulation flowing. She could handle this.

Gathering up the bags of ice, she stood and walked to Jake's room. She knocked. No answer.

She opened the door to find Jake, lying on his bed, facing the wall. "Honey, you need to keep this ice on your face to keep down the swelling."

"No."

"Come on, Jake."

"Go away," he yelled. "I want Dad."

"Well, Daddy's not here. I am. And I want you to—"

"I don't care what you want."

Bam. The hurt just kept on coming. Inhale. Exhale. "Are you in pain?"

No answer.

"What would you like for dinner? I can make soup or—"

"I'm not hungry."

"You will be later."

"No, I won't," Jake yelled.

Victoria stood in silence, couldn't move, appalled by her son's behavior. After a minute or two Jake asked in a small voice, "Did you call Dad?"

"Not yet."

He started to cry. Tiny sniffling tremors quickly turned into heart-wrenching sobs that shook his small body.

"Oh, honey. No. Don't cry." Victoria hurried to the bed, sat beside him and rubbed his back.

"Can I...have his phone...number...so I can...talk to him?" he asked in between choppy breaths.

"Of course you can." Victoria leaned in to kiss the back of Jake's shoulder. "I'll write it down for you so you can call him any time you want. But let me get in touch with him this time. I'll do it right now. Promise. I'll ask him to come over as soon as he can. Okay?"

Jake nodded.

"I love you," Victoria said.

Jake sniffled in response.

Late Monday afternoon the 5E staff was abuzz about Victoria, running out of work early with no explanation. If anyone knew why, they weren't talking. Kyle went about his business, visited two patients, and tried not to worry. If something'd happened to Jake she would call him. Wouldn't she? His cellphone vibrated in his pocket.

He stood to retrieve it, looked at the screen and opened a text message.

From Victoria: "Please come over. ASAP. Jake needs you."

Kyle punched his timecard, left the hospital, and was in Victoria's driveway in thirteen minutes. With a stern "Stay", he left Tori in the truck.

He ran up the front steps, whipped open the screen door and knocked. After waiting what he thought was a reasonable amount of time considering the circumstances, maybe two seconds, he tried the knob and pushed open the door.

"Victoria?" He climbed the stairs.

"In here," she answered from the kitchen, where she sat at the small square table with a mound of shredded napkin strips in front of her, half meticulously folded into tiny accordion pleats.

She looked up at him with sad, exhausted eyes. "Jake got beat up at school today. And before you say anything, I checked with the teacher. He was over by the swing set when it happened." She stared out the window and added quietly, "Not playing hopscotch. Or using pink chalk."

"Is he okay?"

She nodded.

The tightness in his chest eased. "It's not your fault," Kyle said.

Victoria looked down at the table and returned her focus to folding. "I can't be sure because he wouldn't tell me or the principal what happened. It turns out he hates me and only wants you."

That didn't sound at all like Jake. What the heck had happened? "Is he in his room?"

"Yes. I think I heard him packing." A tear made its way down her cheek to her chin and dripped onto the table. "You can't have him," she said. Another tear followed the path of the first. "He's all I have and I won't let him go."

"Ah, Vic." Kyle knelt beside her. "I'm sure this is all a big misunderstanding. Let me talk to him and see what's going on."

Victoria took his hand and squeezed. "Thank you for coming."

"I'm here for both of you. Any time. Always."

With a kiss to her palm he went to knock on Jake's door.

"Go away," Jake yelled.

Kyle walked in. "That's some greeting, kiddo," he said.

Jake rolled over. "Dad."

It took a significant amount of self-control not to react to his son's bruises. "So what's got your mother all upset?" Kyle asked, keeping things laid back, ignoring the suitcase by the foot of Jake's bed.

"Mom's mad I got beat up at school," Jake said.

Understandably. "You want to tell me what happened?"

"Only if you promise not to tell anyone."

"If you don't want me to, I promise I won't."

Jake sat up in bed and Kyle sat down beside him.

"The other week, a kid in my class tried to copy my answers on a big spelling test. I raised my hand and told the teacher. It wasn't the first time and he got in trouble." Jake looked away. "After that he wasn't in class for a bunch of days. I thought he got kicked out by the school. But when he came back he said his dad got real mad at him so he was real mad at me." Kyle leaned in and whispered, "He had a cast on his arm. Do you think his dad broke it?"

"I don't know. I hope not." But he intended to look into it.

"Today the kid's brother, he's a fifth-grader, snuck out of lunch when he saw my class on the playground. He said his brother got beat because of me so I deserved to get beat."

Violence bred violence. "No child deserves to get beaten." Kyle caressed Jake's uninjured cheek with a loving hand, the only way he would ever touch his son.

"After the fifth-grader ran back into the school the kid in my class said he was real sorry and begged me not to tell. He said if his brother got in trouble then their dad would beat him even worse 'cause he's older. I don't want anyone getting beat up because of me," Jake said with a shudder. "I've seen their dad and he's big and scary-looking."

Now it all made sense. Jake wouldn't reveal a name out of concern for the *bully's* safety. Kyle couldn't be prouder, but trying to protect children from an abusive parent was an awfully big undertaking for an eight-year-old. "Why didn't you tell your mom what you told me?"

"She got all crazy and wanted me to tell the principal so the kid's parents got told. She would have made a mess of everything."

"Well, she's not crazy anymore. Now she's mostly sad because for some reason she thinks you hate her."

Jake dropped his head into his hands. "I didn't know what else to do to make her stop. She kept asking and asking. I'm sorry."

"It's not me you need to tell. It's your mom," Kyle

said. "And while we're at it, those two boys sound like they have it pretty bad at home."

Jake nodded.

"Like they need help."

He nodded again.

"And who better to make sure the school helps them than your mom? She'll make sure they do it."

"Or she'll nag them and nag them." Jake smiled.

"I say you tell Mom. And then we talk about what we can do to see those boys don't get hit by their dad again. I bet she'll have lots of ideas."

Jake thought about it for a minute and said, "Okay," then added, "And, Dad? I don't like getting beat up. Will you teach me to fight?"

Kyle didn't want his son following in his confrontational path. So he said, "I have a better idea. Give me a few minutes with your mom then we'll come in and discuss it. Okay?"

Jake climbed onto his lap and wrapped his arms around Kyle's neck. "I love you, Dad." The words danced through his mind and cavorted with his skin cells before settling in his heart. A contented warmth spread throughout his body. Kyle held Jake close. He was responsible for this child. To love him, care for him and help him, and he was determined to be the very best dad he could be.

"I love you, too." He kissed Jake's head.

Now to deal with Victoria.

He found her still at the kitchen table, all the accordion pleats flattened and neatly stacked in rows. When she heard him she looked up.

Kyle pulled out the chair opposite her and sat down. "As upsetting as it is that Jake confided in me and not you, this one time, I think it's important to point out that he told one of us. He has two parents who love him and he needs to know he can come to either one of us."

"You're right," Victoria said, but her eyes didn't meet his. "It's just...the first time he wouldn't talk to me, wouldn't let me fix the problem. I feel so...helpless. I don't like it."

"Part of the reason he wanted to talk to me was to ask me to teach him how to fight."

Victoria jerked up. "Absolutely not. Animals fight," she snapped. "Uncivilized people fight. I will not have my son thinking it's okay to resolve a conflict with his fists." She didn't say it, but "like you were about to do Saturday night" hung in the air between them.

"I didn't say I would." Kyle sat back in his chair. "But what if I wanted to? Victoria, you need to understand you are not a single parent anymore. You do not get to make all the decisions. I'm Jake's father and I have a say. Fifty-fifty."

She tried to say something but Kyle held up his hand to silence her.

"Let me finish. I know I wasn't here for the first eight years of Jake's life. But I'm here now. And I expect us to discuss things, to compromise and present a united front."

She rubbed the back of her neck. "I can do that. But I can't condone Jake fighting."

"I know that. And neither can I. I'm thinking more along the lines of signing him up for a martial arts class. I've taken a few over the years and the focus is on personal safety. He'll meet some new kids, gain confidence. I'll sit in on the classes so I can keep tabs on exactly what they're teaching him."

"How does Jake feel about it?"

"I haven't mentioned it, yet. I wanted to discuss it with you first."

"I appreciate that. Thank you. If he wants to take a karate class, would you see if you can find one on Wednesday nights when I have class?"

"I'll look into it tomorrow."

"Yay," Jake said, running into the kitchen. "My friend Jimmy takes karate. He's not scared of nothing."

"Not scared of anything," Victoria corrected. "You snoop."

"I'm sorry, Mom," Jake said without any prompting. "I don't hate you. I love you every piece of sand on every beach in the whole wide world."

"Wow." Victoria opened her arms, her lips curving into the first smile he'd seen in days. Jake stepped into her embrace. "That's an awful lot." She kissed his head. "I love you, too, sweetie. A million, gajillion, patrillion red M&Ms."

"Yum," Jake said.

Victoria whispered something in Jake's ear. They each held out an arm to him. "Come on, Dad," Jake said. "Family hug."

Kyle wedged himself in, staking his place in their family unit, surrounding Victoria and Jake in his love. He kissed each one on the top of the head.

Victoria gazed up at him with heartfelt appreciation and mouthed the words, "Thank you." Then she set her cheek to his chest. He held her close, feeling the bond between them that nothing could break, feeling hope that a future together was still possible.

"I'm hungry," Jake said.

"I'll get dinner ready." She turned to Kyle. "Will you join us?"

There was no place he'd rather be. "If I can let Tori chill out downstairs."

"Sure."

Over dinner Jake retold his story to Victoria and the three of them hashed out a plan for what to do. The following morning Kyle accompanied his family to meet with the principal and the school social worker.

Afterwards Jake said, "My eye is sore. Can I take today off from school?"

Victoria glanced at her watch. "I've got a hospital-wide quality-assurance meeting in twenty minutes."

"I have a patient meeting I can't miss at eleven," Kyle said. "If Jake can hang with you in your office from eleven to twelve, I can take him now and stay with him for the afternoon," Kyle offered. "And if you could wrap your day up a little early, I'll work an evening shift tonight."

"You will? Are you sure?"

"Positive. Parents have been flexing their schedules for years. It won't be a problem." Victoria stepped close and said, "You were very impressive in there." She flicked her head toward the principal's office. "Very fatherly."

"Thank you."

She fingered the knot of his tie and added, "Have I told you how much I like your new look?"

"Actually, no. You haven't."

"Well, I do. A lot."

Which is exactly what he wanted.

For the rest of the week Kyle barely saw Victoria. At work she spent hours behind her closed office door working on some super-secret project. And at home, after dinner, she holed up in her home office, leaving Kyle to occupy Jake and get him ready for bed. Kyle loved every minute of it.

On Thursday night, while lying in Jake's bed listening to his son read from one of his favorite books, Kyle decided that no matter what the outcome of Friday's vote, whether he could continue to take Tori to work with him or not, he would accept the full-time position the hospital had offered him. He needed the job, needed to be close to his family, and, if he had to, he'd find a way to make his program effective without Tori's assistance.

After an unusually restless night, on Friday morning Kyle sat outside the administrative conference room with Tori, waiting to learn her fate, hoping he hadn't made a gross miscalculation by making his hire contingent on Tori's acceptance as an official hospital therapy dog. If the nursing director had her way, Tori *and* Kyle would be sent packing. And since he'd refused to sign on for anything more than a thirty-day temporary work detail, there wasn't anything he'd be able to do about it.

The door opened and Victoria, dressed in a high-powered tan business suit, stepped out.

Wow. "What's going on in there?" Kyle asked.

"They're about to vote."

"Then what are you doing out here?"

"I recused myself. I didn't want there to be any question of the validity of the results based on partiality."

That left three for and three against.

"I've done all I can." She walked toward him. "Bend down."

He did and she wrapped her arms around his neck

and kissed him. Right there in the hallway for the administrative offices.

"Good luck," she said.

"No matter what happens, I'm not leaving town."

"I'm glad." Victoria smiled. "Jake likes having you here."

"And what about you?" Kyle asked. "Do you like having me here?"

"You're growing on me," she teased.

The door to the conference room opened and four people funneled out. The nursing director said, "You can come in now, Dr. Karlinsky. And you..." she pointed at Victoria accusingly "...meet me in my office at four o'clock."

"Can you pick up Jake?" Victoria asked with no show of emotion.

What the heck was going on? "Sure."

"Come, Dr. Karlinsky. Let's get this over with," the director said.

Her "Let's get this over with" did not sound promising. "I'll meet you at home," Victoria said.

Kyle liked the sound of that—*home*—and found himself grinning like a fool as he entered the conference room. Only Dr. Starzi and the nursing director remained.

"Have a seat." The director motioned to the chair on her left.

Dr. Starzi slid a thick report in a shiny blue cover across the table at him.

"What's this?" Kyle asked.

"A forty-two-page report, complete with bar graphs and colored pie charts, detailing the minutiae of all you and your dog have accomplished in the month you've been here," Dr. Starzi said. "Articles and dissertations highlighting the benefits of therapy dog programs in hospitals across the country. Testimonials from your patients and hospital staff. Mine is on page thirty-two, I believe." He leaned his elbows on the table. "You, my friend, have won the girlfriend lottery. Much to my chagrin."

Kyle picked up the report and flipped through it. "Victoria did all this?" For him?

"I hope you realize what you have," the director said. "By daring to go behind my back, by presenting this report without my prior knowledge and recusing herself from a vote I insisted she participate in, that girl put her future as director of nursing in jeopardy. For you."

Kyle didn't know what to say. He stood. Had to get to her, thank her, tell her how much he loved her, appreciated her. But first... "I don't want this position if Victoria has to pay for it by forfeiting her dream."

"True love. How sweet," Dr. Starzi said in true cynical form. "Tell him the outcome of the vote so I can get out of here." He checked his watch. "I have a sudden urge for a drink."

"Five for. One against," the director said. "Welcome on staff, Dr. Karlinsky. And you, too, Tori." She looked under the table where Tori lay curled at his feet. "The paperwork is waiting for you in Human Resources."

Kyle should have been thrilled. But... "You won't find anyone better to replace you," he said to the director. "Victoria is the best candidate you have and you know it. No one will do as good a job as she will."

"You let me worry about my replacement, Dr. Karlinsky. Good day." And with that she collected her papers and left the conference room.

Kyle checked every place in the hospital he thought Victoria might be. Every place but where she actually was. And by 3:45 p.m. he couldn't put off leaving any longer. He had to pick up Jake.

Victoria dropped her briefcase, slipped off her heels, and unbuttoned the top two buttons of her blouse. It was good to be home.

Kyle met her at the top of the stairs, a beer in one hand, a glass of white wine, which he held out to her, in the other. "You've had a busy week," he said.

Yes. She had. "Where's Jake?" Obviously not rushing to welcome his mother home with a hug and a kiss.

"At Ali's. I wasn't sure what shape you'd be in when you got home." He studied her like he could find the answer in her expression.

"What would you say..." she took the wine, walked past him to the couch in the living room and sat down "...if I told you I quit my job and as soon as I can sell my house I'm leaving town?" She took a sip of the Chardonnay.

Kyle sat down beside her, placed his beer on a coaster on the coffee table and lifted her feet onto his lap. "I'd say let's try someplace warm where Jake can play baseball year round."

Good answer. He worked his thumbs into the arch of her right foot. "Man, that feels good." She closed her eyes, dropped her head against the back of the sofa and let him massage away the stress of the day.

"I saw the report you did," Kyle said. "Impressive stuff."

"Interesting subject matter."

"You shouldn't have put your promotion in jeopardy because of me," Kyle said.

She looked into his eyes. "It was the right thing to do. The hospital needs you and Tori."

"Is that the only reason you did it, because the hospital needs us?"

"It's the only reason I'll admit to." She smiled. "Do the other one." She slid her left foot into his talented grip. "I'm not an easy woman," she said. A gross understatement. But if he planned to stick around he needed to know the extent of it.

"Nothing worthwhile comes easy," Kyle replied.

"I'm a fiercely independent, high-strung perfectionist with a compulsive need to succeed. And when I get focused in on something it's hard to get me to stop."

Kyle moved his hand up her left shin. "That last one's not always a bad thing."

"And I still have…issues." That she hadn't managed to work all the way through. She took another sip of wine.

"You're also a deeply passionate and compassionate person." He caressed her knee and thigh. "An excellent mother, a loyal friend, and the woman I've fallen in love with."

Her eyes shot open.

"We all have issues, Victoria," he continued, as if he hadn't just professed his love for her. "As much as you strive to be, no one is perfect."

"Back up," Victoria said. "You've fallen in love with me?"

"To be honest," he said, "I think more correct phrasing would be I'm still in love with you. I'm not sure I ever stopped."

"Lord help you. Do you have any idea how high maintenance I am?"

He smiled confidently. "I can handle you."

She moved her feet to the floor and climbed onto his lap, straddling him. "You think so?"

"I know so."

"Good." She leaned in. Millimeters from his lips she said, "Because I love you, too." And she kissed him.

When they finally broke for air Kyle asked, "So are you going to tell me what happened in your meeting with the director?"

"It was all a test." Victoria unknotted Kyle's tie. "To see if I would blindly follow her or cave in to the pressure, or if I would stand up for what was in the best interest of the hospital."

Kyle stiffened beneath her. "Why, that conniving..."

"Shh." She put a finger to his lips. "She's the last thing I want to discuss right now." She slid his tie out from his collar and unbuttoned the two top buttons of his shirt.

"So you're still up to replace her?"

Victoria nodded and proceeded to work her way down the row of buttons keeping his beautiful chest from her view.

He grabbed her hands to stop her. "I need you to know I can be an asset at your fancy dinners. I promise I will do my best to never embarrass you again."

"All I want, Kyle Karlinsky, is for you to be the wonderful man Jake and I love." She thought about it for a second. "Well, there's something else I want, too."

"Anything," Kyle said.

"Make love to me. Like you did that night in your

car. I need to feel your weight on top of me, to know I can get through it."

His eyes met hers. "Are you sure?"

"I'm ready. I love you and I trust you."

Kyle lifted her off his lap. Her foot landed on a pack of Jake's baseball cards. Shoot. "When do we have to pick up Jake?"

Kyle took her hand and led her toward the bedroom. "I packed his overnight bag and told Ali if we weren't there by eight he'd be sleeping over."

"A planner," Victoria said. "How *did* I get so lucky?"

"That's nothing," Kyle said as he pulled her through the doorway toward her bed. "In about twenty minutes I'll show you the full extent of your luckiness."

She didn't need to wait. She already knew.

EPILOGUE

Three months later

"WHERE'S KYLE?" Roxie asked.

The employee of the month recognition dinner was due to start in five minutes, and Kyle, Mr. April, had yet to arrive. "Jake had his championship baseball game this afternoon." Victoria had stayed long enough to watch her son score the winning run and wave up to him when the coach walked by, carrying Jake on his shoulders. Then she'd run home to shower. "Afterwards, Kyle took him for pizza with the team while I came early to set up. He promised he'd be on time."

With another surprise. She'd begged him not to. She inhaled. Exhaled. It'd be fine. Whatever he wore would be fine, because she loved him and accepted him. And what could be worse than jeans?

"Who's Mr. Freakishly Tall, Pale, and Bald?" Roxie asked.

"Kyle's friend, Fig. He's in town for the week. Come, I'll introduce you."

"Fig," Victoria said to the polite, well-dressed man she'd met fifteen minutes earlier. "This is my friend

Roxie, a recipient of your generosity in sponsoring our table."

"Nice to meet you." Fig held out his hand.

Roxie shook it. "Man, you're all bones. You feel like you could use a good meal."

"Right back atcha," Fig countered, without missing a beat.

"So take me to dinner," Roxie said. "Friday night. You choose the place."

Gotta love Roxie.

"I'm dying of cancer," Fig said without emotion.

Victoria tried to tell if he was joking, but his expression gave nothing away.

"Do you plan to do it before Friday night?" Roxie asked, because no one rattled Roxie.

Fig shrugged. "Not sure."

"Tell you what. I'll plan for you to pick me up at six. If you're not there by seven, I'll say a prayer."

Fig's smile showed a warm, playful side that matched Roxie's. "Deal," he said, holding out his hand again. Roxie shook it, again.

"Come on," Roxie said to Fig. "I'll give you my address."

"May I have your attention?" The MC's voice came through the speakers.

Kyle was late. Had something happened?

"If you all would turn your attention towards the lobby doors," the MC added.

Victoria turned. Her heart stopped, her breath caught in her lungs. There stood Kyle, gorgeous in a form-fitting tuxedo and shiny shoes. And he'd brought Jake, his mini red-haired replica in an identical tiny tux. Both carried one long-stemmed red rose. Jake also held a small white paper sack that looked to be from her favorite chocolate shop.

A hush fell over the room.

Kyle scanned the crowd until he found her. They locked eyes. He held out his hand, Jake took it, and together they started toward her. Father and son. Her two favorite men, the loves of her life, Kyle with a half-smile, Jake, shoulders back, chin up, proud to be part of something important.

When they got within five feet of her, Victoria quipped, "You can't keep from making a spectacle of yourself, can you?"

"Baby, you ain't seen nothing yet." Standing an arm's length away, he reached into his pants pocket, took out a black velvet ring box, and went down on one knee.

His face very serious, Jake went down on one knee, beside him.

Victoria sucked in a breath. Her heart started to pound. Her eyes burned to let go of some tears.

Kyle looked up. So did Jake, full of hope.

Kyle held out the ring box and flipped open the lid to reveal a beautiful pear-shaped diamond set in an ultra-modern white-gold tension setting. Magnificent. A ring she would have chosen if given the opportunity.

"You have to say yes, Mom." Jake held up the white bag. "He even got you chocolates." A few laughs broke out in the silence.

"Say yes to what, Jake?" She raised her eyebrows and tilted her head, looking straight at Kyle. "No one's asked me anything."

She hoped she could hear him over the pulse pounding in her ears.

"Don't be difficult." Roxie elbowed her in the arm.

"Victoria Forley," Kyle said, "I don't deserve you, but I love you and Jake more than anything. And if you agree to marry me I promise to make you smile when you're sad, calm you when you're mad, and hold you in my arms until you're glad."

Jake tugged on Kyle's jacket. He leaned down and Jake whispered in his ear.

"You sure?" Kyle asked. Jake gave a solemn nod.

Kyle turned back to Victoria and added, "And I promise to give you a baby girl so you don't feel like it's two against one."

A few more laughs ensued.

Victoria smiled through the urge to cry, touched by their sincerity and Jake's concern.

"Well, in that case," she said, "how can I refuse? Yes. I'd be honored to marry you."

The crowd erupted in cheers.

"Thank you, Mommy. Thank you!" Jake said, jumping up and down.

Kyle slipped the ring onto her finger. A perfect fit. People tapped silverware against their glasses until she and Kyle kissed.

"Congratulations to the happy couple," the MC said. "Now, if you'll all take your seats, we can get started."

After the award ceremony the director came over to their table, rubbing her hands together. "Young love makes people feel generous. Come on, you two. Let's mingle."

Not sure if Kyle would want to, Victoria turned to him. "Of course," he said with a congenial smile, placed his napkin on the table and stood.

Later, standing in the arms of the man she loved, her fiancé, swaying on the dance floor with dozens of other couples but feeling like she and Kyle were the only two people in the room, Victoria looked up and said, "Tonight was supposed to be *your* special night. In so much of a hurry you couldn't wait until tomorrow to propose?"

Kyle looked deeply into her eyes and replied, "You saying yes is what made tonight special. And long engagement, short engagement, big wedding, small wedding, courthouse wedding or Vegas wedding doesn't matter to me, as long as when it's over you're my wife."

She felt exactly the same way. "The sooner we're married, the sooner we can start working on that baby girl."

He lost the beat of the music, tightened his hold to keep her from tripping. "I've been thinking," he said. "Maybe we should hold off on that for a while, or I'm fine with us only having one child."

"You don't want another child?" While Jake's suggestion had taken her by surprise, the more she'd thought about it, the more she'd started to love the idea of having another baby, of having Kyle there with her this time.

"No. I mean I do. But..." He spun her to the edge of the dance floor where it was less crowded. "I think you should apply to medical school. I can help you study for the medical college admission tests. I'll support us and take care of Jake. It's been your dream since you were a little girl. Now there's nothing to stop you from going after it."

Victoria settled her ear against his chest, and while listening to the wild beat of his heart considered it— for less than thirty seconds. The long hours of study and residency that would have her working around the clock and keep her away from her husband and son. Years ago she'd wanted to become a physician to find cures for diseases, to help people. And she was helping people as a nurse. As director of nursing she'd have the ability to improve the quality of care provided to hundreds of patients at a time.

She looked up at the man willing to put their lives together on hold, to forgo having another child so she could pursue her childhood dreams, and fell even deeper in love with him.

But her dreams had changed. "Are you trying to renege on your promise to make a baby girl with me?"

"No, I…"

"Because I love you, Kyle Karlinsky. And if you think you can marry me then send me off to medical school, you've got another think coming."

"I thought…"

"You thought wrong. I'm happy with my life, sharing each day with you and Jake. And the only thing that would make me happier is a baby, girl or boy, within the next two years."

"I love you, too, Victoria, soon to be Karlinsky. And since I'm all about making you happy…" he pulled her close and nuzzled her ear the way she liked "…I promise to do everything within my power to meet that goal, or die from exhaustion, trying."

* * * * *

A sneaky peek at next month...

Medical Romance™

CAPTIVATING MEDICAL DRAMA—WITH HEART

My wish list for next month's titles...

In stores from 6th January 2012:

❏ The Boss She Can't Resist – Lucy Clark

& Heart Surgeon, Hero...Husband? – Susan Carlisle

❏ Dr Langley: Protector or Playboy? – Joanna Neil

& Daredevil and Dr Kate – Leah Martyn

❏ Spring Proposal in Swallowbrook – Abigail Gordon

❏ Doctor's Guide to Dating in the Jungle – Tina Beckett

Available at WHSmith, Tesco, Asda, Eason, Amazon and Apple

Just can't wait?